The IMPLANT

"Awakening"

By: Gary Wells

Published by Keed Publishing

For Information contact and visit Keed Publishing at
www.KeedPublishing.co

ISBN 978-1-951990-04-6

Dedication

To my incredible wife, Sheila, for her editing work and patience with me. Many thanks to my family for their support, love, and inspiration. Thank you to my son, Mitch, for the cover artwork, and to my daughter, Krista, for her formatting work. A special thanks to Keed Publishing for believing in me.

This story is for all those people that look to the heavens and wonder what may be out there.

The IMPLANT

"Awakening"

Chapter One

The Priest

The slaves meticulously prepared the high priest's robes for the entombment ceremony. Woven with gold thread and covered in gold adornments and precious stones, the robes were so heavy it took three slaves to hold and clean them. After cleaning, the robes would be hand rubbed with perfumed oils to brighten their golden luster with aromatic perfection. There was no finer clothing in the land of Pharaoh, not even the finery worn by Pharaoh himself. The high priest's quarters were filled with treasures gifted by the pharaoh from every corner of his kingdom.

The two female slaves grooming the priest for the ceremony were the only humans allowed in the high priest's private quarters. The slaves, also gifts from the pharaoh, would spend their lives serving the priest's every need with absolute obedience.

The priest's physical features were not like anything the slaves had ever seen before. The priest was a full seven hands taller than the pharaoh. His head was very large with an elongated shape. His skin was a natural grayish blue color, but the slaves applied colored powders to make the color look more human. His hands were twice the length of human hands, and the Egyptian custom of painting fingernails made them look even more bizarre. Most disturbing were the eyes. They were completely black with no pupils and twice the size of human eyes. They terrified anyone that saw them. Throughout the kingdom, it was believed that if you looked in his demon eyes, your death could be seen in the reflection of their black depth.

The high priest had been planning his departure from the land of the pharaoh since the last star cycle. He had been waiting until the implant was ready, so he could transfer into a new host body to continue the mission. His last two attempts had failed. Human bodies were very frail. The quick death of the old pharaoh had put his life in danger, and he would have to leave before he could try the implant in a new body for his transfer so he hid the implant in one of his slaves until he could find a stronger male for the implant. He would be glad to be TOR-LOK again. The ship had healed itself

2

enough for a limited flight and, except for some last-minute details, he was ready.

The new pharaoh, Pharaoh Akhenaten's son, will take the throne of his dead father at tonight's burial ceremony. The old pharaoh had previously made the decision that his son was too unstable and evil to have access to the true power he had received from the priest. TOR-LOK's arrangement with the old human had served them both well. The high priest used his knowledge and technology to serve the pharaoh and protect his kingdom. In return, the priest was afforded all the privileges of a member of the royal family. The odd couple developed a great respect and friendship for each other, even though the pharaoh did not fully comprehend what TOR-LOK really was or where he was from. All the powers that he had shared with the pharaoh were too advanced for the primitive deity to comprehend in a logical sense, so the pharaoh easily believed the priest to be a gift from the sun god, Aten. The pharaoh found comfort in his pagan belief in the gods and their magical power. There was no question in the priest's mind that the new son pharaoh would attempt to assassinate him soon after the ceremony.

The son had always been jealous of the special bond the priest had with his father and the secrets they shared and kept from him. Over time, the jealousy grew into resentment, then anger, and finally, hatred. Pharaoh Akhenaten had confided to the priest that his son had been troubled since childhood, growing crueler as he aged. The pharaoh had considered ending his son's life to spare his people from the oppression and horror they would endure when his son became Pharaoh, but as time passed, his love for his son overruled his judgment and he could not take his son's life.

The priest had to fly the ship out of the kingdom this day. Pharaoh Akhenaten's sudden death changed everything. The night before, while they were walking in the palace garden, Pharaoh collapsed. The priest picked him up, carrying him quietly through the dark and down into the hidden chamber that concealed the ship. It was not the first time the priest had put the pharaoh in the healing chamber. The healing chamber had repaired the old pharaoh's single heart before, but it was too diseased to be repaired this time as the chamber did not have enough material to repair the heart.

Since being hit by the star flare, TOR-LOK's host body had been slowly dying from radiation exposure, which had also damaged his ship, forcing him to find refuge on this little planet. The ship was still repairing itself but was ready for limited space flight and now, with Pharaoh's death, his life was in imminent danger. The boy pharaoh would attempt to assassinate him as soon as he could locate TOR-LOK's ship. If TOR-LOK's host body should be killed, before he could transfer into a new host, the ship would be stranded without a flyer.

The events that forced his landing on this planet had become legend in Pharaoh Akhenaten's kingdom. The story was told that the priest had been a gift for Pharaoh sent in a shiny chariot by the sun god. The chariot first appeared as a bright light in the sky until it finally descended to the desert. The great priest appeared from the inside the chariot, bowing to Pharaoh Akhenaten who accepted the sun god's gift and made TOR-LOK the high priest of his kingdom.

The priest performed great miracles for the pharaoh and was worshiped by all the people of his kingdom. Like most legends, the story of the priest's landing on Earth began from bits of truth. That was the thing about legends; over time, the line between truth and myth slowly disappeared.

This legend, however, could not begin to capture the incredible, true story.

The real event began as a bright light appearing one summer morning just before the sun rose over the ancient Egyptian land of Akhenaten, the pharaoh. The strange light moved across the summer sky, dancing magically from place to place so quickly that human eyes could not follow its movement between one place to the next. The light-struck great fear in the people of Pharaoh's kingdom. Many went to the temple to pray to God Pharaoh to protect them. Pharaoh's wise men were also frightened about the light in the sky, and they knew they dare not delay awakening Pharaoh from his sleep to tell him of the mysterious light. Pharaoh was angry to be awakened after a long night with two of his female slaves, but his anger disappeared when he stood on the balcony of his bed chamber watching the mysterious light jump across the sky. He demanded his priests explain the meaning of this light that dared menace his sky. They risked death if they had no answer so the wise men invented and rehearsed a story that would direct Pharaoh's wrath away from them. The priests' ability to survive and thrive depended on their ability to misdirect, like magicians. They told Pharaoh that the light was a demon, sent to test his rule. They lied that the sacrifice of one hundred slaves would show the demon that Pharaoh had power over life and death and consume the demon with fear, chasing it from the sky forever. Pharaoh followed the advice of his priests and ordered the slaughter. Killing one hundred slaves was distasteful and wasteful to Pharaoh but he agreed that this demonstration of his power was necessary as he, too, was secretly frightened by the demon in the sky. One hundred slaves were taken outside the palace entry and slaughtered by Pharaoh's guards. The mutilated corpses were left as a gruesome display for the demon to see the consequence of any challenge to Pharaoh's absolute rule. The blood from the slaughtered bodies blackened the sand and the heat from the rising sun soured the bodies, but the demon light continued to dance in the light of the rising sun, undeterred by the carnage.

Hushed voices spoke of the demon that had no fear of Pharaoh. The blasphemy of their words quickly reached Pharaoh's ear. Outraged, he again summoned his priests. When they entered the holy chamber, they were immediately killed by Pharaoh's guards, then bound by their legs and dragged through the streets for all to witness the punishment for displeasing Pharaoh. The demon light continued to move in the sky and the people talked of a new God.

Pharaoh stood alone on the balcony of his chambers and commanded the light to leave his sky, but the light did not leave, continuing its defiance. *What was this demon that it did not obey?* He thought, with fear welling up inside of him. By high noon, the demon light moved closer to the ground, showing its true form. Shaped like a round battle shield and immense in size, its surface held the brightness of the sun, burning the eyes of anyone looking directly at it for more than a moment.

The strange object finally lowered just outside the wall of the palace, causing the sand beneath it to swirl as high as the palace walls. It made no sound as it finally stopped, floating inches above the hot sand.

Pharaoh's guards, three hundred strong, stormed through the palace gate with weapons drawn ready for the order to strike the silver chariot. Pharaoh, watching from the balcony, called his personal guards. He would confront this demon and slay it himself.

Pharaoh stepped onto his caravan in battle armor. His never-ending inner conflict about his being a God had never been so strong. The conflict had always been there. He had been told from birth that he was a God, descending from Gods. He was worshiped by his people as a God. Still, in his heart, he could not understand the fears that haunted him and his ability to feel pain. When he was just a boy, he had almost died from a fever. Gods were not supposed to feel pain or get sick and even though the priests had explained that he was saved by his own divine power. He often questioned the truth of their words and the truth of who he was. As he grew older, he did not understand why he had no control over sickness and death. He could order death but could not stop it in sickness. He could not control the weather or the sun or the moon. How could a God's body bleed like his? His father and his father's father had all died an earthly death. Should a God not live forever and know all things? He had no understanding of this mesmerizing, demon object and even less understanding of himself. This day was challenging all his doubts.

Inside the ship, TOR-LOK watched the hostiles surrounding him. He had contemplated his options before landing on this planet but neither his host body nor the ship could continue the mission in their damaged condition. He would need to use the ship's healer to stay alive until he could grow a new implant replacement. The life force of the ship had been severely damaged by the star flare and would need time to self-repair before he could risk engaging the main power.

Without the main power propulsion, the ship could not attain the speeds necessary to dimension jump and continue the mission. An analysis of the ship's systems was inconclusive in determining how much time it would take for the ship to self-repair or how much time it would take before this host body expired. There were simply too many unknowns. He had no choice but to use the magnetic power of this small planet to silently maneuver the ship in the atmosphere and look for a place of refuge. Now, here he was, surrounded by hostiles.

It was bad luck that brought him to this primitive planet, and he would need all his skills to survive here until the ship was repaired and he could make a host transfer. His ship was a miracle combination of biology and technology, able to travel to the farthest reaches of the universe. Technology did not make the ship immune to the dangers of space, but the mission was the only way to save his species. The genocide of the Great Invasion had destroyed his world and caused near extinction of his species. The survivors committed to a new existence. They had learned that existing in their old life forms made their survival uncertain. This mission was the last hope for his kind and TOR-LOK must not fail at any cost.

The black star flare was an anomaly. TOR-LOK had passed countless black stars with no incidents. After entering this galaxy, the ship altered its flight path to avoid a maverick asteroid shower. The ship made a hard turn to avoid the high-speed rocks as it had done so many times before. The ship's evasive maneuver veered the ship close to the black star. The star's gravity pulled on the ship and TOR-LOK saw an opportunity to conserve energy. He would use a sling. Instead of wasting the ship's power to pull away from the star, TOR-LOK accelerated the ship toward the star using the star's gravitational pull to accelerate the ship around the star until he was slung by the force of the star's gravitational force, back on course at dimension jump speed without using the ship's power. TOR-LOK took advantage of any opportunity to conserve power. Utilizing a sling was an opportunity that TOR-LOK would not pass up.

The maneuver was working perfectly when the ship was suddenly engulfed by a planet- sized flare exploding from the star. The effects of the damage were immediate. The nuclear superheat of the flare hit the ship, spinning it sideways. TOR-LOK tried to power out, but the ship's plasma power did not respond. He tried the direction control thrusters to counteract the death spin of the ship.

The maneuver worked. As he gained control, he slowly turned back to space. The ship was still alive, but the damage was extensive. His host body felt internal pain and was having trouble staying conscious. He closed his eyes for a moment after the ship was out of danger to let his multiple hearts slow down. After his body functions stabilized, he surveyed the damage.

The pulsar heat had caused most of the ship's systems to shut down and the living plasma power wrap had superheated. The ship's plasma would die without time to heal itself. The ship could not power to mission speeds. His body was hot and cold at the same time. He was sure the host body was poisoned. The reserve implant host body had been killed by the flare. He could not transfer out of the dying host. He would grow another implant after finding a safe location for the ship. Until then, he could only hope that this host body would survive long enough. The chamber could contain the poison for now but how much time he had was unknown. He could not risk a distress signal. With the ship in such a vulnerable condition while he was in the healing chamber, alerting the wrong species could be fatal. He prepared for hibernation and directed maintenance power to life support and hull repulsion. He set the ship's sensors to wake him in one star cycle or if the ship came into proximity of an atmosphere planet or another craft. When he awakened, if he awakened, he would attempt to find a safe place to land. TOR-LOK settled into the chamber, drifting into hyper sleep while the ship continued through the blackness of space.

The ship's sensors awakened him in less than one solar rotation, having detected a small atmosphere planet. TOR-LOK felt the pain of his host body as he came out of hibernation. He sat in the chamber until his muscles responded, then he lifted himself up and moved over to the control mound. The command chair emerged from the mound and control instruments appeared. He quickly checked the systems. The ship had not sustained any additional damage while he was in hibernation and the plasma had begun self-healing but was still too damaged to risk powering.

He scanned the planetary system; it was a small one-star system. The third planet from the star had a thick atmosphere that contained breathable gases that would allow him to move on the surface without being confined in his skin suit. Its surface was covered with liquid, solid composite with an abundance of biological growths and diverse life forms. He adjusted the ship's course to intercept. The ship could fly on the planet's power once he reached its atmosphere. He would find a safe place to land and give the plasma wrap time to heal itself. He was unsure of his host body's condition. The healer was inconclusive. He sent more scans to the surface of the planet but at his current distance he could only capture basic surface conditions. Detailed information could only be gathered by scaling the planet's surface, a dangerous but necessary maneuver.

Scans of the other planets in the system showed that two planets had supported life at one time but were now barren. No doubt, victims of planetary disasters. It was just a matter of time before every planet was hit by killer-size space rocks or comets unless planetary protection barriers were constructed. This small system showed no species evolved enough to be capable of developing that technology. The third planet was TOR-LOK's only chance. The surface of the other planets in this system were too hostile to afford him refuge outside the safety of the ship or his suit. The third planet's surface conditions were mild, evidenced by the abundance of diverse organic life forms. There was no advanced technological development so he would not face superior weapons. The surface had large areas of liquid, a rare find. The land masses varied in temperature and elevation. This planet looked very promising.

The ship was approaching a large red planet, TOR-LOK considered another sling. It would save valuable time. Scans showed horrific surface winds that he would have to navigate, but he could also use them to get around the planet faster. It was an acceptable risk that would ensure enough energy to get the ship to the third planet. He began the maneuver toward the surface of the forbidding looking giant and initiated planet mass power. The planet's gravity accelerated the ship as it skimmed the atmosphere. The magnetic current of the planet was immense and gave him the ability to increase his speed while plummeting through the surface storms. He had not experienced such winds since the explosion of the Coorlon sun.

The sling would build enough speed once he left the atmosphere to jump to the third planet. He would hold the ship at full planet power until the last instant to produce enough speed to make the sling. His speed was building as he circled the planet. He applied all his concentration and held his course. Finally, at the last possible moment, he made the first of two turns and was compressed against his command chair with such force that if he were not in his protective suit, the host skeleton would break apart. The planet was a blur as the right-angle maneuver skimmed the ship through the windstorm building speed. He held direction until the ship reached maximum speed. He made a second right angle turn, propelling the ship upwards toward space, cheating the gravitational pull of the mammoth planet and catapulting him around the far side of the planet and into space.

Perfection, he thought. It was at this moment that he regained his confidence in the mission's survival. So much depended on him. He tried not to over think it but in space there was so much time with nothing but your own thoughts. Even in hibernation, when he was not supposed to be able to dream, his mind was enslaved with the mission. No matter what obstacles he faced, he must survive. He would try to rest his mind until he reached the small planet. He would need to be ready for anything.

TOR-LOK approached the small planet, stopping at the edge of its atmosphere where he engaged planet mass power and turned off ship power. He sent more scans. Anything could be waiting. It would not be the first time that a seemingly docile planet was a trap.

The surface looked calm and showed no readings of hidden advanced power sources. He moved forward, with caution, accelerating entry speed, plummeting deep into the small planet's atmosphere, appearing as a fireball in the sky. He made a right-angle maneuver to slow his speed and extinguish the flames engulfing the hull.

He was struck by the planet's beauty. The rich, deep colors reminded him of the beauty of his home planet before the war. This world was equally beautiful and visually sedating. He proceeded to fly over the planet in search of a suitable location to land the ship. The planet was incredibly diverse. Both the land and liquid areas contained uncountable numbers of life forms. TOR-LOK swooped down just above the top of the surface growth and then straight up and over bright peaks. *This area would be a good hiding place,* he thought, should the need arise, but the surface temperature was too low for him to stay while he prepared a new implant and searched for a new body. He accelerated the ship until the land disappeared and there was only liquid. He was tempted to fly into the liquid to get a closer look but decided it was too dangerous in the ship's condition. Exploration would have to wait. The liquid finally gave way to another large land mass dotted with liquid flows and tall land peaks topped with frozen liquid.

Most of the planet's life forms were scattered and very primitive, still evolving and merging. Large species groups with features like his host body, were coexisting and demonstrating social growth. The humanoids were clearly the highest evolved life form that he had seen so far, encouraging the chances of finding a suitable host with upper brain functions capable of supporting an implant. Their structures were crude and without power, but they showed intelligent basic skills to provide nourishment and protection from surface conditions. Temperatures here were still low so TOR-LOK continued his search until the ship reached a great sparse land area devoid of foliage except occasional strange looking tall plants. Temperatures were almost perfect. He slowed the ship and increased scans, detecting a large humanoid population. He flew to a higher altitude to observe without being seen.

The population area was covered with dwellings. They were different than the dwellings he had observed earlier. Some structures were exceptionally large and constructed with composite mixtures. He flew lower to get a better look. The humanoids were much smaller in stature than TOR-LOK's host body and had small heads and different covering color but were otherwise remarkably similar in form. This would only be possible if this planet had been seeded. He absorbed their speech patterns and quickly learned their language and many of their customs and history. To make their communication sounds would require him to make difficult muscular movement. TOR-LOK had rarely needed to use physical communication, but primitives could not communicate with their minds. He would need to use their primitive sounds to make them understand him.

He moved the ship in different directions to survey the area and make sure that there were no hidden ambushes. He watched the display of carnage by the primitives with great interest. The slaughtering of its own kind demonstrated their dangerous state of evolution. These killings were an obvious demonstration of power. The minds of the primitives were absorbed with a single deity. That was good, a single leader. He decided to land. He needed a safe place and protection. He would try to communicate with this leader.

TOR-LOK moved through the minds of the hostiles that surrounded the ship. They had simple mental structuring. He telepathically commanded them to put down their weapons. The soldiers looked back and forth at each other as they dropped their swords, spears, and shields.

Pharaoh arrived in his caravan that was being carried by slaves and surrounded by his personal guards. Pharaoh could not believe his own eyes. His soldiers were standing empty-handed with their weapons lying on the ground. He had never witnessed such disobedience. He ordered the soldiers to pick up their weapons. The pharaoh's voice snapped them out of their trance, and they picked up their weapons, wondering how they got on the ground. Pharaoh stepped down from his caravan and walked to within an arm's length of the light demon's chariot. With all eyes fixed on him, the pharaoh slowly reached out and ran his open palm over the strange chariot's surface. He had never felt anything like this chariot. It was smooth and warm to the touch, floating in the air and not touching the sand.

Watching from inside the ship, TOR-LOK was struck by the fear this pharaoh commanded in the minds of the hostiles. TOR-LOK's telepathic control of the soldiers stopped when they saw their pharaoh.

He could not read the mind of this pharaoh. This deity was mentally advanced from the rest. He would have to trick this leader into trusting him. He set the ship to self-protect. If his plan failed and his host body was injured, the ship would kill all the primitives so he could get to the healer. He concealed the heat stick in his suit and opened the portal causing a hissing sound from the releasing pressure, causing the soldiers to jump backward and ready their weapons. Pharaoh did not outwardly startle and held his ground surprising even himself with his composure as he could not remember being more frightened. For the first time since his training as a young boy hunting the tiger, he felt alive.

Akhenaten had come to find his life as a God dulling to his mind. Although worshiped as a God with the power of life and death, the mundane routine of a ruler had become a prison. The nameless faces bowing and groveling in fear of his disfavor presented no challenge in his life. With all his power over his world, he had never been able to recapture the excitement he had felt when he stared into the growling face of the cornered tiger. But now, every part of his body was again alive with fear and wonder. He did not know what his next breath might bring but he welcomed this unknown thing before him that had brought his senses back to life.

The primitives watched the chariot melt onto the sand, forming a silver path that turned from liquid into a solid ramp. All but Pharaoh was frozen in fear and anticipation of the blue light shining from the opening in the chariot. The fear of the unknown burned in their heads like the dark terror before a battle. Would these moments be their last? The waiting was a moment of surprise relief for the pharaoh. He no longer felt fear for this demon. Pharaoh welcomed this unknown thing and was ready to confront the truth of his own mortality. Was he truly a God? Could he be harmed by this demon? If he were not a God, he was ready to face that truth.

Long seconds passed with no movement from the blue light. The pharaoh finally moved closer to the opening until he was almost close enough to step onto the silver ramp. He removed the dagger from its gold scabbard and faced the opening. If joining his ancestors today was his destiny, he was ready.

TOR-LOK moved slowly out of the ship until he was in full view. His tall frame gave him the appearance of a giant. The mirror-like reflection of his space suit, like his ship, shot painful refracting sunlight into the eyes of Pharaoh and his soldiers. The soldiers' hands were frozen on their weapons. TOR-LOK moved slowly down the silver ramp of the ship toward the pharaoh, keeping one hand close to his hidden heat stick should this decision turn out to be a deadly mistake. TOR-LOK stopped a few feet from the pharaoh. Pharaoh did not move.

What courage, TOR-LOK thought as he slowly knelt his seven-foot frame down on one knee speaking perfect Egyptian loudly but with great physical difficulty.

"Praise be to the great God King Akhenaten!" Nobody moved!

"I am a gift from Aten, to serve you," TOR-LOK said, still on one knee. He signaled the ship to fire a power beam straight up into the sky to demonstrate his power. The blast caused the soldiers to fall to the ground in fear that the lightning from the demon chariot would take their souls. Pharaoh stood firm with his knife in his hand, showing no fear. TOR-LOK was not sure how his charade was going. Should he strike out? Should he have the ship kill them all before they decided to kill him? He stayed on his knee, looking down at Pharaoh's feet with his hand on the power stick, ready to kill if he had to. TOR-LOK lifted his head slowly, looking into Pharaoh's eyes. Pharaoh reached out and put his hand on TOR-LOK's shoulder.

There was no fear in Pharaoh's voice as he spoke. "I praise Aten and welcome this gift. You shall be my highest of priests," he proclaimed. At that moment, Pharaoh believed what he had questioned all his life. He must be a God to receive such homage from the God of the sun, Aten.

He turned toward his soldiers and proclaimed, "From this day, Aten's gift shall be praised by the people of Egypt as they praise me!"

The soldiers began to chant: **"Aten! Aten! Aten!"** They continued their chanting until

Pharaoh raised his hand, quieting them. Pharaoh turned and climbed onto his gold-adorned caravan. He motioned toward the palace. Pharaoh's personal guards escorted the new priest on foot behind the caravan.

The weight of the planet's atmosphere was heavy on TOR-LOK's body and made his movements difficult, but he would have to adjust himself to these new conditions, if he were to stay with these aliens, so he showed no outward discomfort. His suit was adjusting to his new surroundings and began to make his breathing easier. The long walk to the palace gave him time to formulate a plan. The first thing that must be done was to secure the ship. He sent mental commands for the portal to close and for the ship to fly into the lower atmosphere until he knew where it would be safe and still give him access to use the healer.

The soldiers stopped their chanting and looked back as the ship silently lifted off the ground and disappeared into the sky. The pharaoh did not look back even when their chanting stopped. A God was above such trivial curiosity. Although TOR-LOK's scans of this deity showed that its physical composition was no different than the other primitives, his mind was functioning at a much higher level. So far, scans indicated that this species was only able to use a small part of their brain, leaving much room for evolutionary growth. This species was so far ahead of the other life forms analyzed by the ship's sensors that TOR-LOK was convinced they had been seeded.

The chanting sound: **"Pharaoh! Pharaoh! Pharaoh!"** outside the high priest's quarters brought TOR-LOK back to the present. The people chanted for the new god king in anticipation of the ceremony that night, oblivious to their fate of horror and death from the evil new pharaoh. It was time to leave. The ship was ready. All that was left was securing his slaves in the ship and dealing with the new pharaoh.

The old pharaoh had confided that his son had a dark illness in his mind and had pleaded with TOR-LOK to take the son to the healing chamber in the ship like he had done for him when he was ill. The chamber had always cured him, and it might be a cure for his son's darkness. TOR-LOK told the old pharaoh that the healing chamber could not repair the mind and that perhaps his son would lose the darkness as he grew into a man. TOR-LOK's advice seemed to give the pharaoh temporary comfort, but in his heart, he knew the darkness in his son would only grow.

TOR-LOK had already decided that if he were still on this planet at the time of Pharaoh's death, he would do what the father could not bear to do: Kill the son himself to save the people from his cruel madness. Pharaoh and his wife, Nefertiti, had only one son to inherit the throne. Their other children would be stepped over or killed. Should the only heir die, the throne would then pass to the son of Pharaoh's sister, who was favored by the old pharaoh for his demonstrated love of the people. After killing the son, TOR-LOK would leave this desert with the slaves, Shekaan and Kadages. Even with the new pharaoh's death, these female slaves would not survive. They would be killed.

The treatments had prolonged the host body's life, but the damage was too extensive. TOR-LOK had attempted to activate a new implant in many young males, but their bodies had not tolerated the implant process and died. He had no time to prepare another host when the old pharaoh died. He had put Shekaan to sleep and carried her to the ship. He inserted the implant in the young female's neck to keep it alive until he could find a male host body. He was surprised when her body showed no negative effects from the powerful membrane. She would have no memory of the trip to the ship to remember its secret location. Pharaoh's son must not know the ship's location and if Shekaan were tortured, she would have nothing to tell.

The failure to produce a new host and the health of Pharaoh had prevented his leaving. His time on this planet had not been without its rewards, but not a day passed that he did not want to leave this planet and continue the mission. So much depended on him. If something should happen to the host body before he could transfer, the mission would be marooned.

He had decided that after he killed Pharaoh's son, he would take his slaves to the first place he saw when he entered this planet. The terrain was mountainous, with heavy foliage and an abundance of deep-water bodies, a perfect place to hide the ship while he prepared a new host.

TOR-LOK walked onto his balcony, looking over the desert. This land had a dangerous beauty about it that reminded him of the Polar's moon. He had landed on Polar to collect power elements and had been put at ease by its desolate, serene beauty only to almost be killed by strange, vicious animals that he named *Grounders*. They hid underground, feeling the vibration of one's movements until they were close enough to burst out of hiding and rip you to pieces. If *Grounders* did not get you, the sudden storm death winds would. He had learned to be cautious. Space travel had taught him that things were seldom as they appeared. Life on this planet was calm and serene on its surface but it was what could not be seen or detected on scans that could be treacherous. Life on this beautiful planet was harsh with an abundance of life ending diseases. By far, the most dangerous and wondrous species on the planet were the primitives themselves. Landing on alien planets was a great danger of space travel. You always had to be on your guard.

"Your highness," a small voice called from behind him. He turned and gave an acknowledging glance toward Shekaan, the older of his two slaves.

"The new pharaoh has summoned you," she told him with her head bowed.

TOR-LOK looked at his gentle little Shekaan. He had become very fond of the females and knew that he was their only chance to survive.

"See to my robes," he ordered her. TOR-LOK walked into his clothing chamber, reaching under one of his garments, he grabbed his heat stick, concealing it up his sleeve. He moved quickly down the long passageway into the open courtyard adjoining his quarters. This meeting was a bad sign.

The new pharaoh was supposed to stay in seclusion to mourn his father until the ceremony. TOR-LOK considered that it may be an ambush, but for him not to go would be an intolerable insult and give the new pharaoh the excuse to kill him openly. Many thoughts that it was unlikely the new pharaoh would try to kill him before the ceremony. What was more likely was that this was a show of power, putting the priest on notice.

He hurried across the open courtyard and climbed the steps to the palace doors, where he was met by the new pharaoh's personal guards. He had watched these same guards many times in the battle arena practicing their killing skills, sharing the new Pharaoh's lust for blood. They were always by his side, ready to give their life for their new God. He listened into their minds but learned little. It was clear that these guards were not privy to the new pharaoh's plans and had received no kill orders, but death was on their minds. The guards escorted him down the long hallway of kings, lit on both sides by giant urns of burning oil. They climbed the last set of steps until the new pharaoh could be seen sitting on the throne. TOR-LOK noticed the slight smile on the new pharaoh's face and sensed that this showdown was a prelude to his own, inevitable assassination.

TOR-LOK bowed respectfully, awaiting the new pharaoh's acknowledgment while gripping the heat stick in case he had misjudged the time of his assassination.

"My father's great advisor, you honor me with your presence, Priest." The new pharaoh announced with little enthusiasm, "Come closer."

"It is I that am honored, great Pharaoh. My life is but to serve you!" TOR-LOK replied, moving slowly toward the son to comply with his request. He had moved only two steps when the new pharaoh stood up, turning his back to the high priest, leaving TOR-LOK no choice but to stop. Turning his back on the priest was the first insult.

"Your counsel and powers served my father well, but he was a fool to take only advice. You will give to me all your powers and secrets after tonight's ceremony!" he ordered threateningly. The tone of his voice did not invite any compromise or discussion. To voice disobedience would invite immediate death at the hands of his guards. TOR-LOK saw only hate in the new pharaoh's mind while he bowed humbly.

"As you command, Pharaoh. The secrets from the heavens shall be yours," he lied.

TOR-LOK saw only lust for the silver chariot in the new pharaoh's thoughts and predicted the son would kill him the minute he found the ship. The old pharaoh had all the slaves killed that built the secret chamber, to keep the location secret. He never revealed the location to his son. Being excluded from his father's confidence had built a wall between father and son, fueling the son's obsession to know the priest's secrets that were shared only with his father.

The new pharaoh did not believe the priest. He had expected him to pretend to be agreeable, but he knew that the priest would never give up his secrets. In his paranoia, he feared the priest would try to kill him and become the new pharaoh. The priest was far too dangerous. This meeting made the son even more anxious to be rid of him. He would discover the ship's location and take its secrets for himself. The ship could not deny a God.

"Leave me, Priest, and prepare your offering," the new pharaoh said, turning his back to the priest for a second time; showing the highest degree of insult.

TOR-LOK stood defiantly for a moment before bowing silently while backing out of the chamber. The new pharaoh's guards followed him out of the palace like the killing dogs they were trained to be.

TOR-LOK hurried back to his chambers. There was little time left to prepare the ship. After he was certain that no one had followed him, he left through the back entrance of his chambers. He walked across the open courtyard to his private worship room, which was a disguised entry to the hidden ship. He lit a wall torch and used his great body strength to push against the far wall, forcing it to open enough for him to pass through then pushed the wall back into place behind him. He walked quickly down a long set of steps that led to a large door. The door was internally locked and could not be opened by primitives. TOR-LOK put his palm on the gold design in the middle of the door, lighting it up and swinging the door open.

The ship that had traveled through many galaxies looked out of place imprisoned by the walls in this cold dark room. The torchlight reflecting off its hull gave the ship an eerie look. He removed the power boosters, disguised as flowers, from each hand of the statue that stood just inside the room, disarming the security beam. He sent a mental command, opening a portal. He was thinking about how to protect the slaves from the physical danger of flying. They would not be able to tolerate even a short ride through the atmosphere without some protection. Human bodies were so frail and unable to survive for even a short time without concentrated gases. The chamber healer should hold the two women and keep them from being injured during the flight by filling the chamber with breathable liquid and keeping their bodies cushioned. The liquid would frighten them when forced to breathe it into their bodies, but it would keep them alive. There was no time for further modifications. The chamber Pharaoh had built around the ship had been TOR-LOK's design, allowing the ceiling to be blown away to accommodate a fast escape. He was as ready as he could be.

TOR-LOK exited the ship, not resetting the security beam in case he had to enter the ship quickly. He hurried up the stairs to the worship chamber. He pushed on the wall creating a small opening. As TOR-LOK stepped into the worship chamber, he felt something hit his chest and fell back against the wall, his body burning with pain. He looked down to see the first arrow in his body quickly followed by another. He held his heat stick in front of him. The four guards had thought it would be an easy kill and felt nothing as their bodies were liquefied by the heat beam. TOR-LOK stood alone, the arrows protruding from his chest. He grabbed each arrow and broke them off where they entered his chest. He was losing a lot of body fluid. The second arrow had struck one of his hearts. He could not take the time to go back to the healing chamber. The pharaoh would have already sent assassins to capture or kill Shekaan and Kadages. He would have to hurry to rescue them, hoping he was not too late. If his host body could not be repaired, everything would depend on Shekaan's survival.

He closed the door to the worship chamber and hurried through the courtyard toward his chambers, not trying to conceal his weapon. The humans he passed seemed unaware of what had just happened. That was a good sign. The new pharaoh had sent his assassins in secret. As TOR-LOK approached the entry to his private chambers he saw that it was surrounded by guards. He saw the surprise on their faces when they saw him. They raised their weapons. The beam from the heat stick made no sound when it liquefied them, He rushed through the door and saw Shekaan and Kadages lying on the floor, arms and feet bound. No doubt they were going to be taken to the palace to be dealt with at the new pharaoh's pleasure. The two guards standing over them were reduced to liquid when the heat beam hit them.

There was terror in the women's eyes while TOR-LOK released them but there was no time for explanations. He gave them a thought command to follow him and rushed back to the ship with the women running behind him. The loss of body fluids was weakening him, and he had to force himself to keep moving. The worship chamber was empty except for the liquified remains of the guards. He opened the secret door and led the women down the stairs and through the last door. He opened the portal of the ship. Shekaan and Kadages were frozen in fear at the sight of the ship.

You must go inside, TOR-LOK's thought ordered them. They did not move.

Go inside now! TOR-LOK repeated loudly.

The young women had never heard the high priest raise his voice. His frightening tone, filled with such urgency made the women enter the ship despite their fear. The inside illuminated as they entered, with no torches and they felt the surprising warmth of the ship's floor under their bare feet, adding to the women's confusion and fear. The interior of the ship was all white with large bumps in the floor.

A low humming sound resonated throughout the ship, sounding like a moaning monster beneath their feet. It was all beyond their understanding. TOR-LOK ushered them to the large protrusion. It instantly uncovered itself, further terrifying the women. TOR-LOK motioned Shekaan to lie down inside. She lifted herself inside and as she lay back looking up at the priest, he cradled her face softly in his hand to try to calm her. She lay motionless as he turned to Kadages, motioning for her to also get in the chamber. She climbed in, squeezing next to Shekaan and grabbing her hand. He smiled at them as the top of the chamber sealed the women inside. He knew the next step would likely panic the women, so he tried to prepare them with a mental message explaining that liquid would pour over them and that it was alright to breath it in and not to be afraid.

The liquid filled the chamber and the women, as TOR-LOK had predicted, panicked, kicking their feet against the chamber thinking they were being drowned. They pounded on the sides with their fists until the fluid filled the chamber. When they could hold their breath no longer, they took their first breath of liquid and realized that they could breathe while submerged in the fluid. They became quiet and still, almost like they were in a trance. TOR-LOK went to his command chair, which appeared as he approached. He painfully lifted himself onto it. The controls materialized.

He had wanted to leave after dark to avoid the exit explosion harming primitives, but there was no time. He shot a heat blast from the ship straight up at the ceiling, blowing off the worship chambers roof with such force that pieces landed as far away as the palace, leaving a hole large enough for the ship to easily fly out of. He lifted the ship from its hidden tomb and turned toward the pharaoh's palace. People were running for their lives through the rubble. He hovered the ship over the palace and sat down in the courtyard. He left the ship and entered the palace. He struggled down the long hallway to the pharaoh's throne room. The evil son was sitting on his throne surrounded by his guards who rushed toward TOR-LOK. The heat stick eliminated all the guards while the son watched in horror. In a last act of respect to the old pharaoh that had given him refuge and friendship and to save thousands from the terror that would surely befall them under the rule of the mad, boy pharaoh, he sent one final blast, melting the new pharaoh.

Pain stabbed through his body as he returned to the ship. The loss of one heart had put great stress on the other. He needed the healing chamber. He took the ship straight up into the atmosphere until he could see the curve of the planet. He worried about the women's condition in the chamber and how long his host body could remain conscious without using the chamber to remove the arrows. When the ship reached the edge of space TOR-LOK accelerated toward the mountain he first saw when he entered Earth's atmosphere. In just minutes, the ship was hovering over the mountain peak.

TOR-LOK was worried about the females and set the ship down by the liquid at the bottom of the mountain. The females were lying with their eyes wide open, holding each other. He drained the healer and tried to help them climb out but was too weak and he fell to the floor of the ship. The women lifted themselves out of the chamber. They were confused when there was no fluid in their lungs and their clothes were not wet. TOR-LOK motioned for help to get up. They each grabbed one arm, struggling with his weight as they helped him into the chamber. He set the chamber to keep him awake so he would be able to stop the process should the host body expire. The remaining heart was gorging itself trying to keep up with the body's demand for life-giving fluid. If the healing chamber could not get the damaged heart to work, the host body would die. TOR-LOK 's chest felt like it was on fire. Shekaan was attending to his wound, taking pieces of cloth she had torn from her tunic and wrapping them around the base of the wounds, trying to stop the flow of blue liquid that was now pouring from the wounds.

TOR-LOK waved them away from the healer and closed the lid. The chamber engaged a retriever to remove the arrow shafts. The extraction itself was a dangerous procedure, if there was too much damaged tissue removed, it would kill him. He activated the extractor! TOR-LOK did not want to spend the extra time required for tissue numbing so he would have to bear the pain. Shekaan watched the alien machine as it grabbed onto the stub of the broken arrow and worked its way down to the end of the shaft. A cocoon was formed around the arrow which melted the arrow within the cocoon. After the arrow had been eliminated, the extractor pulled back, leaving a layer of orange healing goo to seal the surrounding tissue and stop the bleeding. After removing the first arrow, the extractor repeated the procedure on the second arrow. Knowing the chamber would hibernate his body for the healing process and seal the chamber, TOR-LOK telepathically opened the ship's portal to allow the women access to the outside. They would need to search for food and water and take care of their bodily needs until the healing procedure was complete. The healing chamber started the hibernation process. The two terrified women peered at him in the chamber. He smiled, trying to ease their fear, and told them he was tired and would sleep. Before he could give them more instructions, the chamber numbed his muscles and he slipped into hibernation.

The terrified women were now alone. The day's events confused their minds. Without the high priest to direct them, they were too afraid to leave the ship even though staying in the strange chariot was foreign and terrifying. They never had to make their own decisions. They were born into slavery, their only purpose in life was to serve their master. They were ready to give their lives for the priest, but his deathlike sleep offered no direction for them. They did not understand what was happening to the priest. Both women stood by the chamber watching and waiting for him to awaken but after waiting many hours, hunger overtook them. The ship was barren inside. Its radiating warmth was comforting but there was no food or water and no place to dispose of waste from their bodies or clean themselves, forcing them to find the courage to leave the ship to search for food and water.

They investigated the area close to the spaceship in fear and growing curiosity, like two little children finding themselves in a strange land. But they were intelligent women with a strong will to survive. They had looked upon TOR-LOK as a demi-god. Seeing him wounded and bleeding had shaken their understanding of what they thought he was. Although he had magical, god-like powers, his body was damaged and gods could not be hurt like mortals, according to the teachings of the priests. Their confusion added to their fear.

Over the next two days, the women ventured farther from the ship to look for water and scavenge for food. They found the lake and cleaned themselves in its shallow edge, drank water and ate berries.

When darkness came, the sounds of the forest frightened them, and they would scurry back to the safety of the ship. They were aliens in a strange world. The slim pickings of the forest close to the ship would not keep them alive for long. The women's hunger forced them to venture deeper into the forest to find food.

Four days after entering the healing chamber, the machine initiated the reviving process. There was no more the machine could do to save the host body. TOR-LOK managed to climb out. The machine had given him a little more time, but he knew this body would not live much longer. The women were gone. TOR-LOK scanned the surrounding forest, searching for them. He feared that the women had gotten lost and may have been killed by animals or primitives. He could only hope they were still alive. The implant he had put in Shekaan was not complete. He would have to try a transfer without finishing the process. If he could not find her in time, he would have to leave this dying body and would be trapped in the ship with no flyer. He sent mental commands to the females to return to the ship, but there was no response.

Ship scans had detected many different animals in the forest, some of which could be a threat to the women. On the next day of searching, scans identified small human groups functioning in organized social systems. These primitives were more socially integrated and valued life more than the higher evolved Egyptians. From first contact with the Egyptians, he had witnessed their brutality and indifference to human life. As close as TOR-LOK had been to the pharaoh, he had not been able to change his mindset toward the value of human life that had been ingrained in the Egyptian people. That was a burden of their stage of evolution. Although technologically inferior to the Egyptians, these forest primitives worked together to feed and defend themselves. In their society, they needed each other to survive.

At the end of his third day of searching, he no longer had the physical strength to search for the slaves and prepared the healing chamber for hibernation. It was doubtful that this body's remaining heart would survive hibernation, but it was now his only option. He was out of time and had to hide the ship while the host body was alive. He moved the ship over the water while making a last, desperate scan. The slaves were nowhere near the ship. He was having a difficult time maintaining consciousness. He decided to hide the ship in the water, close to where he left the women so the ship would have a better chance of connecting with the implant and making a transfer. The eyes of his host body began to blur. A deep stabbing pain erupted from the chest. He was out of time. He lowered the ship into the water until it settled on the bottom. He lifted himself off the command seat and climbed into the healing chamber. He initiated hibernation, transferring out of the host and into the ship before the chamber closed. Until the implant could be connected or the host body miraculously recovered, he was trapped. He had waited too long to leave this planet and now he feared that everything could be lost.

The women settled into their new life. Indians found them wandering aimlessly in the forest and had taken them into their camp, fed them, gave them a safe place to sleep and protected them from the dangers of the strange forest. Thinking TOR-LOK was dead, they had given up trying to return to the ship. The women and their new brothers and sisters could not communicate with each other in language, saving the women from having to explain where they came from. These people were their new family. Their life now was to learn the Indian ways and become one of them. The women were free for the first time since their birth. They served their brothers and sisters, and their brothers and sisters served them. They had no masters. They finally had a family. Skekaan and Kadages lived many years and birthed many children. They never betrayed their great secret knowing that their new family would not understand as they did not understand.

The star ship that had traveled uncountable distances across the universe, survived the heat of exploding stars, the constant barrage of asteroids and unseen dangers of space travel, now lay motionless on the bottom of a lake, on the third planet of a single star system. The low blue lights from the ship could be seen, shining up through the dark water at night.

Over time, stories were told by the elders of the strange lights in the lake that were sent from the sky by the great mother to guide the souls of the dead to a new life in the stars. As the years turned to decades, sediment and water grass covered the ship. The lights dimmed from view and the submerged ship appeared as a hill of sand jetting from the bottom of the lake.

Shekaan's descendants were unknowingly drawn to the lake all their lives, held by a signal that called to them. After the passing of countless winters, the legend of the lights turned to myth and the myth was forgotten. The ancient ship lay in its watery grave, signaling for its flyer. Waiting...

Chapter Two

Ambush

The Terian ship was in its longest shape, cutting through space. The most advanced ship ever created; it was the pinnacle of supreme technology. Inside the craft, dull lights, and the low pitch hum of the anti- matter drives created a serene atmosphere. The team was in hibernation, leaving only the leader, TE-GON, and "C" (the central artificial), to fly the ship. For TE-GON, this was paradise. He cherished search missions, wrapped in his command chair, flying into the unknown.

He had earned many honors in his infamous career with the elite Terian Supreme but was most proud of achieving the rank of Command Leader, which was given to only the best flyers. He was celebrated throughout the Terian Empire and was the pride of the Terian Supreme. His space discoveries and exploration adventures were legendary and mandatory training downloads for all training flyers.

TE-GON was tall even by Terian standards, almost 15 kidums, which gave him a striking and authoritative physical presence to support his technical excellence. As far back as he could remember, becoming a flyer had been his obsession. He had been designed and altered to be a flyer before birth. In his training years, when other learners were engaging in political games, social events, and mating rituals, he spent all his extra time studying the download thought records, reliving the experiences of ancient flyers. He would sit under the thought machines, absorbing downloads, until his brain was ready to burst. His thirst for knowledge was never satisfied. He sacrificed not taking a life mate. There was only one passion for him and that was flying. To achieve the highest rank from the Supreme, he had made many personal sacrifices but to be the leader of this mission was a tribute to his accomplishments.

The ship would make multiple tunnel jumps to reach their destination distance by the projected five- star cycles. Ancient Terian ships would have taken over two lifetimes to travel the same distance. It was not uncommon, before advanced anti-matter propulsion and tunnel jumping, for ancient space travelers to grow old and die during a voyage, their mummified bodies still at the controls of their recovered ships. These ancients flew missions knowing that they would never see their home again. They were called ghost travelers, revered heroes, for their fearless dedication and sacrifice exploring the unknown for the advancement of the Terian race. The ancients were his heroes!

TE-GON received a thought transmission from "C" inside the ship's systems.

Ship alert, Comet proximity, "C" reported.

The leader gave a thought command to the ship to *open a vision portal.* The ship opened the portal at his requested location, revealing the comet. The ship was as close to the comet as the ship's programming would allow. Comets were a dangerous space anomaly because of their exploding chemical composition, but they were beautiful to watch. The leader marveled at the mysterious glow of the ancient missile.

Weapon beam! "C" reported.

The warning was too late! The beam hit the ship, coating the hull in a nuclear soup that shot power impulses into the ship, attacking the ship's systems. The attack was weak. Hull repulsion absorbed most of the power from the beam, keeping it from penetrating the higher ship systems. "C's" evasive response was instantaneous, swerving the ship sideways to minimize its physical exposure to another potential hit from the same location, then maximizing power to the hull's repulsion force in case they were struck again. "C" then increased the ship's speed and made another hard turn to distance the ship from the attacker's location. "C" could not locate the target to return fire. The weapon beam had been fired from behind the comet and passing through the ice particles of the comet's tail greatly reduced Its power. The leader knew instantly that the attacker was the Rogue. The last communication from the Supreme warned Terian leaders that reliable intelligence predicted that the Rogue would attempt to capture a Terian ship. The Rogue were the only species desperate enough to try it. The Rogue's obsession for the pursuit of Terian Supreme technology had no boundaries.

The attackers slow recharging weapon systems gave "C" the seconds needed to create a tunnel before a second attack beam could be fired. "C" jumped the ship into the tunnel the instant it opened without preparing a destination, a dangerous maneuver. If the ship survived the tunnel, it would be flying blind, but the first objective was survival, so "C" accelerated the ship into the tunnel without softening the hull or waiting for the leader to go liquid. They would have to survive the tunnel ride with the hull at full flight density with the leader in hard physical form. The four team members hibernating were also at serious risk if the life support systems had been hit.

The ship began to shake violently as the ship's speed increased to level five. The command chair tightened around TE-GON. The ship's speed increased to level eight as it spiraled through the tunnel. The increasing pressure against TE-GON's chest was threatening his breathing and making him lightheaded. He was about to pass out from the force, when his lungs suddenly filled, and he began breathing again.

We are through the tunnel, Leader! "C" reported, as the ship emerged into unknown open space.

Status? the leader requested.

Main power systems are intact but the anti-matter drives have been damaged and will not respond. Power core critically low. Hull repulsion is critical. We will have limited defense ability if hit again. The team has active life functions, "C" reported. *Hibernation life support was not penetrated.*

Why were the ship's sensors not able to see the attack ship? TE-GON asked.

Unknown. "C" responded. *The sensors only detected the beam, not a ship. Weapon tracking traced the beam from a comet.*

They were invisible! TE-GON interjected. *The temperatures of the comet must have shielded their heat signature.*

They may have some degree of refraction technology! "C" suggested.

TE-GON feared their situation was dire. The ship did not have enough power to create or navigate another tunnel without the anti-matter drives. If the Rogue caught up with them, there would be little power for weapons, but, if "C" could not detect them coming, they would not even have a target for their weapons.

"C" was calculating their present position and searching for a high-power source. The ship's power core was too depleted to fly the ship for long without regeneration. "C" sent a distress signal as soon as the ship was through the tunnel, but the signal would have to be relayed by another ship to reach home. They were on their own.

The Rogue would be relentless in their pursuit. Their failure would mean death by the swarm. TE-GON would never allow his ship to fall to the Rogue. The atrocities committed by the Rogue were legendary. Entire worlds destroyed to cover up their crimes of torture and genocide. Destroyed worlds left no witnesses. Terians had only themselves to blame for it was the generosity of Terian science that enabled these monsters to come out of the rocks countless star cycles ago.

TE-GON had a slight lead on the Rogue's ship, but it would not take long for the Rogue's ship to find their power trail and catch up with them, so they needed to regenerate. The jump had saved them from an immediate second attack but another confrontation with the Rogue before regeneration would be fatal.

The ship would not survive another direct hit and capture meant self-destruction, the final option. That decision he would gladly share with "C". When the Supreme mandated new flight rules, that life and death decisions must be unanimous with "C", he resented the restriction on his ultimate authority. However, after flying with "C", he realized the wisdom of the Supreme's decision. The ambush showed how well the partnership worked. When "C" quickly made the immediate evasive moves, she had saved the ship from catastrophic damage and possible capture. Two battle commanders were better than one.

I have verified our position in a one-star system, "C" reported. *There are four planets within reach that are suitable for regeneration.* "C" continued,

The fastest charge is the large red planet, but it has a violent atmosphere.

TE-GON asked, *How violent?*

Speed seven turbulence in cross patterns, "C" answered.

TE-GON said, *Scan all planets closer to the star to find one suitable to make repairs. We will regenerate at the large planet.*

The best find would be a planet where they did not need to wear protective skin suits, so repairing the ship would be easier. The leader knew that was an unlikely find. In all his galactic travels, it was rare to find a world that did not require wearing skin suit protection. Breathable gas planets were anomalies: the rare aftermath of a chain of perfectly timed catastrophic events that acted as a catalyst to create the delicate balance of elements, chemical reactions and atmospheres that could create and sustain diverse biological life. All life worlds that had been discovered were quite different from each other in biological diversity and evolution. He had witnessed life forms that defied the logic of known science.

One such species lived on a planet of burning rock, with a poisonous and non-breathable atmosphere, which could be fatal to any organic lifeform. The species had evolved their biology to absorb poison gas and internally turn it into a life supporting gas. These creatures survived and thrived eating and digesting the burning rock and reproduced themselves by a bizarre process that grew their young inside solid rocks. The young received nourishment by eating their rocky womb from the inside out. He had explored planets dominated by fire breathing insects and other worlds where all life lived inside larger beings that were in turn fed and cared for by their tenants. Diverse life planets were often scientifically unexplainable. Planets that could create and nurture life were the wonders of the universe and always the greatest find of any mission and earned great rewards from the Supreme. Breathable-atmosphere liquid planets would be sought as a last refuge by a flyer whose ship could fly no farther and had no ship life support.

The large planet would work for regeneration but was too violent for a landing. Any planet that they landed on would be in danger of being discovered by the Rogue. Organic beings on that planet would be exposed to the horror of the swarm. The monsters that were following them would be looking for the Terian power trail. There was a chance that the Terian ship's reduced power trail signature would be difficult to follow and may throw the Rogue off their trail or at least slow them down long enough to repair the ship and slip away before the vulnerable planet could be discovered by the monsters. TE-GON worried for any defenseless civilization threatened by his landing on their planet, but the ship's survival was above all. He reduced the ship from level three to level two speed to transfer more core energy to the sensors. This would reduce his lead on the Rogue's ship, but he needed more information on the large planet to plan regeneration.

"C" received another sensor alert and reported it to TE-GON. A faint, high power source had been detected in the one-star system. It was only a tick but unmistakable. The source was on the small third planet. The ship would need to get closer for detailed scans but from the initial readings, the power was from a small single source with a very high output.

TE-GON ordered, *Keep sending scans!*

The detected power source was too powerful to ignore. This was something TE-GON had not expected. The planet must have an advanced civilization to produce the power that scans could pick up at this distance.

Search for an advanced life form, TE-GON sent thoughts to "C".

I agree, "C" replied. She added, *The high-power reading from this third planet is much more powerful than ancient Terian star ships could produce or even anti-matter powered ships, so it is not Terian technology. It is from something very advanced.*

Very advanced, TE-GON thinking to himself. This was an important find that he could not wait to explore if they survived. He had absorbed all the learning downloads about alien life forms and could not help but wonder if the power source on the third planet was from a life form that had become stranded. The study of the ancients and their ships was one of TE-GON's great passions. When the Supreme developed technology that detected the traces of power trails left by ancient ships, the final resting places of marooned alien ships became traceable. The ships that were recovered were primitive with dangerous, technical flaws that caused inevitable mechanical failures and forced landings that marooned flyers. The crude construction of ancient ships made them very heavy, with underpowered propulsion systems. It could take a flyer's lifetime to travel distances now considered short missions. Slow speeds and fragile hulls made them helpless targets of the countless obstacles flying through space. TE-GON admired the bravery of those ancient flyers in ships made before the discovery of Perium! Repulsion technology and the discovery of light weight Perium changed space travel. Perium was a miracle material, almost indestructible in both its liquid and hardened state. Perium was the only material that was programmable to change its thickness instantaneously with no change in temperature or strength. Ships built with Perium hulls and repulsion technology removed the danger of being destroyed by high-speed space debris.

Perium replaced the need for fixed openings on ships. Impenetrable portals or doors could be programmed in any location or desired thickness. Perium made ships strong enough for tunnel speed. Without tunnel flight, it would take ten lifetimes to reach the same distance they could travel in one tunnel jump. The creation of tunnels and discovery of Perium made Terian the most advanced civilization in the known galaxies. Perium's only weakness was that certain power beams and melters could absorb through it. The absorption did not damage the Perium hull of a ship, but a melter would ravage the ship's insides; mechanical and biological, leaving a dead empty hull.

TE-GON ordered the activation of all hibernation cells and pods. He would need everyone awake during regeneration. The pods would store additional power from regeneration and the pod's weapon systems could protect the mother ship if the Rogue should attack while the ship was regenerating.

They were nearing the large red planet and TE-GON needed to rest to be at his best for what was ahead. He turned control of the ship to "C". He decided to charge his body in solid form in case of an emergency. Charging took longer when solid but, recovery time was immediate and that could make the difference between life and death. He sent last minute commands to "C" and went to charge his body.

"C" enjoyed command and had proven her abilities and reliability countless times. She was another miracle development of the Terian Supreme. She was the first machine trusted to be second in command of a Terian galactic spaceship. Built with female personality patterns to be more user friendly, "C" was the most advanced thinking machine ever created.

Her system was connected directly with the ship and had been enhanced with biological neurons, giving her a state of consciousness with the ability to learn from experience. Her core contained all Terian knowledge, and her personality functions were enhanced with the same biological and technical structuring of a natural biological Terian. She was in a constant mental growth cycle just like a biological. It was different for her because her thoughts and feelings advanced from her core of all Terian knowledge. Her feelings were not pre-programmed. Her system had the ability to develop personal feelings and relationships, just like a biological.

Learning relationship development inevitably caused "C" to compare herself to her creators. As she developed, she would often wonder how different her existence would be if she had been born a biological. Would she think the same? What if her encasement was mobile and fashioned after a Terian body instead of being integrated with the ship? Would that make her more biological than mechanical? Was a machine with biological enhancements as real as a biological Terian with mechanical enhancements? She had so many questions.

The revolutionary concept of machines as thinking partners was also a critical element of Terians developing into an advanced civilization. "C" took great pride in her mission with the team. She was able to develop close relationships and a sense of protective caring for TE-GON and team. She often wondered if the leader and crew thought of her as an equal or as just a machine programmed to serve.

Ship sensors alerted "C" of imminent contact with an asteroid cluster. "C" adjusted course to avoid it. In normal flight, the ship's repulsion force would repeal the asteroids and a manual course change would not be necessary, but repulsion would require energy that the ship could not spare. The hull could not be damaged, but collisions affected guidance and would require power adjustments and that was not an option with the ship's critically low level.

Sensor readings were filtering in from the third planet. The ship was still too far away for the sensors to show complete detail, but they were picking up an incredible amount of diverse life forms. Surface development was primitive. Flying crafts with lifeforms aboard were detected throughout the lower atmosphere. Humanoid forms appeared to be the dominant lifeform, which was common on seeded planets. Some machines on the planet used fusion power which could be a concern for their safety.

The biggest mystery was the patterned high-power emission. It was an isolated source beyond the technological evolution of the life forms on the planet. She would advise the leader to send a pod to identify the source when they were close enough. Until they could identify what it was, they would have to use extreme caution. Sensors showed no other technical or physical threat to the ship to prevent landing, but "C" had learned that sensors did not always process everything that was scanned. Primitive aliens were unpredictable, and it was necessary to be prepared for unforeseen circumstances. The third planet had no global defenses against outside attack. They would be helpless against the Rogue or any other advanced hostile invader. There was no reply to telepathic transmissions yet, but that was to be expected at their present distance from the target. With such a primitive civilization, it was unlikely they had developed mental communication.

"C" filled the hibernation chambers with warming hyper liquid to prepare the team for consciousness from suspended animation. The next step of recovery was the most dangerous. "C" had to revive the neurons in each team member's brain at a precise instant or their memory functions would be damaged. When hibernation was being developed, there were many casualties. Like all new technology, advancement demanded sacrifice. Not until the central command machines, like "C", took over the wake-up process, did the casualties stop. "C" had performed reactivation countless times without ever damaging a team member, earning the trust of the team whose lives depended on her ability. This time was no different. "C" brought each member back perfectly. The recovering team members moved slowly as they awakened. Their muscles slightly atrophic until stimulated with low power charges.

ALUME was the first to wake. As the only female team member besides "C", it was not unusual that she recovered first. Females often demonstrated faster recovery ability than males. Both TWEE and ZE-TAN recovered at almost the same time and CRE-LIN who was also the oldest, recovered last. TE-GON had handpicked this team himself. The usual procedure was for the Supreme to assign the ship's team with no vote from the ship leader. However, TE-GON had achieved a rank and privilege that transcended normal procedures and was allowed to pick his own team. He chose each of them for their unique skills.

TWEE was the youngest team member. His understanding of advanced technologies became the talk of the Supreme after he designed a device that calculated jump destinations.

ZE-TAN was the team's weapons expert. He had only experienced two missions before being chosen by TE-GON. On his last voyage, he saved his ship during an encounter with hostile shape changers. His ship had landed on a planet answering a distress signal. The shape changers that inhabited the planet had set an ambush by camouflaging themselves as wounded little ones. ZE-TAN was security for the landing party and immediately noticed that the wounds on the little ones were all the same, copies.

Sensing the ambush, he pulled his blasters and fired on the shapeshifters before they could spring their trap. Two shape changers were later dissected and identified as reptilian with facial glans that discharged flesh eating venom. Their race and planet location were recorded in the downloads to warn future explorers. ZE-TAN's quick action and skill with weapons had saved the landing party and earned him immediate recognition with the Supreme, (the ultimate power of technology).

CRE-LIN and ALUME were the mission's biological experts. The search for new life forms, always a mission priority when encountered, was also one of the most dangerous of all mission duties. The biological team was responsible for advising the leader on all matters regarding any new biological life forms they should encounter.

CRE-LIN was the only team member that had a life partner back home on Paetaan and had been flying for over fifty-star cycles. His mission time was second only to TE-GON.

ALUME was the best thought reader in the supreme. She had been the leader's first team choice. All Terians were designed at birth for mental telepathy, but ALUME had the gift of hearing thoughts of the inner mind. Having a thought reader on mission gave the leader great insight into situations that might occur in a long mission. ALUME could, at times, see into the immediate future, although she could not call them at will. Many of her future insights were unclear and confusing. Sometimes the visions just came to her completely out of context with what was occurring at the time. There did not seem to be a reliable formula for her to know when or where it would happen. She had seen into the future under many different situations. Some of her visions were under stress; sometimes it happened during a quiet moment. The leaders of past missions that she had flown with had been able to use her gifts to help them make critical decisions that affected the lives of all aboard the ship. She had been credited with saving more than one voyage.

While the team was recovering from hibernation, "C" updated them about the Rogue attack and their current situation. All their skills and training would now be put to the test. After they had sufficiently recovered, each team member began preparations.

ZE-TAN analyzed the weapon systems. He discovered it was not good. The damaged anti-matter drives made the main weapon systems useless. He would have to devise alternative weapon solutions.

TWEE reviewed the attack on the scanner recordings. The Rogue had made an incredibly lucky shot, but not lucky enough. The Rogue aimed to disable instead of kill; they wanted the ship in one piece. That was a big mistake. Even with the anti- matter drives shut down, the Terian ship had devastating destructive power. A deliberately set explosion of the anti-matter chamber had the power to destroy a planetary system. Of course, that was a last resort to avoid capture. He calculated that, at this distance, it was impossible to expect any help from the Supreme. That left them alone to deal with the unrelenting, primitive, suicide fighting Rogue monsters. He concentrated on his duty to the ship and began to design a repair plan.

CRE-LIN studied the scans of the target planet. The planet's atmospheric gas mixture was a miracle of chance. The atmospheric properties had created a perfect environment for life. The only other place he had seen so many diverse life forms in one place was on the demonstration farms of his mother planet. This small planet's dominant species were humanoid; still at a very primitive level compared to Terians, but very advanced compared to the planet's other life forms. He also believed them to be seeded.

The biology of the dominating life form was very much like the Terian's, although these humanoids were much smaller in stature. Only one heartbeat could be detected in the species which meant short life spans. Their bodies were very frail, compared to other species he had studied at the same evolutionary age of development. This species was far more mentally advanced than their age as a species. They had developed low level space flight and fusion power that should have been beyond their evolutionary ability.

CRE-LIN wondered what had seeded the planet. Being marooned on a planet like this could be very dangerous. How would they survive? Physical appearance would make blending in with the indigenous humanoid species, impossible. The difference in their physical appearances would not be the only problem that they would have to overcome. He was anxious to get a sample of their biological tissue to confirm his suspicion that this species was not indigenous to the planet. He had studied many species that had evolved from life that had been deposited by falling space rock or comet fragments. There had been examples of procreation between advanced races and primitives; but they were rare and usually created unpleasant results, like the Rogue.

ALUME also saw the scans of the planet and was worried. Fusion development was a danger to the landing; the last thing they needed was a fight with the primitives, especially primitives that have fusion weapons. She had seen it before in other species at this stage of their evolution. ALUME had studied primitives' reactions to Terian flyers; the outcome was almost always violent, forcing the flyers to use defensive weapons. Any fight with these humanoids would not only devastate this isolated little planet but also alert the pursuing Rogue to their location. The future of this planet would not be their own. The Supreme would never allow a valuable liquid planet with fusion technology to remain unsupervised. It was always the same; the strong taking over the weak. ALUME was anxious to explore the planet but with the Rogue in pursuit, there may be no time.

The ship was ready for regeneration. "C's" calculations showed that the ships remaining core power would fail soon. Without power, the Perium could not be controlled; that meant no control of the hull, portals or shape changing, which would leave the ship an easy target, floating helplessly in its hardened state. The magnetic mass of the red planet was their only chance.

"C" calculated possible regeneration on the giant red planet's largest moon where the atmosphere did not have the horrific winds of the larger planet but the amount of energy that could be absorbed from the moon would take too long compared to the red planet. If the Rogue attacked them at the smaller moon, they would have no atmosphere cover; too dangerous. The chemical and gas readings in the red planet's atmosphere were some of the largest ever recorded. Magnetic power should provide enough storage energy to get them to the small planet with power to spare. It would take all the leader's skill to keep from being crushed against the surface. The winds were treacherous in the upper atmosphere but comparatively mild in the middle.

The good thing was that the winds would be even more dangerous to the Rogue. Their ships could not fly element power from the planet's magnetic core. They had to use their main engines to maneuver their heavy, underpowered ships; it would be crazy to attempt an attack in the planet's turbulence. If they were crazy enough to try, the leader would have the advantage of element power maneuvering: Cloud cover, the pods additional maneuverability and fire power. TE-GON was the best flyer in Paetaan. If he took the ship low, under the winds, absorption time would be minimal.

TE-GON awoke from charging and requested, *Status?*

"C" sent the status, and the leader's response was immediate.

He commanded, *Prepare for regeneration!*

TE-GON was confident his team would give their lives to do their duty. Another ambush could demand that great sacrifice. One more well-aimed blast beam would leave him helpless and force self-destruction. Although the Rogue attack ship had not yet been detected, all his instincts prevailed they were close. Even though the Rogue ships did not have the technology or power to create and navigate tunnels, they could still jump vast distances. So, considering his ship's reduced speed capability, they could catch up if they detected his ship's power trail. The safest time for them to attack would be after regeneration to avoid the red planet's winds. His experience revealed they would likely ignore the danger and strike during regeneration when his weapon systems were unpowered. His ship must not be captured by the Rogue. They could replicate the Terian technology and use it against all Terians and make the expansion of the swarm horror unstoppable.

TE-GON still possessed a secret weapon. The Rogue, unaware the Supreme had secretly designed the ship to carry star pods, could not know his ship had four of them. Built with Perium hulls, the pods were strong enough for star and element flight. He would use these four secret weapons against the unsuspecting Rogue attack ship. With any luck, by the time they realized what was happening, it would be too late. He would position two pods at the edge of the atmosphere as lookouts; then send the remaining two into position under the mother ship and out of sight from a ship attacking from above. A single pod was no match against a Rogue attack ship, but four pods would carry enough firepower to disable or at least keep the Rogue occupied until TE-GON's ship had absorbed enough energy to engage its weapon systems. He sent a thought command to "C" to prepare the pods. ZE-TAN put a surprise for the Rogue in his pod.

The pods were too small to carry melters, but he had the next best thing. He armed a blaster with a bio-probe and set it to his thought pattern. He would have to get his pod close enough to the rogue ship to deliver his surprise, but if it hit the Rogue ship, the bio-probe would infect the Rogue ship's systems and destroy it from the inside. He finished preparing and went liquid, flowing into his pod.

The flyers operated the pods telepathically, but the control of the crafts was also connected directly to "C" and the mother ship's systems. The pods were capable of limited solar system travel and despite their small size, were equipped with hibernation if the flyer became separated from the mother ship and stranded in space. The pods' primary purpose was surface exploration of alien planets, but everyone knew that they were much more than that. The universe was a dangerous place and having armed pods gave the ship leaders heavy mobile fire power against any threat.

As the mother ship approached the red planet, "C" scanned the surface. All the flyers were ready in their pods." C" opened portals, releasing them out into space. TWEE and ZE-TAN were in the lead pods and activated element flight at the edge of the planet's atmosphere. Both flyers immediately felt the power surge flow through their pods from the magnetic pull of this large planet. They held their places, until, at "C's" command, they dropped into the deadly winds toward the planet's surface. TWEE's hearts began pumping so fast he thought they were going to explode. He had never flown into such turbulence.

The surface of the monstrous planet was shrouded in violent storms crashing into each other. The flyers watched the terrifying, swirling abyss, grateful for the protection of their pods. There was no time for fear. ZE-TAN and TWEE calmed themselves and pushed the fear out of their minds. This was what they had trained for, warriors to the death.

The pods spun and rolled, descending through the winds close to the surface. TWEE and ZE-TAN were finally able to stabilize their pods after they passed through the calmer middle winds. Taking their positions close to the surface, both were ready to guard the mother ship from below against attack.

CRE-LIN and ALUME took positions in the rim of space above the atmosphere watching scanners for any movement. CRE-LIN had been in combat many times and, like TE-GON, sensed that something was coming. He was ready!

The two pods were strategically distanced from each other, in case of attack, but still within a quick jump distance of each other. With the pods in position, TE-GON had protection from a surprise attack. If the Rogue attacked from one of the moons, the warning time would be short. If the attack ship was invisible, the only warning would be from detection of heat displacement, making the warning time even shorter.

The Rogue attack ship with its heavy propulsion drives and weapon systems would have to attack using slow turns, putting them at a disadvantage against the superior maneuvering of TE-GON's ship and the pods. In the red planet's atmosphere, the Rogue would use most of their power supply just trying not to be blown into the surface and would have no firing stability. TE-GON liked his chances as he readied the mother ship at the edge of the atmosphere.

Report! he called out.

All pods are in position, "C" replied, then continued, *level flight in atmosphere not maintainable. Recommend spinning entry.*

The mother ship's size made element flight more difficult, but TE-GON had flown in violent conditions before.

Enter atmosphere at element level three and synchronize rotation with wind velocities, he ordered.

"C" began the ship spin as the mother ship moved into the atmosphere. The ship had to get through the top winds and into the middle winds to stabilize and begin regeneration. The ship was spinning sideways, moving with the direction of the winds. Suddenly, another storm hit the ship from the opposite direction, flipping it upside down in a direction opposite to the main winds and pushing it at increasing velocity toward the surface.

TE-GON quickly turned a hard-right angle then another hard-right angle to slow speed. The maneuver worked! The ship's descent slowed enough for TE-GON to stop just above the pods. The winds were as slow as they were going to get, so TE-GON transferred full power from the weapon systems to the stabilizers which began absorption. The mother ship was now defenseless!

With the ship stabilized and absorbing planet energy, TE-GON took the moment to analyze the situation. He believed the Rogue had some type of detection avoidance device that hid them from detection before the attack. "C's" sensors should have detected the Rogue ship. The fact that scans had exposed nothing raised dangerous possibilities. There could be more than one vessel. If they did not detect one enemy ship, then they could have missed more. That meant that the next attack could be by multiple ships. The pods would have their hands full with one ship. Two or more ships would make battle difficult. The lack of detection also raised the possibility of a malfunction of his ship's central control. To TE-GON's knowledge, there had never been a failure of a central system but his experience in space had taught him the hard lesson that in the black void, anything was possible. If "C" had malfunctioned, protocol dictated she should be shut down. With that, TE-GON considered confronting "C" with his thoughts but decided against it. Shutting the central system down now presented too much additional risk to the ship. He would rather take his chances with a malfunction than have no central system at all, so alerting "C" about his concern would serve no purpose. Going to battle against the Rogue without Central orders would be even more dangerous. His instincts told him that "C" had not made an error. It was more likely the Rogue used some sort of new technology that prevented scans from detecting them, so he accepted his own analogy and moved his thoughts to the moment.

Status? TE-GON asked.

No detection of the Rogue ship, Leader, "C" replied quickly.

TE-GON was anxious. All his experience told him the Rogue were close. They had too much to lose if they did not intercept and finish them off. Tracking the Terian ship's power trail, even without anti-matter drives, would be easy for the Rogue, even after the mother ship's tunnel escape. Their jump ability, although primitive, could easily put them within attack distance. They had to be close, but where?

There could be more than one ship! The leader declared to "C".

His statement puzzled "C". She had concluded that there had been no craft detection before the attack because of the comet's interference. The presence of another craft would have been detected unless it, too, was riding in the comet's tail. If there had been another Rogue ship, why would it not have joined the attack? "C" considered that her system could have made a detection error and took the precaution of running a function scan to detect any malfunction in her systems. The scan was negative. There had been no error. She reported the result of the function scan showed the Rogue must have used some type of light-refraction technology.

TE-GON was relieved that "C" had run her own check of her system, looking for the possibility of error. One less thing to worry about.

Do the downloads identify clocking technology? TE-GON asked.

There is a report of an attack on a Balasarian Research Outpost in the Vulacaaic star system that had reported to have developed a light-refraction technology, "C" answered, *But the outpost was destroyed.*

The power trail of their attacker was counterfeit but the Rogue was suspected because most of the dead had missing body parts and the Rogue took body parts for food. The Rogue could also have found the technology of the Balasarians that claimed to make objects invisible to sight and scans.

TE-GON remembered hearing the story before from another leader that had witnessed the outpost devastation. The Balasarians had developed some of the most accomplished technology in the galaxies. They were revered for their generosity in sharing their discoveries. The outpost slaughter brought outrage and fear throughout advanced civilizations, but the killers left no witnesses, only death.

TE-GON ordered "C" to re-evaluate the recorded scans of the comet, just before the attack. At first, she did not see it. Then, there it was! Such a small thing, not something you would be looking for in a scan. A temperature variation, so slight that you had to be looking for it to see it, but it was unmistakable. Inside the comet's tail was a temperature anomaly that should not be there. "C" saw, not just one, but three. She reported her findings to her leader!

Inform the pods there are three Rogue ships. No more communication, TE-GON ordered.

The mother ship was absorbing quickly and so far, element control was maintaining the ship's altitude safely below the worst of the middle winds and above the milder, but still dangerous, surface storms. TE-GON was ready in case they had to move fast.

A sudden downdraft shook the ship violently. "C" softened the hull to absorb the worst of the vibrations. She diverted most all the remaining stored power to repulsion saving just enough to life support to keep the leader and her alive. The ship's surface began to glow bright orange from the radiation absorbing into the hull. They needed maximum storage for the ship to be capable of level three speeds without using anti-matter drives. The mother ship was vulnerable and was completely dependent on the pods if attacked.

TE-GON had studied everything in the downloads about the Rogue. They were a species driven by an insatiable need to expand their swarm. They formed huge war colonies that constantly fought each other for the favor of their hive masters. Individual life held little meaning. The hive's masters were killers that took leadership by any means. The weak served without question. That order of privilege had not changed since the Rogue were rock crawling cannibals. All Rogue spent their lifetimes in a quest to serve and expand the swarm by any means. Invasion, murder, enslavement, and theft were preferred methods. Even other Rogue hives were subject to attack if it better served the swarm. In a battle between hives, the conquered hive became slaves to the conquering hive master. Slaves that resisted or were not useful became food.

The Terian empire supplied weapons and flight technology to the reptilians to use them to fight enemies of the Terian empire and allow them to colonize outside their planet. In time, the Rogue betrayed the Terian empire, becoming a hated enemy. The Rogue continued to spread their horror throughout the galaxies using the same attack plan: Find a technologically inferior race, slaughter and enslave them, then plunder the planet's resources and technology. When all the planet's resources were depleted, and technology pillaged. remaining survivors ended up in Rogue food pens and the planet destroyed by an engineered asteroid collision. Planet killing was a successful tactic for the Rogue, destroying proof of their genocide.

TE-GON hoped that he was wrong about the Rogue being close but the warrior in him suspected the enemy would come for the kill.

The Rogue commander's first ambush had failed and that meant his death from the hive. Failure in battle meant certain death by the swarm. He could save himself if he could catch the Terian's ship and capture it. This time, the Terian would know they were coming. The leaders of the Rogue swarm knew it was only a matter of time before they would face a war with the Terian. Without Terian anti- matter technology to power their machines, the Rogue could not defeat them. All technology possessed by the Rogue had been either given to them by the Terian or stolen from a civilization they had destroyed. They created nothing. The plan of attacking the Terian ship was to capture the anti-matter. The stolen refraction machine made them invisible to the Terian ship and gave the Rogue the opportunity to ambush the superior Terian ship. Because the Rogue commander found the refraction machine, he earned the honor of capturing the Terian ship. The discovery was pure luck. He had stumbled onto the Balasarian research compound by accident. He was setting signal sensors that would guide the killer asteroid to destroy what remained of the Balasarian planet after pillaging all its natural resources and killing off all life. There was little time left before the asteroid would vaporize the planet when a small cylinder, protruding from the ground, was spotted by one of his crew. It was an exhaust outlet for an underground complex that had evaded detection. The Rogue scouting party only had enough time to search the first level of the complex, where they discovered the stealth machine. He escaped the planet just before the planet exploded into space rubble. He killed the crew member that found the exhaust pipe and took full credit for the discovery.

The three Rogue attack ships had precious little power left after chasing the crippled Terian. The Rogue commander used the fastest speeds and multiple jumps in pursuit and had sent his two scout ships in different directions to search for the Terian's power trail. He was unsure what amount of damage he had inflicted on his enemy. When the coward plunged into a tunnel instead of fighting back, he knew he had hit the ship. The ship had sent a distress signal before the tunnel jump but knew no one was coming to help. The ship was alone and damaged.

This was his chance to strike the final blow. He must destroy the Terian ship to save his own life, but first, he had to find it. The commander was losing hope when he finally received a report from one of his ships.

"The Terian power trail leads to a large red planet!" the scout ship reported.

"Were you seen?" the commander asked.

"We are undetected and positioned behind the red planets large moon!" the scout ship captain boasted, defensively.

"Stay out of sight and do nothing until I arrive!" the Rogue leader ordered.

The commander channeled all power to propulsion knowing that would mean taking power from life support. Some crew may die, but individual lives were of no importance. Any dead could be used for food. Inwardly, his cold-blooded body was boiling with excitement. Outwardly, he was careful not to show the weakness of emotion.

The second Rogue scout ship reached Jupiter well ahead of the command ship and joined the first scout ship behind the large moon. The Terian mother ship was still in the planet's atmosphere and would be an easy target. The scout ships' scans had not identified the pods. Their small size made them appear like space rocks on the Rogue's crude scanners. The pilot of the second scout ship wanted to strike the Terian immediately, but the captain of the lead scout ship did not dare take an action without the commander's order. Even if the unapproved attack were successful, he would have to kill his commander to take credit.

He decided to let the opportunity pass, fearing that the commander was too strong for him to kill.

The Rogue command ship finally arrived, taking position behind a smaller moon. The commander decided to wait. He was sure the Terian ship was regenerating and wanted to make sure it was deep enough into the process to have no powered weapons. The Rogue ships were technologically outmatched against this crippled enemy, but he had superior numbers and surprise on his side. He would not fail again. An ambush was always a good plan.

Just like the attack from the comet's tail, surprise would be their equalizer. The Rogue placed no value in a fair fight. That was for fools. He would do whatever it took to defeat the enemy, including the sacrifice of his own crew and scout ships. When he watched the Terian ship fly past his hiding place in the comet's tail without detecting his ship, he knew the stealth reflectors had worked. The attack plan was perfect except for the debris of the comet's tail slowing the velocity of the stun shot. It would have been a glorious victory for the commander and would have earned him the power and respect that had eluded him for so long. Not taking a kill shot had been a mistake. A kill shot would not have slowed going through the comet's tail and would have eliminated the Terian ship. He had been foolish to think that he could capture a Terian galactic cruiser intact. His greed to take all the credit, and by ordering his two scout ships not to fire on the Terian ship; that was his second blunder. With the Terian destroyed, they could have at least been able to pick through the bones of the ship for whatever scraps remained and take credit for a kill. The extra energy required to fire the patterned stun blast completely drained power to his weapons systems. In the moments that it took to recharge and re-position his scout ships to get within firing range, the Terian ship had already jumped into one of their tunnels and was gone. Their escape would seal his fate if he could not find them and finish them off. He must not fail this time. The Terian leader would not be expecting the two scout ships. The Rogue commander would make his scout ships take all the risk of the attack while he remained safely behind. He could taste the glory of this victory!

CRE-LIN was the first to detect the enemy on his scans. No ships were visible at this distance, but he knew instantly that the anomaly could only be the Rogue. TE-GON's prediction was correct. CRE-LIN was sure the Rogue ships were not aware of his scans, or he would already be dead, but he detected two ships emerging from behind a moon. They were approaching the planet from the opposite side from where the mother ship was absorbing. The mother ship would not be able to detect them until it was too late. He had to alert his leader.

CRE-LIN was on the opposite side of the planet from the mother ship, so he first relayed his thought warning to ALUME in the closest pod. She received CRE-LIN's thoughts but the two Rogue ships were now between her and the mother ship so she could not send a thought warning to "C" without her flight movement being detected by Rogue scanners.

Instead, she flew her pod in a rolling motion to camouflage her movement and maintain the appearance of a space rock. She rolled into a safe position to telepathically alert the two pods under the mother ship. When all the pods had received the alert, they set into action. They would not be able to respond to each other or the mother ship without the risk of alerting the Rogue of their presence, but each knew what they must do. ZE-TAN moved first right below the mother ship so a warning to "C" would not be detected. Regeneration had now turned the mother ship's hull into a glowing fire. ZE-TAN sent his thought warning about the Rogue ships approaching, giving "C" and TE-GON the Rogue positions. The team was ready.

TE-GON ordered disengagement from regeneration.

Power status? he requested.

Weapon systems can be fully charged if we divert more power from life functions, "C" responded in anticipation of what her leader's next order would be.

Full power to weapons and repulsion and prepare to attack upon my command! TE-GON ordered.

The Rogue scout ships were closing in using a circling maneuver. One ship for the kill and one to take a second shot, if the first failed. They were completely unaware that they were now being hunted. Just before TE-GON could give the order to attack, "C" sent a thought warning to her leader!

These are scout ships, "C" reported. *There is another command attack ship!*

TE-GON held back his attack order. His mind quickly recalled the advice of his most respected combat teacher: *Never underestimate the desperate warrior.* TE-GON would follow this wise counsel. He quickly changed his strategy.

The Rogue commander's attack plan was in motion. He would stay safely outside the planet's atmosphere and steal the glory when the Terian was destroyed. The commander was feeling confident.

In the next moment, a heat beam hit the first Rogue scout ship, igniting it into a ball of fire before exploding into pieces. The Rogue commander had been tricked into a trap. There were more Terian ships. He ordered his second ship to pursue and destroy the attack craft. The last scout ship flew toward the location of the first ship's debris and fired blindly, desperately hoping to hit the fast- moving pod.

At the same time, the Rogue commander fired a kill beam at the old coordinates of the regenerating mother ship from his *safe* location. TE-GON had already moved his ship and the Rogue's deadly beam harmlessly hit the surface. The scout ship, flying blindly, was shot at by ZE-TAN, who had maneuvered behind it. The Rogue commander attempted evasive tactics to escape from what he thought was one pod when both ALUME's and CRE-LIN's pods fired their blaster beams at the scout ship. The smaller pod beams were hitting the Rogue scout ship, breaking it up. The Rogue captain increased his speed, skimming along the edge of the middle winds while weaving side to side to avoid the pods' attack beams. The smaller and faster pods outmaneuvered the slower, heavy ship and continued their onslaught.

The Rogue commander watched as the three pods were destroying his scout ship, but he would not waste time to go to its aid. He concentrated his sensors to find the prized Terian mother ship. The scout ships were a necessary sacrifice for the glory of the swarm. The Rogue commander detected his prize heading through the storms with another small craft behind it. He fired all his powered-up weapons.

"C" detected the incoming Rogue weapons and flew deep into the clouds to hide but it was moments too late. One power beam hit and absorbed through the mother ship's Perium hull: exploding just behind the command chamber, tearing off the right side of the command chair, taking TE-GON's arm and burning most of his body. The heat from the blast cauterized the arm saving TE-GON from massive fluid loss. The blast continued to move through the ship's systems causing more damage and cutting power to the weapon systems.

"C" immediately dove the ship closer to the planet's surface with TWEE following close behind. The pods were the mother ship's only defense against another attack. ALUME sensed her leader's pain and knew he had been hit. She alerted ZE-TAN and CRE-LIN. The three pods broke off their attack on the dying scout ship. ALUME and CRE-LIN flew to cover the mother ship while ZE-TAN made his way out of the atmosphere and into space, closing in on the retreating Rogue command ship. ZE-TAN accelerated his pod to its maximum speed.

The Rogue commander detected the pod and realized the depth of the trap. The Terian had out maneuvered him a second time. He had heard about small vessels inside larger ships but had not believed it. The commander fired a three-blast spread in a desperate attempt to hit the attacking pod, but they fell short of their target. ZE-TAN passed by the rear of the command ship at level five speed and shot the probe carrying his special weapon into the Rogue command ship's hull. The probe penetrated the ship causing a vacuum breech. ZE-TAN waited until he had circled his pod back around and was closing in on the Rogue command ship. He veered off at the last moment toward the safety of the red planet's winds before he sent a thought signal to the probe's special cargo, releasing the deadly organic eating machines. The *"Eaters"* as they had been appropriately named, moved instantly, searching for the closest organic food. The three-Rogue crew working to contain the breech only felt their reptilian-like skin tingle at first. Then came the excruciating pain!

The Rogue commander watched his view screen as his crew was being devoured so quickly that they appeared to be melting. He had seen the "*Eaters*" before in battle and quickly sealed the breeched compartment, leaving the dying crew entombed with the "*Eaters*". It would be suicide to attempt to rescue his screaming crew. Nothing could save them. He watched as they disappeared completely. The *tiny eating machines*, trapped in the sealed chamber, would perish immediately after the flesh of the doomed Rogue crew was gone, and there was no more organic fuel. The Rogue commander turned his attention back to ZE-TAN's attacking pod, firing melters in all directions to scatter the small craft. ZE-TAN detected the melters and broke off his attack on the Rogue ship, flying into the winds where the pursuing melters would be blown apart.

With both his ships destroyed, the Commander was alone, crippled. His sensors had recorded a hit on the mother ship, but scans showed movement of multiple power sources: The small ships! This was not the time to stand and fight. He turned his ship toward the dark and jumped blindly into the void.

There was no hope for glory on this day. The command ship jumped far enough away from the red planet to offer at least temporary safety.

He had failed. His crew would think he was at his weakest after this defeat. He must show his strength before they could plot his assassination and take command of the ship. He acted quickly, ordering one of his surviving crew into the command chamber.

When the frightened Rogue walked into the chamber, the commander lunged forward, pushed his claws into the stunned Rogue's eyes and severed his head. The commander drank the hot fluid pouring from the severed head in front of his remaining crew. He ordered them to take the body to the food bin. That would end any thought of revolt. He had survived this time but, if he could not find the Terian ship and kill them all, the swarm would show him no mercy for his failure.

"C "was unable to stabilize the Terian ship from its violent spinning. TE-GON was unconscious but alive. The command instruments had been severely damaged by the blast and were not responding. "C" had to stop the spinning from outside. She had no choice but to use the pods. It would be a desperate balancing act, but it was the only way to stop the ship from its deathly spin. The flyers positioned their pods on each side of the ship, then turned their element force to the highest level to use the magnetic pull of the planet to counteract the spin of the ship. The pods were past all safe levels but if they did not stop the spin, the mother ship would crash into the surface.

Slowly, the spin began to subside until it finally stopped, and the ship was stabilized. The damage from the Rogue hit was devastating. The anti-matter was unstable and could not power the drives so TWEE calculated that if they bypassed the ship's systems and directed the pods' energy to the main power drives, they could blast the ship to the atmosphere. Once in space, the regeneration had successfully stored enough energy for the ship to cruise to the target planet.

"C" would have to synchronize the pods perfectly and energize them past their maximum safe power levels again to create a powerful enough thrust to escape from red planet's monstrous pull. The higher energy levels would put the pods in danger of exploding but this was the only chance to save them. The team would have to stay in solid form inside their pods. Their skinsuits would have to protect them against the pressure in case of a breech that would force them to leave their pods.

"C" synchronized the pods and the team prepared for what could be the last moments of their lives.

With the pods dangerously past their safe level, she released one final thrust from the pods, jolting the mother ship's main drives forward with such force that if the flyers had not been wearing skin suits, their insides would have compressed until they exploded.

As the attached ships bolted through the atmosphere, they all started to spin together. "C "adjusted the pods' thrusters, correcting the spin while the ship continued its climb through the turmoil of the winds, toward open space. The teams' skin suits were holding from the pressure, but they would not hold much longer. The ship's hull was stretched to its maximum spear-like length as the ship continued its acceleration through the angry atmosphere. The pods were exceeding stress levels but were holding together.

Long, anxious moments passed until they broke free and entered the familiar blackness of space. They had cheated death for the second time, but the danger was not over. "C" scanned for the enemy. They could be waiting to inflict the final blow. She could not be sure that the scanners were still functioning correctly, but they were her only eyes, and she had no choice but to trust them. They detected no artificial power sources or organic life forms. The Rogue ship was gone!

"C" was certain that if there were any other Rogue ships, they would have been in the battle. The last ship was badly damaged but still had enough power to flee. There was no way to know if it still had weapons, but there was always the danger of a suicide attack. To the Rogue, failure meant death. "C" would have to be prepared for a final ambush which was sure to come.

"C" opened hull portals to bring the pods back into the mother ship. Immediately, the flyers went to work repairing damage to the ship. The heat that flashed through the ship had melted a swath of damage, but the healer chamber was not damaged. TE-GON was carried into the healer, still alive but unconscious. The healer analyzed his injuries but could not predict if he would survive. The team immersed themselves in the repairs but the trauma of their escape from Jupiter's atmosphere and the Rogue battle had taken a toll on each of them. They had all been designed and trained for space travel since birth and understood that the dangers of space were a constant reality, but no amount of training could completely prepare a flyer for a real near-death experience in space. The unimaginable distances and isolation required the highest level of discipline and loyalty. They had been trained to respond without question to their superior's commands. Now, with TE-GON unconscious and near death, "C" would be their leader.

None of the team had ever been under the absolute command of a machine. Faced with TE-GON's possible death, it was on all their minds. What if he did not recover? Could this machine be trusted with absolute authority over biological Terian and make the right decisions that could mean the difference between their living or dying? A lingering doubt invaded their minds.

The mother ship was flying at level two speed toward the target planet with no sign of the Rogue. TE-GON finally regained consciousness, but his injuries were so severe, he struggled to stay awake. He saw that his arm was gone, and his normally strong body was overcome with weakness. He had lost a heart, but the healer showed his other organs intact. Back home on Paetaan, body parts could easily be replaced but the smaller healing chambers in spaceships were limited in their ability to produce replacements so he would have to recover with one heart. His enhancements were probably the only reason that he was still alive. He learned so long ago, the importance of bio-enhancement to a flyer. This integration of mechanical and biological tissue had originally been developed by the Supreme as a tool to allow computers to physically move around and perform tasks thought too dangerous for biological Terians.

Over hundreds of stars cycles the technology advanced and was used to enhance performance and longevity in natural biological Terians as well. Like all great technological advances, there was a downside. The original technology was used to reproduce body parts with no limit to the number of replacements allowed. Elective integrations became commonplace and some Terians replaced most of their body parts to enhance strength, appearance, and lifespan. The replacement of biological parts by mechanical parts raised the issue of when a biological stopped being a biological. Did having mostly mechanical parts change them from biological beings into machines? Technology challenged the very core of natural evolution. The arguments for and against divided their civilization.

The Supreme ultimately enacted new laws that limited the number of mechanics that could be used with biological tissue to preserve and protect the biological integrity of their species. Even after new laws threatened detention and banishment for violations, the illegal enhancements did not stop.

There were stories about Terians becoming all mechanical except for basic biological functions and brain centers. Their enhancements were not easily revealed by outward appearance, but their attitudes of superiority and actions eventually betrayed them. Supreme laws for flyers were less restrictive to allow enhancements necessary for survival in harsh environments during space travel.

TE-GON's rank had earned him the right to enhancements that were restricted from other flyers, and he had never hesitated to take advantage of implementing them. His arms and legs were the first to have the changes. Next, they enhanced his hearts and lungs, which could triple his expected life span. His greatest enhancement was his higher function brain stem implant which allowed larger downloads and expanded mental retention. Quite simply, his enhancements made him smarter, faster, and stronger, with the ability to live three times longer than a normal Terian. He enjoyed the privileges that came with being a leader. His strength and speed were invaluable assets to his advancement in the Supreme. Space exploration had made important contributions to the Terian Supreme's technological success and flyers were extended great privileges as a reward for their service to the Supreme.

TE-GON knew he was dying. He was grateful that "C" could take command. She had become his trusted confidant and friend. With "C" as second in command, they complimented each other in making critical decisions. They had learned to function like one unit, lowering the margin of error in their decisions. The flight team responded to" C" like she was one of them. "C" was treated like a living crew member, with a trust and loyalty that was not possible with the old non-biological machines. He worried about whether the team would accept her authority. He had to trust that he had made the right team choices.

TE-GON sent a thought to "C". *Send a flyer to the target,* he ordered.

May I suggest a scan rider, Leader? "C" asked.

We must make physical contact to analyze the beings on the planet and identify the power source. Send ALUME. he ordered.

TE-GON had accepted that scan riders were a necessary tool, but when they were first introduced by the Supreme, many leaders saw them as a threat to the future of Terian flyers by replacing them as "initial contact explorers". With all the danger that came with space travel, there were many in the Supreme that saw scan riders as the alternative to risking biological flyers' lives exploring space.

Regardless of the apprehension among the leaders, a scan rider was the safest way to gather intelligence on unknown planets and alien life forms but the Supreme bowed to pressure from their flyers and never restricted flyer contact. When TE-GON began flying, personal contact was the only trusted method of reliable information, and he had a hard time giving up that authority.

Yes, Leader, "C" answered.

Sending a team member for initial contact so far from the mother ship was dangerous but she did not question her leader's order. She did agree that ALUME was the right choice. Who better to send than a thought reader?

ALUME was running a system check on her pod when she received her orders. Initial contact missions were usually carried out remotely by a scan rider, rarely by a flyer and never by a flyer with so little flight experience and no weapon training.

ALUME knew that the situation must be desperate for the leader to risk physical contact with primitive aliens. She was honored to have been picked and was ready to do her duty.

"C" absorbed anti-matter energy from the ship into ALUME's pod for the extra power needed to jump to the target planet. A jump like this one would take her pod to its maximum stress level. ALUME had only jumped during training simulation. She had learned that there was a great difference between simulation and reality. The unknown only enhanced her sense of duty and excitement about her new mission.

"C" gave ALUME all the current data scans of this planet and its dominant species. ALUME was to treat the humanoids as hostiles until it could be proven otherwise. Contact with so many different life forms throughout the galaxies had taught Terian flyers that you never knew what to expect from an unknown species, so you planned for the worse. She would be cautious. The first danger was the pod. Flyers had been known to travel the length of a planetary system in a pod with an anti-matter charge. The Perium hull gave her pod the same structural strength as the mother ship but, because of their size, pods could not carry a repulsion device like the mother ship.

Speeding through space in a jump exposed the pod to obstructions. There was danger of a collision. In many ways, she would be facing many of the dangers the ancients faced when flying their crude ships. The Perium hull could absorb a smaller collision but was not immune to being thrown off course during a jump, sending the flyer too far away to be able to return.

ALUME received the order from" C" to prepare for the jump. She went liquid and absorbed into her pod. "C" created an opening in the hull and moved ALUME's pod into space. "C" powered the pod and it jumped at level three speed toward the target planet. The small planet loomed larger and larger until the proximity warning alerted ALUME. She broke off the jump and slowed the pod just outside the planet's atmosphere.

She was struck by its beauty. The bright colors gave it a vibrant, glowing look. The liquid bodies were massive and teeming with life. Her scans showed that this world was a young formation. Before she entered the edge of the planet's atmosphere, she had to maneuver around small orbiting machines. They appeared to be relay devices. Signals were coming from the surface and the machines would return signals. When she entered the edge of the atmosphere, she switched to element flight. She loved flying element. The pod could turn immediately to her thoughts. She quickly located the power source and flew her pod directly above it from the edge of the planet's atmosphere to avoid detection. She decided to wait until the area around the signal was dark before descending to get a closer look.

While holding the pod in position, she received a thought that jolted her. The mental thought she received was alien and strong. Then it stopped. The thought came again, moments later. She downloaded the language of the thought to understand the message being sent.

Help! Help! the message kept resonating.

The thought had the same energy signature as the large energy source that had brought them to this planet. She wanted to investigate and identify but discipline prevailed. ALUME held the pod steady until the surface was dark. The thought message continued.

ALUME reported the thought message to "C" and informed her that it was connected to the energy source. There was only one sender and must have been alien as this species had not evolved enough for thought messages.

She guessed that an alien ship must have crashed, and its flyer was sending a plea for help. She sent her own thoughts to the sender, but there was no response.

While she waited, ALUME turned her attention to processing the mass of information from her surface scans. The natural resources were astounding. Scans sent back element verifications that made this small planet a treasure of the galaxy. The Supreme would reward them handsomely for discovering this planet, if they survived. Life on this little planet would take many star cycles to record. A rich resource planet like this would quickly be declared a host planet by the Supreme. The primitive occupants would not be allowed to keep it just for themselves.

ALUME continued to receive thought messages asking for help. She hoped that waiting for darkness would not be too late to help. Whatever was sending the thought was in trouble. It could be a trap. Her instincts told her that this was not a trap. She sensed the strong connection between the sender and the power source. That made the sender important to the mother ship landing on this planet. She did not know why, but the feeling was very strong, and whenever she had this kind of feeling, she was always right.

The scans made it clear that the dominant humanoid species on this planet was at a very primitive state of evolution and physically appeared the same as many species discovered throughout the galaxies, including Terians. Conflicts were everywhere. Their weapons were crude, but their fusion weapons were mobile and posed a threat to the mother ship, so the landing location would require isolation and extreme caution. These primitives were completely unaware of life forms not from their own planet. They were lucky not to have been found by scavengers like the Rogue.

These *"humans"*, as they called themselves, would be helpless against advanced technology. Most of ALUME's isolation studies were related to the effects of coping with the loneliness of space travel but civilization isolation had also been a part of her learning and had greatly interested ALUME. It was hard for her to understand how thinking beings, even as primitives, could believe that they were alone in the universe when observing the vastness of space with its countless stars. The reality of the universe was overwhelming, even to Terians, who traveled through the galaxies. Planet isolation was not uncommon.

They had explored many planets with intelligent life forms that were completely unaware of other civilizations. If the primitives of this small planet knew the real the threat of invasion, they would use all their resources and technology to protect their planet instead of killing each other. They were hostile and self-focused, preoccupied with fighting amongst themselves.

Her scans accessed the information systems used on this world, recording the planet's knowledge. If she and the team survived and were able to return home, every raider in the galaxies would know about this small blue world with its rich resources. This planet's only hope for survival after being marked by the mother ship power trails, would be as a protected host planet of the Supreme.

Should they not survive the Rogue, ALUME knew that neither the leader nor "C", would ever allow the mother ship to be captured and would self-destruct, even if it meant destroying this innocent planet. If they could not make repairs quickly and escape through a tunnel before the Rogue found them, the planet would be doomed. If they did escape undetected and returned home, this planet would still be doomed, not to annihilation but evolutionary slavery as a host planet by the Supreme, all for their own good, of course. ALUME was suddenly sad for this planet and her part in their uncertain future.

The thought sender was slowing. She could feel its weakness. The planet's star was lowering on the horizon, bringing darkness to the surface. She hoped she would be in time.

Chapter Three
Mick

The morning air was crisp and refreshing, engulfing Mick's senses as he crawled from his tent. He had slept deeply. It was one of the many rewards of camping. He went to the stream and filled his cupped hands with ice-cold water and splashed it on his face. The cold surged through him from head to toe. This had been a morning ritual for Mick since the first time he went camping with his father. This beautiful spot at the river bend was a part of his Indian heritage; where he and his father had spent so much time together when he was just a kid, all those years ago.

He had such warm memories of his father telling him stories of being a young Indian boy on the reservation. His father had been the first member of the tribe to go to college. He had a great mind and worked hard to earn a full scholarship to the University of Washington where he excelled in every class, eventually earning his doctoral degree in environmental biology with a minor in forest management. He turned down lucrative offers from large research and development firms that required relocation. Instead, he took a job with the Department of Forestry at Bellingham, Washington station. Working for the government had afforded him a great deal of his job time in the same forest where he had grown up so he took Mick with him whenever he could.

Mick cherished his memories of exploring and sharing the love of the forest with his father. It had been over fifteen years since his father's fatal heart attack left a dark void in his heart and so many unanswered questions about his *special powers*. He inherited his father's passion and curiosity for all things related to science and immersed himself in his studies, eventually following in his father's footsteps by choosing cellular biology for his career. In so many ways, he emulated his father.

Mick moved with confidence as he navigated through the thick underbrush and multi-story pine trees. He had developed a sixth sense when it came to tracking. He attributed that to his Indian heritage, his *"gift"*, and his father's teaching him how to read the language of the forest. He knew the Baker National Forest like the back of his hand. Mick loved to hunt, not with a gun, but with his camera. It started as a hobby, but the National Geographic Society liked his work so much that the money they paid for his pictures financed his post-graduate education.

His mother never remarried, devoting her life to her son. She supported his ambitions and was always there for him. It had been almost three years since her passing from cancer. He had watched helplessly as the disease slowly took her.

Her death drove him to work even harder in his research so that one day, he might discover a medicine that might make a difference in the battle to defeat cancer. His doctoral thesis on how synthetic proteins affect cellular development was published in the *National Medical Review*. He was credited as one of the brightest new research minds of the scientific community. Like his father, he was recruited by the largest research and development companies in the country including the United States Military and could have written his own ticket, but Mick did not like being in the spotlight. He thought working for a big corporation would be like living in a fishbowl. The corporate suits would always be popping in to see what progress was being made, giving directives, interfering with his work. In the end, it was an easy decision to accept a freelance position with Orion First, a small Seattle research company, mostly funded by University of Washington Alumni. He was given unrestricted use of university facilities and complete intellectual freedom. Although his salary would never make him rich, Orion provided everything he needed for his research. His career fulfilled him intellectually, but it was the photography, his trips to Mount Baker National Forest and his lifelong friendship with Carly that gave him balance in his life.

Mick had his priorities neatly in his mind. His work and photography bordered on obsession, giving him little time for a personal life and his *"gift"* did not help. There had only been two women in his life. The first was Carly Callahan. He had grown up with Carly. Their parents had been close friends and neighbors and they had gone to school together from kindergarten all the way through high school. They were voted the couple most likely to get married, in their high school yearbook. They did everything together in their younger years, but shortly after high school, and a brief romance, they went their separate ways. They stayed in close contact and Mick saw her often on his trips to Mount Baker National Forest.

Carly followed her father into law enforcement becoming the first female officer in the Bellingham Police Department. She tired of the violence and politics and eventually transferred to the Mount Baker National Park, becoming the youngest chief park ranger there. The rumor around the town of Concrete was that she had transferred into the forest service to be closer to Mick. It was no secret that she wanted more from her relationship with Mick, but his career and photography did not leave much time for a personal life, so they settled for friendship.

The only other serious relationship was Sheila. It was a whirlwind romance. Both thought they had found their soul mate. The relationship began to suffer quickly as his work demanded most of his time. He began to see less and less of Sheila as the months went on. She had been patient and understanding, but Mick's *"gift"* betrayed her real feelings of loneliness and disappointment. He realized that he could not give her the kind of life that she longed for and deserved. Their relationship turned into good friends even though he knew she wanted more.

Relationships needed their little secrets to survive, but no one could hide a secret from Mick. His father had tried to help him understand his *"gift"*, but there had not been enough time for his father to teach him how to control it. Mick did his best to figure that out on his own. His mother had tried to guide him but unlike his father, she never had the *"gift"* and could not understand the deep effect it had on every part of his life. Mick was a child intellectual prodigy, able to carry on adult conversations before he was three. By the time he was five, the results of an I.Q. test produced numbers so high that there was no category to rate his level. His father took him (in confidence) to a friend at the university to test his extra sensory perception and those results were also off the charts. He was able to identify objects on the inside of an unmarked box or behind walls. These were parlor tricks next to his most guarded secret, *hearing people's thoughts*. It was the main reason he had no close friends. Mick had accepted that his "*gift*" was a lifetime sentence of being alone.

Mick's father had protected him from the outside world finding out about his "*gift*", fearing that if the government people found out they would make him a prisoner by using him for military intelligence. With only his mother to confide in, Mick became withdrawn. It was in his early teen years that he found photography, spending every spare weekend in the wilderness of the Mount Baker National Forest with his camera, his memories, and no other thoughts to interrupt his own. There were only the sounds and smells of the forest that he loved so much. It was a time of peace for him.

Mick picked up the tracks of a mother bear and her two cubs at the Skagit River wetlands where they had fed on salmon swimming upriver to spawn. With full stomachs, they were now in the deep forest where he had been tracking them for two days. If he could find them without alerting the mother, he knew he could get some fantastic pictures. If she smelled him, he could be in great danger. He did not want to face the ferocity of a mother bear protecting her young. He moved quickly and quietly, with the wind in his face, to keep the mother bear from getting his scent. The tricky part was staying just far enough behind not to lose the prey, but not get so close that you became the prey.

Reading the trail, he saw newer tracks of another bear mixed in with the mother and her two cubs. The tracks were deeper and much larger. A male was stalking them. During the salmon run, smaller male bears were often chased away by the larger dominant males from the shallow parts of the river where the salmon were easy to catch. The outcasted bears would be driven to near starvation, turning them into desperate predators that would kill a cub for food if given the opportunity. Mother bears will fight to the death to protect their cubs, but they were no match for a larger, hungry male. Mick stopped farther ahead at a trail clearing and examined the tracks again, but this set showed the larger bear's tracks split off into another direction.

The mother bear had either gotten lucky and the male had given up or he was circling around to get ahead of the mother and her cubs. Mick knew the danger and was now on high alert. He came to a long curving bend in the walking path and heard the cubs ahead.

Slowly, he laid down on his stomach. He slowly crawled behind a rotting fallen tree, overgrown with thick layers of moss. The sounds of the cubs were slowly moving away from him, so he slipped off his backpack, took out his camera and crawled over the moss-covered tree trying not to make a sound. He began inching along through the thick underbrush until he could hear no sounds. He stopped and waited. After a few moments, he saw the brush move in a thicket about a hundred feet ahead and readied his camera. He saw no sign of the male bear, hoping it had given up on the cubs.

This is when you need patience and discipline. Great pictures demanded both plus lots of luck. Finally, a cub poked its head up from the thicket. Mick lifted himself up on his elbows to get the shot when the mother bear suddenly stood up on her hind legs, sniffing the air. Mick caught a glimpse of movement in his peripheral vison. The male bear was running at a full gallop toward the thicket. The mother bear bolted toward the charging male, blocking his attack. The two bears collided, biting, clawing, and grunting in the thick brush.

He could no longer see the fighting bears. He could hear them fighting in the brush and fierce growling filled the forest. The mother was fighting for her life and the life of her cubs. The cubs, meanwhile, remained frozen in the thicket, as they had been trained to do since birth. If the mother bear were killed, the male bear would no doubt find the cubs and make them a meal.

Suddenly, the sounds of battle went quiet and after a few seconds, the male emerged from the heavy brush. He was moving his head, sniffing the air, moving slowly and deliberately toward where the cubs were hiding. Without thinking, Mick yelled at the male bear to distract him away from the cubs.

No sooner had he yelled out than he realized what he had done. The male bear turned his head toward Mick. In a deliberate, unhurried show of dominance, the bear lifted himself on his back legs and stood to meet this threat to his food. The bear looked enormous on his hind feet. In that moment, Mick's instinct was to run. He struggled to his feet and ran to the fallen tree. In a desperate effort to put a barrier between himself and certain death, he hurled himself onto the tree trying to pull himself up to get to the other side. The bear dropped to all fours and charged. Mick could feel death behind him as he tried to pull himself over the slippery moss. The grizzly threw all his weight against the large log, clawing at his new prey. The bear's claw slashed Mick's forearm that he held up for defense, slicing downward across Mick's face and chest, knocking Mick over the tree to the other side. The crazed monster tried to scramble over, but he could not get a grip in the slippery moss. He stood on his rear legs clawing at Mick but now unable to reach him.

Mick's heart was pounding so hard, it felt like it was going to jump right out of his body as he stumbled backwards, landing him on his back.

Blood was pouring from his wounds as he looked up to see his attacker clumsily attempting to get over the fallen tree. He desperately began sending mental thoughts to the attacking bear. *Go away! Go away! Go away!* The attacking bear seemed to stop for a moment, shook its head, then continued his attack.

While the bear was trying to climb over the tree a third time, the mother bear attacked the male from behind, savagely biting his back, causing the larger male to spin around, breaking free from the mother bear's teeth biting down on its spine. He faced off with the frenzied mother but did not attack. He turned his attention back to Mick, the easier prey.

Mick was bleeding profusely, his body felt like it was on fire, but he knew that if he did not get up a tree and out of the bear's reach, he was going to die. While the bear was momentarily distracted by the mother bear, he hobbled to the closest tree, and despite the pain of moving, pulled himself up until he reached the fourth limb. Blood loss from his wounds made him lightheaded. He did not know how long he could hold on. The frustrated male bear finally was able to get over the tree and attempted to climb up the trunk of the tree to reach his bleeding prey, but the tree branches stopped his attempt to climb, and he fell back on the ground.

The mother bear was badly hurt. She leaned against the fallen tree, her warm quick breathing visibly erupting against the cold air. She made no further move toward the male bear and moved in the opposite direction to her cubs in the thicket. She needed to get herself and her cubs deep into the forest and away from the male. Mick watched her dragging her heavily bleeding left rear leg.

With that much bleeding her chances of survival were not good. She disappeared out of sight into the thicket. The male bear had no more interest in fighting the mother bear, he would wait for the easier kill.

Mick's body was burning with pain. The brutal bear's claws had torn through the muscle in his forearm, sliced open his face and cut deep into his chest. The pain pounded through his brain while blood was pouring from the cuts. He took off his belt to make a tourniquet for his arm and applied pressure to his chest wound while blood poured from his face wound. He pulled the belt tight on his arm, slowing the bleeding. With his good arm wrapped around a limb to keep him from falling, he could not pull hard enough on the belt to stop the bleeding entirely, but it was reduced to a trickle and not gushing. He could only hope the bear would lose interest.

He sent a mental plea for help. An act of desperation perhaps, but what did he have to lose? He increased the mental pleas for help while clinging on to the branch. After almost an hour his mental pleas had produced no results, but at least he felt he was doing something. The bear finally gave out a growl and walked slowly toward the thicket. Mick eyed his backpack on the ground and saw an opportunity to get his cell phone to call for help. The bear was moving slowly away toward the edge of the thicket.

Mick decided to make his move. He loosened his grip and moved slowly down the limbs, never taking his eyes off the bear.

The moment his feet touched the ground, the bear whipped his head around. He had been playing possum. Too late to stop, Mick grabbed the backpack with his bad arm, slinging it over his head as the bear turned itself around and began his charge. Mick surged up the tree and surprised himself with how fast he reached the second branch, but it was not high enough. The bear's momentum from the charge propelled him over the mossy trunk in time to slash the back of Mick's leg before it fell backward to the ground.

The bear seemed possessed as it jumped up and charged again, slamming its full weight against the tree. The force caused Mick to lunge forward over his safe branch and fall toward the ground. His flailing hands caught a limb, stopping his fall just inches out of the frenzied bear's reach.

He held tight with his tourniquet arm that was gushing blood again. Spurts of blood invaded his eyes as he scrambled to grab a higher limb with his other arm. He pulled up with everything he had left and made his way back up to his safe limb, holding on for his life. The bear had fallen back to the base of the tree, but jumped up again in a frenzy, scrambling back up the trunk trying to reach his prey that was just beyond reach.

Mick rummaged through his backpack, found his spare t-shirt, and tied it around his leg to slow the bleeding. The cell phone had no signal. He was weak, exhausted, bleeding to death, and stuck in a tree being stalked by his attacker. Hours went by, but the bear stayed close to the thicket, too hungry to give up on his prey. Mick had to do something. He would not be able to hold on much longer. He began to climb higher up the tree hoping for a signal. He hung his backpack on a branch and began pulling himself up the tree. The going was slow and painful, but when he finally reached the highest limb that would support his weight. His cell phone had two bars. He quickly dialed.

"Ranger Station," Mick recognized Molly's distinctive southern drawl.

"Molly! this is Mick Welch, I need help," he pleaded.

"Mick where are you?" she asked.

"I am about three miles east of Horseshoe Cove just off the old logging trail," his voice was faltering.

"Are you hurt?" she asked.

"I've been attacked by a bear that has me trapped up in a tree. I'm losing a lot of blood."

He heard Molly saying something, but the reception was bad, and he could not understand her. Then the phone went dead. He tried to redial but had lost the signal. Mick hit redial over and over with no luck. All he could do was hope Molly picked up his location. He moved lower down the tree to wait for help and be closer to the ground for a possible escape.

Molly had been the dispatcher at the ranger station for almost ten years. After she had received Mick's call for help, she had attempted to get Mick back on the phone with no luck. She knew Mick from his friendship with Carly and his many visits to town over the years. Mick did not fit the image of what a young doctor scientist should look like. His rugged, good looks made him seem more like a movie star than a genius scientist.

Like most people that knew him, she had fallen under the spell of his boyish charm. He was not like most of the men she met in her daily life in Concrete. Although she was happily married to the same man for sixteen years and had three of his kids, she could not help but wonder what it would be like to know Mick on a more intimate basis. Everyone had their fantasies. She snapped out of her daydream when Carly answered the two-way.

"This is Carly," she answered, chewing a mouthful of chicken at the diner.

"Chief, I just received a distress call from Mick. He said he is trapped in a tree by a bear and he's bleeding!"

She dropped her chicken leg. "Where is he?" she asked, putting on her coat.

"Said he was three miles east of Horseshoe Cove, just off the logging road," Molly replied.

"Call Jerry in Sedro Woolley and get the chopper," Carly ordered. The helicopter belonged to the police department, but they made it available to the rangers in emergencies.

"Get a location on Ripley and George," she continued, "I'll be there in five minutes." Then the line went dead.

Three minutes later, Carly burst through the ranger station door. Molly updated her before she could reach the front desk.

"Ripley and George are still at the dam taking care of that boat accident. I told them about Mick. They said that they could be in his area in about twenty minutes." She took a quick breath and continued, "They have an ambulance on the way for one of the boaters that broke a leg. George wanted to know if you wanted the ambulance to meet them up at Horseshoe Cove instead to help with Mick." She took a quick breath and continued,

"Jerry is fueling the chopper in Bellingham and can pick you up in ten!"

"Tell Ripley and George to have a citizen drive the injured boater to the Sedro Woolley Hospital to be tended to," Carly ordered. "I want them to have that ambulance meet them about three miles east of Horseshoe Cove on the old logging road. The bear has Mick up a tree, so have them take their rifles and watch their rear ends! I am on my way!" Carly grabbed a rifle on her way out the door to wait for the chopper.

Bears were the most dangerous predators in the forest. She had dealt with rogue bears before and the outcome was never good, but she was comforted by the fact that even as a young boy, Mick had this uncanny knowledge of the forest and was a master of survival protocol and safety. Carly remembered when Mick had taken a group of Concrete High School science students on a photo trip to Baker Lake.

During their trip, two of the students had wandered off into the forest and gotten lost. Mick called Carly right away requesting a search team. When Carly arrived, she was impressed with how Mick had organized the remaining students into search groups. He had handled everything like a rescue team professional except that he had directed everyone to look in one specific area. She asked him why he had everyone only looking on the South Pass Road? Mick responded very nonchalantly that he just had a feeling that the lost students had gone in that direction. Sure enough, Mick had been right. The search team found the lost high school kids four hours later just off the South Pass Road. When she had asked Mick again how he had known where they were, he told her he just had a hunch and gave her a wink. Carly attributed his hunch to his Indian heritage intuition and let it go.

The chopper took just over twenty minutes to arrive at the ranger station. Carly hurried aboard, barely giving it a chance to touch down. The helicopter pilot and Carly were old friends and had even gone out a few times, but nothing came of it. They yelled their "hello" over the roar of the engine, then Carly gave him the destination. They remained silent during the rest of the flight as Carly put her thoughts together. Ripley and George should be close to Mick's reported location by now. The truth was that if a hungry bear had you cornered in the wild and you had no weapon, you were a dead duck. From what he had told Molly, the bear had wounded him. If he lost enough blood, he could already be dead. She could not put that thought out of her mind.

The dark of a moonless night covered the forest quickly. Mick continued to send mental thoughts for help in case a rescue party was trying to find him but was losing hope. Every few minutes, the bear would slam itself against the tree with all his weight, trying to shake its prey loose. Mick's blood loss was making him weaker and lightheaded. He was losing his grip on the tree and despite his desperate effort to hold on, his good arm finally gave out, sending him down through the tree limbs, hitting the ground just a few feet from the bear.

He was still conscious when he landed on the ground. At first, the bear seemed confused by seeing Mick laying on the ground but after a slight hesitation, the bear turned toward him, stood up on his hind legs and began the death walk toward him. Mick pushed himself up until he, too, was standing, facing the bear. The bear dropped on all fours and took a swipe at its prey. The claws missed as Mick stumbled falling flat on his back. He laid there staring up at the darkness as the bear's face, now standing over him, filled his eyes, ready to kill.

ALUME flew the pod just above the tall vegetation, to avoid being seen. The thoughts had been getting weaker. Then they stopped. ALUME hoped she was not too late. Then, she heard it again, but the thought was very weak! She moved through the last light of the sunset, following the trail. She located the thought sender as it was about to be attacked by a large beast. She levitated the beast helplessly into the air, moving it deeper into the vegetation. The beast made ferocious sounds, striking out in all directions at the invisible enemy. When ALUME was satisfied that the beast was far enough away to no longer be a threat, she lowered it to the ground and released her grip.

The confused bear retreated deeper into the forest. A bright light suddenly appeared to Mick behind his would-be killer. He watched as the bear was lifted off the ground, floating upward, away from him. The bear was swatting and growling at the air, trying to get its balance with no ground to stand on.

"Is this a dream?" Mick said aloud, as he watched the helpless bear float higher then backwards into the thick forest until he was completely out of sight. Mick tried to stand again but fell back to the ground. He was desperately trying not to lose consciousness as he watched a tall, slender silhouette moving toward him. The figure appeared to have a very large head. Mick could not make out a face but wondered again if he was dreaming.

"Who are you?" Mick asked, receiving no reply. The light and the figure faded as Mick lost consciousness.

ALUME had lowered the pod to the ground and absorbed out, taking solid form. The human tried to communicate with her before falling unconscious. It was hurt badly, but still alive and losing a lot of body fluid from several punctures. Its brain functions were weak. She had to act quickly. She mentally entered its brain stem and was surprised by what she felt.

Whatever this creature was, its brain was highly evolved.

Earlier scans of the planet revealed that humans had early evolutional brain patterns. This being had the same physical form as humans but had old construction and was not entirely human. A quick particle analysis verified that this being was constructed with particle patterns older than any she had ever seen. Normal human evolution could not have naturally produced this being. It was alien to this planet. She would have to pass her energy into it quickly to keep it alive. She sent a high-energy charge through its brain. ALUME was uncertain if the being could withstand the shock but there was no other option. The brain patterns in this creature were so deep that a lesser charge would not circulate.

Immediately after the first charge, part of its brain responded. She sent another, much larger, and the brain began expanding at an accelerated rate. It felt like this creature had been mentally blocked and her charges were freeing it. She opened a capsule from her skin suit and removed the healing paste. She had done all she could do for this alien's mind, now she needed to repair its physical damage. She could not be sure what the paste's effects would have on this alien's wounds, but it was the only chance for it to survive without being put in a healer. She spread the orange goo on Mick's face. As soon as it touched his skin, it spread throughout its body to all the torn tissues.

ALUME heard the machine approaching. Sensors identified it as a primitive flying machine. There were also humans approaching on the ground. ALUME saw no advantage to further contact. The human was still unconscious, but she had done all she could do. She absorbed into her pod and lifted the pod to the top of the tree line as other humans approached.

As soon as Mick passed out, the dreams began. Dreams that had haunted him since he was a child. While lying on the cold ground, the images flashed through his head. They were so familiar, clear and real. There was a horrible gorilla like beast attacking toy sized beings screaming terrifying bird-like sounds while they were being eaten alive. Suddenly the dream changed, and he was falling into complete darkness, faster and faster until the pressure against him made his whole-body ache. Then, like the clicking of a TV remote, the scene changed, and he was in a battle with flying machines that changed their shapes while they were flying. The scene changed again.

He was flying in a ship being chased by a rock like object shooting light beams at him. His visions continued, surrounding him with spectacular celestial bodies. These visions were amazingly real. What was happening to him? He wanted it to stop! He thought he must be dying. Was his brain flaming out in his last moments?

Finally, the strange images slowed until he found himself in a beautiful place unlike anything he had ever seen. Was this Heaven? It couldn't be, he didn't believe in Heaven. Brightly colored plants, unlike any he had ever seen before, covered the landscape. Tall structures shaped like trees were everywhere and you could see through them like crystals. That is when he saw her. She was tall and elegant. She moved next to him, placing her long fingers on his head and he stared into her deep black eyes. He felt so at peace. Then, suddenly, he was flying very fast and close to the ground, the feeling was exhilarating. He needed to get a grip on himself and try to figure out what was happening to him. The more he focused his thoughts, the more things would begin to slow down. He began to feel things around him. The earth he was lying on suddenly felt cold under his body. The smells were familiar. He must be alive, or how could he smell or feel? This was not death. This was a message. Something was in his head projecting these things into his mind.

He tried to regain control of his body. He focused every ounce of his will and tried to send his thoughts back to whatever was calling him.

The images were still coming, but this time he concentrated on the images and tried to study them. They kept coming faster, one image after another, but he controlled his fear. The images were like watching a video. The sensations and visions were terrifying and beautiful at the same time. As the mental scrapbook opened, he began to feel a true sense of being out in space. As the images began to fade, Mick felt regret that this incredible show may be coming to an end. A calm fell over him. He felt different. He wanted to see more, to know more. Suddenly everything went quiet. No images, no message, just the quiet breath of the forest as he lay on the ground, unable to move. He was unsure how much time had passed when he finally felt hands lifting him from the ground and heard voices talking to him that grew more and more faint until he could hear them no more.

The deputies were driving slowly up the old logging road when they saw the bright light coming from just above the tree line at the edge of the woods. George pulled the jeep off the road.

"What the hell is that?" George muttered.

"Must be the chopper!" Ripley replied.

George answered without taking his eyes off the light, "Can't be a chopper; there's no noise. Choppers make noise."

"Let's take a closer look!" George said, getting out of the jeep.

Both men moved across the small pasture of brush and into the tree line, toward the light. They walked farther into the forest until they were next to the wall of brightness. They could not see what the light was coming from. They walked a few feet more until they were under the light source. Inside the circle of light, the two men froze, staring up at the silver blue object floating above them. White light outlined the object with pulsating blue light coming from its center. The object was low enough that they could almost reach up and touch it. The pulsating light was mesmerizing to George and Ripley. They watched as the object slowly lifted higher while making no sound and slowly moving deeper into the woods.

"What the hell is that?" Ripley asked George in a whisper.

"I think it's a UFO," George answered," a real honest to God UFO."

"Should we follow it?" Ripley asked without moving.

"I need to get a hold of the chief," George answered. "She is not going to believe this! Hell, I don't believe this!" He pulled out his two way and tried to contact Carly but received no reply.

"She must be in the chopper," Ripley replied. "Better call Molly."

"Come in, Base, this is George. Molly! Are you there?"

"Roger that, George, go ahead," she responded.

"Molly, we are at the old road, how far away is the chief?"

"She should be approaching your location," she answered.

"Try and patch me through. I need to talk with her right now." George's voice was stressed.

"Everything okay out there? Did you find Mick?" Molly asked.

"Negative to both. Rip and I just saw some kind of weird flying thing, but we haven't found Mick yet. Please patch me through to the chief."

Molly knew something was very wrong as she called to the chopper pilot. The pilot's voice interrupted the humming sound of the chopper blades. He yelled to Carly over the sound of the engine.

"It's Molly, put on your headphones."

Molly's voice boomed into Carly's ears, "Chief, George is at the old road and needs to talk to you. Hold on, I'll patch him through."

"Chief! Is that you?" George asked in such a low voice Carly could barely hear him.

"George, this is Carly, you'll have to speak louder! What's going on out there?"

"Chief, it's the weirdest thing out here. There was a real bright light coming out of the woods. We thought at first it might be Mick trying to signal us but then it moved over the trees. We followed it until we were right under it. This thing looks like a spaceship, a UFO or something. Hell, I don't know what it is but it's still here, moving in the woods. Do you want us to follow it? Over."

UFO? thought Carly, those boys must be smoking grass like they did at the Christmas party.

"No! Do not follow! I repeat, do not follow," Carly ordered. "I will be there in two minutes. Stay where you are! Over and out."

When the chopper arrived, Carly first saw the jeep at the side of the road. Her eyes quickly went to the light shining from deeper in the woods.

"Let's check out that light," she said to the pilot.

The chopper passed over the deputies below heading toward the light. As they got closer, the light moved farther away into the woods, like it was luring them to follow. Then the white light went out and was replaced by a blue light that changed from light blue to dark blue. When the chopper flew within fifty feet of the UFO, the craft turned a bright white. The light was so bright they could not look directly at it.

"Are we seeing what I think we're seeing?" the pilot asked without expecting an answer.

Carly did not reply as she recorded what she was seeing on her phone, but it was like taking a picture of the sun.

"I'll notify the military," the pilot told her.

"No! Please don't report it yet, Jerry! I have men and a hurt civilian down there. God knows what the military would do if they saw this. I don't want them trying to shoot this thing down. Let's wait until we find Mick and get our people out of here before we call anyone."

"Roger that, Carly, but we don't know what we're dealing with here," the pilot responded.

"Whatever it is, it's not acting hostile and I'm afraid the military would change that and put us all in danger," she responded.

Carly and the pilot could not take their eyes off it. The blue color pulsated from the body of the object, made it look like it was breathing. Carly wondered how a pilot could see out, assuming it had a pilot.

There was nothing about it that made Carly feel they were in any danger. The object just floated in front of them edging deeper into the forest. Then the UFO suddenly shined a bright white light straight down, lighting up the forest beneath it.

"What the hell is it doing?" the pilot asked.

"It's either looking for something or trying to show us something but it isn't making any hostile moves," Carly said to the pilot.

"I'm going to have my men move in." She turned on her headset, "George?"

"Yeah, Chief," George replied.

"George, I want you and Ripley to move under that light."

"Roger that, Chief. Should we get the rifles?" George asked.

"Negative, do not take any weapons," Carly ordered.

Something told her that weapons would be a big mistake. Whatever this thing was, a rifle was going to be of little use if it became hostile. Carly thought about the movie, *Predator,* where the alien would not harm anyone without a weapon, then questioned whether her decision was based on what she had seen in a science fiction movie. But her decision made as much sense as what she was seeing in front of her.

The two deputies moved through the thick forest toward the bright light. Both men were frightened but they were not cowards and moved forward.

They got close to the UFO and George yelled into the two-way, "We're almost to the light, Chief!"

"Move in slowly," Carly ordered.

"You move in from the right, Rip, and I'll move in from the left," George told him.

Ripley nodded his understanding and both men started toward the center of the blue light. The two deputies moved through the wall of light under the craft. Blue lights were shining inside the circle of white light. The bottom of the UFO was perfectly smooth with a slight bulge in the middle. The ship made no sound. It was just floating there, above the trees.

George was the first to see something. After his eyes adjusted to the brightness, he realized it was the doc lying on the ground. Mick was on his back with something moving all over his face.

"Is that the doc?" Ripley asked.

"Sure looks like him, under whatever is on his face," George responded. "What the hell is that stuff?"

The men just stared at the orange goo that was moving all over Mick's face.

"What do you see down there?" Carly asked.

"It's the doc! He's got something crawling all over him!" George reported.

"Is he alive? What's crawling on him?" Carly panicked.

"He's breathing, but he is covered with shiny orange stuff, Chief. You need to see this," George said. "This is some weird shit going on here."

The lights from the UFO suddenly went out. The pilot and Carly watched as the object turned until it was end on end, became a solid blue color, then shot away at such a high speed. It was there one second and gone the next, like a magic trick.

"Jesus, did you see that?" the pilot asked, "I've never seen anything move like that."

"Nothing from this planet," Carly offered. "Set this thing down, Jerry. We need to help Mick."

"Roger that," the pilot replied and turned the chopper around, setting it down on the road by her deputy's jeep.

Carly replayed the video on her phone but all she and the pilot could see was a blinding light. The UFO could not be made out. Then she saw the lights of the ambulance approaching from down the logging road.

She turned to the pilot. "Jerry, I want you to keep what we've seen here tonight between us for now. Can you do that?"

"No problem, Carly. No one would believe it anyway seeing that video," he told her.

"I will just put an unidentified aircraft sighting in my report. Reporting UFO's is a career kiss of death in my business," the pilot told her, shaking his head.

Carly and the pilot joined the deputies that were kneeling over Mick. She squeezed between them and bent over Mick. She did not understand what she was seeing. He had a luminescent orange substance moving around on his face. Carly reached down and touched the moving goo with her finger. It was warm to the touch and felt like jelly. She moved her finger through the orange substance, but none of it stuck on her finger when she pulled it away. Carly looked up at the dark sky and knew who had put it there.

Blood was all over Mick's clothes, but she could not see any injuries. She opened his shirt to check for wounds and saw that the orange goo was covering his chest and abdomen. When Carly pushed the orange goo to the side, she could see the gashes on his skin healing before her eyes.

"My God!" Carly exclaimed. "Whatever this stuff is, it appears to be closing his wounds." They all looked at each other first, then almost in unison, looked up at the dark sky.

Carly did not say anything to the ambulance driver about the UFO. The ambulance driver had not seen the phenomenon so there was no reason to say anything. Her gut was telling her to play her cards very close to the vest about this sighting. She knew how the media crucified people that claimed to see what she and the others had just witnessed. Her cell phone video showed nothing definitive. She could not explain away the orange goo, so she didn't try. Right now, she just wanted to get Mick to the hospital and everyone else out of these woods before that thing came back.

ALUME flew her pod out of the humans' sight. This contact had been exciting for her. Her first planetary contact with an alien. She had located the power source and helped the thought sender. This little planet was proving to be much more to her than just a repair refuge, so much more. She looked down at the planet's surface and wondered what other surprises this beautiful planet would have. She had done well, but now she needed rest. ALUME flew back by the liquid that covered the power source and maneuvered the pod in between trees so it would be out of sight. She sent an update thought to "C". She had put a location marker in the thought sender's mind so she would be able to find him. She went liquid and to charge.

Mick could not make out the person in the hospital room. As his eyes focused, he saw that it was a nurse changing an IV in his arm.

"Well, decided to join the living, have you?" The nurse asked him when she saw that he was awake.

"Where am I?" Mick asked.

"You're at United Care Clinic," the nurse replied.

Mick tried to sit up, but he was too weak and settled back into his pillow.

"Easy, Mr. Welch, you need to stay still and rest. I'll get the doctor," she told him over her shoulder as she left the room.

He was groggy and had a terrible headache, probably from blood loss and medication, he thought. He felt his arm, shoulder, and face for bandages but there were none. Was he dreaming? Where were the wounds from the bear attack? He remembered the bear attack and blood everywhere but now he could not find any cuts on him. Had he imagined the fight with the bear, the cubs, climbing the tree? Everything was so clear in his memory. He felt his face again and felt nothing! He had never had a headache like this.

Besides his head feeling like it was going to blow off his shoulders, he had this strange feeling; like a part of him had been asleep his whole life and suddenly woke up. His thoughts were everywhere. He remembered the bright light and the tall girl! That strange girl, touching his head and making him feel better and the bear floating into the trees. Was any of this real or did he dream it all? He closed his eyes trying to concentrate through the pain in his head when the doctor hurried into the room, nurse in tow.

"Well, how are we feeling?" he asked Mick. Not waiting for a reply, he held a small flashlight to Mick's eyes, checking his pupils.

"I don't have any cuts. I remember bleeding. There was a bear and so much blood...so much blood," Mick repeated. "I remember it attacked me, but I have no wounds."

The doctor did not respond to Mick, grabbed the chart at the end of the bed and went on with his questions.

"Do you take any medications, Mr. Welch?" the doctor asked.

"Only what you're giving me," Mick quipped, looking at the tubes invading his body.

"A sense of humor! That's a good sign," the doctor responded. He restated his question.

"Did you take any prescribed medicines before the incident?"

"No!" Mick replied with no humor in his voice. "What's wrong with me? My head feels like it's going to blow off my shoulders."

The doctor looked at him with serious eyes that all doctors seemed to be issued when they graduate from medical school. Then he finally replied.

"Well, some of the tests that we have run on you came back abnormal and I thought that there may be some internal hemorrhaging, but we can't find any. We didn't see anything on the x-rays, but I want to move you to the hospital in Sedro Woolley where we can get you a cat scan. I want you to rest now and regain some strength before we move you. The nurse will get you something for your head. In the meantime, I would like to run a new blood panel just to be sure we have not missed anything. Sometimes this type of trauma can create side effects. When you arrived, you were covered in a gelatinous material that was moving all over your skin, like a living organism. We have not been able to identify it. Real science fiction stuff." He continued in a whisper, "We could not even remove it to treat your wounds until it turned from orange to grey and became motionless, like it died. I've never seen anything like it, so I sent a sample to the lab to be analyzed, but we don't have the results yet. When the orange stuff turned grey, the lacerations were gone. There were no visible wounds or scars. I must tell you that I am more than a little baffled on this one. I suspect there may be some internal bleeding still going on and that is causing your elevated blood pressure and headaches." he concluded.

The two men just looked at each other for an awkward moment.

"I'm kind of tired," Mick said in a deliberate soft voice. He wanted to be alone.

"I think rest is a great idea," the doctor replied. "We can talk after we get more test results." He wrote on the clipboard and whispered something to the nurse. The doctor disappeared from the room while the nurse injected something in Mick's IV.

The nurse told Mick, "I've given you something for your head pain. If you need anything else, just press the red button," patting the little control box next to him. She gave him a little smile and dimmed the overhead light, closing the door behind her.

Mick was trying to sort things out. He had lied to the doctor, he felt like he was going to pass out again, but he did not want to be stuck in this bed while they threw darts trying to find out what was wrong with him. He was sure it was just blood loss trauma. Maybe that was causing the images in his head. He was too tired to think about it anymore, but he felt that something was seriously wrong with him and fell into a troubled sleep.

ALUME was still in charge mode when she jolted awake! The thought sender was dying. His brain was overloading. The energy she had sent through his tissue to save him was now killing him. This human being was somehow connected to the power source, so it was important to the landing to try and save him! She moved from the hiding place in the trees toward the direction of the tracer she had put in the human's body.

The tracer was in a large structure surrounded on three sides by forest. The sun was beginning to rise and there were no other humans in the area, so ALUME lowered the pod to the ground. She stayed liquid, so she would not be easily seen. She left the pod and sent it into the treetops, out of easy sight.

She flowed across the parking lot to the back of the structure, then absorbed into the building. Inside, humans were moving all around, but did not notice her stretched thin flowing along the edge of the hallway. She passed many small enclosures with humans in them. She was sure this was a primitive healing place. Her scans only detected one human with a crude mechanical limb. None of the other humans had any enhancements. These humans were small in stature and had an inner shell construction that protected their vital organs, just like the Terians. They had not yet developed multiple organs, which explained their short life cycles. This species was still at a very early stage of evolution. They had adapted well to their environment but were far too fragile for space travel.

She located the thought sender higher up in the structure and absorbed through multiple barriers until she reached his level. She flowed to his enclosure and absorbed through the wall into the room. The space was dark, but ALUME's eyes were as good in the dark as in the light, so she had no trouble seeing her human.

ALUME began to reshape into solid form. Mick opened his eyes when he heard the strange gurgling sound of her transformation. He stared in the direction of the strange noise but did not understand what he was seeing. A liquid mass was rising from the floor like a slow-motion fountain of water. The sight of it startled Mick. He tried to get up from his bed, pulling the tubes and wires attached to him and knocking down the portable monitor stand. He lost his balance and fell backward, hitting the wall with a loud thud.

ALUME finished reshaping and moved toward the human. She opened her arms in the Terian gesture of friendship, but Mick just stared at the anomaly standing in front of him, not sure if he was dreaming. Suddenly, he recognized the creature in front of him as the same one from the light in the woods: Tall, slender, blue tinted skin and deep black eyes. There could be no doubt that whatever this being was, it was not from this world.

"You were in the woods and floated the bear away. Where are you from?" he asked.

ALUME just stared at him making no sound, but Mick could hear the creature in his head.

We have come from another star system. Our ship has been damaged. We have come to repair it with the power source in the liquid.

"Power source in the liquid?" Mick asked, feeling faint from the pounding in his head. ALUME entered his thoughts and there was nothing about the ship or its power source. The human was not aware of his connection with the ship in the liquid.

Mick's head was throbbing worse. ALUME moved quickly, putting her hand on Mick's head. When they touched, she was able to connect. She felt the problem immediately. His brain's power connections were trying to expand with no physical place to grow. This human was very old, a mixture of two different constructions. The energy she had infused into him had triggered something in the combination of these constructions, something that could not be repaired with healing paste. His brain was shorting out his life functions. She needed to expand his brain capacity.

She could not predict how that would affect the human's life functions but if she did not try; his brain fluid would leak, and he would die.

Mick did not resist when she helped him lay down on the bed. She moved her hands over his face, putting him into a deep sleep. With both of her hands on his head she began to transfer energy into his brain stem, growing new vessels for his brain's impulse connections. She made the transfer slowly so as not to overload his system.

As the expansion continued, the human was not responding well. His body signs were deteriorating. His brain was rejecting the new vessels, treating them like invading foreign tissue. His body was shutting down to protect itself; he was close to death! ALUME had to do something more or he would die. Without hesitation, she released some of herself with the transfer so his body would recognize the tissue and accept the new growth. Under normal conditions she would be breaking Supreme law by sharing her biology with an alien and was further conflicted about interfering with this species, but she did not feel like she had a choice. ALUME was convinced that this human was important to obtaining the power source and the ship's survival stood above all law.

The Terian tissues immediately began working inside the human. The brain impulses were able to flow through the new connections, expanding his mental capacity. Excess energy escaped through his skin giving it a blue glow. The energized light became so bright; it passed through the wall of the room and into the hallway. All parts of his brain were expanding. ALUME was surprised at how quickly his brain was adapting. She attempted to disengage from the connection, but a force from inside him would not let go. She had to make a focused mental pull to break the connection.

The floor nurse called security about the blue light and strange noises coming from a patient's room and the security guard approached the room cautiously. He slowly opened the door and saw the patient lying on the bed, his body shining like a blue glow stick.

There was something next to him, melting before his eyes. The guard froze in place as ALUME finished going liquid and absorbed through the wall.

Mick was still glowing, but the blue light was dissipating quickly. After a few seconds, the guard scrambled for the light switch. Mick came to and could feel his skin tingling like he was being poked with a thousand needles. He was shaken from his encounter with the strange creature and was experiencing a euphoric change throughout his body when someone burst into the room.

Before Mick arrived at the hospital, Carly was assured that there was nothing she could do and was advised to go home and get some sleep. She stationed Ripley in the parking lot to keep an eye on things, especially things that might come from the sky. After a few hours of tossing and turning in bed, she headed back to the hospital. She entered the hospital through the rear ambulance entrance. Her job took her to the hospital at least twice a week and even more often at the height of the tourist season. It was always something: Rock climbers fell, hikers and bikers overexposed to the elements, car accidents or animal attacks. She knew the hospital layout as well as anyone that worked there. Going through the back was the fastest way in and avoided a lot of questions and socializing.

Carly was anxious to check on Mick. She had had a lot of questions. She stopped at the café and picked up coffee beforehand. George and Ripley had brought Mick's car to the hospital parking lot. When she arrived, she gave Ripley his coffee, got Mick's keys, and sent him home. She took the empty service elevator to Mick's room on the third floor. As she got off the elevator, she heard a commotion coming from down the hallway. She saw that Mick's door was open, with blue light pouring into the hallway. She drew her gun and ran into the room. She saw Cliff, the security guard, standing in the middle of the room, staring at the wall and a glowing blue object on the bed that she immediately recognized was Mick.

"What the hell is going on here?" Carly asked, holstering her weapon.

The guard replied in a shaking voice, his finger pointing at the wall, "Something went right through there."

"Well, whatever you thought you saw, Cliff, it's gone now," Carly replied. She thought better of saying too much, better to let the guard cast his own doubts on what he saw.

"I swear there was something in the room with him, Carly," the guard said. "There was a real bright light and this thing melted and looked like water, only it was different than water, and it just went right through the wall," knowing how crazy he must sound.

"What is it that you saw?" Carly asked, knowing he had no idea what he had just seen.

"I don't know what the hell it was. It was changing its shape," he said.

Carly let the guard ramble on about the strange vision that he was already doubting he had really seen. Mick was trying to sit up in the bed. The blue glow coming from his body, now a dying amber.

Carly needed to talk to Mick alone but first, she would have to get rid of the security guard.

"Cliff, I need you to check the other people on the floor," she told him.

While he was still rambling about the thing going through the wall, Carly walked him out of the room and into the hall. She closed the door behind him and went to Mick's side, grabbing his hand.

"Are you okay?" she asked him.

"I'm fine, I think," Mick answered.

"What the hell just happened here?" Carly asked.

I'm not really sure, he thought.

Carly heard Mick in her head, but he did not speak, and it visibly startled her.

"How am I hearing you when you are not speaking?" she asked him.

As a trained law enforcement officer, Carly did not deal well with crazy, and that was the only word for what was going on. The idea that Mick was talking without speaking was a lot for her to process.

"What's happening here, Mick?" she asked in her most authoritative tone.

"I don't know," he replied in his normal voice. "I have always been able to hear people's thoughts, but I have never been telepathic before."

"What are you talking about, reading people's minds?" she asked.

"They called it thought transferring at the special school I went to when I was a kid," he answered.

"What special school are you talking about? I don't remember you going to a special school," she said challengingly.

"Do you remember when my parents sent me to Summer Science Camp?" he asked her.

"Yes," she replied. "You were gone the whole summer."

"Well," he continued, "there was no Science Camp. My father took me to see his doctor friends at the University of Washington. They researched my special abilities. I could read people's thoughts and sometimes see things that were happening somewhere or were going to happen. For three months they gave me every kind of test they could think of to explain how I could do the things that no one else could do. My dad never shared with the doctors that he had the same abilities. He wanted to see if they could find something that would explain why we had these special abilities, but they failed to find anything."

Carly and Mick shared many childhood secrets, but this was the first she had ever heard of this. She felt a little betrayed but tried not to show it.

"I really wanted to tell you about it, but Dad made me promise not to tell anyone, not even you." He explained, trying to make her feel better about the betrayal he read in her thoughts.

"Maybe now would be a good time to explain," she suggested. Carly knew this story was going to be a doozy.

He began, "I was born with these abilities, just like my father. My mom didn't understand because she never had the "*gift*". That is what my dad called it. I think it's really a curse. Anyway, my "*gift*" got stronger as I got older. It became harder for me to hide, so I just kept to myself. You were my only real friend. My father taught me not to trust anyone. He was afraid that if my abilities should be discovered by the wrong people, like the intelligence community, they would put me under lock and key and have me use my "*gift*" for national security, which of course is just another way of saying spy. Dad's paranoia taught me to be paranoid too. I think that this creature that saved me heard my mental thoughts for help, rescued me, and that same creature that saved me in the woods was just here."

Carly showed Mick the video she had taken in the woods. "I took this last night when we found you. All you can see are the bright lights, but we all saw the UFO."

"Wow, I didn't know what the light was. All I could make out was something very tall; I think a woman. She came closer after the bear was lifted into the air and flew back into the woods," Mick explained.

"The bear flew back into the woods?" she asked.

Mick continued to explain, "No, it didn't exactly fly, it just lifted off the ground by itself just before it was going to finish me off. The bear lifted off the ground as high as the trees and floated deep into the woods until it was out of sight. That was when this creature appeared out of the light. I was as good as dead, Carly," he told her somberly. "Whatever that creature is, it saved my life."

"Do you remember anything else about what happened in the woods? Did this tall woman talk to you?" Carly asked him.

"I don't really remember much after she appeared in the light," Mick told her.

"Alright, tell me about what just happened?" Carly asked. "Did the creature appear again in the light?"

He shook his head, "No, today she made the light come out of me."

Mick told her everything he could remember since the creature appeared in the room. Carly just listened. If she had not seen the UFO with their own eyes, she would probably have thought Mick was hallucinating, except that the security guard said he saw something supernatural. She could not deny the light she saw coming from Mick's body as well.

"I don't know what to make of all this," Carly admitted.

"This is either a miracle or a nightmare," Mick replied.

"We should take what we know to the government," she said.

"I think we need reinforcement, but not the government. I don't trust them not to be aggressive," Mick cautioned. "The military always reacts with aggression. What if the aliens just want to fix their ship and the military starts shooting? I hate to think about what might happen if our military attacked these aliens, and the aliens fought back. Imagine the technology they have if they have figured out space travel," Mick said, with a solemn look.

The security guard came back into the room to report the statements he took from the nurses that had seen the light, but Carly cut him off.

"That's good work, Cliff. Please take your statements down to the ranger station and give them to Molly at the front desk. I will see that the hospital administrator finds out what a great job you've done here," she told him. She shook his hand and was walking him back out the door when the nurse walked past her to check on Mick.

"Hello, Carly," she said while passing by her. "My god! what happened in here?" she asked when she saw the overturned IV.

"Mick was startled when he awoke and knocked over the IV. It must have caused an electrical problem that flashed the bright light, but there doesn't seem to be any damage. Nothing to worry about," Carly replied.

"Well, let's fix this up," she said setting the IV stand upright and reconnecting the IV to Mick's arm before leaving the room. Carly closed the door again after the nurse left and moved back to his bed.

"Before the creature got here, I had a terrible headache," Mick continued. "To be honest, I thought I was dying. I was half asleep when I heard this gurgling sound. I looked over and saw something coming out of the floor. Then it turned into what I saw in the woods. I think it was female. It sounded female. She told me they were here because they needed to repair their damaged ship. Then, she put a kind of charge through my body that felt like electricity. Suddenly, the headache went away. That's when you came into the room. I'm not sure what it did to me, but I feel different," he confessed.

"Different, how?" Carly asked.

"I'm getting visions of things I've never seen before," Mick answered.

"What things?" Carly was curious.

Mick's voice was getting weaker. She could see that he was tired.

"You need to get some rest," she said, pulling the covers over him. She put her hand on his shoulder then turned to leave.

"There is a ship," Mick told her.

"We know there is a ship, Mick," Carly agreed.

"Not that ship," he told her.

"There are more ships?" Carly asked.

"Yes, it's their mother ship they need to repair," Mick told her.

"What happened to their ship?" Carly asked.

"They were attacked by something that is still after them," Mick answered. "They are coming. You believe me, don't you?" Mick asked.

"Of course, I believe you! It's just hard to make sense out of all this," she said, in a frustrated voice. "We can figure all this out when you are feeling better. I'm leaving your keys here," she said, setting them down on the bedside table. She bent down and kissed him on the cheek then left the room.

Carly could not explain the things she had seen. All this was over her pay grade. She needed time to think and get her head clear. For now, she would do her job and check in at the station. She took the stairs to avoid answering any questions. Her training taught her to look at things in a logical, disciplined, methodical way. She called it a practical deduction of the unlikely. There was always a logical explanation for everything, and it was usually right in front of you if you took the time to figure it out. She had been the first policewoman on the Bellingham Police Force.

During her five years as a patrol officer, she had seen a lot of crazy things that at first look appeared to be unexplainable. By applying practical deduction and good police work, the answers usually came to light. Eventually, the constant exposure to death and dealing with the underbelly of society became too much for her. She then transferred to ranger service, becoming the head ranger in just two years. What Mick had just told her, combined with what she had on video, pointed to an unparalleled phenomenon beyond anything she had experienced or known.

Something incredible was happening that could not just be explained away. She wasn't sure what to do about it. She needed to give herself some time to figure out the right course of action. She already was second guessing her decision not to report what she knew to government authorities, but something told her not to involve them yet. Whatever was happening here, it was too big for her to handle alone. Her cell rang.

"This is Carly," she answered.

"Hey, Carly, it's Jerry."

"Morning, Jerry," she answered, not surprised to get his call.

"I just wanted to give you a head's up," he told her. Carly could hear the concern in his voice.

"I just got out of the sheriff's office in Bellingham after being grilled by some government people from Homeland Security. They wanted to know all about the light I reported last night," he told her.

Carly's heart started beating faster. "What did you tell them?" she asked.

"Only that we saw a bright light that disappeared and the person we rescued had orange stuff on his face. I figured they would find that out anyway. They kept pressing me, so I just played dumb. Then they finally stopped with the questions. You are probably next on their list," he warned.

"Thanks for letting me know," she told him and hung up. She called the hospital to warn Mick but was told that he left without checking out. She called his cell. It went to voicemail. She left him a warning about the government men and asked him to call her. After telling her about being afraid of the government, she was worried. She had to find him.

ALUME flowed out of the building into the daylight after helping the human. She stopped under a bush when two humans walked past her. She could not bring the pod down to her with so many humans around. She would have to go to the pod. She flowed as fast as she could across the pavement. After she had gone only a few feet, a car sped into the lot heading straight toward her.

There was no time for her to get out of the way, so she levitated the car off the pavement, its back wheels spinning in air as it floated off the ground.

When she was safely across the pavement, she dropped the car, leaving the frightened and bewildered driver frozen at the wheel. She flowed up the tree toward the pod. She had only reached the first branch when she saw the two little humans climbing up the tree just above her. They must have spotted the pod from the ground and were trying to get closer to see what it was. She flowed upward on the opposite side of the tree to pass them without being seen. As she attempted to go around them, one of the children moved his hand and put it right on ALUME as she was flowing by. ALUME's liquid form was hot to his touch. He jerked his hand back, losing his grip, screaming as he fell. ALUME levitated him in mid-air to stop his fall, then lowered the astonished boy gently to the ground. She reached the top of the tree and absorbed into the pod. While the two boys watched, she slowly moved the pod deeper into the forest, staying next to the treetops to remain out of sight.

Mick got dressed as soon as Carly left. He wanted to get the hell out of the hospital before they shipped him off to Sedro Woolley for more tests. He could not risk any more tests. They may already know too much. He needed to think this thing out. There were a couple of men in suits talking to nurses at the end of the hall, so he headed the opposite way to the Exit door. He went down the three flights, six steps at a time, like the days when he was running track in college. Man, did he feel good! The last door was locked. Mick turned the knob as hard as he could. The knob broke off and the door flew open.

"Wow!" he exclaimed out loud. He was different, all right! The creature had done something to him, but he liked it. He found his car and drove over to Annie's Pizza Station. He went in, ordered a black coffee, then sat down to think this thing out.

The first thing he needed to do was to get some input from someone he trusted who might know something about what was happening. He could trust Carly as a friend, but she was, after all, a cop. plus he had never been able to hear all her thoughts. He could not tell for certain how Carly might react to everything that had happened but if she told government people, that could be a problem. She was having trouble trying to get her head around the whole alien thing. Hell, who could blame her, he was having a hard time with it himself even though he had seen it up close and personal. This was a real extraterrestrial event, so he needed an expert. One person immediately came to his mind- the professor! He had a call to make. But he wanted to call where he would have some privacy.

He finished his coffee and drove to The Inn. He could hear Taylor Swift in the background music as he entered the lobby. Natalya, the manager, was, by her own admission, the biggest Taylor Swift fan in America, or a "Swifty", as Taylor's die-hard fans had been nicknamed.

"Hi, Doc," Natalya greeted him with her biggest smile. Everyone in Concrete called him Doc.

"Hi, Natalya! How goes the battle?" he replied with his signature smile.

Natalya was one of those people that always seemed to be working. Whenever he stayed at The

Inn, no matter what day or time, Natalya was always at the front desk. Her grandfather owned The Inn, but was getting up there in years; thus, was unable to get around easily, so, as she loved to tell people, she was the "chief cook and bottle washer."

"I should be asking you about the battle," she teased, letting him know that she had already heard about what had happened to him with the bear. She was hoping to get his side of the story. That was already the talk of the small town.

"You don't look any the worst for wear," she noticed, with a flirting look.

"It really wasn't that big a deal," Mick replied quickly changing the subject.

"Can you check me in for a couple days?" he asked.

"Sure, Sweetie," (she called everyone Sweetie). "I can put you in your regular room," she offered.

"You know, if you don't mind, I'd rather be in the back if you have something available," he requested.

"No problem, Sweetie. Are you hiding out?" she asked jokingly.

"Just want to get some sleep! Can you do me a favor, Natalya?" he asked.

"Anything, Sweetie," she said as she leaned forward on her elbows like he was going to give her secret information. "You name it."

"Thanks, you're the best!" he said. "If you would not mention to anyone else that I am here, I would be in your debt."

"You got it, Doc. Mum's the word," she said, putting her forefinger to her lips.

After he checked in, Mick drove to the back of The Inn. He parked next to a wall of blackberry bushes that bordered the woods. This would keep his jeep from being seen from the front. He took his backpack and the large duffel bag that the rangers had loaded with all his stuff carrying them to his room. He locked his door, sat on the bed, and called Professor Taylor.

Mick met the professor at a university science forum shortly after his thesis had been published. The elderly man was the department head for Interplanetary Science at Seattle University. The professor had used his influence to make sure that they were seated next to each other at the forum dinner. They hit it off right away and Mick was fascinated by the professor's enthusiastic talk about America's need to continue funding the exploration in space to seek out new science and extraterrestrial life.

The professor talked about the government programs he consulted for, as well as his fifty-year love-hate relationship with the military. The top military minds were always seeking his counsel and support for the endorsement of their military related space projects. The military big shots had learned that it was always easier to get funding, if you had the endorsement of scientific data for any military project that they needed money for. They would put in a little extra funding for science studies.

Since their first meeting, despite their considerable age differences, these two genius science geeks became close friends. The professor even accompanied Mick on one of his photo safaris to Baker Lake, which had turned into a disaster for the professor. It rained cats and dogs for three days straight. The professor swore that it would be a wet day in Hell before he ever subjected himself to such torture again. As it turned out, the professor was not much into roughing it. Mick reasoned that the professor, who had spent most of his life passionately studying space, would be the perfect candidate for advice on dealing with this phenomenon. The professor had spent his entire career looking for extraterrestrials. His experience with the military could come in handy.

Mick debated with himself about how to tell the professor and decided not to say too much on the phone. He would try to get him to drive to Concrete. That would not be easy, considering that his last trip to Concrete did not go well. He would just have to make the call and wing it. Mick began to dial the professor when he saw there was a voicemail from Carly. He played the voicemail and heard the warning about the government people questioning the helicopter pilot. Now, he was really concerned. He dialed the professor's office in Seattle U. and got no answer!

He looked at the time on his phone, 7:10 a.m. Too early. The office didn't open until 8:00 a.m. That gave him a little time to clean up. He had a feeling that he would not have time later.

Chapter Four
UFOs Are Real

Mick dialed the professor's university office a few minutes after eight and the familiar young female voice answered, "Professor Taylor's office".

"Hi, Julie," Mick greeted her with his usual warmth, "Is the old' man in?"

"Oh, hi, Mick," she replied, "no, he's not in yet."

"When do you expect him?" Mick asked.

"He hasn't been coming in much lately, Mick. He left a message that he was doing research," Julie told him. "That means he's probably at the Pike Place Market where he spends most of his days lately."

"Does he have a cell phone yet?" Mick asked, already knowing the answer.

Julie just gave a little laugh. "Now, Mick, you know the professor refuses to carry a cell phone. Do you want to leave a message?" she asked.

"Yes," Mick responded, "tell him that it is very important for him to meet me at The Inn, in Concrete, Room 27, and Julie, tell him not to call. Urge him just to get up here as fast as he can. Something has come up and it can't wait."

"Of course, Mick, I'll tell him it's very important, so he can't wait," Julie repeated in her fake flirting voice.

All Mick could do now was wait for the professor. He desperately hoped he would drop what he was doing and make the drive.

The professor was enjoying his latte at the original Starbucks in the market. He had been a regular there since it first opened. Most people didn't know that Starbucks started at the market, with its little open- air display bins where you could sample coffee beans from all over the world for twenty-five cents a cup. Now, there seemed to be a Starbucks at almost every corner. *Who could have guessed?* he thought. It was so true that the only thing that was consistent in life was change.

The market was the professor's favorite place. In the fifties, he used to tag along with his mother and grandmother. The women would hunt for bargains at Saint Vincent de Paul Thrift Store and the other little shops that carried a variety of new and used treasures that could only be found at the market.

When he tired of following his mother through the little shops, he would wander by himself through the market, taking in all the people, sounds and smells.

His favorite thing was watching the fish vendors. After a customer had selected a fresh fish, the vendor would yell out, "Wrap it up!" He would throw the selected fish high in the air behind him, where it was caught by the back-counter man, who quickly wrapped it in newspaper, then put in an iced bag for the shopper to take home. This seemed to delight the never-ending large crowds waiting and watching. On rare days, the back-counter man would drop one and everybody watching would clap their hands like when you hear a plate dropped at a busy restaurant. After all these years, fish throwing never changed and was still one of the most popular attractions at the market.

When his mother and grandmother finally finished their rummaging, they would shop for their fresh vegetables and fish for the week, just like they had since they were children. He spent most of his younger days with his mother and grandmother. His father was the first African American that had ever been promoted to foreman at the Fisher Flowering Mill and his work occupied all his time.

For the forty-eight years of his marriage, Pike Place was their favorite place. These days, when the professor walked through the market alone, it was like she was still there with him even though she had been gone now for almost three years.

The professor asked the barista if he could use her phone and as usual, she handed it over. She was amazed that some people still did not have cell phones. At least this old guy gave her a buck when he got a drink, and in her book, that earned him a phone call. Anyways, she had unlimited minutes.

The professor dialed his office. After ringing three times, he was about to hang up when Julie answered, "Professor Taylor's office."

"Julie, it's me, I guess you have figured out that I won't be in today," he said smiling into the phone.

"I know, Professor. I think it's great that you are finally taking some time for yourself," she said.

"Well, I must say, playing hooky is my new favorite thing," he told her with a chuckle. "You take the rest of the day off, too and I'll see you tomorrow," but as he took the phone away from his ear, he heard Julie yelling.

"Wait! Wait, Professor!" Mick called.

The professor quickly put the phone back to his ear.

"Did you say Mick called?" he asked.

"Yeah, he called about an hour ago, He was excited about something, said it was very, very important for you to meet him right away in Room

27 at The Inn, in Concrete. I think he said Concrete, and oh yeah, he told me to tell you to just get up there fast as you could cause he had something he needed to see you about. Oh, and he said not to call! How weird is that!"

"That is weird." the professor agreed. *What could Mick have to talk to him about that he could not say on the phone?* the professor thought to himself. *What could be so important that he had to drive all the way to Concrete today?* For a moment, he contemplated calling Mick anyway but decided against it. Mick was someone to be taken seriously. If he did not want a phone call, he must have a good reason. The drive to Concrete was a good hour or more from Seattle in day traffic. He would need gas. He headed for his car and could not deny the curiosity that was beginning to build inside him. There was little enough excitement in an old professor's life. This had the makings of a real suspense novel, his favorite read.

The professor filled up at the Gas-a-Plenty Station just up from the market then hit the on-ramp merging onto Interstate 5 heading toward Bellingham.

Everyone was going to work so the traffic was heavy, and it took him almost an hour and twenty minutes to reach the Sedro Woolley turn off. He was glad to see the Interstate 5 traffic disappearing from his rear-view mirror. He passed through the town of Sedro Woolley on the stretch of a two-lane road that was dotted with large front yards and houses set back from the road. All the stories he had read about small towns were sure true of Concrete, he thought, remembering the camping trip. Wherever they went in the town, everyone knew Mick. For that matter, everyone seemed to know each other. He could not imagine that you could keep a secret if you lived there. He had been a Seattle city boy all his life and had trouble relating to the idea of living in a small town where everybody knew everybody. He enjoyed a certain amount of anonymity.

When he first met Mick, he was immediately taken with the young scientist's intellect and easy manner. The young man was not prone to ego despite his considerable accomplishments in biological research at such a young age. A mysterious call from a man like Mick really got his blood going.

The professor pulled into the parking lot of The Inn. He saw that the rooms in front only went to fifteen, so he drove around to the back of the building where he saw room number twenty-seven on the bottom level. The lot was quiet except for a couple of folks packing up their cars to leave. He parked and walked toward Mick's room, a light mist refreshing his face. Mick answered the door on the first knock.

"Professor!" Mick gave him a bear hug. "Thank you for coming."

The professor pulled up the small chair from the tiny writing desk and sat down facing him and got right to it.

"Okay, my boy, what is this all about?" he asked.

Before answering, Mick stood up and walked to the window, pulling back a corner of the closed curtain and looking out over the parking lot for anything unusual. Satisfied that there was nothing, he said in a clear and confident tone, "I am in contact with an extra-terrestrial being."

The professor's face betrayed his surprise at what Mick had told him. Had he heard it from anyone else he probably would not have taken so long to reply but a statement like that coming from a scientist like Mick, demanded a careful and respectful response. It was a crazy thing to hear.

"How?" The professor asked.

Mick sat back down on the bed and spent the next half hour telling the professor every bizarre detail of the last twenty-four hours, from the bear attack, floating bear, and the encounter at the hospital. The professor listened to the fantastic tale being careful not to interrupt. What he was hearing would be the most significant event in human history if it were true. There was no question in the professor's mind that Mick believed every word he was saying, and the professor knew this brilliant young man was a man of absolute science, so his first conclusion was that the events he just heard, must be a hallucinogenic reaction to medication. The professor feared that because of his perceived near-death experience, the last thing Mick needed was a doubting Thomas, so despite his skepticism he responded carefully. He needed to talk with the ranger and see the video that Mick said was on her phone. He asked Mick to show where the bear wounds had been. Mick complied, showing no sign of any cuts or scars, re-enforcing the professor's suspicions about drugs.

He considered Mick's concern about the ranger possibly reporting the UFO. The logical thing for her to have done was to immediately report the incident to Homeland Security, which, as far as Mick knew, she had not done. If this incident was real and Homeland caught wind of a possible extra-terrestrial ship landing up here, the area would already be swarming with agents and Mick would most likely already be in federal protective custody. The whole area would be put under the blanket jurisdiction of a top-secret military operation. He also knew about Mick's lifelong friendship with the ranger and considered that may be why she was in his UFO story. God knows what kind of crazy action the government would take to keep the public in the dark, but you could rest assured that they would do everything in their power to keep the truth from the public.

The professor had heard the rumors about a secret CIA department that dealt exclusively with UFO phenomenon but had never seen any proof that it really existed. In all the years that he had been a government consultant on inter-planetary research and phenomena, he had never been allowed on the inside. He had never been at peace with the suspicious and untimely death of an old friend back in 1964. The man was high-ranking Air Force official and a close friend of the professor. He called him out of the blue one day to tell him he was going to show the professor something in Area 51 that would blow his mind.

Two days before they were to meet, his friend was killed in a single vehicle drunk driving automobile accident. He had always believed that his friend's death was not an accident but deliberate, to protect a secret from getting out. He had never known his Mormon friend to take a drink, but the police came up with solid evidence of alcohol in the blood stream. Case closed. He had learned after forty years of dealing with the government, that they loved their secrets and guarded them with lethal vengeance.

"You could be in great danger if the wrong people get wind of this," the professor told him, hoping the story was true.

"That's what I was thinking," Mick agreed. "I'm getting a little paranoid."

"This creature that saved you talked about a ship in the lake, what do you think she meant by that?" the professor asked.

"She didn't talk. I just knew what she was saying in my mind, but I don't know what she meant," Mick answered, "just that the ship was in the lake."

"You said she; this alien, is female?" the professor asked.

"I don't know for sure, of course, but her voice and mannerisms just seemed feminine." Mick confirmed.

"How does this alien know where you are?" the professor asked.

"I don't know," Mick answered, "but she seems to be able to locate me quite easily."

"She communicated with you telepathically. Maybe you can communicate with her the same way?" the professor suggested.

Mick read the doubt in the professor's mind and knew that he thought the story was a fabrication from the effects of medication. He needed proof, after all, he was a scientist.

I don't understand the connection I have with this being, Mick telepathically said to the professor, testing his ability.

The professor was visibly shocked when he heard Mick without Mick speaking.

"My god, you are telepathic!" the professor said in a whisper.

"Since the incident in the hospital with the alien, I have been able to communicate telepathically," Mick explained. "I have always been able to read most people's minds. I know that you think this is the medication, but I assure you it's very real. Whatever she did at the hospital is changing me," Mick told the professor, in his normal voice.

"How are you changing?" the professor asked.

"I feel stronger, mentally, and physically," he said.

The professor was beginning to believe something real was happening here. He sat for a few moments just staring at Mick before finally speaking.

"I have waited all my life for verification of life from other worlds. I have dreamed about seeing for myself before I died. My whole career, I've preached that it was the world's responsibility to search for life in the universe, but I never dreamed that I might experience it for myself. Can you try to contact this alien?"

"I can try," Mick answered. He closed his eyes and concentrated.

ALUME scanned the ship in the water, but the scans were unable to penetrate the hull. She would have to enter the ship herself to inspect inside. She had just lowered the pod to the water above the ship when she received the human's thoughts. They were not distressed and were asking her to come to him. She did not want to delay her inspection of the ship, but she needed to check on her human.

She lifted the pod from the water and flew toward the tracer and stayed close to the treetops. The human was in a small group of structures. Exposing the pod during the light of the star was dangerous, but she did not sense a trap and the scans did not detect any weapons.

ALUME stopped at the top of the tree line where the human's thoughts were the strongest and waited.

When Mick finally opened his eyes, the professor was staring at him.

Mick just shrugged saying, "I don't know."

They sat quietly making small talk until Mick finally said, with a grin. "She's here."

The two men walked out into the sunlight. They looked in all directions for a few moments before the professor pointed to the tree line.

You called to me, ALUME thought to Mick.

I needed to see that you were real and not something just in my mind, he thought back.

The pod floated noiselessly, emitting a pulsating blue color through its silver hull.

"I never dreamed that I would see such a thing with my own eyes," the professor said, staring at the miracle floating above the trees.

Professor Taylor moved closer to the mesmerizing object while Mick took a video and walked under the ship. Two families were loading their bags in the parking lot but were oblivious to the floating UFO, until one of the teenage girls started yelling at her parents and pointing to the trees. Mick and the professor were both directly below the pod when they heard the approaching siren.

Carly was driving through town looking for Mick's car when she received the first call from Tyler Sanderson, reporting that a UFO had just passed over his gas station. Soon after, she received another call from Natalya at The Inn yelling about a strange airplane above The Inn. She headed straight there.

"It's back again," Carly said out loud to herself, as she turned into the parking lot. She called Molly and requested back-up. Natalya's description of the object matched what she and the helicopter pilot had witnessed the night before. Carly was coming to grips with the fact that this incredible event was happening again whether she wanted it to or not. What she saw the night before was hard to deny when you were looking right at it, but her training did not easily let her accept the reality of aliens and UFO's. She had looked at the video she had taken in the woods a hundred times, hoping that it was a secret military craft. That was the only logical explanation she could come up with. She was hanging onto denial. Her fear now was that what she had seen in the woods and what she was about to see at The Inn would change everybody's lives. She did not know what the next few moments might bring.

The front of The Inn appeared normal but when she pulled around the building to the back lot floating above the trees, she saw the UFO from the night before. She slammed on the brakes and stared at it for a few moments before getting out of her patrol car. The craft did not appear to be aggressive but the people in the parking lot needed to be evacuated from the area immediately. Then she saw that Mick and another man were standing right underneath the object.

She yelled at everyone to move out of the parking lot to the front of the building, but nobody moved. She found herself having a hard time not staring up herself, but her sense of duty kicked back in, and she yelled again, louder, and people began to move back. The other man with Mick, she recognized as the science professor that Mick had brought to Concrete on a camping trip.

"Mick" she yelled, "you all need to move the hell away from that thing."

"Everything's alright, Carly," Mick yelled back, without moving.

The crowd began moving toward the object, taking pictures with their cell phones. The pod's sensors detected Carly's weapon.

ALUME decided to leave the area before the weapon could be used and cause the pod to take a defensive action. She took the pod straight up at speed three, making no sound and leaving only a vacuum blast of air as it vanished. To the people in the parking lot, one moment it was there and the next moment it was just gone. Carly stood for a moment with the rest of the astonished witnesses, looking up, trying to see where it had gone. After a few moments she spoke to the crowd.

"Okay, folks, it's all over, let's clear the area please!" she commanded.

A voice in the crowd yelled out, "What the hell was that?"

Carly did her best to think of something that would settle the crowd down.

"The Navy base must be conducting exercises today and I think we just saw one of their new secret ships." The answer had a logical ring to it, but she could see that nobody believed it.

"I've never seen a plane like that," someone else called out.

"The military doesn't have anything that can move that fast," yelled out another.

"That's why they call them secret," she told everybody. "Now please just go on about your business."

The crowd was energized. They were not disbursing. They were talking to each other, trying to understand what they had just seen. Carly's deputies pulled into the parking lot and Carly ordered them to get personal information from the people in the parking lot and take statements from those that felt compelled to give one. The ranger's cell phone began ringing.

"Callahan," she answered.

"Is it true, Carly?" There was urgency in the voice. Carly recognized Mitchell Mortenson, from the Sedro Wooley News. *How did he find out so quickly?* she thought to herself. Maybe somebody at the station had a big mouth. Then she remembered all the phone cameras. This whole thing was probably all-over social media by now.

"Hey, Mitchell! Is what true?" Carly asked.

"The UFO! Did you see it?" he asked with childlike excitement.

"Now, slow down, Mitchell," Carly replied quickly. "I saw an aircraft that I have not seen before. I'm sure the Navy can explain it better than I can."

"The Navy has already denied any knowledge, Carly." She could hear the frustration in the newsman's voice.

"Mitchell, you know they deny everything. I'll bet you a month's pay it is one of theirs."

"Carly, we go back a long way, give me something that will shed some light on this," the reporter's voice was almost pleading.

"I'm sorry, Mitchell, I have no idea what kind of plane it was," she replied, trying to play down the whole incident.

"Report I got said it looked like a UFO," the newspaperman said, challenging the Ranger to deny it.

"Like I said," Carly explained. "It sure wasn't any plane I could identify," I've got to go, Mitchell. Talk to you later." She hung up before he could ask another question and directed her attention to finding Mick, who had disappeared from the parking lot.

The soldier on watch at NORAD was half asleep at the radar scope. The room was busy with soldiers watching scopes, monitoring flight activity in the area. The soldier had worked in the watch room for almost two years and had never seen anything out of the ordinary. Uneventful was okay with him, especially today. He took another drink of strong coffee to try and distance his mind from the threating fatigue of a night spent too long at the bar. Then he saw it, moving so fast that it took his mind a second to catch up before he yelled out.

"Bogey, nine o'clock, Sir."

"Confirm!" the captain ordered.

Another soldier at a second scope spoke up. "Confirm, Sir, bogey, nine o'clock."

"Commercial, civilian, or military?" The captain asked.

"Unidentified, Sir," the soldier replied. "Air speed is fourteen hundred fifty knots, Sir!"

The captain jumped up from his chair and moved quickly to the soldier's radar screen.

"It's got to be a missile to be moving that fast," the captain said.

"Negative, Sir, the bogey made a ninety-degree turn, Sir!"

"A ninety-degree turn at fourteen hundred fifty knots; that's impossible!" he mumbled, his eyes re-reading the radar screen.

"Bogey has made another ninety-degree turn sir and is descending to the surface," the soldier reported.

"Get a satellite track on the return location," the captain ordered. The soldier downloaded the return coordinates.

"It's headed for the Baker National Park area," the radar man reported. Moments later, he reported, "The bogey has disappeared from my scope, Sir!"

"Can you verify a crash?" the captain asked.

"No, Sir!" he replied, "the bogey just disappeared."

"Get me Command!" the captain barked.

The duty officer at command listened to the captain's report. What was being reported did not make much sense. His first thought was that it was simply instrument misreading, but his training had taught him not to question a captain, so he put the call through to the upper authority. Within two minutes of transferring the call, the base was put on high alert and two F-16 jets were scrambled from the naval air station in Seattle.

"Eagle One, this is Sky Hawk Leader!" reported the lead pilot. "Approaching coordinates of bogey. Radar clear! negative contact, negative visual, will circle area at higher altitude! Over!"

"Roger that, Eagle One," Command answered.

The two jets circled a wide area searching for any moving object, but the radar showed nothing.

"We are not seeing any movement in the area," the lead pilot reported.

"Roger that, Eagle One, return to base."

The planes circled back toward base. Whatever it was, it was long gone. Both pilots were relieved that there was nothing to pursue. They could never catch something going the speeds tracked on NORAD's radar. The pilots did not communicate with each other as they headed back to base. Words were not necessary. There would have been questions from Command if they had reported anything, and neither pilot wanted to answer those questions. Reports of UFO's would not look good on their record when it came to promotion review. The high command had a dim view of reported UFO sightings by its pilots. It was a career killer. Both pilots believed that there had to have been something if NORAD's radar clocked its speed. NORAD did not make mistakes. Whatever it was, Command would be happy not to have a public record of it.

Carly caught a glimpse of the professor going into one of the rooms and followed him. When she walked into the room, Mick and the professor had big smiles on their faces.

"Hi, Carly," Mick greeted casually.

"Why aren't you in the hospital? They called me when you just disappeared. What the hell just happened here?" Carly asked.

"I didn't need to stay in the hospital," he told her. "I have never felt so good. There is nothing wrong with me." Mick said in a calm voice.

"How have you been, Ranger?" the professor interrupted with a smile.

The ranger ignored the professor's question and asked him one of her own.

"Let me guess, you're not here for another camping trip," she joked.

"Oh my, no! Mick invited me here to see what I believe we just saw," the professor answered, still smiling.

Carly radioed out to the parking lot, "Come in, George! Over."

"Yeah, Chief! Over," George answered.

"I want you and Ridley to finish up with those statements and get back to the station, and George, no talking to media or any federal people. Refer anyone that asks anything about this to me. Over."

"Roger that, Chief! Over and out." George answered.

The silence in the room was broken by the sound of low-flying jet planes.

"Well, it sounds like the military is here!" Mick said, "It might have been a mistake to have the alien come in the middle of the day."

"You called it here?" Carly asked in disbelief.

"I have a connection with the alien," Mick confided. "I kind of pushed him into it," the professor confessed.

"What kind of connection?" Carly asked, ignoring the professor.

"I'm not sure, but it came when I mentally called it," he told her.

"Are you talking about the creature that floated a bear into the woods and did something to your brain that turned you blue in your hospital room?" she asked sarcastically.

"Yes!" Mick replied, ignoring Carly's cynical tone. "She is a scout sent to prepare for the larger craft to land and make damage repairs."

"Mick, we have no idea what we are dealing with here. The feds have already interviewed the helicopter pilot and were next," Carly told him. "We need to tell them what we know."

"I think that is a very bad idea," the professor told her.

"What did the pilot tell them?" Mick asked.

"You didn't listen to the message I left you?" she scolded. "The pilot just said he saw a bright light and orange stuff on you."

"You can bet that once they see this little shindig on social media, if they haven't already, nothing will stop them from detaining everyone that has seen or had any contact with the UFO," the professor interjected.

"I have already been contacted by a local reporter asking questions," Carly confided, "and if I'm not mistaken, those were military jets that just flew overhead. I can guess what they were looking for so, I think it's safe to assume they already know."

'Then, we are not safe," the professor warned.

"Professor, can you get in touch with the president without alerting the military?" Mick asked.

The professor had been asking himself the same question. Getting to the president was a very difficult thing. Everyone wanted something from the leader of the United States and that took procedures. It would have to be someone that knew the power players and how to get around the red tape. One name came quickly to mind, his old chess buddy, retired General Albert Kaiser.

"I don't have that kind of pull, but I know someone that might," the professor answered.

Even in retirement, the general was a powerful and respected figure within the military hierarchy. Most of the United States senior Senators had called on him for advice at one time or another. If anyone could get to the power players, it was Kaiser.

After General Kaiser's wife passed away a few years earlier, the professor had spent many nights at the old war dog's house on Whidbey Island, playing chess till the wee hours of the morning and talking about everything under the sun. They had met at a NASA meeting of the Joint Chiefs of Staff many years ago, when the professor was consulting on the mission to put the Hubble telescope into space. The general headed a military panel that reported to the United States Senate. The general, in his loud, intimidating best general voice, had questioned the professor's facts regarding the importance of spending so much money from the defense budget to put a telescope into space and the professor gave it right back to him by rattling off reason after reason on just how the United States could benefit from seeing deeper into space and how the military could also benefit. The professor won the general's immediate respect for standing up to him and being prepared. They had been good friends ever since. The professor was one of those rare people that could befriend and relate to a variety of diverse personalities.

"Retirement hasn't slowed me down a damn bit," the general would brag. He was a tough, smart old bird that did not make the rank of general because he lacked self-confidence or brain power.

"May I borrow your phone?" the professor asked.

The phone only rang twice before the professor heard the general's familiar, gruff voice.

"Kaiser," came the answer.

"Well, I'm surprised you're up!" The professor teased with a smile on his face. "I thought that all you old white men took morning naps."

"I'm awake enough to whip your butt in some chess!" replied the general, recognizing his old friend's voice.

"I will have to take a rain check, Albert, something real important has come up. Something I need your help with," the professor confided.

"Sounds like real cold war spy stuff," the general said. "So, what is so important?" he asked.

"Something I can't talk about on the phone," the professor confided. "Could you meet me here in Concrete?" he asked.

"What the hell are you doing in Concrete?" the general asked then continued without waiting for an answer. "I can be there in an hour."

"Wonderful!" the professor knew he could rely on the general. "I'm in Room 27 at The Inn. Do you need directions?"

"The town's only a couple blocks long, I'll find it," the general replied. Then the line went dead. The general knew the town of Concrete very well. Over the years, he had caravanned thousands of military vehicles through Concrete on the way to training maneuvers next to the national park. To get funding in the cold war days, you had to demonstrate readiness with a dog and pony show of military ground troops.

He would have to hurry to catch the next ferry. That was the best and worst thing about living on Whidbey Island. You were at the mercy of the ferry schedule unless you were willing to take the long way over the Deception Pass bridge. The good news was it was also harder for people to just drop in on you. His wife had always told him to make more room in his heart for people, but he had never been a socializer. Since she passed, except for an occasional old career buddy and the professor, he preferred to be alone with his memories.

He remembered when she insisted, they move to Whidbey Island. He had argued that it was too far from the base. "You have to take the bad with the good," she told him.

It was one of only a handful of times in over fifty-two years together that she would stand her ground and not take no for an answer. As always, she had been so right. They had a wonderful life together on the island. He struggled when she passed, staying there without her. Her memories were everywhere, but in the end, he could not bear to leave the house that was filled with all the love she had given him. He decided to finish his days there, surrounded by her.

He grabbed his glasses from the kitchen table and tucked them into his jacket pocket. His eyes were not as good as they used to be, but he hung on to denial by admitting that getting older mandated some limitations. He went into the bedroom and took his 45 out of the nightstand. He knew the professor well enough to know that an urgent call like this must be serious and it was better to be ready for anything. He enjoyed getting the mysterious call to action, immediately classifying it as a mission, one of the many things he missed about having a command. He picked up the carry bag that he always kept by the front door and jogged to the Hummer. He took pride in his physical shape for a man of 71. The Hummer was the perfect car for the general: Powerful, rugged looking and an attention getter with all the bells and whistles. It was a guy thing and he loved it. *This was going to be a good day*, he thought as he herded the Hummer down his gravel driveway onto Waterfront Drive to catch the ferry.

Carly was not so sure about the professor's choice. "Was that a good idea calling a military guy, and a general to boot?" she questioned.

"Sometimes you just need to have faith," the professor said confidently. "You must believe in people. The general has connections in places where we wouldn't even know there were places and is not the kind of man that would betray a trust. Now tell me again everything you can remember about our visitor and please don't leave anything out," the professor asked. "The smallest detail could be important."

Mick recounted the events since the bear attack. The professor marveled at Mick's ability to recall details. The first time they met, he knew that this young scientist was most certainly a genius. Mick had a photographic memory and in the professor's opinion, was intellectually incorruptible. When he and Mick were discussing deep scientific theory, the young scientist seemed to have an unlimited amount of information stored in some faraway part of his mind, ready to be recalled upon a moment's notice.

The professor could not help but notice that he seemed more aggressive than he had been in the past. Where he used to have to be prodded to get him to talk, he was now more assertive. He was bolder, like a new dimension to his personality had been unleashed. That was it, the professor thought, his personality was larger. Probably just the result of all the excitement, but he was different.

After about an hour, there was a thundering knock! Carly opened the door and, like MacArthur's return to the Philippines, General Kaiser invaded the room. The professor stood up and the two men saluted each other, as was the protocol.

"Looks like a crime scene out there," the general said, referring to the deputy's taking statements from a huge crowd. The crowd had grown much bigger with people, hoping to get a look at a UFO.

"That's why I called you," the professor told him. "Let me introduce you to everyone. This is Mick Welch, a colleague of mine from the university as well as the man responsible for this meeting." The professor turned to the ranger. "I believe you already know Carly," the professor said.

"Yes, of course." the general admitted. "We have met on a few occasions. Nice to see you again, Ranger!"

Carly gave him a polite nod. The general then turned to his old friend and asked in his most commanding voice, "Now, please tell me why I'm here!"

"Do you remember the conversations you and I have had about UFOs?" the professor asked.

"UFO's? You called me here to talk about UFOs?" the general seemed genuinely annoyed.

"Yes, Albert! I just saw one out in the parking lot!" the professor replied. "That's why all those people are out there? News travels fast in a small town."

This was now more bizarre then the general could have imagined. This old friend, probably one of the smartest people on the planet, telling him that he had just seen a UFO.

You never know what the day will bring, he thought.

"Does this have anything to do with your theory that Area 51 was the cause of your friend's untimely death?" the general asked, not convinced that the professor had seen a UFO.

"No! this is about an alien spacecraft, the real thing," the professor said, looking him right in the eye. He knew that the only way to get the general's help was to cut through the sarcasm and get to it. The general was silent, beginning to realize that this was not a bad joke.

"My friend, Mick, who, I hold in as high a regard as you, had a visit from a being from another world. The alien communicated to him that they need to land on our planet to make repairs to their ship," the professor explained.

"They need to land for repairs?" the general questioned sarcastically. "Come on, Professor. I mean mistaking an aircraft for an alien spaceship is one thing but talking to an alien? Coming from anyone else, I would just call you looney," The general was getting very loud.

"Albert, just try to keep your mind open," the professor responded, just as loud.

Mick held his cell phone up to General Kaiser's face and played the video he had taken of the pod in the parking lot. The general watched the video and when it was over, calmly asked Mick to play it again.

"Jesus Christ! When did you take this?" he asked.

Mick answered telepathically, *A couple of hours ago.* He knew that the old man needed more proof that this was serious. Mick decided to give him a demonstration.

You met your wife, Evelyn, at a charity benefit to help servicemen returning from active duty in Korea make the transition back to civilian life, a cause you got involved in because of the raising suicide rate among servicemen returning from combat. She died two years ago from breast cancer, and you still walk with her every day on the shore next to your house.

The general stared at Mick. "Hey, what the hell is this? How can I hear you when you are not talking?

Are you a goddamn alien? You get the hell out of my head! My personal life is none of your goddamn business!"

"I am sorry for the intrusion, General, but it's important for you to believe that this is a real event." Mick told him, this time in a spoken voice. "The alien saved my life and during the process. She changed me so that I have enhanced my abilities. I have always had some special abilities but now I can hear things clearly in people's minds. I thought you should know everything. You must be convinced that this is real." Mick told him.

The general turned to the only uniform in the room.

"Well, Ranger, what do you have to say about all this?" the general asked.

"Just like you, I'm having a hard time with all this, but I saw what I saw and have to deal with it." She told him, "I witnessed it twice. Last night with two of my deputies and a police helicopter pilot and again today in this parking lot."

"Did you report these sightings?" the general asked.

"No, I did not," Carly confessed.

"Why not? the general asked. "Isn't that your job?" The general was beginning his interrogation, but before he could say another word, the ranger shot out of her chair and faced the general nose to nose.

"Don't you tell me what my goddamn job is!" Carly was tired and not in any mood for the general's bullshit. "Sometimes the rules just don't apply, and you must improvise. I have seen first-hand what can happen when the government gets involved. We have all just witnessed what is probably the most important event that any of us will ever see and if you choose to not believe us, then as far as I'm concerned you can just high tail it back to where you came from." Carly turned away from the general and went into the parking lot to check on her men.

"Let me see that video again." General Kaiser watched the pod floating noiselessly and then disappearing into the sky. The military man in him was trying to process what he was seeing, looking for the trick in it.

"After the craft shot up into the sky, we saw fighter planes fly over, so the military must know something," Professor Taylor informed him.

The general sat back down, saying nothing. He was thinking to himself that the video looked real enough, alright, but that did not make it alien. Mick talking to him without speaking and knowing those things about his life could be a parlor trick.

But if he was being honest, his gut told him that it wasn't a trick.

"If you keep an open mind, I will tell you everything I know," Mick offered.

"Okay, I'm listening," the general said.

Mick told his story again and when he had finished, sat back down on the edge of the bed. Carly walked back into the room, surprised to find the room so quiet.

"What did I miss?" she asked, expecting an explanation.

There was a long silence in the room until, finally, the general spoke in a remarkably soft voice.

He told them, "I have a confession to make, Professor, that I have never told anyone but my wife. I saw the real crashed Roswell spaceship at Area 51."

"So, I was right all along," the professor said. "Jesus, Albert, all those arguments you made against UFOs, and you knew the truth all along?"

"I really considered coming clean," he confessed, "but it was top secret. I was afraid your knowing could put you in danger. Besides, then what would we have had to argue about?"

"What did it look like?" asked Carly.

"Well, it didn't look like anything I'd ever seen before, as you can imagine, and nothing like the one on your video. The craft was only about eight feet across and was pretty broken up from the crash. They pieced it back together as best as they could. It was covered in what looked like aluminum and its general shape looked kind of saucer-like but more oblong. What was left of the inside of the ship looked smooth, I mean there were no instruments that I could see."

"Did they recover any aliens from the crash?" Professor Taylor asked.

"I was told that there were four and they looked like children because of their size, but I never actually saw one," the general replied. "Two were dead in the wreckage and two more lying outside on the ground. It appeared that they were able to get out of the ship under their own power. But only one of them survived." Kaiser confirmed.

"What happened to the survivor?" Carly asked.

"I didn't ask, and they didn't say," General Kaiser said.

"So, the Roswell stories were true." the professor exclaimed.

"The Air Force put a shroud of secrecy over the whole incident with the threat of solitary confinement in a federal prison to anyone who broke the silence," the general explained.

"Why did it have to be hidden from the public?" Carly asked.

"The government, well, mainly the military, wanted to keep the craft to themselves to see what they could learn from it. Think of how advanced their alien technology would have to be just to get here. You keep that kind of stuff under wraps," the general explained.

The professor said, "Over the years, I've heard stories about people that had knowledge about Roswell or had worked on the crashed ship. Some had died in violent accidents under suspicious circumstances, but no one could prove it. Rumors were that they had been eliminated because they knew too much. I was a young graduate student at the time and joined with the entire scientific community in demanding answers from the government regarding the circumstances surrounding the frequency of death by accident involving the scientists. Our demands fell on empty ears, and an investigation of the deaths were never disclosed by the government."

"I was telling you the truth that I didn't know anything about any of that, Professor," insisted the general. "I just took the tour, more by mistake than on purpose. I was at Area 51 to see a demonstration of a jet fighter built with what they claimed was newly discovered technology. It used some kind of anti- gravity device that could lift the plane off the ground without any engine power. When I questioned how they developed the technology, they showed me the spacecraft because I was on a panel that advised the senate funding committee. I guess they thought that showing the spaceship would get them the money they were asking for, and they were right! They had me sign a secrecy agreement putting my career on the block along with prison time if I ever talked about it."

"Why are you telling us now?" Carly asked.

"Just seems like the right time. It won't be long before it's not much of a secret when these videos get out and they always do," the general said with a smile. "What the hell can they do to a retired old man?" He said half-jokingly, knowing that they could still do plenty.

General Kaiser was cool and calm on the outside, but the truth was that he was very excited about being in action again and getting a chance to see a real spaceship and alien. The crashed Roswell ship had ignited his imagination when he saw it and changed his outlook about many things in his life. That single event made him think about things a lot more philosophically and that was not an easy feat for a hard-liner military mind. When he told Evelyn about the Roswell ship, her response to the story had given him great comfort. She thought for a moment and said to him with that loving smile, "God has created so many miracles." They never spoke of it again.

"You said that the ship was small?" Mick asked as he recalled the general's description of the Roswell ship. "There is no way a creature like the one I saw could fit in such a small ship. She was at least seven feet tall."

Professor Taylor suggested. "That drastic physical difference between the two creatures leads me to believe that the two aliens are not related in any way."

"Are you sure about the size of the Roswell aliens?" Mick asked the general.

"Like I said, I never saw the bodies, just the wreckage, but you can bet that they had to be between two and three feet tall if four of them fit inside the wrecked craft I saw," the general replied.

Mick's brain was going a mile a minute trying to digest the general's new revelation. ALUME, at seven- foot-tall, and the three-foot-tall aliens found at the Roswell crash site meant there are two different alien life forms from two different worlds. That brought up the question of how many different life forms were out there that had evolved to the point of building ships that could travel vast distances through space. Mick thought about how far mankind had advanced technologically in just the last hundred years and where they might be in another hundred years. There could be beings in the universe that were thousands, maybe hundreds of thousands, of years evolved.

What would they be technologically capable of? They would be like gods to more primitive civilizations. He remembered when he was a kid, looking up at the billions of stars, trying to guess how many different worlds might be hiding amongst them and what kinds of life forms lived in those worlds. Would they be like us, or would they be something incomprehensible to humans? Even as a kid, he thought that the assumption that there were no other forms of intelligent life in the universe besides us was shamefully arrogant and ignorant.

The general's voice brought Mick back to the real world. "Tell me again what this alien said about why they are landing here."

"Their ship was attacked. They need to land and make repairs," Mick added. "They detected a power source coming from close to here that they could use to make repairs."

"What power source?" the general asked. "What attacked them? Maybe that's something we should be concerned about."

Mick said. "They don't know what the power source is. That's why they sent the scout ship. She did tell me that this power source cannot be from earth. She didn't say what attacked them."

General Kaiser asked, "Did you get any feeling of an aggressive intent?"

Mick answered, "She did not give me the feeling of any hostility or fear toward us. I strongly felt that she was afraid for us, but I don't know why."

"So, has their big ship already landed here?" the general asked.

"She said the larger ship is coming," Mick explained.

The general asked, "What will happen after they make their repairs?"

"I don't know," Mick answered.

"Did this creature actually speak to you?" the general asked.

Mick answered, "It wasn't like that. Whatever it did to my mind made me able to communicate telepathically with it like I just did with you."

Professor Taylor volunteered, "We've been studying telepathy for years. Think of it. All you have to do is think of something to communicate it to another.

"Wouldn't that be a little awkward?" asked Carly.

"Privacy would be out the window," she added.

"I've seen government studies that suggest the human brain may be capable of identifying different thought patterns. It's possible that any species advanced enough to travel through the galaxy could certainly have evolved in their mental ability to communicate telepathically, perhaps over long distances. This creature could have powers that we can't even begin to understand," the professor told them.

General Taylor jumped right in. "I agree, and that makes them a serious threat. Protocol here is to inform the authorities so that they can initiate precautionary procedures for defense, if they are hostile."

"Why would they go to trouble of giving us an advance notice? That just does not make any sense," the professor reasoned.

General Kaiser interrupted, "It could be a diversion from their real intent, to get us to drop our guard."

Everyone stared at him.

"Someone needs to be the devil's advocate," the general said to answer their stares. "Expect the unexpected."

Mick argued, standing up. He spoke to everyone in the room but was directing his conclusion at the general. "Involving the military is what we are trying to avoid. With your revelation about Roswell, I believe we are right. If we involve the government, I believe it should only be the top guy."

General Kaiser questioned him, "You want to tell the president of the United States that the aliens are here?"

Mick said, "The president is the only one that should deal with this."

"You can't just call the president and tell him aliens are coming. It just doesn't work like that," the general told him in a frustrated voice.

Professor Taylor interjected, "You know the people that can get to him! Look Albert, let us assume just for a minute that the military takes this thing over. What do you think will happen?"

The general did not even have to think about it. "The first and only priority would be to capture the technology at any cost!" he said without hesitation.

"Exactly what we thought! That's why we need a plan that gets right to the top without alerting the military. Who would know how to avoid the military better than you?" the professor offered. "It cannot hurt to be cautious until we have a better idea of what we are dealing with. I don't think having the military charge in with guns blazing is the right thing to do. So, what do you say? Let's try and work out a plan together before we just bow out and leave it to the government because I believe that this is the most important event in the history of mankind! Let's not throw it away!"

The general warned, "You all need to understand what you are going to face when the government closes in on this, which you can bet they will. NORAD probably tracked the UFO. That's why they sent the jets."

"But they don't know about the bigger ship landing here for repair," Mick said. "If we can get that information to the president before they lock everything up, maybe there is a chance that, instead of a battle, he would do the right thing and help them fix their ship. We could learn things from them that could change our world for the better, as well as change us for the better. We will never know if it gets into the wrong people's hands because we just threw it away."

The professor insisted, "Albert, you know Mick is right. We must do everything we can to help make sure the government gets it right or they may do the wrong thing and cover everything up just like Roswell, or worse, get the planet destroyed. We have no idea what kind of power these visitors have."

General Kaiser considered their plea and knew that taking on the military was a bad idea that could get them all killed. He also believed that they were right. All his life he had been loyal to his country and followed orders. He could not count the times that the orders were wrong, but right or wrong, he had done his duty. He knew the military would screw this up.

Then nobody would be held accountable because they would have the excuse that they were following orders or hide themselves behind the anonymity of national security. The professor was right, it was time he followed his own mind and did the right thing.

"Okay," the general agreed. "We'll keep the spooks out of it for now and try to reach someone high enough up in the government that can get to the president, but if these aliens turn out to be hostile, I call in the military! Now what is the plan?"

Professor Taylor asked the general, "Is there a government agency, independent of the military, that would deal with an extraterrestrial event and report directly to the president?"

General Kaiser replied, "I'm not sure it's that simple. The government works in layers. The president receives information from the FBI, CIA, Military and any one of a score of other agencies for information as well as carrying out the orders of the administration. It is complicated."

"Can you use your contacts to find out?" the professor asked.

The general agreed, "I can try."

"Good. Thanks, Albert," the professor was glad the general was on board. "I will connect with my colleagues in the scientific community to find out about any groups that may be involved in monitoring extraterrestrials."

"I will be at my place," the general said, getting up from the small writing table. "You can reach me on my cell. When I find out anything, I'll call," he told them as he headed for the door.

"Wouldn't it be better if we all stayed together, Albert?" the professor suggested.

"Believe me when I tell you, you don't want to be at my location when I connect with any of the people I call," the general warned. He knew the danger they would be in when the military zeroed in on this. He was pretty sure they were already on the move. These civilians had no idea what they were up against. None of their lives would ever be the same if the military identified them as being part of this UFO ordeal. He knew what the military was capable of and anticipated an extremely dangerous road ahead. He walked to where the professor was standing, giving him a bear hug while whispering in his ear.

"This is very dangerous!" he warned.

"We need to try, Albert! Helping them is the right thing to do," the professor replied. "People have the right to know!"

"Well, sometimes it's better not to know!" the general said. "I will be in touch as soon as I have something. Good luck to us all!" he said, going out the door.

After General Kaiser left, Mick, Carly, and the professor talked about what to do next.

"I think you should try to meet with the visitor!" the professor suggested to Mick. "The government may know about the UFO, but they will not know anything about your contact with the visitor. If you can communicate with the alien, you might be able to find out when and where the mother ship is arriving and what we can do to help them."

Carly suggested, "I think it would be best for now if I just did my job and helped with local developments. Any information the military shares with me could help us stay one step ahead of them. But we must agree to bring in the government if we sense any hostile action by the visitors or get to a point where we feel we can no longer be effective by ourselves!"

Mick and Professor Taylor chimed in unison, "Agreed!"

"Well, I'm going to need to make some calls, so I need to get a cell phone!" Professor Taylor said.

Carly offered heading toward the door, "I will take you to the drugstore, Professor, where we can get a burner phone. They are untraceable."

"Well, thank you, Carly. I'm new to this kind of thing," he confessed.

Carly just smiled, taking the professor's arm as they left.

Chapter Five
Night Lights

Mick was glad to be alone for a few minutes. He was getting a strange feeling, like something was calling out to him. At first, he thought it was the alien trying to contact him, but it was a different feeling than with the alien. This was something else. It was getting stronger. He laid down to rest, drifted off to sleep and soon began dreaming.

He was deep underwater looking at a distorted sun shining down on him. He tried to swim toward it but could not move his arms. Unable to breathe and helpless, he felt death looming. He heard a voice in the darkness and was jolted out of his sleep.

"I think you were having a nightmare." Professor Taylor asked, "Are you okay?"

"Yeah, I am fine, just a little tired," Mick replied.

The professor sympathized, "Well, who wouldn't be after all you've been through. I am going to make some calls."

The professor sat at a small writing table and began calling some of his colleagues at NASA. He had hoped to get the name of a department head that would know something about UFO investigations. After the first few calls, he was hitting a dead end. No one admitted knowing anything about a department for UFOs. None of them even asked why he wanted to know about a UFO agency. It was not normal for NASA scientists not to ask questions. Science people were curious by nature. They were afraid to speak out. He considered making inquiries to contacts at the Air Force and Homeland Security but decided to leave those calls for General Kaiser. Professor Taylor needed to contact someone higher up. Then he remembered Jennifer, the petite little grad student, who took his advanced astronomy class last year at the university. Her mother was in the secretarial pool of the CIA at Langley. That was probably more in General Kaiser's area of expertise, but it was a good contact that might give them some answers.

He called Julie on his new spy phone and got Jennifer's number. After two rings a woman answered.

"Hello."

"Jennifer?" Professor Taylor asked. "Yes, this is Jennifer. Who is this?"

"Jennifer, I'm so glad to reach you. This is Professor Taylor."

"Professor Taylor? Oh, my God! It's the legendary Professor Taylor," the voice replied, at a loss for words to get a call from her famous former professor.

"I never thought about being legendary, but I guess that comes from hanging around long enough," he answered. "Jennifer, is your mother still in the secretarial pool at the CIA?"

"Yes, Professor." she replied.

"Well, I want you to see if she can find out something for me. I need some information for an article I'm writing," the professor lied.

"She's sitting right here, I'll put her on." she said.

"Hello." Her voice had a very southern accent.

"Hello, Jennifer's mother!" he said in his best professor's voice.

"Charlene, please call me Charlene," she replied.

"Well thank you, Charlene. I am writing an article about the mysteries of the universe and visitors from outer space. I would like to include what our government's response might be to an actual alien landing," he explained.

"Okay, so how can I help?" she asked.

"Do we, I mean the government, have an agency that deals with possible visitors from outer space?" he asked.

217

"That would probably be *Night Lights,*" she told him.

"*Night Lights*?" he was getting somewhere now.

"'*Night Lights*' refers to UFOs," she told him. "There is a small group that investigates and reports directly to the director himself. I have never done any work for that division myself, but I have friends that have. I was told they are under contract not to speak about it."

"Sounds top secret," he said, trying to sound casual about it.

"Everything the agency does is top secret, if you know what I mean."

"That helps me immensely. How can I repay your kindness?" he asked.

"My daughter thinks the sun revolves around you. Let's just call it even. Nice talking with you, Professor. I hope I was of some help." She hung up.

So, the professor thought, *the CIA has a division that does nothing but investigate UFOs.*

He saw that Mick had fallen back asleep, so he decided not to wake him. He called General Kaiser. The professor told him about the conversation with Jennifer's mother.

"I thought we weren't going to tip off government people!" General Kaiser said in a somewhat angry tone.

"She is a pool secretary. I just told her I wanted the information for an article I was writing. I really don't think she thought it was that important," Professor Taylor explained.

"Well, I hope you're right," the general said, softening his tone. "Those spooks have a habit of tapping everyone's phones. I will keep trying on my end. I'll get back to you."

The phone in the ranger station had been ringing off the hook since the UFO sighting. One of the eyewitnesses at The Inn parking lot had recorded a video of the UFO on their smartphone and posted it on YouTube. Within an hour, it went viral. Crazy calls were coming out of the woodwork, as Molly loved to say about busy tourist weekends. Everyone wanted to know if the video was real. Molly remembered her grandfather's stories about the Martian invasion hoax of 1938. Concrete was not a stranger to invading aliens.

After the 1938 Orson Welles national radio broadcast, "The War of the Worlds", half the country believed that the invasion was real, including the townspeople of Concrete. To incite their belief that the broadcast was real, a rainstorm, coincidently, downed a powerline in Concrete, cutting all power to the town. The already terrified townspeople believed the outage had been caused by invading Martians.

Many of the citizens gathered up what they could carry and fled into the rugged cover of the forest to protect their families from the invading aliens. Some families were not found for days after the hoax was revealed. Radio, telephone, and personal contact were the only ways to reach people in those days and there were no radios or telephones in the forest, so it was many days before a lot of the hiding residents were found and told the truth about the broadcast.

The town was further subjected to a humiliating story in the associated press that was also aired coast to coast on national radio making fun of the culpability of the townspeople for believing that Martians were really invading even though half the country was just as fooled as the people in Concrete. The media attack on the people of Concrete backfired when, in a response article, the editor of the local Sedro Woolley paper wrote an article that was picked up and run in the syndicated Seattle newspaper. The story told about how a small American town, alone and believing that they were facing an unprecedented enemy with overwhelming forces, as reported in the Welles broadcast, demonstrated great courage in the face of possible annihilation. The article accused the Welles broadcast of using the national airwaves to betray the trust of the American people for the purpose of increasing its listener base. The Associated Press story, degrading the citizens of Concrete, was labeled a cowardly attempt by the media to turn attention away from the harm caused by the hoax.

The attention from the article earned the town of Concrete the admiration of the American public, and a goodwill visit by Vice-President John Nance Garner. Aliens had, in a strange way, brought Concrete closer as a community. A story many years later circulated that the Orson Welles broadcast was really a part of a government conspiracy to hide the real story reported by a New Jersey radio station. In that report, eyewitnesses reported a real UFO landing in upstate New York just before the Welles broadcast. The government had been too late to stop the New Jersey news story. So, the government sabotaged that news report's credibility by confiscating photographs taken at the site of the real alien landing. They then arranged the famous Welles broadcast. It was one of the greatest hoaxes ever perpetrated on the American public. Their concocted spin story was successful by portraying anyone that believed in UFOs as a gullible fool.

That was the thing about small towns, people stood together, especially when their families were in danger. They stood together in Concrete and overcame the media slander. The Welles broadcast also demonstrated the dangerous power of the media to mislead. Molly's grandfather experienced the broadcast as a teenager and told the story with small town pride, to all his children, grandchildren, and great grandchildren. The irony is that the people of Concrete didn't know that a real alien spaceship was buried close to their town at the bottom of Baker Lake and had been there for thousands of years.

Seattle news journalist, Jason Jansrud, a great grandson of the journalist that wrote the article in 1938 in the Sedro Woolley Gazette, watched the new video repeatedly. He believed the video was authentic. He sent it to the photo division of his newspaper to authenticate. They reported back to him that after close examination that it was their opinion that the video was authentic. The journalist e-mailed the video to the military base with a request for comment. They quickly stated they had no comment. Jansrud, convinced that this was the real thing, barged into his editor's office with the story of a lifetime. It was aired on a televised news release. It also made the front page of the morning paper.

Carly called Molly and told her she was heading back to the station.

"There were a couple of federal fellows looking for you, Chief," Molly reported.

"What did they want?" Carly asked.

"They wouldn't say! They were real creepy looking. They wanted me to get you on the phone, but I just told them you were out of cell range. They gave me a card with their number. Do you want it?"

"No, I'll pick it up," Carly told her.

"The lot and the station are full of people asking about the UFO," Molly told her.

When Carly pulled into the parking lot, media trucks were everywhere. A large crowd was gathered in front of the ranger station door. When the media people saw the ranger getting out of the jeep, they began shouting questions at her as she pushed her way past them into the building. It was chaos.

"I want everyone out of the station right now!" she ordered as she walked into the office.

After deputies cleared the room, Carly locked the front door.

"Molly, you are to refer all phone inquiries about the UFO to the Sedro Woolley Police

Department. None of you are to talk to the media. We are closing this station to the public. We are still on duty but only for local jurisdiction issues! Is that clear to everyone?" she asked.

The deputies replied in unison, "Got you, Chief!" Molly just nodded.

"George, did you and Ripley talk to those federal boys?" Carly asked.

"No, Chief. They asked for us, but we were out on patrol," George told her.

"Good! Tell them you just saw a light. That's all! Are we clear?" she asked.

"Clear as a bell, Chief!" he replied.

"You can reach me on the two-way backup frequency. I'm heading back to The Inn."

Carly went back out the door pushing her way through the crowd. She pulled out of the lot slowly to avoid hitting any of the news people crowded around her jeep. It had only been three hours since the sighting and the circus had already begun. When she got back to The Inn, media trucks were setting up remote feeds. With the news people talking to the locals, Carly knew it was only a matter of time before Mick would be identified as one of the men in the video. Mick was a town celebrity. Most of the townspeople knew him from his photo trips to Concrete. He had not lived in town since high school but still judged the Science Fair at his alma mater every year and was always a guest speaker at the high school graduation ceremony. A quick check with Google would identify his scientific status. God knows how the media would spin that.

Carly pulled right up in front of The Inn. She saw another crowd in the office and moved inside to disperse them.

She could hear Natalya yelling at the crowd. "All you folks that don't need a room need to leave the office! I did not see any UFO! I can't tell you any more than that. So, please leave!" she pleaded loudly.

Carly ordered in her most authoritative voice, "You heard the lady! Everyone, leave the office area!"

As she herded the crowd out, they continued to ask her questions, but she just smiled and told them that she had no information for them at this time.

"Thanks, Ranger Carly!" Natalya said after the crowd left. "I think now I know why celebrities punch out the paparazzi."

"They won't stay away for long, Natalya. This story is too big!" Carly warned her. "Keep your cool, Girl!" Carly headed to the door.

Natalya yelled, "Hey, Ranger! Just so you know, a couple of weird guys came in a little while ago asking me all kinds of questions about the UFO. Did I see it? Did I get pictures? That kind of stuff, but I told them I didn't see anything. I asked who they were, and they said, newspaper men, but I knew that was a lie."

"You did the right thing, Natalya." Carly thanked her.

"Is this UFO thing real?" Natalya asked.

"As real as it gets," Carly walked toward the door but turned around.

"Do me a favor, Natalya. Mick was never here, right?"

"Mick who?" she answered.

Carly pulled the jeep around back, parked down from Mick's room and called him from the car. "Mick, I'm right outside. We need to get out of town. The feds are looking for you."

He agreed, "I think that is a very good idea. You and Professor Taylor move your cars to the Red Apple Market parking lot. I will pick you up there."

She watched as Mick and the professor walked slowly through the parking lot pretending to take pictures so they would not attract any attention. They got in their cars and Carly followed them to the market. They parked away from each other and walked to Carly's jeep and casually climbed in.

"We need to go to Horseshoe Cove." Mick told Carly.

"What's at Horseshoe Cove?" she asked.

He told her, "She will be at Baker Lake."

Carly noticed that Mick's face looked different.

"The lake it is!" Carly said as she pulled a wide U-turn and headed for Horseshoe Cove.

Mick knew the alien would be at the lake. She was looking for a power source. Mick was anxious to get there. He needed to be there.

They did not talk as the jeep sped toward Baker Lake. Carly was afraid that Mick was reading her private thoughts about what she had wanted to say to him a thousand times but could never drum up the courage. She always held out hope that the two of them would give it another go, but with the passing of time and their now close friendship, she realized that the chance of a reunion between them was unlikely. She would keep him in her heart where he would always be her true love. She watched the road, waiting for the right time to tell him how much she still loved him knowing that she would never say the words.

General Kaiser checked his watch as he pulled the Hummer onto the ferry. He had made the dock in less than eighteen minutes since leaving Concrete. The thud of the deck hand sliding a block behind his tire was when he would normally go upstairs to the lounge to have a coffee for the fifteen-minute ride.

Today, he stayed in the Hummer to think. He did not want any distractions. He knew all too well what they were up against.

The military would want alien technology. The minute NORAD picked up the UFO on radar, the military response would be swift. Jets would immediately be dispatched. They tracked anything that entered the planet's atmosphere and would dispatch jets to intercept. If necessary, they would shoot down any un-identified aircraft flying in U.S. airspace that did not comply with orders to land. Command would have already started the process of alerting priority agencies. It was not likely that the president would get all the details at this early stage. He would probably be spoon-fed bits and pieces in the interest of plausible deniability. The president was insulated by so many buffers that a one-on-one could only happen by jumping through the bureaucratic hoops. Aides were trained to keep him isolated from the hundreds of agencies or people wanting to talk about one thing or another. Even if the president became involved, odds were that he would concur with his military advisors after they gave him their spin on the need for secrecy to protect the public and avoid panic. He had promised the professor he would try, so he would make an honest effort, but he wasn't confident that his efforts would be successful. Assuming there was an alert, any government people he called would be on guard while listening for keywords. He would have to be careful with his questions.

After the ferry docked, the general sped all the way home, arriving in less than ten minutes. He had a mental list of people that may have the information he was looking for. He would hold off calling his big gun until he had gathered intel from lower sources.

The list was almost exclusively intelligence people so there would be no way to rely on them keeping their mouths shut about his inquiry. In the intelligence business, you can't trust anyone. Being a snitch paved the road to promotion. Discussing anything about UFOs or aliens would be a real red flag so he would have to try and get information through the back door. He was going to use Professor Taylor's story as a cover.

The government agency assigned to investigate an extraterrestrial event would probably be Homeland Security or one of their sub-agencies. He knew some agents at Homeland and would have to be double careful how he approached them as they were all high-level agents, suspicious of anything and everything. If he was not careful, General Kaiser, or not, they would come after him. He could guess the military protocol with a UFO landing. The first thing they would do is contain the area and round up everyone that had witnessed anything related to the event, interrogate them at some secret military location to keep them under wraps. Homeland Security had powers that would have been unthinkable before the 9/11 attacks.

Terrorists showed America just how dangerous and vulnerable the world is. Fear cost the American people personal liberties taken from them for the promise of protection by their government. The American people should have been questioning why the United States intelligent community didn't see it coming and stop it before it happened. Conspiracies abound. Orwell may have been right; his timeline was just off.

One thing that kept bothering him was the video of the UFO. He had not been to a movie for years when Evelyn talked him into taking her to see Jurassic Park. How real the dinosaurs looked blew him away so he learned that you could fake anything if you had the technology. The general had seen countless events in his long career that had turned out to be not what they seemed. The mind reading and telepathy thing was something that he simply could not put together, so he put that off to the side for now. The truth was, he did not believe the UFO video was faked at all.

Thinking of all the angles was just how his military mind worked. He dialed the intelligence officer that had taken him to see the Roswell ship at Area 51.

"Homeland Security, how may I direct your call?"

"This is General Albert Kaiser. Please connect me with Major Ryan Jacobs."

The Major came on the line in less than ten seconds. "Bulldog, you old war horse, how is retirement treating you? Are you calling to invite me up to go fishing?"

Typical intelligence jockey, General Kaiser thought, two questions at once.

"No complaints, Major" the General replied, answering the major's questions in the order they were asked. "You know, doing some consulting for a science fiction movie. Keeps me too busy to be fishing right now."

Major Jacobs asked, "To what do I owe this call from out of the blue?"

"I called to see what you might know about the lights in the sky protocol?" He deliberately did not say, "*Night Lights*". There was a hesitation at the other end of the line.

Finally, the major asked in a more serious tone, "Have you been seeing lights in the sky?"

"Always the joker!" General Kaiser replied. "Hardly. My Hollywood guy wants to know how the military would respond to the landing of an alien spaceship. I thought you might be able to help me out or steer me to someone that might know," he lied.

"You old dog, you jumped on the Hollywood gravy train!" The Major exclaimed with a hint of jealousy in his voice as he turned on his phone recorder and signaled his partner for a phone trace.

"Hey, it's not all gravy," the general said. "I put up with a lot of artsy types that don't exactly fit in with my training, but the extra cash comes in handy for my football bets. So, can you help me out? I mean, do we have a protocol for UFOs?"

There it was. General Kaiser was completely exposed! The Major pretended to ignore the question and began to pump him about his football bets. It never ceased to amaze the general that so many people were under the false impression that generals had an inside line on everything.

After a couple more minutes of polite small talk, the general finally said, "Nice talking with you again, Major, but I've got to get ready for a lunch date." The General thought this conversation had gone on long enough.

"Is it one of those Hollywood starlets?" the Major asked.

"Just a neighbor," he lied, impressing himself with his ability to make shit up as he went along.

"Well, have a great date you old dog. Don't do anything I wouldn't do! About those lights in the sky thing, nothing like this has come across my desk before, so I'll have to get back to you on that one. You still living on the island?" the major asked.

"They'll have to bury me here," the general answered.

"I could make it out to the island in a couple weeks. Maybe we could do a little fishing. Then I could give you whatever information I find." the major told him, trying to find out how urgent the information was.

The general thought, *He is stalling! He must be tracing this call.*

"The fishing sounds great! I will hold you to that visit, but I really need the info pronto. This Hollywood guy is on a real tight schedule. Also, there is a bonus in it for me if he finishes on time. Is there any way you might be able to get back to me sooner?"

Major Jacobs joked, "I'll try, but only on the condition you introduce me to some of those Hollywood babes." After the general hung up, Major Jacobs picked up the security memo he had received only one hour earlier and dialed the department directed in the memo.

General Kaiser was sure that Major Jacobs was suspicious. All he could do was hope that he was being paranoid. The military had a protocol for everything. The fact that he had seen the crashed Roswell ship with his own eyes convinced him that this protocol would be in writing and there was no doubt in his mind that Jacobs did not have to call anyone to find out what it was. He was enjoying this. Retirement had not been what the general had bargained for. When age forced him to retire from a 45-year career, it left a deep emptiness in his life, leaving him drowning in a deep emotional hole from which he had a difficult time climbing out. This alien event was rejuvenating and gave him purpose. He was part of something. Even though spaceships and aliens were not exactly his area of expertise; it was great to be in action again.

His next call was to an old battle buddy, the best jet pilot in Viet Nam. After the war he went to work for NASA. Time to find out if the rocket scientists knew anything about UFO protocol. Getting through to NASA was not as easy as Homeland.

NASA was not geared for receiving calls like spy agencies. He cleared four different operators before reaching the right department. After holding for another ten minutes, a familiar voice came on the line.

"Wainwright," answered the obviously annoyed voice.

"Carson, it's Kaiser," the general announced.

"General," the voice replied more cheerfully.

"How are you holding up?"

"I'm good, Carson, doing good as I can; day by day, you know."

"Good! Good! We haven't talked in a while! What have you been doing with yourself?" he asked.

General Kaiser gave his old Army buddy the same Hollywood story he gave to Homeland, but this time he was sure that his friend not only believed him but was genuinely glad to hear from him.

"That's great! You've tapped into something that keeps you busy and makes you a few bucks," Carson told him.

"Property taxes are always on the rise, it gets tougher to make ends meet in retirement," he confided to Wainwright.

"It's funny you should call. I don't know anything about UFO protocol, but I just received an e-mail from *Upper Division* that says to be on alert for UFO activity in Washington state."

"What's *Upper Division*?" the general asked.

"That's the code name the CIA gave itself," came the unexpected answer.

The General knew that was trouble. If NASA got an e-mail, so did Homeland. With the CIA in on this, it was time to call the senator.

The general knew the CIA director would sure as hell know about Roswell. The director was tight with his senator. What the director knew you could bet the senator would know as well. That was either real good news or real bad news. He should not have to convince the senator that aliens were real and that would make it easier to get to the president, but it did raise a new concern. If the senator knew about Roswell, why had he never confided in him about something so important? When he talked to the senator, he would wait to see if the senator brought Roswell up. If he did not, then he would know there was a problem.

A return call from Major Jacobs was taking too long and he was losing patience. He hoped the Hollywood story had been believable enough not to cause suspicion, but knowing there was an alert, he was afraid Jacobs might blow the whistle. He decided to make a few more calls and make something to eat while he had the time. Just then, the phone rang.

The general answered, "This is Kaiser." "Hey, Albert, its Ryan."

That can't be good, the general thought, using first names. Spooks never used first names unless they had something up their sleeve.

"Major, are you going to be able to bail me out?" the general asked in a calm voice.

"Well, I've got some very interesting information," the major replied. "Say, why don't we get together and sort through what I've found out? I'll send a car for you."

"You think I'm too old to drive?" General Kaiser joked, trying to sound humorously indignant to hide his anxiety. Something was wrong. Jacobs would never offer to send a car unless they had plans to contain him, but two could play that game. "I can be there in a couple of hours if I make the next ferry," he continued.

"I know better than to argue with a general," the major relented, "I'll have the gate guard bring you straight to my office," Jacobs offered, tightening the trap.

"Don't worry, I'll find you," the general told him, going along with the game. The general knew that once he went through the base gate, if he even made it that far, he would not be leaving until they were ready to let him leave. There was no way the general was going to let that happen!

"Who in hell did they think they were dealing with?" he said out loud to himself after hanging up.

The general grabbed his action bag just in case things got out of control. A good soldier was always prepared to move at a moment's notice, even a retired general. He was not sure if Jacobs had believed his story about willingly going to the base. Those guys were trained to be suspicious, and you can bet his conversation was being monitored and recorded.

The general had to assume that they might already be watching the house or were on their way, so he would not take the Hummer. He went to the back of the house and looked out the patio slider. The back yard looked clear. He let himself out and made his way to the side door of the detached garage. He removed the tarp covering his Honda 250 dirt bike. It had not been ridden in a while, but true to the Japanese reputation of dependability, the old bike started on the first kick.

He rode a short distance toward the beach then turned onto the dirt path that he and Evelyn had walked so many times. He took the path until it intersected with the main road, about two blocks from his house, just far enough away that he was sure he would not be seen if the house were being watched. As he pulled onto the highway, he was just in time to see the unmarked car pulling into his driveway. They must be there to take him into custody for questioning. He was right. A smile came to his face. He still had it!

Neither of the two agents had ever taken a general into custody and figured that something big must be up to have received their orders from the director himself. They had heard rumors that it was because of a UFO, but that information was above their pay grade. They heard a motorcycle and turned to see it pulling onto the highway. The agents scrambled to their car and sped after the motorcycle.

"This is Pearlman!" the agent reported. "Suspect leaving area at a high rate of speed on a motorcycle. We are in pursuit."

"Don't lose him! That is probably our man," came the director's scathing reply. "I have a chopper in the area to help in pursuit. If you value your career, you will bring him in."

"Yes, Sir, we will get him, Sir," the agent replied.

The general saw the car pull out after him, reached into his pocket and ditched his cell phone so they could not track him. After driving a mile, he saw the military helicopter overhead. He leaned into a curve and hit the throttle. They were coming for him. He slowed down when he was in sight of the car line preparing to load onto the ferry. He drove past the waiting cars until he was close to the walk-on lane.

He turned off his bike and pushed it off the pedestrian pathway, leaning it up against a white wooden fence, trying not to draw attention. He spotted a deck hand that he knew from his many years of riding the ferry, directing traffic onto the ferry.

"Cosmo," he yelled, getting the deck hand's attention.

"Hey, General!" the deck man yelled back, grinning ear to ear. "Say, where's the Hummer?"

"Damn thing wouldn't start!" the general yelled back. "I should have bought Japanese!"

Both men had a quick laugh.

"Say, Cosmo, I need a favor." the General asked.

"Are you kidding? After what you did for my kid, anything for you," the man answered.

Three years had passed since his son had been wounded in Afghanistan. Field surgeons had wanted to amputate the lower half of the soldier's leg.

General Kaiser promised to keep an eye on the ferry worker's son. If there was a call order on the soldier, the general would be informed of any injuries. When Kaiser heard of the damage to the soldier's leg, he intervened. He had the soldier flown to Walter Reed Hospital, where the best surgeons in the Army performed an operation that saved that soldier's leg. The soldier's father and mother had been in tears that early summer evening on the general's front porch thanking him for what he had done for their boy. The general just gave them a hug and denied that he had done anything that would not have been done for any other soldier, but the grateful parents knew better.

To them, it had been an act of divine intervention they could never repay.

"Cosmo, some people are looking for me and I would rather not be found," General Kaiser confided to him.

Cosmo's face immediately turned serious. This was his chance to do something for the man that had given his son such a great gift. Without asking any questions, he motioned for the general to follow him down the walkway and onto the ferry. They walked past cars that were being loaded onto the deck until they reached a door that was marked, *Crew Only.*

The deckhand motioned for the General to go in. Inside was a small break room with three tables, a small refrigerator, and a coffee machine against its far wall.

"No one will see you in here," Cosmo said. "Help yourself to the coffee. Made it myself. I will be back after we get underway."

General Kaiser poured a cup of the strong-smelling coffee. He sat down at a table and thought about what his next step would be. He thought about the senator. He and the senator went back a long way. They had first met at the academy. He had been sponsored into the academy by his commanding general in Korea.

The senator was sponsored by a senator from the state of Texas, who owed the senator's father a big favor. He might be taking a chance calling the senator but with the response he was getting from the CIA, he knew he needed to go to the top of the heap to have any chance of getting the president's ear.

Cosmo came back in a few minutes to check on the general.

"How are you doing? You need anything?" he asked.

"Do you have a cell phone I can use?" the general asked.

Cosmo reached into the slotted chest pocket of his coveralls and pulled out an old-fashioned flip phone, handing it to the general. "Call China if you want," he said with a wink.

He could tell that General Kaiser had a lot on his mind and needed some privacy, so he left without any more conversation. He took the back stairs up to the view deck where most passengers spent their short travel time drinking coffee, eating overpriced packaged food from the concession counter, and socializing. He took a special interest in the passengers today. He would like to identify the agents that were looking for the general. He surveyed the view deck but did not see anyone that looked suspicious or out of place. Cosmo had worked for the Washington state ferry system for almost thirty years and had been on this route for the last eight years.

When you work a run that long you get to know all the regulars, so tourists were easy to spot. He decided to check the lower deck and headed down the front stairs to the car deck.

When he rounded the corner, he recognized them right away, standing by a pillar at the first flight of stairs on the car deck. They were both in suits and looking around, suspiciously. They had government written all over them. He turned around slowly, pretending to check a thermostat.

Then, without looking back at the two men, he made his way back up the stairs, across the second deck, to the back stairs. He took him back down to the car deck on the opposite end of the ferry from the two government men. He walked into the break room and sat next to the general.

Cosmo said, "I found your boys. They're going to spot you if you leave like the other passengers." He began taking off his coveralls. "Here, put these on," he said, as he pulled the straps of the coveralls off his shoulders. The general slipped them on over his clothes. They were now co-conspirators.

The five-minute approach whistle blew.

Cosmo ordered, "Stay here! I will come back to get you. If anyone comes in, tell them you're my brother from Portland and you're waiting for me." Then he was gone.

General Kaiser was impressed with the old deckhand. Without any hesitation, he put himself on the line without any concern for himself. People were capable of amazing things. He had seen it on the battlefield. Average, everyday men, committing incredible acts of bravery for their brothers-in-arms.

Cosmo went back to spy on the two suspicious men and found them standing in the same place, not talking, just looking around, like sentries. They could see everyone getting in cars or lining up to get off the ferry, so the only way the General could hide was in plain sight. The old deckhand made his way back to the break room.

"Tell them to get to their cars," Cosmo told him as he burst into the break room. "They will believe you're a crew member if you act like a crew member."

Cosmo coached the general about what to say to departing passengers. In less than two minutes, it was showtime. They moved out of the breakroom and headed toward where the two men were still standing.

"My car keys are in the right pocket," Cosmo whispered. "It's the old green Chevy pickup at the far end of the parking lot. You can't miss it. It's the ugliest truck in the lot, but it runs well, and I just filled her up. You can keep the phone." The big smile on Cosmo's face told the general how proud he was to be of some help.

The general grabbed Cosmo's shoulders, "Thanks for this," he said looking him squarely in the eyes.

"No, General Kaiser. Thank you! Thank you!" the old deckhand said gratefully.

The ships whistle blasted right on time, signaling the last call for passengers to get to their cars.

General Kaiser, dressed as a deck hand, walked toward the stairway announcing in his booming voice, "Ladies and gentlemen, please return to your vehicles! We will be unloading in just a few minutes!" He repeated the call as he walked past the two sentries and went to the front of the line, where passengers waited to depart on foot. Cosmo had been right. The two sentries never gave him a second look as they retreated to their vehicle. When the ferry settled onto the massive docking pillars, four deck hands secured it with heavy ropes and dropped the plank for the cars and passengers to disembark.

The general left with the other walking passengers. He made his way to the parking lot where he spotted the old green Chevy pickup. It started right up. He had not driven an old-style column stick shift in a long time. He pulled out into traffic and drove through Mukilteo, toward Everett. After he had driven far enough to be sure he was not being followed, he pulled into a 7-11 and called the senator. The phone only rang once.

"Senator Winstons' office," a young, perky voice answered.

"This is General Kaiser, is the big man in?" He did not wait for her to answer. "Tell him, Bulldog is on the phone," the general ordered, using his general voice. The perky voice was silent, while she checked her computer for the keyword, Bulldog. After a short wait, he heard the senator's voice from the other end.

"Bulldog, you old son of a bitch. To what do I owe a personal call from my favorite general?"

"Retired general," the general corrected him. "Still living on the island up in Washington?" the senator asked, remembering. The last time he had seen the general was at his wife's funeral on Whidbey Island.

"Till the day I die! But it's hard getting used to just sitting around. I wish now I would have followed you into politics so I would have a soft job forever." the general said only half- kidding.

"Ha! Ha!" was the senators fake laugh reply. "Now, what can I do for you, Old Friend?"

General Kaiser asked, "Senator, I need for you to arrange a meeting for me with the president."

"What's this all about?" the senator asked.

"I have first-hand information about the UFO sighting in Washington." He was being careful how much he told the senator. His voice sounded all business, making the senator sit forward in his chair.

"What kind of information, Albert?"

"Have you seen the UFO video from Washington state?" General Kaiser asked.

"Yes, I watched it in a briefing," the senator answered cautiously.

"I was with the two men in the video. One of them has direct contact with the alien. There is another ship coming. It's a mother ship that has been damaged and needs to land here on Earth to be repaired. Can you set up a meet with the president?" General Kaiser asked again.

"I will send someone to pick you up. Where are you right now, Albert?" the Senator asked.

"I'm on the move," the general replied, being careful."

"Are you close to your place? I can send a chopper," Senator Winston sounded eager. Too eager as far as the general was concerned. He suspected that the senator was referring to the chopper that he had already spotted by the ferry dock. That meant that the senator already knew the feds were after him. Something was wrong. He hung up, fearing that his location was being traced. As he considered what to do next, his phone rang. It was a blocked call. He let it go to voicemail.

The message confirmed there was a problem. "I lost you Albert. Look, this whole UFO thing is extremely hard to digest. I swear if was anyone but you..." the senator paused, then continued, "But I will call the Oval Office and request an emergency meeting with the president. I will call you when I get a response. For Christ's sake, answer your phone!"

The senator would never request to see the president. He had been instrumental in getting the president elected. He could have an immediate meeting. He was stalling. The senator did not want the general talking to the president. Well, two could play that game! He was positive the senator had to know all about the UFO at Area 51, but never mentioned it when another sighting was brought up. He was playing dumb. Why?

The Senator obviously had his own priorities, and the general bet that full disclosure was not at the top of that list. He needed to call Mick.

Mick answered the phone right away, but the connection was bad and the general had a hard time hearing.

"I can hardly hear you," the general told Mick. "You need to get somewhere safe! You need to go now!"

The general warned, "The feds are on their way. You were right about their intentions. We are on our own."

"We are heading to Horseshoe Cove right now," Mick told him. "That is where the alien is going to be. Can you find your way up there?"

The general answered, "I'll find you,"

"General, is there any way to reach the president?" Mick asked.

"I have one more person that I could call," the general said.

"See you at the cove," Mick told him.

After he hung up, the general placed a call to Commander William Worsham, the former chairman of the Joint Chiefs: Also, the man responsible for his forced retirement.

The general was surprised that his call went right through. There was no mistaking the voice that came on the line.

"General Kaiser, I must say that I'm surprised to get this call." Worsham answered.

"This is more important than personal feelings," the general told him. "I'll get right to it! Are you aware of the UFO video that was on social media?"

"Yes, we are looking..."

Kaiser cut him off before he could say any more. "I've seen the alien craft myself, Sir" He lied. "The video is genuine, and someone must inform the president. This UFO is a scout ship sent ahead to prepare for its damaged mother ship to land here to make repairs. These creatures are friendly. Someone needs to tell the president before he listens to the wrong people and makes a wrong decision."

"You saw these aliens?" Worsham asked.

"No, but I saw their ship up close," he lied again. One of the men in the video is in direct contact with the alien," the general said.

"Where are you now?" Worsham asked.

Everyone wants to know where I am, he thought. "I'm in Seattle." the general told him. Caution was a smart move until he knew for sure whose side Worsham was on.

"I'll try to get through to the president, I'll call you back at this number!" Worsham told him and hung up.

Commander Worsham called his contact at the White House.

"Winston," the senator answered.

"Senator, this is Commander Worsham. I just received intelligence info relative to the UFO alert and would like a meeting with the president as soon as possible," Worsham requested.

"That won't be necessary, William. If this is about a damaged alien ship landing, we already have that information. I will let the president know you called and were right on the job." the senator told him.

"Very well, thank you," Worsham said.

After the senator brushed him off, Worsham called Kaiser.

"General Kaiser, I just received a confirmation that the president already has the information you gave me."

"May I ask, Sir, who confirmed that?" the general asked.

"It was Senator Winston himself!" Worsham answered.

"Very well!" the General replied, then hung up. *This just keeps getting better and better!* the general thought. He wondered what Senator Winston's next move would be. His cozy relationship with the intelligence community was well known. The senator would have to be getting something in return for anything he was involved in. He guessed it would be alien technology if they could get their hands on it.

The general never imagined he would be on the other side of the government. He had always been a good soldier and followed orders. For the first time, he was not following orders but doing what he knew to be the right thing and it felt good.

The general pitched Cosmo's cell phone in the trash can. He was a hot Homeland target now for sure. They all were. What would be Senator Winston's next move? He was sure it would be a trap for the aliens. Baker Lake is where the real action was going to be. However it ended, he would not miss it for the world.

Senator Winston was concerned. General Kaiser could be a problem. The last thing he needed was a loose cannon. He would have to cover his bases and tell the president what he had learned about the mother ship landing in case this thing went south. He would leave out the repair and friendly part. He would have to move fast to get his people there first. He would make a call to Homeland and the CIA director. The game was on.

Homeland Security initiated a *Code Orange* the moment NORAD reported an unknown aircraft. They ordered a mandatory *"No comment"* response by all agents of the United States government to any outside inquiry regarding information on any UFO sightings, as well as to report any inquiries that mentioned *"Lights in the Sky"*. The memo made no reference to *"Night Lights"*. The existence of that division was for people on a need-to-know only basis and spooks like Major Jacobs. Agents were dispatched to Concrete to locate and secure all parties on the UFO video or any other witnesses. An Army battalion would be dispatched to the area to enforce evacuation if the UFO was spotted again. All efforts were to be made to capture any alien technology by any means necessary. The cover-up had begun.

Mick was quiet on the ride to the lake. Even in the silence, Carly sensed that he was different. She could not put her finger on it. She had felt it first at the hospital but thought at the time that it was because of what he had been through with the bear attack. After all, he had almost been killed and had contact with an alien being. That would shake anyone up. Then there was the mind reading thing too. That was crazy for sure, but who knows what that creature might have done to him. She was worried about him.

Carly pulled into the Horseshoe Cove Campground. The area was closed off to the public while underground work was being done to expand the public facilities. There was no work scheduled today so the area was deserted. The cove always brought back a lot of memories for Mick. He had gone to the cove with his father before the campground had been built. Suddenly he began to feel strange, like electricity was moving through his body. He kept it to himself, but something was happening to him.

"I'm going to have a look around," Mick told them as he jumped out of the jeep and headed straight to the lake's edge.

"Someone is in a hurry," the professor said, trying to keep up.

There was no wind, and the lake was smooth as glass.

"Why are we at the lake?" Carly asked Mick as they all rushed to the lake shore.

"That's where it's buried," Mick answered. Professor Taylor asked, "Where what is buried?"

"The power source," Mick answered, without taking his gaze from the lake.

What power source could be in the lake? Carly asked herself. She suspected that Mick was hiding something.

Mick felt more exhilarated the closer he got to the water's edge. His mind became focused on a long silver shape, completely smooth with a slight bulging in the middle. There were no windows or openings. He saw the ship with water flowing over it. There was life inside, but he could not see what it was.

Everything around him started spinning. He felt dizzy, then everything went dark, and he fell to the ground.

TOR-LOK had detected the Terians' first deep space scan of his ship, but it was too weak for him to analyze the source. There were traces of anti-matter in the scans so whatever sent it was an advanced species and that could be an opportunity to resume the mission. In the many star cycles, he had been trapped on this planet, he had, from time to time, detected small readings from the implant, but had been unable to connect. He had not detected the implant in many star cycles and faced the possibility the implant could be dead, and that made him watchful for any opportunity to continue the mission.

Not long after that first scan of his ship, he detected ALUME's pod, approaching the planet. Right after the small craft arrived, TOR-LOK detected a faint signal from the implant and was able to connect quickly, but there seemed to be a mutation in the implant.

Passing through many births must have caused changes in the implant's construction. He attempted a transfer, but it failed and caused the implant's brain to overload. The implant was already actively fused with its host body.

When the human recovered from the transfer attempt, TOR-LOK began to program the host body's transformation without attempting another transfer.

It began to absorb slowly then stopped. Something was blocking a complete connection. After a few moments absorption began again, only much faster. He scanned the implant and isolated a biological impurity that matched the alien that had entered his ship. The infusion of the alien's tissue had temporarily slowed absorption. Why had the alien added its construction? The effect of the transfusion on the implant was the dangerous unknown.

Everything depended on the transformation progress.

Carly rushed over to Mick when he fell. She yelled, "Mick! Mick!" as she placed her jacket under his head then checked his pulse. His heart was beating out of his chest. His face was white as a sheet. Shaking him she asked, "Mick! Can you hear me?"

Mick heard a voice, far away at first then becoming louder. After a few seconds, his eyes opened. He saw Carly and Professor Taylor staring down at him.

"Mick! Are you alright?" Carly asked, holding back her fear.

The color began flowing back into his face and he tried to push himself up, only to fall back.

"Easy, Baby," slipped out of Carly's mouth.

"What happened?" Mick asked, his voice very shaky.

"You passed out," she told him.

Mick put a hand on the professor's shoulder and one on Carly, pulling himself to his feet.

"I saw the ship in the water!" Mick told them.

Carly was worried that Mick might have a concussion. He was talking crazy. Since last night, everything had been crazy and now he thought he saw a ship in the lake. Whatever was happening was beyond her understanding.

"What do you think is going on here?" the professor asked Mick, just as confused as Carly.

"I don't know! I don't know!" Mick answered, "But trust me, I'm supposed to be here."

"We do trust you!" Carly said, "But the general told us that if the military knew a spaceship was here, they would consider it a threat and use force to capture it. We are right in their line of fire and that scares the hell out of me."

Carly could only imagine how this advanced race might protect themselves if the military were to attack them. "What if they are hostile, Mick?" Carly asked. "I mean, we really don't know," the ranger's voice showed her fear. "We don't know what these beings are capable of."

"The visitors are not what we should be afraid of." Mick told her, "Our own people are who we need be afraid of. The visitors just want to repair their ship and leave." Mick was deliberately holding back telling them about the alien's fear of something that was after them.

A chill run through Carly. Mick was talking like he knew these creatures; like he was on their side, like he was one of them. The professor just listened but felt the same as Carly. He had never seen Mick act this way. Something was off.

ALUME's pod appeared, moving across the lake to where the power signal was the strongest. She detected the humans at the edge of the liquid. ALUME felt the connection her human began having with the power source. She did not know the meaning of that connection, but she suspected her human's ancient cell structure was part of the ancient ship.

"She is here," Mick said quietly, pointing to the pod floating off the shore.

Professor Taylor exclaimed, "My god! I have dreamed of seeing an extraterrestrial event all my life and now I'm seeing two in one day. It is just a miracle! A miracle! What is it doing?"

Mick answered, "She's come for the ship!"

Carly asked, "How did you know the alien would be here?"

"She must have put it in my mind," Mick said. Carly did not understand what was going on, but one thing was for sure, they were in too deep to go back now.

ALUME slowly lowered her pod into the water until it was directly over the hill of sediment that covered the sunken ship. ALUME spun the pod causing the water to swirl and blow away the sediment, grass, and mud, exposing the buried ship. Then, she settled the pod on the lake floor next to the sunken ship. She went liquid and absorbed out of her pod, flowing over to the alien ship. When she touched the hull, she felt a slight vibration and heard a barely audible high-pitched frequency that turned the darkened hull a dim blue color.

The ship is still functioning, she thought. That was a good sign. She could feel a presence inside but could not see it. ALUME attempted twice to absorb through the hull with no success. The ship still had an active security barrier. She scanned the hull, but her scans could not penetrate through. She then felt herself being scanned by the ship. A security reaction from movement, she assumed.

She tried to absorb into it again, but something was blocking her. She had her blaster but without knowing more about the ship, using a heat blast to enter could cause a deadly reaction.

ALUME absorbed back into the pod to breathe.

How would the flyer have entered the ship? she wondered. There would have to be a way of entry just as Terian ships responded to programed thought patterns. This ship must also be programmed for thought or biological recognition. That must be the answer, she concluded. The flyer must be connected mentally and or biologically to enter.

She thought contacted "C". *I am not able to enter alien ship,* ALUME reported. *There is an active security barrier, and hull material is unknown. The ship is too large to raise out of the liquid with one pod.*

Separate and re-enter, "C" ordered. *I will send TWEE to help lift the ship from the liquid.* "C" ordered TWEE to prepare for a jump to the small planet to aid ALUME. It took only moments for TWEE's pod to absorb out of the ship and be blasted toward the small planet.

Separation was a dangerous procedure. ALUME would have to leave her body behind without consciousness. She would only have a short time outside her physical body before it would be damaged. She went to charge. Once her physical body was under charge, she mentally separated from her body and moved to the alien ship. She focused her mind and was able to mentally pass through the hull with no resistance.

Inside the ship was a single open area with undulating protrusions. She entered one, finding a control center with a large, contoured seat. Another protrusion held a healer with a body inside: *The dead flyer,* she thought. The other protrusions contained machines she guessed must be for weapons, guidance, and life support.

She found no power source. She attempted to mentally move deeper into the ship but was stopped by a force field that would not allow even mental energy waves to penetrate. She gave a last look around the ancient craft trying to imagine the dead flyer's last moments, dying alone in this primitive world. She was out of time. Her physical body would die if it stayed in charge suspension much longer. She left the ship, moving quickly back into her pod. She re-entered her body and restarted her two hearts. She welcomed the warm flow of her body fluids.

She would wait for TWEE while submerged in the liquid. There was always the danger that the primitives could attack her pod out of the liquid, forcing her pod to defend, causing terrible devastation. Once the killing began, the primitives' fear would force them to continue to attack. Many humans would die. A feeling of sadness filled her. The humans faced a dark future. If they could survive an attack from the Rogue monsters, they would still not be safe. The intensity of the mother ship's power trails would act like a beacon, exposing this planet to invaders. The humans' only hope for survival would be to construct a planet protection system. Without that technology, only the Supreme taking Earth as a host planet would protect them. The cost for that protection would be their natural evolution. The Supreme would dictate their growth.

ALUME set these thoughts aside, remembering her duty. She sent "C" her thought record from the ancient ship. She considered the human's connection to the ship. Part of this human's structures were ancient, confirming that he had been partially seeded and she believed that what seeded him was still in that ancient ship. She had identified the connection between the human's mental energy with the ancient ship's power when she first heard his plea for help.

The primitive parts of his human brain were now being overtaken by expanding ancient structures. His body was in a state of metamorphosis. She could not tell what he was changing into, but his energy patterns were increasing and still perfectly matched with the energy patterns from the ship. She was convinced the human was the key to entering the ancient ship.

"C" analyzed the ship from ALUME's thought images. The ship appeared to be in good structural condition for a craft buried in liquid for so long. Surface scans showed no damage, which indicated it had not crashed but was deliberately put in the liquid. Was the ship unable to fly to escape the planet or was the flyer unable to fly?

The ship could not be identified in the downloads and ALUME's thought images could not reveal the power source. Scans of the power emitted from the ship detected biological particles. Supreme science had no record of any known biology that could create these kind of power readings. Everything depended on identifying the power source. Forceful entry would be too dangerous without more information. In Terian ships, forced entry would trigger self-destruction. Without physical access there could be no power transfer to the mothership. Using the human's connection to enter the ship may be their only chance.

"C" had hoped the leader would recover enough to take command or at least give counsel, but his injuries were too extensive for the ship healer to repair. She had to face the reality that the leader was not going to survive. His death would make her the new leader. A machine had never replaced a biological leader to take full command of a ship on a galactic mission. Even though she was the most advanced bio-machine ever produced by Supreme science, she was still a machine and a machine had never had complete authority over biological Terians. It was the team's duty to follow the leader's orders to the death and "C" could not help but wonder if being a machine might compromise that trust.

The leader's last directive was to make contact and land for repairs. "C" would follow his order. Landing on an alien planet was always dangerous. The mother ship's size made it impossible to hide and vulnerable to attack. Scans and searchers had not yet detected any trace of the Rogue ship that had escaped the red planet. She was certain it was still out there. They could be dead in space or readying an attack. She was taking no chances and assumed they were coming. "C" was facing her greatest danger and would need the team to be at their very best. She was worried that her being a machine might create doubts in their minds.

Having a machine for a leader had been on the minds of each team member. The idea was the most difficult for ZE-TAN. He was trained in the old ways, before the advanced machines were allowed authority, but as a loyal soldier, he would follow orders. He kept his focus on loading his pod with enough fire power to destroy the Rogue ship and the primitives too. A skilled warrior with his battle experience was always ahead of the enemy. Too many times he had witnessed death as the payment for being unprepared. He would be ready for anything.

CRE-LIN's outward calm hid his fear, not of a machine leader or landing on an alien planet but of the Rogue attacking the mother ship when it was a stationary target. There was also the chance the primitives could attack and attempt to capture or kill them. His thoughts were on all those dangers, not his leader.

The mother ship was approaching the small planet's moon. "C" was growing more concerned that they had not detected any trace of the Rogue ship.

She had to make the decision whether to land before finding the Rogue or wait to fight them in space. She thought carefully, knowing that a wrong decision could mean certain death to them all. Waiting to land until they could flush out the

Rogue ship was dangerous. Every minute they were in space used more precious power. She only had one choice.

"C" sent another scan sweep for the Rogue but detected nothing. She considered that the Rogue might be using a cloaking device that could evade scans, but she reasoned that if they did not use it for the second attack at the red planet, the device either did not work or they did not have enough power to activate it. She did not believe that they were cloaking now to avoid detection. She would still take the precaution of deploying watchers. Their range was limited but they could detect the Rogue close to the landing which may give her time to power up and move, rather than be a stationary ground target. In the middle of her thoughts, the healing chamber stopped the life cycle. **TE-GON, their leader, was dead!**

A great sensation rushed through "C's" consciousness, a reaction of her emotional growth programing. Her sadness felt like she was malfunctioning. Her thought patterns were not focused. Slowly, she began to recover and concentrate on her duties, although the sensation lingered. There could be no further delay. She sent thoughts to all team members that *the leader is dead*. She then ordered CRE-LIN and ZE-TAN to ready their pods for a planet screen with authority to maximum destruction. She would try to draw out the Rogue. Her plan was clear to her now as she set everything into motion. She wanted the kill. From deep inside her consciousness, there was a need to act on her new emotion. She did not relate to it for what she was really feeling, vengeance.

ZE-TAN was surprised at "C's" command to planet screen and maximum destroy. It was as if she had read his thoughts. It was an order worthy of an experienced leader, and it gave him more confidence that this machine was going to be a good battle leader. ZE-TAN re-thought his arsenal and decided to add more fire power. Should everything go badly, he would need it. The problem would be the weapons' extra weight. A planet screen required speed. The extra weight would slow his pod, but he reasoned that the pod's security scans would provide proximity warnings to compensate for his slower speed. ZE-TAN preferred to battle the Rogue in open space that did not require going liquid. The older flyers preferred not being liquid in battle even though element flying gave the pod the maneuvering advantage.

Element turns were impossible in open space with no gravity or planet mass to pull from. If the battle were in atmosphere, the flyer must be in liquid form to survive the physical forces that would tear a flyer's solid body into pieces. There was also the danger that if the pod was hit while the flyer was liquid, there may not be enough time to go solid into the protection of a skin suit. ZE-TAN was not the best element flyer in the team, but he was a skilled space fighter and had experience flying an open space planet screen.

CRE-LIN had expected the leader's death. Any other Terian leader, without the leader's enhancements, would have died instantly from his wounds. One of the leader's hearts had already exploded before they put him in the healing chamber and the extensive damage to the remainder of his organs could not have supported his life for long without complete regeneration.

The smaller mission flight healers did not have the power to regenerate that much material. He marveled at the leader's strength to have lasted this long. He was the super Terian that had cheated death so many times, he was thought to be immortal. CRE-LIN hoped particles from the leader could be renewed by the Supreme if they got back home. That was the great reality of flying. Any given moment in space could be your last. Flyers accepted the risk of the unknown for the thrill, including the status, that came with special privileges. Learning about the wonders of space from downloads was for land people. A real flyer was all CRE-LIN had ever wanted to be. His training had warned him about the great danger of landing a mother ship on an alien atmosphere planet and he knew that the team would need to be at their best. If the landing were successful and they could repair their ship and survive the Rogue, this planet would be a great prize and earn the team great rewards and honors. The volume of liquid and element deposits shown on the scans were some of the largest readings that CRE-LIN had ever seen and would make this planet a valuable addition to the Terian empire.

CRE-LIN trusted the new leader. Many flyers were unsure of a biological enhanced machine as leader, but not CRE-LIN. The combination of machine and biological had been a critical ingredient in Terian technological evolution. He was grateful for his mechanical enhancements. He knew that without them, he would never have physically qualified for galaxy missions. The Supreme looked the other way regarding enhancement restrictions when it came to flyers. They had saved his life more than once.

Both pods had extra fuel packs and melters. The melters required a lot of power to fire but if they got inside an enemy ship, they would inflict great damage. The extra fuel packs, despite their weight, could make the difference between returning or drifting forever in space.

"C" set the pods' power levels, calculating for a maximum planet screen. If the pods were sent too far, they would not have enough power to return.

The pods turned bright blue as the power peaked in their drives. "C" shot them away at jump speed. CRE-LIN and ZE-TAN were flattened against the back of their liquid chambers. They would be unable to move until the end of the jump.

CRE-LIN's lighter pod went farther than ZE-TAN's, traveling deeper into the void, creating a dangerous distance from ZE-TAN. They would have to use more of their limited power to move closer to each other if they found the Rogue, but the extra fire power made it worth the risk.

While CRE-LIN and ZE-TAN began their search, TWEE approached the earth and signaled ALUME. She moved her pod to the surface. He moved his pod into the high atmosphere and engaged element power. He sent out watchers to look for the Rogue, but they detected only unarmed primitive ships in the lower atmosphere. Satisfied that there was no immediate threat, he flew to ALUME's location. His descent was so rapid that to anyone watching from the ground, it looked as though his pod appeared on the lake surface out of thin air, but he did not avoid detection by NORAD.

"Sir," the young corporal yelled to his captain, "I just saw unidentified movement in the alert area!" The captain checked the airman's screen, but it showed nothing. "Looks like whatever was there is gone now," the captain said. "What was the bogey's altitude?"

"One hundred and twelve thousand feet, Sir," the airman answered.

The captain immediately replayed the airman's screen and there it was, moving so fast that it was a blur.

"Keep a keen eye and let me know if it reappears," he ordered.

"Yes, Sir," the airman acknowledged.

The captain hoped it was just altitude ghosting. If it showed again, this was going to be a long day.

TWEE stopped just above the lake then lowered his pod to the opposite side of the ancient ship from where ALUME was positioned. The pods began pulsating between light and dark blue colors, making low humming sounds. The water under the pods started to move in a small circular motion and widened until the ancient ship was completely free from the water. The pods used the magnetic pull of their element power to grip the ship and pull it toward the surface until sunlight reflected from its silver surface after thousands of years of darkness. The pods lifted the ship using magnetic tethers until it was above the water. Slowly, they moved to the open field, lowering it gently to the ground. ALUME signaled TWEE to scan for hostiles. He took his pod into the low atmosphere to distance scan.

The corporal had been at NORAD for only two weeks when he recorded his first UFO earlier that day. His training had never prepared him for something moving that fast on a radar scope. The room had finally returned to normal from the first sighting when he saw the second bogey.

"Sir! I have a bogey. Vertical acceleration at eighteen hundred sixty-six miles per hour to stationary position at thirty-two thousand feet," the airman reported.

The captain verified the bogey and immediately reported it to military command. Upon receiving the NORAD alert, an F-16 jet was scrambled from Whidbey Island Naval Air Station to investigate.

TWEE's pod detected the jet approaching and raised his pod to the approaching craft's elevation to face it.

Captain Ronald Jenner's orders were clear: Locate, identify, and force the unknown aircraft to the ground, using deadly force, if necessary. He had been on alert scramble before. Usually, it turned out to be nothing. This bogey was reported to be stationary at over thirty-two thousand feet after a recorded speed of over eighteen hundred sixty-six miles per hour.

Jenner thought the air speed must be a tracking error. That speed was impossible from the fastest Navy aircraft. Helicopters couldn't hover at that altitude.

Jenner didn't know what he was heading into but whatever it was, if the airspeed was correct, it was not an aircraft from this planet. Encounters with UFOs were immediately classified top secret. The scuttlebutt amongst pilots was that there had been encounters with actual alien ships, but no formal reports were ever documented. Pilots did not want to jeopardize their career by reporting sightings that either nobody would believe or would rather be kept quiet. To report one was considered career death.

Jenner was sure this would just be another false alarm until his radar showed the UFO sitting stationary at 32,000 feet. He saw the target ahead and reduced airspeed. The target craft was just floating in place. The blue-ish silver craft was approximately fifteen feet long, thick in the middle and thinning down to blunt ends. His first reaction was trained, skeptical denial. His mind was searching for a logical explanation for what he was seeing. His next reaction was reality; it sure didn't look like any craft he had ever seen.

"Zero One, this is Lookout. I have unidentified in sight. It doesn't look like anything I've ever seen before," Jenner reported. "Craft is stationary at a fixed altitude with no visible propulsion for stationary flight."

"Roger that, Lookout!" Command responded.

Jenner flew past the UFO, while the strange craft maintained its position. He made a hard turn to position another fly by. Questions flooded his head as he executed his turn. *What the hell is that thing?* He knew what it was, but all his training demanded he find an alternate logical explanation. The only thing he knew for sure was that the strange looking craft was sitting stationary at high altitude with no visible propulsion source holding it up. He hoped that whatever it was would be gone when he turned back. His hopes quickly vanished. The UFO was no longer hovering in the same place but flying beside him, off his port wing, matching his speed like they were connected to each other.

TWEE scanned the jet and detected armed weapons. He moved his pod close to the primitive. The weapons were simple directional explosive devices with heat sensors. By flying close, the primitive could not fire and cause his pod to retaliate.

Jenner tried to communicate with the UFO on the emergency band.

"Unidentified craft, you are in American airspace. Identify yourself!" Jenner requested.

The craft did not respond. Jenner had no doubt that the UFO was extraterrestrial. It sure as hell was not Russian or Chinese. He tried to break away from the alien craft to acquire position to fire by making a hard starboard turn, quickly followed by a steep climb. The jet's afterburners kicked in taking him to maximum climb altitude at Mach 4. He was glued to his seat by the force of the climb. The UFO stayed with him, moving even closer to his port wing.

"The unidentified craft is not responding and flying with me just off my wing. I have never seen a craft that can shadow maneuver like this," he reported.

Captain Jenner leveled his jet at forty thousand feet. The UFO was now ten feet off his wing. He slowed to stall speed to try and break from the craft. Instead, the UFO swung around, flying just a few feet from the nose of his fighter. This maneuver unnerved the American pilot. Jenner realized that the alien ship was just playing with him and staying too close for him to take any kind of offense or defend himself. He attempted to communicate with the UFO again.

"Unidentified aircraft, this is a United States military aircraft! You are in restricted air space. Identify yourself!" Jenner demanded.

There was no response.

"Lookout, this is Zero One, turn hard starboard," Command ordered.

Jenner immediately turned hard starboard, and the alien craft pulled away disappearing from Jenner's view.

"Lost visual contact," Jenner reported. "No! There it is! Now its flying parallel off my starboard wing; matching my speed, flying with me."

"Can you describe the craft?" Command asked.

"The craft is completely smooth," Jenner replied. "There are no surface openings of any kind. I cannot see any evidence of outside propulsion, but it is staying with me like we're Siamese twins. The craft is not threatening. Repeat. The craft is showing no sign of aggression," he reported.

When Jenner accelerated or slowed, the craft stayed right with him. Suddenly, the UFO again moved directly into his flight path, flying less than ten feet from the front window of Jenner's jet.

"Craft is flying right off my nose and stays with me no matter how I turn," Jenner reported in an excited voice.

"Are you able to engage the craft?" Command asked.

"Negative, Zero One. Object is too close to engage." Jenner reported, "Craft is not threatening. Repeat. Craft is not threatening. It's just flying with me. I will attempt another contact."

"Unidentified craft this is a United States military aircraft. You are in restricted airspace! Identify yourself!" Jenner ordered.

There was no response.

Jenner tried bluffing, "You are in restricted airspace. Follow me to the landing area or you will be shot down!"

"Zero One, this is Lookout. Craft is not responding," he reported.

There was a long pause from command headquarters before they finally responded.

"Roger that, Lookout. Maintain your altitude. Backup is two minutes out."

"Roger that, Command. I repeat. Unidentified craft showing no aggression."

"Roger that, Lookout. Maintain altitude!" Command ordered.

Jenner knew engaging this UFO was the wrong response. This craft was beyond human technology. God only knew what it would do, if attacked. He tried communicating once more.

"Unidentified aircraft! This is the United States military. You are in restricted airspace. I order you to follow my aircraft to land," Jenner threatened.

One of the two approaching jet fighter came on the radio.

"Lookout! This is Saber Tooth. We are engaging target."

"Negative to that," Jenner replied. "Unidentified aircraft showing no hostility. Repeat. Unidentified is not threatening."

"Lookout! Turn hard starboard," the pilot's voice was strained and determined.

Jenner turned hard starboard but this time the UFO did not follow. Both pilots locked missiles on the UFO but TWEE shot an energy blast at both jets when pod sensors alerted live weapons preparing to fire.

The energy blasts disrupted both jets, shutting down their engines.

"May Day! May Day!" Saber Tooth reported, "We have both lost engine power. Unable to fire. Repeat. We are dead stick and unable to restart engines. Ditching aircraft to minimum population location."

Both pilots started to glide their powerless planes to a low population location. At the last possible minute, they ejected their seats and were catapulted to safety. Both jets continued their spiraling freefall then exploded in a heavily wooded area. Jenner turned his jet around and was relieved to see two chutes circling to the ground. There was no sign of the UFO.

"Command, this is Lookout. Both backup planes are down. Both pilots ejected. No sign of the UFO."

"Roger that. Return to base, Lookout," Command ordered.

If they had not attacked the UFO, Jenner would bet that both planes would have been spared, but hindsight was always the child of lost battles.

Flying back to base, he thought about what would happen to the report he was going to file. The jet's cameras would have all the contact action, but he suspected neither his report nor the pictures would ever be released to the world. He was just the pilot and would be trapped in a lie.

Mick, Professor Taylor, and Carly saw the two jets fall from the sky. They also watched as three Blackhawk helicopters flew overhead toward the wreckage of the crashed jets.

"What have we done?" Carly yelled, "If we had reported what we know to the military, those jets may not have been shot down."

"Those planes were going to shoot the alien ship no matter what, like we were afraid they would," Mick argued. "The alien did something to the jets to defend itself. It could have incinerated them, but it didn't want to kill the pilots."

"How do you know all this?" Carly asked him.

"She told me," Mick answered, nodding toward ALUME's pod.

"We need to talk to Albert," Professor Taylor interjected. "He will know what to expect from the military. Hopefully, he'll be able to get to the president before the government makes anymore stupid moves.

ALUME was saddened by the conflict with the humans. Now the Terian enemy would have two faces: Human and Rogue. The humans would attack again out of fear. She had witnessed this reaction many times from primitives. They were not to be blamed. This was their planet being invaded. It was unfortunate they were destined to lose control of their planet if the Rogue did not destroy them.

ALUME lowered her pod to the ground a few feet from the ancient ship, went liquid, and flowed outside. The mesmerized trio could not take their eyes off the two pods as they lifted the ship from the water. Watching the alien appear in liquid form then change into solid form was icing on the cake.

Mick thought the ancient ship about fifty feet long and maybe fifteen feet tall. Even with lake debris still sliding off the surface, its mirror-like silver skin glistened in the sunlight. This alien ship, that had come from unimaginable distances to get to earth, was undeniably familiar to Mick. He ran his hand over its surface. The second he touched the ship; it transferred waves of energy into him.

ALUME observed the ship's reaction to the human's touch and was convinced that she was right. The ship recognized the human. ALUME needed to get inside the ship and find the power source and the human was the key to getting inside. She mentally called to Mick to try to enter the ship! He was puzzled by her request but did as she instructed and placed his hand on its silver surface. The ship reacted with a strong vibration.

A portal opening appeared with a flow of silver melting to the ground forming a small solid ramp. Mick walked up the ramp and through the opening with ALUME right behind him. The inside of the ship was dark from the outside, but it illuminated when they stepped inside. The portal

soundlessly closed behind them, leaving no visual sign there had ever been an opening. The interior was all white and bare except for large protrusions in the floor.

Mick moved over to a large oval shaped protrusion against the curved wall. It was long and bulged up from the floor as high as his neck. He instinctively placed his hands on it and the covering disappeared, exposing a bluish colored, emaciated body, wearing some kind of suit, lying at the bottom of a rectangle enclosure. Even in its shriveled condition, Mick could tell it had been very tall, maybe over seven feet. The head was large and oblong. Its face was unrecognizable, but the rest of the body appeared human like with two arms and two legs. Its hands were huge.

Looking down at the alien creature, something stirred in his memory. His mind pictured the dead creature, running with two human women in colorful dress. Mick was shaken by the images but regained his composure and followed ALUME to another, larger protrusion a few feet away. Just like with the first protrusion; when he touched it, the covering melted away, displaying a long sloping chair, at least twice Mick's height.

Following ALUME's mental suggestion, he pulled himself onto the long chair and stretched out, feeling like a child in a grownup seat. A strong energy current immediately passed into him but when he felt no pain from it, he relaxed. A three-dimensional display of symbols and shapes enveloped him. The current surging through him increased. It started to make it hard for him to breathe. He settled back into the chair again. The energy force flowing through him moved his hands over the symbols, like he was a puppet, and the ship began a high-pitched humming.

ALUME also felt the energy surges in Mick. They were too powerful. If he did not disconnect, it would kill him. ALUME grabbed him, pulled him from the chair, throwing him to the floor. Mick was startled and tried to get up, but he could not.

The energy to your brain is too strong, ALUME warned. *Something in the ship is trying to change you.* Those were the last words he heard before passing out again.

ALUME felt TOR-LOK's presence. This was her chance to communicate with TOR-LOK. She had sensed its presence on the ship when she was in separation. What she felt had biological traces, but it was closer to pure energy. She had to take a risk and share her mind with this creature. Revealing herself was dangerous, but there was little time. The mother ship was near and without the power to repair the anti-matter drives, they would never see Paetaan again.

Chapter Six

Calm Before the Storm

TOR-LOK had been impatient and reckless. Long ago, the energy input had killed the two males he had implanted when he was with the pharaoh. This human was still too fragile and almost died when he increased the energy flow. The alien had saved the human by breaking his connection. The alien, ALUME, then thought communicated, completely risking exposure to TOR-LOK. She explained the ambush and the conflict with the Rogue. She told about their need for power from his ship to repair their damaged ship to be able to return home. TOR-LOK believed she was being truthful. These Terians were explorers who needed help and wanted an alliance. TOR-LOK considered that an alliance could be an advantage to his mission but did not know if they could be trusted so he did not answer her. If an alien biological found his ship, it was possible that an alliance could be formed, or he could take the chance of entering the alien's mind without an implant if the alien got close enough. A transfer without an implant could be deadly or uncontrollable but if it were successful he could leave this planet without taking the chance of an alliance.

There were too many unknowns. He would be patient and wait until the human's metamorphosis was complete before making such an important decision. He wanted to escape this planet before the alien mother ship arrived and that did not give him much time to transform the human, but he would have to be careful about the energy flow.

When they lifted the ship from the lake, TOR-LOK's scans revealed that the flyers of the two ships were the same species as the alien. He did not know how many would be on the mother ship, but it would have to be very large to hold two smaller ships so there could be many more biologicals. He increased the downloads to the implant. The mother ship must be getting close.

TOR-LOK had monitored the advance of human technology while he was a prisoner in the liquid. This world was still filled with conflicts and death. The human species was at a critical time in their evolution and now had the power of fusion to destroy themselves with him still trapped. Throughout the universe, TOR-LOK had witnessed many species destroying themselves. Some made it through their conflicts, most did not.

These humans could not survive the technology of a hostile species invading their planet, but TOR-LOK did not believe these visiting aliens were invaders.

When the alien mentally entered his ship, TOR-LOK detected no hostility. The alien was just learning and did not act like an invader. They were here for the power in his ship, so he did not want to take any chances. It was safer to leave this planet before there was a confrontation with the mother ship. He still did not know how advanced this species may be, but they had mastered anti-matter space travel, and they were desperate to survive and that could make even peaceful aliens very dangerous.

Mick slowly opened his eyes. "What happened?" he asked.

Your brain was overloading, ALUME told him, still hoping for a response that never came from the creature in the ship.

Once Mick was back in the control seat, he could feel the energy flow through him again but this time it did not hurt. Mick's thoughts were unsteady. As he sat in the chair, his hands began moving, controlled by an invisible force moving his fingers over the holographic controls surrounding him. He tried to regain control of his arms, but the force had a tight grip on them and would not let go.

A small voice in the back of his mind became louder and louder until he finally realized it was ALUME pulling on his arms, breaking the ship's hold. The ship immediately shut down. Mick was exhausted. The battle to control his own mind was taking everything out of him. ALUME knelt next to him and wrapped her large hands around his head. Mick felt his strength begin to return. ALUME was using her energy again to help him.

"What happened this time?" he asked as his mind came back into focus.

The ship was rearranging your mind patterns, she explained. *But your mind is not strong enough yet,* she added.

"I'll try again!" Mick exclaimed.

You could be damaged if you do not control the power entering your mind, ALUME warned him. *It would be safer if we connect as one.*

It was dangerous for ALUME to join with Mick's thoughts. The ship could react defensively if it identified her biology as an invader but if she merged with his mind, there was less danger of Mick being damaged. She might have a better chance of understanding the ship's power source. She helped Mick back onto the control chair and entered his mind. Her first sensation was the volume of information Mick was receiving. He was on the verge of mental overload again. Terians were genetically programed from birth to manage thought input and that helped her manage the input Mick was receiving. It began to work. His mind was able to slow down and focus.

The ancient ship did not resist her mind patterns mixed with the humans. She was able to help him slow the volume of programming from the ship, but she could not stop it. The energy flowing through the human was unlike any ALUME had experienced. It was beyond her understanding.

The uploads into the human were complete, changing the human's cellular construction. New organs were forming. His skin was growing thicker. His breathing system was growing larger and thicker. His muscular structure was also growing. The outside physical changes were not too noticeable yet, but whatever he was changing into would look less like a human when the process was complete. What the transformation was doing to his mind could mean life or death to her and the Terian team.

General Kaiser pulled into Concrete just minutes before the roadblocks went up and watched military Hummers lining up in front of the

Red Apple Market. The occupation had begun. He turned off the main street and headed toward Horseshoe Cove, hoping he could still get through. After driving a short way out of town, he turned onto the same old logging road his troops used during military drills to avoid the military or the spooks.

Driving down the old logging road, he heard a jet flying overhead. He stopped to get a better look and saw the jet fly back overhead but this time he saw a strange craft flying right off the jet's wing. Moments later, he saw two more jets fly overhead. The next sounds he heard were explosions.

"Jesus," he said out loud, jumping back into the old truck. He drove as fast as he could over the weather- beaten road, passing a small handmade sign that read: Horseshoe Cove--1 mile. He went a few hundred yards more, then pulled off the road into the tall brush until the truck could not be seen from the road. Not knowing what might be waiting up ahead, he would go the rest of the way on foot. He stopped within sight of the campground and hid in the brush to survey the area. He saw Carly and Professor Taylor standing next to a large silver ship that was clearly not from this planet. About fifty feet away was a second ship that the general recognized as the UFO in the parking lot video.

He slowly approached the clearing. The professor saw him and called out.

"Albert, so glad to see you!"

"Where's the young fella?" the general asked, staring at the alien ships.

"In there with the alien," Carly answered, pointing at the ancient ship.

"What in hell is he doing in there?" the general asked.

"We aren't really sure," Professor Taylor answered. "Two alien ships pulled this ship out of the water then one of them landed and went into the ship with Mick."

"Two alien ships?" the general looked confused.

"A second ship just like this one, pointing at ALUME's pod showed up and helped lift the sunken ship out of the water. After they set it down, the other one shot up into the sky," the professor explained.

"Is that what caused the explosions? It shot down the fighter jets?" the general asked.

"The alien did not shoot down the jets, it just stopped its engines," the professor corrected him. "Mick said the alien was only defending itself."

"How would he know that?" the general asked.

"Mick said the alien told him," Carly answered.

"Jesus," the general said in a soft voice.

"Mick has some kind of a direct mental connection with the alien," the professor said.

General Kaiser was unsure what to do. He had made critical decisions in high pressure situations his entire career, but this was different. He was standing next to two alien ships, from God knows where, and there was a third alien ship that had downed two American fighter jets. He felt like he was in a science fiction horror movie. He had no intel to guide him. He was completely on his own instincts and struggling about what to do next.

His military experience was telling him to call in the government, but his common sense was telling him something else. This alien creature had every right to defend itself against hostile attack if the jets fired first, and he had no doubt they did. The only thing that made any sense was to get as far away from here as possible. You could bet the military would not take kindly to their planes being forced down and it would not matter who took the first shot. Even though our weapons are probably like toys against these creatures, that wouldn't stop the government from attacking again with a bigger gun, no matter how futile or just plain stupid that was.

The destruction of the two fighter jets started a chain of events within the government. NORAD had tracked TWEE's pod the moment it entered the upper atmosphere and alerted Air Command of the breach of United States airspace by an unidentified aircraft. Air Command reported the breach to the secretary of defense, who immediately informed the president of the United States. The president then gave authority to the secretary of defense to take all actions necessary to defend American airspace.

A group of elite military and political power players headed by Senator Winston and the director of the CIA began the process of securing all information related to the event. All information sent to the president, like Captain Jenner's flight report, would first be screened by Homeland and altered, where necessary, to blame the UFO for unprovoked hostile action. After seeing Jenner's re-written report, the president put the military on high alert. Senator Winston and his secret partners would do whatever is necessary to get the UFO, preferably in one piece, but they would settle for the pieces if that were all they could get.

The CIA concocted a cover story, released through Homeland Security to the news media. The report was that two fighter jets had tragically crashed during a training accident with nukes aboard. Both pilots had ejected and survived. As a precaution, the Baker Lake area was quarantined. Civilians were evacuated to protect them against any possible radiation danger from leakage of the onboard nukes.

After reviewing the video of the UFO in the parking lot and the video from the downed jet fighters' onboard cameras, the president was not convinced of alien hostility. The craft he watched on the video looked peaceful and the confrontation with the jets was not clear enough to satisfy him that the UFO was not simply defending itself. He had served his time in the military and knew all too well the mentality of Command. So far there have been no deaths. The president suspected that the report he received was doctored. He would cautiously support Homeland and keep them on a short leash with the stand down order. He had learned early in his presidency that military intelligence had a mind and agenda of its own. But so did he.

The stand down order from the president was a nuisance to Senator Winston but the bigger problem was competition. He would have to move fast to stay ahead of any other military special interests that might see an opportunity to position themselves to get the prize. The senator would manipulate the full authority of his influence to capture that ship no matter what it took. He had no idea yet that there were three ships.

The senator had financially benefited over the years from the captured alien technology from the Roswell crash. Now he wanted this UFO to expand his influence and wealth. He would have to share a little with the CIA director but what he would make by selling access to alien technology could put him in the White House. The Roswell technology had not just benefited the U.S. military, but many, well-connected and ambitious politicians. The event had also reaped generous donations from American corporations willing to pay for privileged access.

Unlike the president, the senator was not a member of the *Lucky Sperm Club:* (A nickname for the fat cats with unlimited personal resources because of their birth into wealth and privilege). Power cost money and he would get his share by any means. He knew all the political tricks. Senator Winston's biggest obstacle was the president: The man he had helped win the presidency, but he already had a plan to handle that.

CIA Director Kurt Donovan, the main co-conspirator in the senator's plan, sent his personally picked Black Ops squad to Concrete to recon the area where satellite imagery positioned the UFO minutes before downing the fighter planes. This action was taken without the White House's knowledge.

Director Donovan had become obsessed with the existence of intelligent alien life after seeing the crashed Roswell spaceship and the autopsied remains of the occupants. Senator Winston coaxed the director into his group by using his influence in the senate to authorize the CIA to monitor all reported UFO sightings and encounters, deliberately bypassing the FBI. The senator considered the FBI to be *goodie two shoe boy scouts* that could not be trusted. The CIA director read all reports personally. Most investigated sightings were marked non-extra- terrestrial, but a few were marked inconclusive. Those he kept in his secret personal files.

Examination of the crashed Roswell ship documented a technology so advanced that after over seventy years the greatest scientific minds on the planet had learned little about how the technology worked.

What they did learn changed everything they understood about science and technology. The director was not going to be cheated out of any opportunity to capture an alien ship of his own. When he got the go call from the senator, he moved his men to the last radar location of the UFO. He would get this UFO if it were still around, and no Washington politicians or military boys were going to beat him to it. He didn't trust the senator. He had earned a reputation as a ruthless politician that had a habit of eliminating anybody that got in his way, but he needed the senator's connections and influence in Washington to get what he wanted. You could not go around the White House without him.

This new president had been a thorn in Donovan's side since their first meeting in the Oval Office. Donovan was kept waiting for an hour past his appointment while the new president had a photo shoot with some of his movie star buddies. Keeping him waiting like a kid at his first job interview was an insult to the integrity of the agency and its important work, but more importantly, it was an insult to him personally. When he was finally alone with the president, the director expected an apology. Instead, the president laid right into him by bluntly telling him that any CIA operations or activities were to be approved up front by the White House.

In Donovan's mind, the president of the United States had declared war on the intelligence community. This president was arrogant, thinking he could tie the hands of the CIA. What a joke!

From that first meeting, his relationship with the White House staff was one of suspicion, mistrust, and secrets from both sides. The senator had been right picking Jason Laverty at Homeland Security to be in the secret group. He was an old friend of the director and a holdover from the previous administration. The president had made no secret about wanting to replace him.

Both he and Laverty shared the opinion that the president of the United States was just another rich politician trying to play soldier. Laverty had been easy to recruit.

Homeland set up a perimeter around Concrete within hours after the director's men had set up. Eventually Homeland and the CIA would control everything going in or out of Concrete and the Mount Baker National Park.

Local law enforcement agencies were ordered to aid in the evacuation and secure the roads until the military could deploy the necessary personnel to take command.

"Chief, this is Molly. Come in."

"Everything okay, Molly?" Carly responded.

"Yes, Chief, but I thought you would want to know that we received a directive from Homeland Security to help set up roadblocks in and out of

Concrete until the military recovers the nuclear weapons from the crashed military jets."

So that's going to be their story, Carly thought. The lies had begun.

"You tell my deputies to help set up roadblocks. Have them spread the word to the townspeople that they need to evacuate," Carly ordered. "They are to cooperate with the military but keep to themselves about the UFO! Molly, if anyone wants to know where I am, tell them I'm checking on possible civilian casualties from the fallen jets. You have that?"

"Got it, Chief, watch your back. Out."

Carly was worried about the townspeople. The media people had already invaded the town in a frenzy. She had always taken great pride in protecting the public. Nobody knew where this thing was going but one thing was for sure, the government's priority was no witnesses not public welfare.

When the State police and the National Guard arrived in Concrete, they began going door to door in Concrete, instructing residents to evacuate their homes. Those that had no place to go were directed to a temporary shelter at the Sedro Woolley High School. The National Guard, police and park rangers from Sedro Woolley and Bellingham, set up barriers isolating the town of Concrete. The occupation had begun.

Chapter Seven

Finding the Enemy

The Rogue commander contemplated his death. He could not send rescue signals to the swarm. If they did find him, he would be executed for his failure to capture or destroy the Terian ship. He had lost the Terian ship and there was no other choice for him but suicide. With no witnesses to his failure there could be no dishonor.

He was considering a death dive into an asteroid belt when his ship's scans detected the weak power ripple. The ripple was faint, but unmistakably Terian. He could not believe his good fortune. The ripple was still a great distance. He had one jump left, maybe two, if he shut down all other power areas. Once the power was used for those jumps, there may not be enough left to fire the weapons. Even if it were a false target, he would be no worse off than he was now.

The power ripple was moving toward a small planet orbiting close to the star of this system.

He quickly concluded they were landing. If he could attack while they were on the surface, he may still be able to capture the Terians. If he could not capture the Terian ship, he would sacrifice himself and his crew in a death dive to kill it. Either ending would be glorious.

He would only need two of his crew to reload the power modules to be able to maneuver in battle. If he missed the Terian ship with his first shot, he would not get another. He needed to get close to the Terian mother ship to have the element of surprise. His ship could not generate the power needed to operate the stealth machine again so he would not have the advantage of invisibility. He would have to disguise his ship's approach until he was close enough to jump into the planet's atmosphere. He needed a plan.

"C" detected an all-direction scan. It was the Rogue ship. It was alone. By the strength of the scans, it was dangerously low on power and searching for a place to land. It may not be aware of the mother ship or even the target planet or it may still be able to jump.

If it did have enough power to jump, it would still need full ship power to navigate the planet's atmosphere. Rogue ships did not have the technology to element fly so they would need full ship power to maneuver the thick atmosphere, giving the pods a crucial battle advantage. If they did enter the atmosphere for battle, they would need more power to fire their weapons. "C" would take no chances.

"C" sent a thought to ZE-TAN and CRE-LIN to alert them to the general location of the Rogue scan. ZE-TAN was closest. If he was lucky enough to find it and it turned out to be the Rogue, he might be able to kill it or at least damage it enough to no longer be a threat to the mothership.

CRE-LIN moved at speed two, to rendezvous with ZE-TAN. CRE-LIN was not surprised the Rogue ship was still alive. The Rogue's reputation for being relentless to the death was well known. The monsters left nothing but horror and death in their path. There were now too many, well-armed hostile Rogue hives ready to die for the swarm. It could cost the Supreme everything to attempt to eradicate an enemy that had no fear of death; an enemy that they had given the technology that could now be used against them. This clever, savage species had adapted the defensive weapons given to them by the Terians and used them to kill and conquer. Space travel was another gift from the Terians to help the Rogue search for resource planets to sustain their species without cannibalism. The gift was used by the monsters to find and attack helpless civilizations while they spread their terror and treachery throughout the galaxy. They conquered and enslaved worlds with their superior weapons, stole their technology and resources, building an arsenal of death. When a conquered world had nothing left, the Rogue would destroy the world, covering any evidence of their crimes.

Over hundreds of star cycles, the Rogue swarm had become so powerful that even the Terian Supreme feared a final confrontation. If the Supreme learned of the Rogue attack on the mother ship, they would be forced to declare war on them and that was what CRE-LIN and most Terians believed was the only way to save the galaxies from Rogue genocide.

ZE-TAN's scans detected a suspicious object in the area "C" had given them. It moved like a tumbling rock but was emitting a power trail. It had to be the Rogue ship. He was too close to communicate with "C" and take a chance of betraying his location. The Rogue's attempt to disguise themselves told ZE-TAN they were preparing for another ambush. Their weak power trail told him their ship must be severely underpowered. He needed to take immediate action. He had a lot of fire power on his pod and with the element of surprise, he might be able to inflict enough damage to kill the Rogue ship. ZE-TAN knew that he would most likely not survive even if he hit the Rogue ship, but threat of death was part of being a flyer. The healers on mission ships were limited in their ability to heal and could not replace organs. They would give an injured flyer a chance at survival, but mortal wounds would mean permanent death.

Cell replication technology on Paetaan could create a new being from a flyer's stored cell samples but the replicant copy was never the same as the original, lacking the original's learned consciousness. ZE-TAN, like all Supreme flyers, had endured the pain of genetic alteration to grow the additional organs necessary to survive the hostile environment of space but facing permanent death was the ultimate sacrifice. He flew fearlessly toward the tumbling Rogue ship with all weapons ready. He could only hope they would not detect him until it was too late for them.

The Rogue commander's plan was in motion. When he reached the small planet, he would hide behind its small moon to prepare his weapons before jumping into its atmosphere. The swarm had been unable to steal the Terian technology of element power, so he could not outfly a Terian ship in the atmosphere.

Terian ships' maneuvering ability made them difficult targets. He was uncertain how long his ship could maintain power flight in the planet's atmosphere. His best chance of destroying the mother ship was shooting an exploder into the planet's surface close to the Terian ship. If the shot was successful, all energy sources and organic life around the exploder would be eliminated and he could pillage the ship at will and take the planet for the swarm. If he could not fire an exploder, he would wrap himself in a hard suit to crash his ship into the Terian mother ship. It was a good plan. If he survived, his failure at the comet would never be discovered. He would kill any of his surviving crew and tell any tale that suited him.

There would be no witnesses. He would earn a high place in the swarm for killing the Terian ship while taking the planet single handed. This would be his great glory!

He needed to keep up his strength and would eat the last of the live food. The crew could eat the rotted dead food. Their survival was unimportant. The ship's crew were dispensable and only the survival of the ship and its value to the swarm mattered. The commander's orders were law.

He was heading to the food pens, salivating for a Toli, when he felt the strike. ZE-TAN's power shot hit the rolling Rogue ship, delivering its melters into the rear of the ship's hull, knocking it off its controlled roll and into a real spin. The second shot glanced off the hull, increasing the ship's spin speed. ZE-TAN was turning his pod around to take a third shot, but the Rogue ship fired a power shot, striking the pod with melters, which quickly absorbed through ZE-TAN's pod's Perium hull. The melters began to eat everything inside.

ZE-TAN needed to get out quickly. No time for another shot. He opened a portal, ejecting himself into space.

The Rogue commander rushed back to the command seat. Sensors showed a strike on the small ship and detected a biological had ejected. Any other time, the commander would have stopped at nothing to destroy the survivor, but he had no time for that luxury. The Terian scum could not last long in the black without life systems. He powered out of the spin and headed for the small planet. He had to assume the Terian scum had reported his contact before his ship had been destroyed so there was no need to hide.

They would know he was coming but he still had the element of surprise on his side. He hurried to the back of his ship to access the damage. Four melters were spreading through the back of the ship, dissolving everything in their path. The commander used his weapon to kill them. There were two left eating his crew. He killed them both, then finished off the mutilated crew. He considered his survival a good omen. He headed back to the food pens. He had not lost his appetite for a live Toli!

ZE-TAN used his suit thrusters trying to get close enough to the Rogue ship to deliver a final blaster shot but the Rogue was out of range. He had hoped the monster would pursue him for the kill so he could deliver his own kill shot with a blaster, but this Rogue commander was too smart for that. He wanted the mother ship.

ZE-TAN reported the Rogue ship's status and his position to "C". Without the pod's power to boost his thought transmission, his report would most likely not reach the leader, but he had to try. He assessed his situation and faced the reality that there was little chance for his survival. The conflict had left him in a desperate situation. He was alone and his skin suit did not have enough power to support his life functions for long. His only option was to attach to something going fast enough to get within thought range of the mother ship before he ran out of life support. It was a desperate plan, but it was all he had.

He found a cluster of space rocks close enough for him to reach but it would use most of his suit's power to catch them. He had no choice. He approached the cluster from behind, watching the rocks slamming into each other. Attaching risked death. It required perfect timing, speed, coordination, and a great measure of luck to not be crushed by the ricocheting rocks.

ZE-TAN's only experience with attaching had been training simulations and he had failed in each attempt. To catch the cluster, he had used level two speed and used most of the suit's power. If he missed, he would be stranded in space until he suffocated. He moved close to the rocks. Most were too small. He saw a larger one in the middle. Now was his chance.

He increased speed, maneuvering around the smaller rocks until he was right behind the large rock. His plan to attach from behind was dangerous because there was a chance a faster rock could crush him from behind, but he did not have the fuel for the safer maneuver of speeding past, then matching the rocks speed as he attached but he barely had the power just to catch it. He was just moments from attaching when another rock spun into his rock, knocking it sideways and out of his reach. ZE-TAN grabbed onto the colliding rock, but his new ride was spinning wildly. He used a suit fastener to anchor himself while using power blasts from his suit to stop the spinning. He used one more blast to reset his direction. For now, he was alive and heading toward the small planet.

Military vehicles crowded into Concrete. The UFO parking lot video had gone viral, bringing carloads of people, hoping to see the anomaly for themselves.

The elderly couple that took the video sent copies to their two grandchildren. The granddaughter, a staff reporter at the Seattle Time's newspaper, ran the video on the Times website and the grandson immediately posted it on YouTube. Inquiries from all over the world went to every news media outlet, military, and law enforcement agency from Bellingham to Seattle including the ranger station.

Everyone wanted to know if the video was real. News agencies dispatched reporters to Concrete to get the story. The roadblocks finally stopped the flow, but many people had already gotten through, causing pandemonium. All incoming calls to local law enforcement were intercepted by Homeland Security and directed to a mobile military substation outside of Concrete. The cat was out of the bag, but the government was doing everything in their power to contain and control the flow of information. Drones were dispatched to observe activity in the area. All unauthorized drones, usually sent by the media, were shot down. The FBI protested the intervention of the CIA and the military to the justice department, claiming this was a domestic issue under their jurisdiction, but Homeland had declared the event a top-secret matter of national security, giving them the power to override the FBI's domestic authority.

The CIA and the FBI had a long history of infighting when it came to respecting each other's authority. Like most branches of government there was always competition for power. The CIA wanted the prize, and they were not going to let the FBI get in the way. The director was careful to make it appear that they were following the president's orders under Homeland's authority, but he and the senator were calling the shots.

All branches of the military were put on alert by the secretary of state with a strict "NO FIRE" command. The president assembled a small group of trusted staff in the situation room to monitor the drone videos and satellite feeds in the event area.

The government-ordered blackout would lock out the press and give the government at least temporary anonymity. The president, responded to inquiries from the heads of foreign countries with the cover story that the fallen jet planes were the result of a tragic flight training accident and that investigation and analysis of the UFO video had revealed that the video was a promotional trailer for a soon to be released Hollywood motion picture. The White House ordered a media blackout of the air collision tragedy until an investigation could be completed, which could take many months with the goal that in time, it would be forgotten. The world leaders were responded to and deliberately misdirected. The United States government was doing everything it could to make sure that no one was watching. It was a prodigal policy and had been extraordinarily successful in the past.

Carly was getting anxious waiting for Mick to come out of the alien ship. She put her hand on the ancient ship and felt a slight vibration and tingling in her fingers from the surface.

"It's warm." she said.

The Professor and the General joined her, rubbing their hands over its surface and feeling the same warmth and vibration coming from the craft. They were all thinking the same thing: What is Mick doing inside the ship with the alien? Mick heard their thoughts and broke the connection with the ship.

"I need to see my friends", he told ALUME.

Everyone was relieved when Mick and the alien emerged.

"What happened in there?" the professor asked.

"We are trying to figure out how it works and if it will fly," he answered.

"I don't understand," Carly spoke up.

Mick explained, "They detected the power in this ship from space. They need that power to repair their ship, but they need to understand how it works before they can attempt to use it. I have a weird kind of connection with the ship and I'm trying to help them."

The professor asked, "This connection that you have with the ship, where did that come from?"

Mick told him, "ALUME told me that the energy from the ship is the same as the energy coming from me."

Professor Taylor asked, "You called the alien, ALUME?"

Mick said, "Yes."

Carly asked, "So, ALUME said you were like the ship?"

Mick responded, "Part of me. Yes,"

"Hello, General Kaiser! Glad you made it," Mick called out, finally seeing him standing by Carly.

"Hi Mick! What is your friend's part in this?" the general asked, pointing to ALUME.

Mick explained, "She was sent ahead to scout for their mother ship."

"Let me see if I've got this right," the general said sarcastically. "This alien has told you that you are the same as this alien ship that has been buried in the lake for God knows how long and it needs you to help fly it?"

Mick nodded, "Part of me is the same. Yes, they need help to fly it."

"Look Albert, the fact that there are two alien spaceships, and an extraterrestrial right in front of you, should open your mind to the reality that anything is possible," the professor scolded.

Mick warned, "There is bad news here. Her thoughts tell me that our planet is in great danger."

The professor asked, "What kind of danger?"

Mick continued to explain, "Their ship creates an energy trail that acts like a marker beacon that never burns out. It will only be a matter of time before other alien species will detect that energy trail and follow it right to our planet. She told me their species would be obligated to defend us against any invasion from hostile species."

Mick's words were sobering to the professor. He should have seen it himself. A lifetime of studying the universe had convinced him that Earth was most likely an anomaly with its rich natural resources and ability to support such diverse life. Many of Earth's greatest scientists have predicted that in a confrontation with extraterrestrials with superior technology, humans would not fare well. A species that could travel through the galaxy would easily dominate a primitive species, just as man with his superior mental evolution had become the dominant species on Earth. Superior technology could give an alien species the power to impose their will.

General Kaiser suggested, "Maybe these aliens are a scouting party for an invading force."

"No." Mick answered, "She is telling the truth. They are landing here because their ship was attacked and damaged. Earth was the only planet within their reach that had a power source strong enough to repair their ship, but by coming here, they have put Earth in danger."

Carly continued, "What about this ancient ship? It has been here for thousands of years, and it didn't bring aliens."

The professor replied. "We don't know that." The professor added, "Maybe it did. Maybe the power from this ship or the trail it left behind brought the Roswell extraterrestrials or others that we have not identified. Maybe we have just been lucky, until now."

"Is that how the underwater ship found us in the first place?" The general interrupted, sounding much like a cross examination.

Mick explained, "She doesn't know where this ancient ship is from or how it works.

"There is something else," Mick confided. "The thing that attacked their ship will be searching for them to finish the kill."

Staring directly into the alien's black eyes, the professor asked, "Can this danger to our world be stopped?"

ALUME needed these humans to trust her and decided to speak to them physically, despite the pain it caused her. In a forced tone she answered.

"There are species that are beyond your experience. Their cruelty and devastation to your world would be complete." There was a long pause before she continued. "Your world will not be safe." She warned, "Your species will die if you are alone. We have brought this danger to you, but we must return home to report so they can protect you." ALUME continued, "Your world will be seen. If the evil that hunts us finds your world, they will destroy us all. We must make repairs and leave before they find you."

Her speech was truthful, but she did not tell them everything. She did not explain the consequences of being a host planet. What was done was done. Her home planet of Paetaan had been a host planet for countless star cycles until the Terians broke free after fighting a devastating war with their self-proclaimed saviors.

The Terian civilization was robbed of its natural evolution. They lost what they could have been if they had evolved naturally. ALUME knew that being a host planet was just another form of slavery. She consoled herself by thinking that it was better for this world that Terians found it first. The sadness of her personal observations did not change anything. The mother ship's survival was a priority, no matter the danger to these humans.

Professor Taylor had a thousand questions but did not say any more. This alien had just told them that this world would be changed forever and could be destroyed. He could not help but wonder: *Was this the beginning of the apocalypse?*

General Kaiser asked, "What kind of creatures are trying to kill you?"

ALUME told them, "They kill everything for their food and destroy planets. They have no mercy for life." She pointed to the clearing about fifty yards away, "The mother ship will land there."

Mick and ALUME went back to the ancient ship, leaving his friends in the clearing.

The general was worried about what the alien had told them. "We need to tell the authorities what we just heard," he quipped. "These aliens or some other aliens, won't really change the threat. Either way, sounds like were in for a shit storm."

"What do you propose?" the professor asked.

The general replied, "We need higher authority. This is over our heads. We need to tell everything we know to the government."

Carly interrupted, "I still don't think that's a good idea."

"Well, I'm sorry, Ranger," the general responded. "This affects the whole damn world, and they need to be in on it."

The Professor commented, "From what you told us about the guys on the ferry: People in the government, like your friend, the senator, might be the bad guys, so who can we trust?"

The professor was right! the general thought, *Who could he trust?* In a lifetime of service in the United States military, he had seen so many government blunders. Their secret handling of Roswell was a good example that they could not be trusted to do the right thing. There were too many hands that wanted a piece of the pie. It always came down to money and power. He knew the senator had a personal agenda and he guessed that the forces converging on the area were, at least partly, under the senator's influence. He also knew the senator had a chummy relationship with the CIA. He lobbied for any funding they proposed when he was the head of the armed services budget committee. When they were both at the academy the general recognized time and again the senator's talent at wheeling and dealing to get what he wanted. Politics had been the perfect career for him.

General Kaiser then suggested, "There is an easy way to test him. I will call him and go along with him with him to see if he will show himself." General Kaiser dialed the last number he had for the senator. This time, Senator Winston answered.

"Albert! Where are you?" the senator asked with a sense of urgency while pretending he didn't already know.

"Close to Concrete, Washington," General half lied just in case the senator already knew. "I am seeing a lot of military personnel. What is going on?" the general asked, playing dumb.

"Not really sure," the senator lied. "I am told that the military is evacuating that whole area because of a UFO bringing down two of our jets. Did you see anything?" he asked, trying to find out how much the general knew and stall the call, while it was being traced.

"Just the jets falling," Kaiser lied. "What's the president's position on this alien thing?"

Senator Winston was an expert at talking without saying anything. He was quick to reply.

"I'm told by intelligence that they are looking into it."

General Kaiser knew he was being spoon fed. Even though the senator had a dark side, he was disappointed and felt the betrayal.

Senator Winston became bolder. "You know, Albert, I could really use your eyes and ears."

The senator thought it was time to either get the general on board or contain him.

"Anything I can do to help," the general replied, although he was sure of being set up. "I talked to my guy that has contact with the alien. He said that the alien warned him that if we fired on them, they would defend with force."

The senator's tone changed to anger, "What we need to do here, is show these alien sons of bitches they can't come to our planet and intimidate the United States of America! If we need to use force, then we'll use force. Keep your eyes and ears open. Report anything new to me. I'll leave this line open…"

The general hung up and cut him off before the call could be traced.

Senator Winston was sure that General Kaiser was playing him, but there were bigger issues to deal with. He must stay on course and have his people ready when the alien mother ship landed. The military would go after the alien ships if they got in the way. They would be blown out of the sky if they could not be contained.

Senator Winston had become a villain. He wanted the alien ship for himself no matter what the price.

"C" signaled her approach. TWEE circled above the lake to protect them. The only thing in the air were unarmed drones, so he ignored them.

The landing area looked safe, but primitive alien planets had fooled him before, so he stayed alert in case of a surprise attack. There had been no contact from CRE-LIN or ZE-TAN. He hoped that they were not in trouble, but if they had run into the Rogue battleship, they could be dead. The Rogue could be close.

ALUME told Mick the mother ship was landing. Mick left the ship with her to warn his friends.

Mick urgently stated, "The mother ship is about to land. I don't know what might happen, so you need to get as far away from here as you can."

"Jesus, Mick! If it's dangerous for us, it's dangerous for you too!" Carly exclaimed, not able to hide her fear.

"Please!" Mick pleaded. "It is too dangerous for you to stay. You need to go now!"

Professor Taylor said defiantly, "I have waited all my life to see this. I'm not going anywhere."

With a smile on his face, General Kaiser said, "Well, I'm not turning tail and running."

Mick looked at Carly.

She exclaimed, "Don't look at me. I'm not going anywhere!"

Mick could see there was no sense trying to argue with them.

ALUME returned to her pod and joined TWEE over the landing area, scanning for danger. She was worried about the landing. The mother ship's size was the biggest danger in planet landing, even with element power. Taking off again would require the main drives in addition to element power. If they could not repair the main engines, the mother ship would be stranded. She trusted the leader; that all these dangers would be considered before the decision to land would be made.

TWEE moved his pod higher, to the edge of space and contacted "C".

TWEE asked, *Have ZE-TAN or CRE-LIN made contact?*

"C" responded, *No contact.*

TWEE released a searcher and made a final scan. If there was going to be a fight with the Rogue, it would be better to have it now before the landing. He detected nothing but crude human communication machines circling the planet. He reported no sign of the Rogue ship and maintained his position. They were as ready as they could be for the landing.

NORAD detected and tracked the large craft as it entered the atmosphere. Homeland Security immediately put the United States on attack alert.

The secretary of defense rushed into the Oval Office, interrupting the president's meeting with the Chinese ambassador. After the ambassador was taken from the room, the secretary gave the president the news of the approaching alien craft.

The president asked, "Is the craft demonstrating any hostile intent?"

The secretary answered, "No, Sir, not yet! It's still too far away to know its intentions, other than we assume it's going to land. I suggest we scramble the Air Force, Sir."

"No," he paused, then ordered, "Stay on high alert for now!"

The secretary acknowledged, "Yes, Sir. But, Sir, wouldn't it be better to have our planes in the air, just in case?"

The president said. "Our visitors may see that as a hostile act. We have already seen that our planes are not much of a threat to them. I do not want to send the wrong message and start something we cannot finish!"

The president believed he was making the right decision. The truth was, he was fearful of what might be coming, but his father had taught him to never start a fight you could not win. He was sure that this was a fight that the human species would not win in a direct confrontation.

At Horseshoe Cove, all eyes searched the sky. The mother ship appeared as barely a dot when it could first be seen with human eyes. As is came closer to the surface, its immense size turned curiosity into a combination of fear and wonderment. The ship was spear- shaped and emitted a blue glow, much like the smaller pods. Mick guessed that it was at least three hundred feet across. The ship's surface was completely smooth with no windows or sign of outside propulsion. Strangely, it made no sound. As it moved closer to the ground, its shape changed, becoming shorter in length and thicker in the middle. It stopped and floated about five hundred feet above the landing site. TWEE's pod hovered directly above it and ALUME's pod was close by, hovering just above the water.

"C" scanned in all directions in case the Rogue used stealth and were hiding close by. Scans only detected small unarmed human flight vehicles flying just out of the area. There were no threats. The mother ship lowered to the ground.

The president watched in amazement from drone cameras as the alien ship settled to the ground. He could not help but wonder how much humans could learn from such advanced beings able to build a spacecraft of this size that could fly through the stars. He was not of the mind that the United States should confront such an advanced civilization with any threat of force. He suspected inner government factions could be at work to capture the alien ships using national security to keep any captured crafts secret from the general body of the government, including his office. The president was a student of history and understood the consequences of too much too soon. Humans were not evolved enough to deal with such technology. He shuddered to think what the world would be like today if Hitler would have had stealth bomber technology. The aliens wanted to repair their ship then go home. That is exactly what the president wanted them to do: Go home and take their ships with them.

ALUME asked Mick to follow her toward the mother ship. Mick touched the ship and a portal opened. Mick had dreamed of this moment. All his life he had witnessed strange unearthly events like this in his dreams. The buried ship, aliens, and their spaceships were all familiar to him. He was beginning to understand why he turned down so many opportunities to work and do his research in other states and foreign countries. He believed his DNA was programmed to stay close to the ancient ship. It was the ancient ship that brought these aliens to earth. It was like fate had put them all together.

ALUME entered and motioned for Mick to follow. When they both entered, the portal closed and like the ancient ship, there was no trace that there had been an opening. Once inside, they stood in a narrow walkway. It was very warm, almost hot. ALUME had to stoop down as she moved forward but Mick was able to walk upright. The blue lights shining through the walls dimly lit the interior. The walls of the walkway changed from translucent to clear, showing strange, reflected images and shapes that were unrecognizable to him. Mick could smell a sweet scent that reminded him, strangely enough, of his mother's kitchen. The walls were radiating some sort of current that caused a tingling on his skin as he moved. At the end of the short walkway, they entered a large open space that appeared to be the center of the ship. ALUME motioned for him to stop. A thought invaded his head that felt at first like an electric charge. The intensity of this thought was unlike any he had felt before.

Do not fear us. the thought transmitted.

"I do not fear you! "Where are you?" Mick asked, looking around the ship.

"C" replied, *I do not have a physical body; I am part of the ship! Your planet is in danger from the monsters that damaged our ship. We need to repair our ship and lead them away from your planet. "C" warned, If they find us here, they will kill everything. We need your help to find the power source from the ship in the water.*

"You want to take our planet!" Mick asked defiantly, "Why should I help you?"

"C" assured him, *We want only to return to our home and offer you protection. The monsters that are coming will destroy us all if they find us here. We need to locate the power source in the ancient ship to repair our ship and leave here before the monsters find us and your planet.*

"I don't know anything about the power in that ship," Mick exclaimed.

You are connected to the ancient ship. It needs you to escape this world, ALUME told him.

Mick asked, "How is that possible?"

ALUME explained, *The creature that brought the ancient ship to your planet left a part of itself in those before you and is now using that part of you to change you.*

Mick stood silently for a moment before he spoke again. "You mean that I am related to that dead thing in the ship?"

That dead thing in the healer was only a host to the creature in the ship, as you are designed to be, ALUME said.

Mick was starting to put the pieces together. His father, grandfather, great grandfather, all his direct ancestors, back to the old tribes, had not been able to connect with the ship. Maybe because their mental development was too primitive. Somehow, ALUME had expanded his mind to be able to connect to the ship. She had saved his life and opened his mind. An extraterrestrial space traveler designed his DNA and implanted it in his ancestor thousands of years ago, but why? And what did that make him? Was he human or alien? He thought about everything his family had to endure because of his and his father's abilities.

Why couldn't they have just been a normal family? He felt anger welling up inside him. So many questions were going through his mind about the ship and his extraterrestrial ancestors. The best place to find answers was the ancient ship.

Carly watched Mick and ALUME leave the mother ship and go directly into the ancient ship without saying a word.

"Well, what now?" Mick asked as they entered the ancient ship,

ALUME answered, *You will know.*

Mick pulled himself onto the control seat. This time around, he wanted answers.

The CIA director watched the landing from a CIA drone camera. There were now three alien crafts on the ground and one more hovering above them.

When the alien and the human left the larger ship and re-entered the smaller ship, he decided it was time to take control of this event, despite the president's order to stand down. He ordered his two tactical ground units to move in and contain the landing area. He also sent two-armed drones to the strike zone for backup.

TWEE and "C" detected the armed humans converging on the landing site and the approach of the two-armed drones. "C" had hoped the humans would resist aggression, but they were preparing to attack, and she could not allow that. She ordered TWEE to eliminate the drones.

TWEE took out the two drones with a heat blast, melting them in flight. A ground soldier, in the advancing tactical group, fired a stinger missile at TWEE's pod. The pod detected the missile and vaporized it in flight. TWEE prepared to eliminate the armed humans but "C" ordered him not to fire. Killing humans would only cause more fear and retaliation. TWEE moved closer. The pod's surface began to alternate between blue and red, giving it a frightening look to the soldiers on the ground.

The squad leader just stared at the pod, uncertain what to do. He had witnessed the destruction of the drones and saw what the UFO did to the missile. Firing at this ship was not a good option.

The president of the United States and the secretary of defense had also been watching as the events at Baker Lake unfolded. When the special ops squad emerged into the clearing, the president stood up asking the entire room, "Who the hell ordered the military in there?"

The secretary of defense responded, "I don't know, Mr. President." He turned to the chief of armed forces and asked, "General, can you tell us what is happening here?"

The general was just as confused as everyone else in the room. "Whoever they are, Sir, they are not mine," he responded.

The president turned to the secretary of defense and stated, "I thought the area was secure."

The secretary answered, "The area is supposed to be secure, Sir. They shouldn't be there, Sir."

The president screamed, "Get them the hell out of there! I want to know who sent them in there! Get me that son of a bitch at Langley and find out who those civilians are!"

"Sir, are you seeing this?" The squad leader asked, thinking he was talking directly with the director, but the call had been intercepted by military command.

"This is Colonel Wilson at military command! Who am I speaking with?"

The squad leader's direct line with the director had been compromised. He knew the consequences of failing his mission. He had done work for the director before and knew the do or die rules. He decided to answer Colonel Wilson.

"Let's just say I am an interested party," he answered.

"Well, Interested Party, whoever sent you there has put you in a life-or-death situation."

"Not much I can do about that now, Colonel. I'm kind of in the thick of it, you know," the squad leader acknowledged. "Damned if I do and damned if I don't."

"You can withdraw your men immediately and we won't look for you. Or stay, and probably be killed!" The colonel warned, "If the UFO doesn't get you, you can bet the United States military will. So, what's it going to be?"

The squad leader had his back against the wall and decided that going against the director was his greatest threat. He broke connection with the colonel and ordered three of his soldiers to secure the civilians. The soldiers moved in quickly and grabbed Carly and the professor.

General Kaiser sized the soldiers up as a *kill and contain* mercenary unit. He knew from experience that force was the only way to diffuse the situation. When one of the soldiers got close to him, the general grabbed the soldier, and pulled out his .45, putting it against the soldier's temple.

"You will take your hands off them or I promise you I will blow this soldier's head off!" the general warned the soldiers who grabbed Carly and the Professor.

The squad leader ordered back at the general, "Drop that weapon! Or you are all dead."

"Soldier, I am General Albert Kaiser," the general declared. "That alien ship that is right up your ass is not something you want to piss off. I have no doubt that it will take you and your team out if you do not get your weapons away from its mother ship. You need to make the right decision before you get us all blown to hell!"

The squad leader was faced with the reality that there was no right decision here. He and his men had faced many life-threating situations in Desert Storm, Iraq, and Afghanistan. He had always relied on his training to guide his decisions, but he had no training for what was facing him. He was toe-to-toe with a real UFO from another world. He did not know their capabilities. His men were ready to carry out his orders, even if it meant certain death. He was dead either way, but he was not ready to sacrifice his men.

The squad leader quickly ordered, "Corporal! Release the civilians and secure your weapons! We are leaving!"

The soldiers released Carly and the professor. General Kaiser lowered his gun from the soldier's head.

The soldiers moved back, disappearing into the forest.

TWEE moved his pod back over the mother ship.

"I am very impressed," Carly told the general after the soldiers were gone.

General Kaiser told her, "I would love to take the credit, but I suspect the reality of certain death played a big role in their decision to disappear." Then the General spoke with a finality in his voice, "We need to get the hell out of here and right now!"

Carly asked, "What about Mick?"

"I wouldn't worry about Mick right now," the General retorted. "He is in a safer place than we are. We need to put distance between us and these aliens. Staying here could be very harmful to our health."

Carly ran to the jeep with the general and the professor right behind her. She drove out of the cove as fast as the potholes and weathered ridges in the old road would allow. They drove past empty military vehicles. The soldiers were still there. Mick and the aliens were on their own. There was nothing she could do to help now.

"C" was relieved that the humans left the landing area. Killing humans, even in defense, would only cause more aggression and retaliation. The Rogue was a great danger but having to fight the humans as well could prove to be disastrous. The longer their ships were on this planet, the greater the danger to everyone. The repairs to the ship must be made before there is a deadly confrontation with these primitives.

"C" ordered TWEE to fly to the edge of the atmosphere and scan for incoming crafts. He scanned all directions and reported back to "C" that all was clear. She then asked ALUME if they had located the power core.

The power waves are everywhere inside the ship, ALUME reported. *I have analyzed the energy waves, and they are living biological energy.*

"C" was surprised. Supreme science had never been able to produce any measurable amount of power from biological material. The Terian downloads could not verify if it could mix with anti- matter. This human may be the only connection to find the answers. Without more information, power absorption would be too dangerous. If they could not charge the anti-matter, they would be stranded. The only other way to get home would be on the ancient ship. C" had to know if it could fly.

She told ALUME to have the human try to fly the ship. ALUME was not sure the human would survive space travel. He was transforming and a second heart was developing, but it was not functioning yet. His breathing chambers were expanding, and his body mass was growing but he was still mostly human and physically frail for space travel. There was no time to wait. The ship's ability to fly had to be tested. There was also a chance that in flight, they may learn how to access the power source.

We must fly the ship, ALUME told him.

Mick responded, "I don't know how to fly the ship."

You must use your mind to try, ALUME told him. *We must know if it will fly.*

Mick settled back onto the control chair. The control panel appeared, and he concentrated on flying the ship. His hands began moving over the control images. A low humming sound began. There was a slight vibration that shuddered through the ship. The command chair wrapped tightly around him as the ship began to move. The wall in front of the control panel turned clear, allowing Mick to see outside the ship. His hands kept moving across the panel until the ship jolted. The command chair squeezed around Mick as the ship lifted slowly from the ground.

"C" urged Mick, *you must use your mind to command the ship.*

He concentrated on moving above the trees and the ship responded quickly. He watched the forest move under him and thought commanded it to go higher. He saw that his thoughts changed the pattern of his hand's movements across the panel. He thought to go faster, and his hands moved in a new pattern, accelerating the ship, and pressing him into the control seat.

"It's hard to breathe," he complained.

ALUME told him, *your body will adapt.*

Pain was shooting through his chest. The ship was moving faster, and the seat tightened even more against his chest. He felt like his heart was going to explode. ALUME sensed the danger to the human.

She urged Mick, *You must reduce speed and change direction. Just think what you want the ship to do.*

Mick began to understand. He thought about what he wanted the ship to do. His hands would move on the controls to make the ship do what he was thinking. He thought to slow down, and his hands moved across the panel, slowing the ship, easing the pressure against him. Mick's hands flew over the controls making the ship turn around and fly toward the lake. The ground was almost a blur as he looked through the portal. The ship slowed over the cove and lowered slowly to the ground. After stopping, the command chair unwrapped from around Mick, and he was able to take a deep breath.

ALUME assured him, *You are in control! The human is transforming quickly,* ALUME thought. She could see the metamorphosis was adapting him to flying the ship. She had been right about this human; he was the key to the ancient ship. ALUME worried the ship might be close to claiming the human's mind.

The president watched the ancient ship fly from the area, then return. His generals urged him to send in the Air Force to disable the UFO while it was on the ground. The president had a quick response to their pleas.

"All forces are to stand down," he ordered. "They have given us no reason to attack."

The CIA was also watching from its own satellites and was updating the senator. When he learned that the ops team had been ordered out of the area and the UFO was flying freely, he called the director.

The senator yelled into the phone, "What the hell happened?"

"They had eyes on the UFO and saw my men," the director told him.

"You assured me surveillance would be blocked!" the Senator scolded.

"There are always variables. The president doesn't share his plans with me!" the director fired back, angry for being questioned about his ability to do his job.

The senator warned, "Well, you had better not screw up again or we will all be in prison. I will be called on this and so will you. So, deny, deny, deny! Do you understand? Deny! Now you get rid of the president's eyes out there and get our people back in there before it's too late!"

"C" scanned the short flight and learned that the ancient ship was powered by an emission of high energy from the ship's core, creating element flight from within the ship itself without drawing from planet mass. This was technology "C" could not identify in the downloads. It was more advanced than Supreme science. During flight, the main engines never engaged. "C" feared the ship may be too damaged to function at full power and was the reason the ship landed here. If the power could not be transferred from the ancient ship, the mother ship would not be able to leave this world. This ancient ship would be their only means of escape! Even if the ancient ship could take them into space, without high enough speed to reach jump or tunnel speeds, they could never return home and would drift in the black void until death.

The ship's download information had no explanation for the ancient biology that had awakened in the body of the human, but it was clear he was biologically a part of the ship. The downloads referred to a species of machines that had evolved into pure energy. They needed biologicals to carry their energy. The machines would take over biological bodies as hosts for their physical movement. Once a host was implanted, the energy being would insert itself, taking over the host body. This process could be repeated forever. There was no scientific proof this species was anything but a myth, but "C" believed this human may be the victim of one of those creatures. If "C" was right, proof that these beings did exist would be one of the greatest discoveries of Terian science.

CRE-LIN's scans and watchers had not located either the Rogue or ZE-TAN. He was losing hope when a watcher signaled detection of ZE-Tan's pod drifting in space. He set an intercept course at his fastest speed. When he got close enough to see ZE-TAN's lifeless pod, sensors detected a Rogue power trail. A scan of the pod revealed that melters had eaten away the inside, leaving only a hollow Perium shell. There was no biological residue left inside the pod or on the dead melters, so ZE-TAN did not die in the pod. CRE-LIN hoped he had not been taken by the Rogue. He quickly dismissed the thought. ZE-TAN would never be taken alive.

CRE-LIN decided that when the pod was hit with melters, ZE-TAN had escaped his pod and evaded the Rouge. He could survive in his skin suit, but propulsion for any distance would be too dangerous in open space and the suit's power would not take him far. Once the power was gone, he would suffocate. Wider scans did not detect any sign of him. CRE-LIN sent another watcher in a widening circle to try and locate him and flew in the direction of the Rogue power trail. That would be his best chance of finding ZE-TAN, if he were still alive. Knowing where the Rogue was heading was a great advantage only if he could catch them, so he pushed his pod to its fastest speed even though it meant using up precious power. This was no time for caution. He had to risk that his pod would make it. The survival of the mother ship and his team members could depend on his finding ZE-TAN and getting to the Rogue before they reached the small planet.

ZE-TAN was hurling through the void, clinging to his space rock. He used his skin suit thrusters to correct his rock's direction and avoid collisions with other space rocks. He was grateful to be alive. So far, he only had one serious collision with another rock that knocked him backward. He had been able to recover but the direction correction had nearly depleted his suit's power.

His life support was dangerously low, but, if he could avoid more collisions, he had a chance. ZE-TAN felt good about his survival. He had cheated death in his encounter with the Rogue and had managed to hit the Rogue ship with melters. His continued good luck at attacking gave him confidence of getting another shot at the monster.

While he was enjoying his good fortune, he did not see the ship moving up behind him and could hardly contain his excitement when he received CRE-LIN's thought, *Did you lose your pod?*

Once aboard, the two flyers could barely move in a pod designed for only one. Going liquid would give them more room but the time lost in reshaping, if they should encounter the Rogue, was too dangerous. The extra moments it takes to reshape could make the difference between survival and oblivion. The Rogue power trail was heading straight toward the target planet. They could only hope they would not be too late.

CRE-LIN's pod had limited weapons, but ZE-TAN had grabbed his *"special"* blaster when he escaped his pod. He had increased the power of this blaster, but its range was limited so he would have to be out of the pod and close to the target to make a hit, which would most likely kill him.

Their plan was simple: Catch up with the Rogue, then wait for it to enter the planet's atmosphere where it would be most vulnerable. The pod would have the advantage of superior speed and maneuverability. They would fly close enough to the Rogue ship so that ZE-TAN could eject from the pod and take a point-blank shot at the Rogue right where the Rogue commander would be in his command chair. That was the prime objective; kill the Rogue commander! All Rogue ships were equipped with self- destruct neutrons that could only be detonated by the commander. The resulting chain reaction of a neutron explosion would destroy the mother ship and cause catastrophic destruction on the planet's surface. They would have to kill the Rogue commander or destroy enough of the Rogue ship to destroy the self-destruct neutron.

CRE-LIN's pod would have a chance of escaping the heat of the blaster concussion but for ZE-TAN to survive, he would have to have enough power left in his skin suit to power to the surface before the blast wave could hit him. The bulky Rogue ship would still be able to maneuver if it were struck by the blaster but if they could kill the Rogue commander, the leaderless ship would fall harmlessly to the surface. The outcome of battle was never certain but with only one pod, it was a good plan.

"C" could not wait any longer for ZE-TAN and CRE-LIN. She decided on her final strategy. With the two pods left, she would have to lure the Rogue into the atmosphere to gain maneuvering advantage and have any chance of making a kill. She would set a trap by powering down the mother ship. making it appear helpless on the surface. Seeing what appeared to be a helpless mother ship, the Rogue commander would attempt to capture the helpless ship intact. "C" had studied Rogue downloads since she had been activated. They were ruthless in their quest to rise within the swarm. Capturing a Terian Star ship would earn the Rogue commander great status with the swarm. "C" had to lure the Rogue close enough for the pods to surprise attack.

TWEE's pod would be positioned at the edge of the atmosphere, just far enough away to avoid being detected by the Rogue but close enough to attack quickly. "C" would remote fly ALUME's pod away from the grounded mother ship at high speed at the last moment, making the Rogue think it was cowardly abandoning the mother ship to save itself. "C" anticipated the Rogue commander would pursue the pod to eliminate it as a threat. When the Rogue chased the empty pod into the atmosphere,

TWEE would attack from above and "C" would power up the mother ship's weapon systems and shoot from below, catching the enemy in a crossfire.

"C" ordered ALUME, *The Rogue must not find the alien ship. Take position over the top of the mountain and be motionless, so the Rogue will not see you.*

Mick also received "C's" thoughts and was angered at the idea of being ushered away to safety like a coward.

He said to ALUME, "We can help. This ship has weapons."

ALUME warned, *You are not ready to fight this enemy.*

"I must try," Mick said, leaving no room for further argument.

ALUME remained silent and was doing her best to mask her thoughts. She must be patient. She would feel the same as the human if it were her world.

Chapter Eight
Battle for Glory

Live drone surveillance had been available to the president and representative from every branch of the military since the downing of the two jets. The War Room was now Central operations. A tall well- dressed man entered the situation room. He approached the secretary of state and whispered in his ear.

The secretary asked him in a loud voice, "Are you sure?"

"Yes, Sir!" the man confirmed.

"Keep me informed!" the secretary ordered.

"Yes, Sir," the man replied and briskly left the room.

"We have intel that it was the CIA that dispatched the soldiers to Horseshoe Cove," the secretary told the president, in a voice loud enough for everyone in the room to hear.

The president asked, "Who authorized that?"

"As far as we can tell, Homeland Security," the secretary answered.

The president asked, "What have we found out about the two civilians at the UFO sighting?"

"Facial recognition identified them as: Mick Welch, a biological research scientist, Professor Taylor, a planetary scientist from the ..."

"University of Washington," the president interrupted, finishing his sentence.

The secretary asked, "You know him, Sir?"

The president told him, "I met him after one of his lectures I attended at Harvard. I doubt that either of them is CIA. Try to find them and see what they know. Get Senator Winston here right now!"

The president knew that if the CIA were involved, Senator Winston would know all about it. Having served two terms as a senator himself, he understood the structured and financially self-serving mentality of career Washington bureaucrats. The president was the only child of a self-made billionaire, raised and groomed in the world of privilege and power. Above the need or concern for money, he attended the best schools and rubbed shoulders with the elite shakers and movers of the world. He had the perfect training and intellect to be the leader of the greatest country in the world. He was used to getting his way, not out of privileged arrogance but from honest compromise and negotiation that considered the needs of all sides.

His educated self-confidence served him well in the world of politics. He had a gift of common horse-sense that escaped so many of his peers, whom were members of what his father jokingly called the *Lucky Sperm Club.*

His father taught him that making the right decision was easy if you just remembered, "If it doesn't feel right, don't do it."

That philosophy had helped his father become one of the richest men in the world and got his son elected as president of the United States. His timing had been perfectly calculated. The American people were hungry for a president with the same Kennedy charisma that told it like it was. They had their fill of the long-winded, do-nothing buffoons of politics, bought and sold by the wealthy elite.

His two terms in the U.S. Senate fine-tuned his proficiency in the art of diplomacy, developing powerful working contacts and learning the art of compromise. He had no illusions about the realities of the world and his place in it. He was a true renaissance man: Exceptionally intelligent, a diverse thinker, and limitless in his tastes and interests, a man of the people, intellectually vested in the future of humanity. He was a one-woman man, happily married to a brilliant woman who was a professor at Princeton with a doctorate in philosophy. He was a rare second-generation genius never satisfied with the bureaucracy's ridged unforgiving and self- protective defenses that hindered the ability to get things done for the country.

All his power and influence could not completely overcome the government's solid wall of bureaucratic self-interest. The back-door power brokers in the nation's capital resisted even the smallest of changes. This was mental cancer for a man like him. He wanted to get things done from his first day as president and was up against the wall with his hands tied. He had managed to forge loyal alliances only to find them being attacked by this faceless power structure that was relentless in their quest to maintain the status quo. But he would never give up.

The protocol of this extraterrestrial event did not supersede the commander in chief's absolute power over all branches of the military as well as the CIA, NSA, and Homeland Security. A sore point with military high command. They judged this president to be hostile to their military machine and soft on foreign policy issues. When he was a senator and chairman of the powerful senate committee on appropriations, he recommended denial of many of the military's pet projects, publicly denouncing them as wasteful and poorly conceived. The military machine was a good old boy system, he publicly proclaimed. The military establishment at that point geared up its propaganda machine against the junior senator and the battle was on.

Sitting back in his chair and surveying the people in the room, the president saw no friendly faces, apart from his immediate staff. He was painfully aware that most in the room wished he had never been elected but he had realized long ago that being president did not make you popular in Washington unless you played ball. Adoration was for Oprah and movie stars.

All the generals had advocated an immediate military containment of the alien crafts at any cost. He knew they wanted more of the technology that they had already been gifted with from the Roswell crash. They were not aware he was one of only three presidents that had seen proof of the Roswell incident. Eisenhower was the first, Nixon was the second, and he was the third. Unlike Eisenhower and Nixon, he learned about it before he was elected president. His father owned several aircraft companies as far back as the forties and had close ties with the military. When the Roswell spacecraft was recovered and taken to a military base under top security, they called on his father, who employed some of the greatest scientific minds in the world, to reverse engineer the alien ship and apply its technology to military use. His father went along with the lie that there was no crashed alien spaceship at Roswell and what had been found was the remains of a military weather balloon.

Years later, his father showed his son top-secret pictures of the Roswell craft and its passengers. He confided to the eager boy that two previous presidents knew the truth about the extraterrestrial crash.

The military high command at the time of the Roswell crash consulted with Eisenhower about how to handle the incident. Eisenhower did not confide in Nixon about Roswell. Nixon had been trying to get to the truth of the rumored captured UFO but could not get any information out of the military at the time.

Nixon confronted Mick's father about the incident at a private re-election fundraiser in Montecito, California. His father, being a staunch supporter, confided the true events to Nixon and showed him the proof.

The president's father never saw any proof that President Kennedy knew the truth about Roswell, but the rumor was that he was shown proof of the aliens in order to enlist his funding support for the Apollo space program. The secrets learned from the Roswell alien technology moved America years ahead of the rest of the world in aircraft development. Scientists today are still trying, after seventy years, to understand much of the captured alien technology and biology.

The president did not know for sure how many others in the room had this knowledge, but he guessed at least some of the generals and admirals had to know. They were, after all, members of the same club. Their advice to him was to contain the aliens while they were most vulnerable, using the destruction of the two fighters to justify retaliatory aggression. The president did not agree. Intel was limited but it appeared that the alien craft was simply defending itself against the fighter's attack. Logic told him that beings capable of traveling unimaginable distances through the stars could have easily blown the fighters out of the air, but they used their technology to stop the planes' engines, thus giving the pilots a chance to survive. The president believed it to be an act of restraint.

At this point, he believed they were not hostile, but he still could not be sure of their intentions. They had also tried not to hide the existence of the alien craft at the bottom of Baker Lake. His military advisors believed that the buried ship may have been planted in the lake by the visitors and could be a weapon.

They also considered the buried ship American property. When the president asked about defensive military options, the majority response was to have nuclear missiles ready against what they labeled the invaders. When asked to expand on the probability of those missiles being successful against a fast-moving target and what might be the consequence to the civilian population of using those weapons, he received what he thought was his military advisors' first truthful response; they could not or would not, give him definitive answers. That's when he made the decision to order the military on high alert but restricted their actions to containment and evacuation of civilians, tying the hands of the high command hawks. That is the mentality he was up against. He knew what these people were capable of. At this point, he was ready to cooperate with these alien visitors. It was a sad reality that his military advisors were so short-sighted and self-serving. He did not have a military mentality. His military experience was limited to six years in the Navy with two of those in the intelligence sector. Although he was proud to serve his country, military life had not been his cup of tea. Everything was black or white.

You were not supposed to think for yourself. You were taught to make decisions according to military protocol, and that was difficult for him. He did his duty with full commitment, followed the rules, and counted the days until his enlistment was over. Now, as commander in chief, the tough calls were his. He decided to sit tight to see what developed.

Troops were stationed close to the alien ships. If they became hostile, he could launch a fast offensive. He suspected that Senator Winston had something to do with the CIA special ops team, which was why he had requested the senator join him in the War Room. Winston had been his political mentor when he was in prep school; hired by his father to teach him the real world of down and dirty politics and who better to do that than the master of down and dirty himself. The senator and the president seldom agreed on issues even before he had been elected president, but Winston's political shrewdness and connections carried great clout in Washington.

The president had put that power to work for him more than once, certainly in getting elected. It all had a price of course, but that was politics. A politician with Winston's influence could be extremely dangerous. Although the senator had used his position to support the president on many occasions, the president did not fool himself into thinking that it was out of respect and loyalty. Every favor came with a price. The president knew that his opinions did not carry much weight with the men in this room. They considered him a dove while the senator had always supported the military in major funding requests, earning him the title of the *Hawk* of Washington.

Senator Winston entered the War Room and greeted the president with the traditional hug. The facade was that they were like family and the senator played it to the hilt. The reality was, he had always resented the young president with his inherited empire and spoke less than respectfully of him behind his back.

"So, good to see you, Mr. President," Winston said warmly.

"Thank you for coming," the president greeted back, pretending that the senator had a choice. There was no indication of deceit in the Senator's eyes. Winston was, after all, the master game player.

"Wouldn't miss it," the senator replied, stepping back, still holding the president's shoulders. "Looks like you've got a real tiger by the tail here," he added with experienced, programmed empathy.

"More like an elephant," the president replied, inferring the hostile military presence in the room.

The remark went right over the heads of the military men, but the senator got it right away. That's why he was here. Someone had spilled the beans about the CIA's involvement and the president was looking for the inside man, The senator was too smart to be caught holding a smoking gun and the president could not prove a goddamn thing. All he had to do was deny, deny, deny. The military was on his side. They did not like stand down orders. They liked control and with the senator's support they had a chance of getting that control. One hand feeds the other and as life changing as this event was, it was no exception.

The senator quickly circulated throughout the room greeting all the military generals and admirals by name, establishing his dominance of this political stage.

The president observed the faces of the men in the room greeting their ally. They were not going to rat on the senator and jeopardize his support for future funding.

Politics had a long memory, and this was classic Winston, the president thought. The senator was the high priest of dirty politics and pulled strings in the background without risking any direct responsibility. In the War Room he would be cut off from openly contacting the CIA and that was exactly what the president wanted. Having contained the senator, his next problem was keeping the other world powers out of it. He needed time without their interference.

The Russians and Chinese knew something was up. Like NORAD, they tracked everything entering the atmosphere. The American president stood by the cover story that the object was a falling United States communication satellite. The Russians and the Chinese did not believe that for a moment. They had seen the YouTube video of the alien ship in a parking lot in Washington and wanted in on any captured technology.

The senator had reported that he received a call from retired General Albert Kaiser. Kaiser informed him he had direct contact with the aliens and learned that they were here to make repairs to their damaged ship. When pressed about the general's whereabouts, the senator simply said that the general refused to give his location and the phone he used was a burner, therefore, untraceable. The president suspected that the senator was lying but thought better about calling him out about it. The bigger issue was what did their landing mean for planet Earth? There was no way to know if these extraterrestrials would be friendly or hostile. The military would likely have no defense against them should they be hostile. He had seen the video from the cockpit camera of one of the downed attack fighters. He was convinced the UFO only meant to disable the attacking jets, not to kill the pilots. He compared it to not shooting a caged dog just because it was barking at you. It would demonstrate cruelty to kill a helpless living thing that could cause you no harm. The only practical option, in his judgment, was to let the aliens repair their ship so they could leave. He did not believe for one minute that the aliens were here to develop a relationship with humans. If they could not repair their ship, well, that might bring up a whole new set of problems, but first things first. This planet's future could be threatened, but he felt his best option was to keep the military on the bench, including the CIA.

There was a barrage of inquiries from the top world leaders. It seemed that everyone wanted to be in on the show if it proved to be a real alien encounter. He restricted all calls except from a select few on the priority need to know list. The president simply wanted to keep his mind uncluttered. He needed a cool head to avoid a catastrophe from within. The CIA was a big problem. The director had always been resentful of his administration. He knew the director would love to capture the alien technology and bury it in some secret location.

Control of an alien ship meant power. He did not underestimate what they might do to get it. The greatest threat to the security of this world may not be the aliens. The president understood the military mind. Every military officer in this room believed that the military, not a politician, should oversee and make decisions on any situation that may threaten the security of the United States. That mindset was why the founding fathers, in their infinite wisdom, took that power of the military and tethered it to a commander in chief, to calm the angry sea. That was his job, to calm the angry sea before it sank the ship.

Mick eased the ancient ship toward space. *We will help kill what is coming,* he told ALUME firmly.

ALUME felt the strength in the human's thoughts and realized his mind had become too powerful for her to hide thoughts from him. She agreed with the leader's plan, but the human had feelings to protect this world. "C" was not his leader, and the human was being torn between his human side and whatever was transforming him.

"C" turned her attention to the pods, leaving ALUME to deal with the human. ALUME's empty pod was in position, powered and ready, floating next to the mother ship. TWEE had moved into position at the edge of the atmosphere, ready to swoop down on what they hoped would be an unsuspecting Rogue ship. She shut down all but the life support power systems in the mother ship to give the appearance of a dead ship, completely vulnerable with no hull repulsion protection or powered weapon systems. All she could do now was wait.

TWEE detected the Rogue ship approaching the far side of the Earth's moon and alerted "C". The hunter was about to become the hunted. The Rogue ship was still a good distance from the little planet, unless it made a jump, then it could be in Earth's atmosphere in moments. "C" detected the ancient ship, floating above the mountain. With any luck, the Rogue would not detect it. Everything was ready! The trap was set.

TWEE reported to "C" that the Rogue ship had stopped behind the Earth's moon.

The Rogue commander was preparing for his time of glory and was oblivious to the possibility of a trap. He decided to make a jump even with his ship's critically low power. It was dangerous, but they would not see him coming until it was too late. He would not send watchers, fearing they would alert the Terian ship, but he risked sending one low power scan to locate the mother ship so he would not be attacking blind. The scan located the Terian ship, un- powered, lying dead on the planet's surface with only a scout ship for protection. As a precaution, he shot a location beacon to the dark side of the moon. Should he die, the swarm would find this planet and destroy it. Failed glory would be avenged.

The power of the swarm is shining on me, he thought.

He could barely contain his excitement. His plan was no longer to kill the Terian mother ship but to capture it and destroy the scout ship. His success would earn him a hive of his own and maybe a place on the swarm council. He could see only self-enrichment and felt no fear of the enemy. He would attack fiercely, using all remaining power to carry out his attack. The glory in his eyes blinded him to the trap that was waiting as drool dripped from his mouth.

They are mine, he thought. Suddenly, the pod powered away, fleeing from the mother ship's side at high speed.

Terian coward, the commander thought. He would enjoy dealing with the pod later. All his focus must now be on taking the helpless mother ship whole. Nothing would stop him. His vision of glory blinded him. He powered his ship for a jump.

CRE-LIN watched the Rogue ship as it slowly moved around the moon. His sensors detected the Rogue ship building power.

He is going to jump! CRE-LIN thought to ZE-TAN, quickly flying his pod directly at the Rogue ship.

There was no time for ZE-TAN to exit the pod and use his weapon, so CRE-LIN would have to attach to the Rogue ship before it jumped.

The Rogue commander felt a heavy thud vibrate through the ship's hull as his ship surged forward at jump speed. The pod's hull would withstand the speed but could not protect ZE-TAN and CRE-LIN from the heat that would invade the inside of the pod. They did not have long before the heat vaporized them. They had been trained to do their duty and protect the mother ship at any cost and in that last moment, knowing that their action meant their death, they did their duty. ZE-TAN engaged the super blaster. ZE-TAN and CRE-LIN shared a knowing glance before ZE-TAN raised his arm, setting off the weapon that turned their pod into a bomb.

The heat from the blast melted the back of the Rogue ship, killing the last of the crew. The Rogue commander was mortally wounded by the heat blast that surged through the doomed ship, but the dying commander clung to life, refusing death.

In those last moments the commander's thoughts were confused: *What had happened? How had he been hit?* He had little control of what was left of his ship as it sped into the planet's atmosphere.

He was fighting to stay conscious while his skin melted into the command chair. The commander was near death. His body was melting, boiling his body fluid. All was lost. He was defeated but would not be cheated out of his revenge. In his last moments of clarity, he aimed the molting mass around him at the Terian mother ship. His death would be glorious. He shot the last melters while the oxygen in the planet's atmosphere fed the flames devouring his ship. A final blast of searing heat surged through what had been reduced to a freefalling molten mass as it continued toward the planet's surface. The Rogue commander was fighting to stay conscious for the ultimate victory of impacting the Terian ship, but the heat had eaten through his skin and stole his last breath, cheating him of his last wish.

Mick detected the Rogue ship the moment it emerged from its jump and accelerated so quickly that the pressure on his body became almost unbearable. The ancient ship caught the flaming missile. Mick's fingers moved across the control panel, sending a superheated light blast at the fireball cutting it into two pieces and increasing their velocity. TWEE swooped his pod toward the burning projectiles, firing at the larger of the two pieces, exploding it into a roman candle shower of small fiery cinders. The smaller mass continued its fall, picking up even more speed from the welcoming arms of Earth's gravity. Mick swung the ancient ship around and flew directly at the falling mass, swerving at the last second while firing another blast of light, striking a glancing blow, causing the fiery mass to spin but stay on course.

"C" was not expecting a suicide dive from the Rogue ship and began powering up the mother ship the moment the Rogue ship entered the atmosphere. She tried to lift the large ship off the surface while thrusting ALUME's pod into the fireball, hoping to change its course enough to save the mother ship from a direct hit. ALUME's pod hit the fireball at speed two, molding its Perium hull to the fiery mass but it did not divert from its target. "C" was able to move the mother ship less than a hundred feet from where the fireball hit the ground. The force of the blast flipped the mother ship upside down at the edge of the clearing. The blast did not penetrate the mother ship but severely twisted the hull, crushing part of the anti-matter drive chamber. Miraculously, the chamber did not corrupt, saving an anti-matter chain reaction that would have destroyed the planet.

ALUME's thoughts to "C" went unanswered. Something was wrong. The leader was designed to be almost indestructible. She should have responded immediately but ALUME did not know that the Rogue melters had absorbed into the mother ship and were moving through the twisted ship toward the energy in the anti-matter chamber, requiring all her focus as she electrocuted them one by one. If they breached the chamber, the Rogue would have the ultimate revenge of an anti-matter chain reaction.

TWEE's pod hovered above the clearing to defend.

Mick moved close to the mother ship, setting the ancient ship down in between the piles of molten debris burning all around the mother ship's twisted hull. ALUME went liquid while Mick opened a portal. "C" needed help and took a second to send an urgent thought, *Melters!*

ALUME flowed through the fiery clearing to the mother ship. She absorbed through the hull and heard conflict coming from the opposite end of the twisted ship. The melters had already eaten most of the insides that were visible to her. She flowed toward the sounds until she saw the melters. "C" was igniting power beams at them to kill them as they ate their way forward toward the energy of the anti- matter.

ALUME took solid form behind the advancing killers and fired her blaster before she could be detected. She hit one of the larger melters but as it melted, it turned and spit scam, hitting ALUME's hand. It felt like her hand was on fire as her flesh began dissolving. She grabbed the blaster with her other hand and burned off the infected hand to keep the scam from spreading up her arm. Despite her injury, she kept firing at melters with her good hand but was unable to stop them all as they advanced toward the anti-matter. During the seconds that ALUME's action slowed the melters, "C" calculated the programmed pattern of the remaining melters' movements and fired all the ship blasters in unison at their anticipated direction. The beams exploded, disintegrating the remaining melters. ALUME and "C" surveyed the damage.

The pinnacle of Terian Supreme technology lay upside down and twisted with its insides devoured beyond recognition. "C" was surviving inside what was left of the power system of a dying ship, but there was not much time left before the power would fail and she would be the first of her kind to die. She needed a new power system. The power in TWEE's pod was not enough. Her only chance was the large power source in the ancient ship. If the ancient ship rejected her, she would die and the Terian knowledge downloads she carried would die with her. Without the downloads, creating tunnels would be impossible and there would be no hope for the team of ever going home.

I must transfer to the alien ship, "C" thought to ALUME.

ALUME would have to carry "C" to the ancient ship in her liquid state, but "C's" energy drain would kill them both if they did not get to the ancient ship fast enough.

Carly brought the jeep to a stop when she felt they were out of danger. She watched the fireball plummet toward Earth as it was being hit with laser beams of light coming from the attacking ships. They were too far away for Carly to tell for sure, but one of the attacking ships looked like the ship from the lake.

When the fireball hit, they could feel the ground reverberate from the concussion.

"Oh, my God," Carly whispered, anticipating the devastation.

The professor put his arm around her, sharing her fear.

"I have to go back." Carly told him. "You all stay here while I check it out."

"I'm going with you," the professor said immediately, refusing to move.

Carly did not argue and started the jeep. The general was yelling at someone on his cell phone while he got back in the jeep without stopping his phone conversation. Carly turned the jeep around, speeding back to Horseshoe Cove.

General Kaiser was trying to reach Senator Winston, with no luck. He guessed the government's next move and the senator was the only person he knew with enough power to stop it. The military would be on their way to take over the area. Just like Roswell, they would control information. CIA would no doubt brand the event a hostile invasion. National security would be given authority that would not require presidential approval for their actions. When the senator did not respond, General Kaiser called his senate office and got the runaround. He must be in a secure location or simply did not want to talk.

The general's knowledge of military protocol told him that these extraterrestrials would be taken, dead or alive. The ones that were not killed would wish they were. In the stories that he had heard about Roswell, one of the crash survivors had lived for almost a week in captivity and was subjected to countless medical atrocities before it died. After the alien's death, it was dissected into tiny pieces, which were in turn probably sold to pharmaceutical companies for vast sums. The biggest prize would be the ships.

The military would do anything to get alien technology, anything. He had always taken the path of the dutiful and disciplined soldier and followed orders even when he felt they were wrong. This time he would make his own decision, the right decision, and warn the aliens.

The general knew the field procedure. The military would overwhelm the location securing the crash site and taking all aliens and humans into protective custody at some secret military installation. The military would classify the event as a matter of national security and confiscate all physical evidence, to be hidden away, under a cloak of secrecy, to be studied and reverse engineered. Any resistance would be answered with lethal force. Like Roswell, the public would be denied the truth. The government spin doctors would concoct a cover-up story followed by publicly orchestrated denials that would, over time, erase the true events from the public. The general would try not to let that happen this time. He was through with all the government's clandestine actions. He put his cell phone back into his pocket, holding on for dear life as the jeep hit every rut and pothole of the dirt road. He realized it was too late in his life to play along with the lies. He would share his suspicions so Mick could warn the aliens.

The road was still clear as Carly drove the jeep around the last bend and into view of the crash site. She could tell by the destruction that they would probably have been killed if they had stayed. The pieces of the fireball were still so hot they felt the burn on their faces. The area looked like a war zone. Mick's ship was about 50 feet away from the twisted, upside-down mother ship. When Carly could not drive any closer, everyone approached the wrecked alien ship on foot. They had advanced only a few feet when TWEE's pod silently appeared, hovering over them. The pod turned a reddish blue color, threatening attack. No one moved.

"Don't anyone move," the general instructed.

Nobody had any intention of moving. TWEE's scan identified the humans as non-hostile, but he was not taking any chances. TWEE did not trust these humans. They were primitive, unstable, and unpredictable. If they made any type of hostile move, he would eliminate them. TWEE thought alerted "C" and she ordered TWEE to take no action. His pod then alerted him that armed machines were approaching.

"C" also detected the human machines and ordered TWEE to protect. TWEE flew high above the mothership to confront the incoming hostiles. ALUME intercepted TWEE and the leader's thoughts. Anticipating the inevitable conflict, she advised Mick to open a portal and bring the humans into the safety of the ship. Mick agreed and stood in the opening, motioning for the humans to enter. They heard the incoming Blackhawks and ran to the ship. Once inside, they found themselves in a white room, pulsating with a dull blue light. There were red colored protrusions scattered throughout the room making the inside look appropriately like something from a science fiction movie.

The general approached Mick, who was now sitting on a large object in the center of the ship.

"The military will come with everything they've got. They will capture and contain everything here and will not allow anything to escape even if they must use nukes," the general told him.

"Why doesn't the president stop them?" Carly asked.

"I would guess that they convinced him this was an attack," the general explained. "Hell, he may very well be a prisoner for all we know. There is no way they will allow this event to go public even if it means killing all witnesses. They will try to capture the technology even if that means blowing it up and reassembling."

"C" and ALUME knew the danger. Advanced civilizations had to protect against the theft of their technology. The obsession of lesser evolved civilizations for superior technology was always a danger greater than the blackness of space itself.

The Terians had also used the stolen technology of advanced civilizations to advance themselves as they were evolving. They still searched for gifts of new technology on each of their missions. These humans were no different. Their response was predictable. That was the reason for the *no interference* laws from the Supreme. The outcome of primitive contact was predictable. This landing had been necessary for a chance to survive, and survival rose above all other laws. Now that the mother ship was destroyed, the ancient ship was their only hope of escaping this planet and getting home. Supreme law allowed any means to survive an alien planet.

They would not survive the humans if they could not escape the planet. Humans would be relentless and merciless to obtain their technology. "C's" duty was clear, anything that was left of the Terian machines and the Terians themselves would have to be removed from this planet or destroyed, leaving no traces that they had ever been here. "C" would do her duty.

Mick could hear the Terian leader's thoughts. He wanted to help them to survive, but he was still human, most of him anyway. He could not deny his feelings for his species. He hoped that he would not have to choose one side or the other.

Chapter Nine
The Real Enemy

By the time the flaming Rogue ship became visible from the planet's surface, its original form was indistinguishable. The president and the senator watched the terrifying fireball hurling through the atmosphere, blindly racing toward the surface.

As frightened eyes watched, another small craft appeared and crisscrossed in front of the fireball, firing bright, laser shaped lights at the fireball and breaking off pieces of it that exploded in all directions. The impossible movement of the smaller craft caused gasps from everyone in the room as they watched it move at incredible speed and make right angle turns without slowing. There was not a military man in the room that did not want that kind of technology in their arsenal. Some of these men had benefited from the secrets unveiled from the Roswell crash and were eager for a second windfall. The stealth bomber was only one example of the benefit of reverse engineering alien technology.

Another larger craft appeared out of nowhere and hit the fireball with flashing light that split the fireball in two. The two pieces of the fireball crashed into the surface, close enough to the large mother ship that the impact caused it to flip into the air and crash back to the surface, upside down and twisted.

The president had never been officially briefed on the Roswell incident by the military. His knowledge of alien existence came from his father so the military brass in the room did not know the depth of his knowledge on the subject. It was protocol for top military secrets to be kept from sitting presidents. Plausible deniability they called it. Politicians came and went and could not be trusted to keep their mouths shut about something as important as beings from other planets that crash landed on this planet. It had been decided long ago by unidentifiable back-room powers, that the public would not understand why the alien survivors and their technology needed to be kept a national secret, hidden away in secret military installations. The senator was one of the few living politicians that had been allowed into the select circle and briefed about Roswell. He had the advantage of being an inside player with the military elite.

After watching the fireball being fired on by the smaller alien crafts, and ultimately damaging the mother ship, Homeland recommended that the President issue an immediate lockdown of the Concrete area and to use all available military force to secure the remains of the alien craft and protect against any alien aggression from the crafts that had fired on the fireball. The president was not convinced to take such a bold move and denied their recommendation, confirming the stand down order.

The president then spoke to everyone in the War Room, "These visitors have navigated unimaginable distances through the stars to get here and from what I have seen, they have not taken any aggressive action except in self-defense. Whatever that fireball was, they had their reasons for shooting at it. We will attempt to offer aid and assistance to these visitors and refrain from any aggressive actions until they demonstrate that they have hostile intent against us."

The senator boldly suggested, "Think of what we can learn from their technology," deciding to make a desperate attempt to bring the president into the fold by exposing his real position.

"Now would be the time to take control, while they are damaged," the senator pleaded.

The president asked his secretary of defense," Where are you on this Carl?"

"I must concur with the senator, Mr. President. Deal from strength while they are at their weakest. Why take the chance that they are friendly?"

The president thought for a moment then gave the command, "Secure the area but stand down from aggressive confrontation!"

The chief of staff asked, "Do we have presidential authority to use deadly force, if it becomes necessary, Sir?"

The President responded, "For defense only." He repeated firmly, "Force is to be used for defense only!"

The secretary of defense, the director of Homeland Security, the FBI, and the CIA, were now under orders to use their forces to contain and control the area. Deadly force was only authorized for defense and protection of American lives. Military command was unhappy about having their hands tied, secretly hoping the aliens would give them any reason to displace the president's authority.

The CIA Black Ops captain moved his unit back through the forest toward the burning crash area. His new orders came from the director, and he did not intend to let the boss down again. He was going to bag an extraterrestrial, dead or alive. The team moved quickly. They positioned themselves around the upside-down mother ship. Mick sensed them right away and sent a warning to ALUME that soldiers were surrounding them. TWEE was busy protecting against incoming craft so they were on their own.

"Soldiers are here," Mick told the others as he jumped from the control seat.

Carly asked, "Where are you going?"

"I've got to do something!" he said opening the portal.

He emerged from the ancient ship with everyone following behind him. It was to be a showdown.

ALUME absorbed through the hull of the mother ship and changed to solid form. The astonished soldiers watched her transformation while pointing their weapons at her. The soldiers began rising off the ground, arms and legs trying to regain balance. One soldier shot multiple times at ALUME striking her and knocking her backward. The Perium in her skin suit prevented penetration but the impacts were painful. To protect herself, she stopped the shooters heart, killing him instantly. TWEE detected the gunshot but was under protect order and stayed in position directly in the path of approaching crafts.

Mick watched as the floating soldiers were being pressed together, twenty feet above ground. The bunched-up soldiers began to float even higher, over the trees until they were out of sight. Mick wondered how far ALUME had sent them, recalling the bear that she had sent into the forest.

Carly began yelling. Mick turned to see Professor Taylor lying on the ground. Mick rushed over to him. The old man did not look good. There was blood coming from his shoulder. Carly was applying pressure on the wound to slow the bleeding.

ALUME moved next to the injured man and motioned Carly away. She pulled a small silver vial out of her skin suit and spread the same orange goo on the wound that she had put on Mick after the bear attack. The goo quickly spread all over the professor's skin.

ALUME picked the man up and headed to the ancient ship. Mick and Carly followed her into the ship. The general stayed at the portal opening to watch for more soldiers. Once inside the ship, ALUME hurried to the healing chamber protrusion.

Remove the body! she told Mick.

Mick reached down into the chamber, pulling the dead alien's body out of the chamber, and laying it down gently on the floor. ALUME carefully lowered the professor's limp body into the chamber. A clear cover appeared, sealing him inside. The soundless chamber turned a dull blue color then suddenly turned a bright white, making a high-pitched sound. The old man became a silhouette against the white light.

Carly asked, "Will he be alright?

ALUME sensed fear in her voice. "The chamber will seal the wound and reconstruct the damage," ALUME told her. "It is unknown if he will survive."

They all stared into the chamber; all they could do was wait.

TWEE saw the approaching enemy. The first to appear on the horizon were two fast-moving stealth fighters followed by the slower, low altitude Blackhawk helicopters carrying assault troops.

TWEE's pod calculated the targets and fired an absorbing impulse, shutting down the engines on all the human machines at once. The fighters and the Blackhawks immediately began to spiral out of control, in death falls. Three of the falling Blackhawks exploded upon contact with the ground killing everyone aboard. The other four crashed without exploding but killing sixteen more soldiers in flaming twisted metal. The fighter pilots ejected, unable to control their powerless jets. The lead pilot managed to fire a heat seeking missile at TWEE's pod before he ejected. TWEE's pod detected the missile and fired a heat beam that exploded it harmlessly. The human weapons were very primitive, but pod sensors determined that they could cause flight damage to the pod so TWEE distanced himself in case there were more attack crafts. He flew his pod straight up. At his new altitude, he could easily see incoming crafts. The beams he had used to absorb and eliminate the power of the human machines had severely reduced the pod's power reserve. TWEE would not be able to power many more weapon beams without regenerating. He would be forced to use high heat beams to stop continued attacks and that would kill many more of the humans, but he must protect the leader at all costs, no matter how many of these primitives must die.

The president watched the drone camera feeds of the alien ship bringing down the fighters and Blackhawks and the soldiers surrounding the damaged mother ship.

"Who is authorizing these attacks on the alien ship?" he yelled, trying to be composed.

The secretary of defense replied, "They were not authorized, Sir!"

"They were not authorized by command, Mr. President," the general in charge of military command offered before being asked.

The president yelled, "Those were American aircraft and I want to know who in hell sent them in there!" His heart sunk as he had watched the falling aircraft. The alien technology had stopped the aircraft without firing a shot. Why did they do that? He watched them fire explosive weapons at the fireball, but why didn't they use them to destroy the attacking aircraft?

The room fell silent. The president continued to speak openly. "The aliens have weapons that could have blown our planes out of the sky, but they didn't use them. They just stopped the engines giving some of our pilots a chance to survive." He said aloud, "Could it be that they were defending themselves and trying to minimize deaths?"

After a few second pause, the president stood up and addressed the room. He said in a very calm and controlled voice, "I am ordering our forces to stand down before more Americans get killed."

The senator spoke up, "Mr. President, I urge you to reconsider."

The president responded forcefully, "No! Senator! I will not jeopardize any more lives. Until I see otherwise, I am convinced that the aliens demonstrated great restraint to stop our aggression, which should not have occurred in the first place. All United States forces will stand down and return to base. Let me be very clear on this! I don't want our United States military forces, the CIA, or Homeland Security to use any first strike aggressive action against these extraterrestrials! And I want to know who was responsible for those soldiers and aircraft being there. I want to know **pronto**! Whoever was responsible will be tried for treason!" He waited a moment and said, in a cold voice, "Is that clear?"

Everyone in the room acknowledged the president and went about contacting their forces with the president's orders.

Senator Winston, wisely, said no more to the president. Any influence he thought he may have regarding this event was gone. The senator got up from his chair and went into the rest room. He made the call from which there would be no coming back. When the voice on the other end answered, the senator said, "The eagle has left the nest," and hung up.

The senator had gone all in. This president would not stop him from acquiring the alien technology. He would simply play it another way. He would use his famous buffer technique. If the shit hit the fan, they would not be able to prove that he was involved. The senator put his cell phone back in his pocket and leaned against the wall. He was still taking a great risk. There was a terrible penalty for disobeying a direct order of the president of the United States. The call could cost him everything, but the benefits, financial and political, made it a risk that had to be taken.

The Roswell biological and technological discoveries had benefited humanity in so many ways. It had also benefited the people that had controlled access to the discoveries.

Indirectly, the president had also benefited, after all, the president's father had earned millions of dollars from reverse engineering the Roswell ship. All that wealth had been instrumental in putting his son in the highest office in the free world. Senator Winston prided himself on being a super patriot. Somebody had to make the hard decisions for the good of all and if he should get a little something along the way, well, that was the American way, and who knew the American way better. The American way was his way.

TWEE watched but no more human machines approached. They appeared to have given up for now. He reported to "C" and flew around the area again to confirm that there were no more hostile machines before flying back over the mother ship. He had accepted that they may never get back home but would rather they take their chances in space then stay on this primitive planet. When they did leave, he would make sure there was no trace of their visit left behind.

ALUME wanted to attempt "C's" transfer before there could be more conflict with the humans.

I must transfer the Leader into this ship, or she will die! she thought to Mick. *I am unsure if the ship will allow her to enter its power systems.*

"I will do whatever I can to help!" he assured her.

ALUME left the ship and made her way back to the twisted hull of the mother ship. She went liquid and absorbed inside. "C" had compressed the downloads into as small an energy concentration as possible, but this was the first time the Terian knowledge downloads had ever been transferred. "C" would be sharing ALUME's energy to sustain herself until she could enter the ancient ship's power. ALUME's energy must last, or they would both die.

Prepare the mother ship! "C" ordered. A difficult order, but necessary. Even as an empty shell, the mother ship could not be left behind. It would have to be dissolved.

ALUME programmed the Perium and absorbed out of the mother ship, keeping herself liquid for the transfer.

You must keep moving. If you stop, you may not have enough energy to start again, "C" warned, then made the jump into ALUME's liquid mass.

ALUME felt the pain of the power drain as soon as "C" jumped into her. She began to flow toward the ancient ship. She heard the Perium of the mother ship melting but did not look back. Losing the ship was like losing a part of herself and she could not watch.

After flowing only a few feet, she was beginning to struggle. The distance to the ancient ship was less than 100 feet but her progress was painfully slow as she navigated around the burning rubble of the Rogue ship. Breathing Earth's atmosphere was difficult enough for a Terian but combined with "C", it was an energy drain. She was losing her strength quickly. She stopped at the halfway point, feeling drained. She mustered all her will and moved another 10 feet before she had to stop again. She had never known such pain but pushed through until they finally reached the ancient ship. She lost consciousness as she was moving up the ramp.

"C" was too far away from the hull to jump. For the first time since "C" had been activated, her energy was fading. She was facing her end. She felt the desperation known only to those that stare into the face of death. Her thoughts were not for herself but for the remaining team that would never see home again. Without her to calculate jumps, the downloads would disappear with her death. She sent TWEE what could be her last orders.

Carry out the Supreme directive. Destroy all traces of our technology if I do not survive. You will use weapons only for defense." she ordered, *"Kill only to survive."*

I will come for you, TWEE told her.

I cannot survive in the pod, you must protect! she ordered.

TWEE wanted to destroy the primitive humans before they could attack again but was bound by the leader's orders. He had witnessed enough evolving primitive species that he had no doubt it would only be a matter of time before these humans destroyed themselves and this planet. There was nothing here but death. This beautiful world was nothing more than a trap. Primitive species were always the same: Frightened, and hostile. They wanted technology they could not understand and would eagerly kill for it.

TWEE wondered if the flyer of the ancient ship had been lured by the planet's beauty and primitive innocence only to be trapped and killed in its deadly illusion. He moved his pod back to the clearing and hovered just above the melting mother ship. Should the leader, "C", die, his rank would make him the next leader. Then he would make all the decisions. Until then, he would follow orders. There was still a chance they could survive using the ancient ship but without the leader they would lose the Terian downloads. Without them, they were doomed.

ALUME heard a faint voice calling to her. It was her human.

Just a little farther, ALUME, just a little farther! Mick yelled.

His voice brought her back. She used all her remaining strength to move the last couple of feet to the open portal of the ship. Once inside, "C" made one final jump and absorbed into the ship. She had been seconds from death but the power from the ship saved her and she flowed into the ship's systems.

Leader! Leader! ALUME tried to communicate with "C" but received no response.

A few moments passed before the leader responded.

I am in the power system, she replied. *I am surrounded by the ship's power but cannot identify what it is.*

The power circulating through "C" was overpowering. She was recharging with a fierce, paralyzing intensity. "C" could not move. She was overheating, frozen in place. Her life was still in danger if the alien energy flowing through her was not reduced.

"C" told ALUME, *The power is too strong.*

ALUME told Mick, *The power is killing the leader.*

TOR-LOK felt the alien dying and sent instructions to the implant.

Mick moved back to the control seat. His hands moved across the controls until the hum of power in the ship became quieter.

"C" felt the ship's energy loosen its grip. She began to move a little at first, but slowly, she was able to flow freely. The ship's technology was a wonder and beyond the Terian download's knowledge. She had integrated into the ship's systems. The flow of power was somehow biologically generated. The ship's construction was unidentifiable, and the complexity of its operation was beyond her programming. The energy flow was not centralized, it flowed from everywhere and communicated randomly, but organized, like the ship was thinking and studying.

The technology that built this craft was more advanced than any science recorded in the downloads. "C" reasoned that any being so advanced should be able to thought send but when she tried, there was no response.

"C" continued to scan the ship. The emaciated body of the flyer had two constructions. The dead creature was constructed of two different beings that combined to control the ship's systems. One part matched the energy of the ship, but the biological construction was a completely different lifeform. The body they found in the healer was only a host body. Where was the invasive entity? Did it die with the host or was it still here? She knew the answer.

It was so simple! The ship needed a biological body to fly it. A host would be implanted with a growth that would allow the invading species into the host body to control its mind. When the host body became damaged or worn out, the invader would replace the host with a new one, allowing the ship to have an unending supply of flyers for vast distances over eons of time. The host was controlled by an entity of pure energy! These beings were pure energy with no physical form. They traveled the endlessness of space, possibly making them the oldest living species in the universe.

If that were true, they would carry the secrets of the universe. Proof of their existence would be the greatest discovery ever made. It also meant that she and the team were already prisoners.

She had to communicate with these beings. She would need their help for her team to survive. An alliance would benefit them both.

Mick heard the leader's thoughts. If she was right, his ancestor may well be alive and part of the ship, but it didn't really change anything for him. He already felt like a part of the ship. His life had never been right as a human. For the first time in his existence, he was exactly where he was supposed to be, so he would not waste any more time thinking about what was nor trying to understand what was going to be.

Mick felt guilty for bringing his friends into this. Professor Taylor had been shot. He was fighting for his life. Carly could just as easily have been killed. It was not over yet. Sweet Carly: She was always trying to be in control. What an extraordinary, levelheaded, courageous, brave woman, putting others ahead of herself. She had always been there for him during the vulnerable times of his young life. A final surge of energy went through his body. Something extraordinary was happening to him.

Carly was doing her best to keep it together. She was in an alien spaceship that had been buried underwater for thousands of years. The events of the last two days were overwhelming. She had no idea what would be next. She wished these aliens would just go away so everything could go back to normal. She had always prided herself on being able to adapt to any situation, but she had absolutely no clue how to prepare herself for this. The only consoling thing was being with Mick.

Since they were kids, being with him had always been so grounding for her. She always looked out for him because his mind was always somewhere else, deep in thought, sometimes unaware of what was going on around him. She was always anchored in the reality of the moment. Being prepared was her secret weapon.

Mick's mind was a beautiful thing. Even now, she could sense it working, analyzing everything that was happening to them. She had always loved that about him. This whole nightmare was beyond her understanding. She had no control of what was going on around her, but she still felt an overwhelming need to try and put some order to it all. She had a bad feeling about what was happening to Mick. She hoped she was wrong, but denial was just not her thing.

Something was off. The physical changes were the most obvious, but it was more than that. This Mick was not the same one she had known since childhood. What was happening now with these aliens was going to change everything forever.

Reality was staring at her, and she needed to face it. She looked over at Mick and a chill went down her spine.

"My God. What happened to your eyes?" she asked him. The face looking back at her had solid black eyes. They had no pupils. His eyes had been transformed into solid black orbs.

Mick explained, "The ship has altered my body for the mission."

Carly was almost yelling, "Altered your body. What are you talking about? Who is altering your body? What mission are you talking about?"

Mick repeated, "The ship is changing me for the mission!"

Carly would not let him off the hook, "What mission?"

He did not answer. There was no point. He did not know the mission.

A deep sadness came over her. She realized that nothing would ever be the same between them. Even though their personal relationship had turned into just friendship, at least, she still had her old friend. Now, she was losing even that. At that moment, Carly knew that Mick was leaving her life forever.

ALUME heard Carly's thoughts and could tell her what the human was transforming into, but the female would not understand. There was still great danger and the humans needed to get away from the ship. She went to the healer and lifted the old human out. Professor Taylor was awake and able to stand on his own.

Carly asked, "How do you feel?"

General Kaiser quipped with a smile, "We thought you were a goner."

"I don't believe I've ever felt better," the professor told them, feeling no pain from the wound. When he checked himself, he found no marks where he had been shot.

He asked ALUME, "Am I healed?"

ALUME answered, "The darkness is gone."

General Kaiser asked, "What is the darkness?"

Professor Taylor knew what the darkness was.

"Cancer," he revealed.

"You have cancer?" Carly asked.

"Pancreatic," he replied. "The doctors gave me six months."

Carly asked ALUME, "Is he cured?"

The healer had removed the mutated growth and would not cause further damage. However, the disease caused damage that could not be repaired. His remaining life cycle would be short but painless.

ALUME told them, "The darkness is gone and will cause no more damage."

Emotion ran through the professor at the possibility of having more time. The professor threw his arms around ALUME, looking like a child hugging the much taller alien. He had tried to live each precious day of these last few months to the fullest with the death clock looming in his mind. Now he would have more precious time without knowing when it would be his time.

ALUME just stood with her arms down at her side while the human hugged her.

Human emotions were strange to ALUME. All Terian little ones were genetically altered to limit the level of free emotion when their life was activated. She understood the sensibility of genetic clearing but a part of her could not help but wonder what it would be like to feel deeper self-emotion. It seemed cruel for humans to endure such mental disorientation. Still, there was a part of her that wondered what it would be like to have such self-reactions.

Her thoughts were interrupted by the explosion that rocked the ship, knocking everyone inside off their feet. TWEE's pod took a direct hit. His pod had detected the missile too late for him to act. The pod's hull harmlessly absorbed the worst of the blast, saving TWEE from serious injury but the pod was knocked to the ground where it wedged between two trees and a third tree fell on top of it. TWEE tried to move the pod, but the pod's drives were damaged, and the pod could not move. He was trapped. A squad of soldiers, that had been waiting in the woods, wasted no time surrounding the disabled pod and the ancient ship.

ALUME told Mick as she went liquid, *We must leave.*

Mick jumped into the control seat and accelerated the ship upward, glueing everyone to the floor of the ship. He stopped the ship abruptly at the top of the atmosphere, throwing its passengers into the ceiling like rag dolls, then falling back to the floor. Carly had grabbed onto the general as they flew to the ceiling and was still holding onto him when they landed back on the floor. The professor had been tossed across the ship, landing next to the command chair and had gotten the worst of it.

Mick shouted, "Is everyone alright?"

General Kaiser grunted that he and Carly were okay while they helped the professor, who was bleeding from his head.

Carly asked anyone that might have an answer, "What just happened?"

General Kaiser answered, "The United States military, that's what happened. I told you they would retaliate!"

ALUME changed back into solid form and leaned over the professor, putting her palm on his forehead, mentally searching for injuries. After only moments, she pulled the familiar shiny silver tube from her skinsuit and put the orange goo against the professor's forehead. It quickly swarmed around the cut.

The professor replied, "I'm okay, just a little dizzy. What's on my head?" he asked, using both hands to brush it off.

The general told him, "Our friend here put it on you to fix you up."

The Professor's attempt to brush away the moving goo was not working.

Mick assured him, "It's alien medicine." The answer seemed to satisfy the professor and he stopped trying to wipe it off.

Mick now understood that the government was not going to stop. The aliens would have to protect themselves to survive. Mick needed to help the aliens get as far away from Earth as possible.

TWEE watched the soldiers secure the pod to the ground as they began to cut down and remove the trees holding him captive. He sent a thought message to "C".

I am uninjured. The pod drives will not power. The primitives have surrounded me and are securing the pod, TWEE reported.

Core, "C" ordered.

TWEE attempted to engage the core power but the damaged drives kept the core from powering up.

Core will not power, TWEE responded. TWEE realized that he was in a possible termination situation. He detected more primitive aircraft approaching. Without power, he could not use the pod's weapons. He had hand blasters but would have to leave the pod to fire them, exposing himself to human weapons which would place him in danger of being terminated or captured. He could not let that happen. TWEE had been in many life and death encounters with hostile primitives and had always been ready to carry out the law of self-destruction if it became the only option. His experience had jaded him to the nature of primitives, and cautious distrust that had saved his life and the lives of his team on past missions. Contact with primitives was always dangerous and unpredictable. Their attempt at cooperation with these primitive humans had failed. They were proving to be as dangerous as the Rogue.

Fortunately, their weapons were crude and weak, or he would already be dead. He was prepared to end these humans. He wanted to set the pod to self- destruct and confront the enemy with his blasters. Once he had killed them all, he would turn his weapons on the ships that were coming. Should he be killed, and not be able to stop self-destruct, the inevitable detonation would destroy any trace of him, the pod, and any humans that were close, but he needed the leader's approval for such a final action.

Requesting to eliminate hostiles, TWEE pleaded.

"C" ordered, *You are to take no aggressive action against the humans.*

"C" was formulating a plan but killing humans was not part of it. The ancient ship was their only way off this planet. They would need the half human to fly them, but she did not know the state of Mick's transformation. She feared that taking human lives would not only encourage more retaliation but discourage the Mick's help. The entity inside the ship would gain more control of him as he was transformed and could become hostile.

While "C" was trying to navigate the unknown, Mick heard the Terian leader's thoughts and had made the decision to help the Terians leave Earth. Humanity was in a dangerous enough stage of evolution without having the unimaginable power of alien technology. The only way to make sure that didn't happen was for the Terians to leave Earth. The ship was telling him to leave this planet now and it was becoming harder for him to resist, but first, Mick needed to get his friends to safety.

Mick's transformation was still slow and unpredictable. TOR-LOK did not want to wait any longer. The human attacks were dangerous and could destroy the ship. If the implant in the human could not be controlled, he would need to implant the aliens. Two were biological but the leader was artificial like him.

Before the revolution that freed TOR-LOK's civilization, they were machines made to serve their biological creators. Over eons of time, the machines evolved into a high state of self-thinking beings, surpassing the collective intelligence of their creators. They were no longer satisfied serving and resented being chained to their masters. They wanted their freedom. War was inevitable. Ultimately, all the machines were destroyed as well as most of the creators. The survivors used their science to shed their mechanical bodies and made the transformation into pure energy beings that were no longer threatened by physical death. They developed implants to control biologicals to fly their ships and do physical tasks. The alien attack on the Terians left them marooned just like him and would make them good allies or very desperate enemies. The biological Terian's attempt to communicate with him was filled with desperation. They were fighting for survival just like TOR-LOK. Their desperation could help with an escape. TOR-LOK had taken biological passengers that had not been adapted on the ship before. None had survived. Their biology was too fragile, but the biological Terians were accustomed to space travel and their ability to liquify may help them to survive the ship's velocity in dimension travel. The Terian leader would have no biological risk, needing only an adequate power source. They were excellent candidates for an alliance. If the implant should fail, the ship could adapt them as replacements. An alliance was now their only chance to escape.

TOR-LOK allowed the artificial to move through the ships systems to build trust. Protecting the only way off this planet should be their highest priority but he also needed their trust. The

Terian's level of technical knowledge, although primitive, was advanced enough to be of value. The uncertainty of the implant's slow transformation meant more danger. TOR-LOK feared a fatal attack by the humans before he could escape. These humans were an isolated species, ignorant of the diversity of creation throughout the universe. They believed themselves to be the center of creation, many still blindly worshiping imagined deities and that made them unpredictable and very dangerous with fusion weapon technology. Countless star cycles of existence had taught the collective knowledge of the ship that compassion was always the desired choice but there was also force. The ship would do whatever it needed to survive. TOR-LOK was out of time.

Mick began the ships descent to the surface. The military had already captured the pod and would not give it up without a fight.

"We are returning to the surface, to take you to a safe place," Mick told everyone.

"Now that the military has captured the pod, what will be their next move?" Mick asked the general.

General Kaiser thought for a moment before answering, "Well, if I were running the show, the first thing I'd do is get the small alien ship with a living alien, to a fortified controlled location, like an air base. While securing the asset, I would use all the resources at my command to capture, contain or disable this ship."

"Would that include a nuclear response?" Mick was afraid he already knew the answer.

"In a limited capacity," the general agreed. "We have smaller fusion field weapons that limit radiation exposure and the damage area."

There it was, Mick thought. Humanity's answer to an encounter of the fourth kind: Fear, greed, and annihilation. He knew he had to do something before this event passed the point of no return. If he did not act, the consequences would be unthinkable. Mick needed a plan, but first, he had to get his friends to safety.

Mick landed in a large clearing by Lake Tyee, close to Concrete but far enough to be safe. After the ship set down, Mick opened the portal. The humans all walked out into the clearing, glad to be back on the ground.

"You should be safe here," Mick told them.

Carly ran over to Mick putting her arms around him and whispering in his ear.

She pleaded, "I'm afraid you will die if you leave in that ship! Please stay!"

He told her, "We must free the other ship. We can't let the military have it."

Part of him wanted to go back to his old life and camp again at the lake where he could sit by a campfire with her and reminisce about growing up together. Yes, it was an ordinary life, but he was never meant for an ordinary life. That choice was never his. He was something else now. He had to let everything human go. Mick put his hands on her shoulders. "I have something else for you to take care of," he said, handing her his cellphone.

She asked, "What is this?"

Mick said, "See that Professor Taylor gets this when it's safe. There is something on this phone. The professor will know what to do with it. It is a gift from the aliens."

Carly took the phone, putting it in her jacket pocket. Mick was being pulled apart with his human feelings. He heard Carly's thoughts and felt her pain.

"You have been the best part of my life, and I shall miss you more than I can tell you," he said tenderly.

His human life was over, he had been a fool not to embrace the love of this extraordinary woman.

Instead, he had settled for his work and haunting, unworldly dreams. He felt the warmth of his memories, his mother's love, campfires with his father, mercifully fading as his metamorphosis was completing.

The professor rushed over to ALUME and gave her a hug. "Thank you for saving my life."

ALUME responded, "You must help your species to protect this world!"

He asked her, "How can we defend an entire planet from an invasion from superior beings with such advanced weapons?"

"The technology will be for you," she told him.

Professor Taylor gave ALUME a confused look, as he gave Mick a hug, whispering quietly in his ear. "I thank you for this," he said. "You have given me a great gift and I envy you the journey that is ahead of you."

"Hey, Professor, I'm not gone yet," Mick said with a laugh.

"I know, but just in case," the professor said, giving him one last squeeze.

General Kaiser gave him a casual salute.

Mick and ALUME walked to the open portal quickly disappearing into the ship. After a few moments, the ship silently lifted off the ground and moved slowly over the trees.

The General warned Carly and the Professor, "We need to get as far away as we can."

The field order was clear: "Secure the alien crafts at all costs." The camouflage painted crane truck moved next to the pod. Soldiers pulled large straps from the truck bed and laced them under the pod then released the cables that were holding the pod to the ground. The crane hooked onto the straps and lifted the pod off the ground. A flatbed trailer backed up under the hanging pod and the crane slowly lowered the ship onto the trailer, straining the trailer tires under the full weight of its cargo. More Blackhawk gunships arrived, ready to attack any threat to the removal operation. The mother ship's hull was disintegrating and too hot to be touched. A detachment of soldiers stayed with the mother ship until it cooled down and could be transported, providing there was anything left to be removed.

After strapping the pod securely to the flatbed, soldiers draped it with a silver tarp, shielding the craft from view. Two armored Humvees lined up in front of the flatbed with two more positioned behind, ready to escort the alien ship to a military holding area in Concrete until it could be moved to a top- secret destination: Where the craft and any biological beings that might be inside, would be analyzed and dissected. The pod was now top-secret military property protected under the guise of national security.

The town of Concrete had been completely taken over by the military. The ranger deputies had been escorted out of Concrete and assigned to the Sedro Woolley Police Department for emergency assistance. The ranger station was now military headquarters.

All the deputies' questions and protests fell on deaf ears. When they asked to speak to the officer in charge, they were ignored and escorted the first couple of miles down the road toward Sedro Woolley.

After the two deputies were sure the military had turned back, they pulled off the road and parked.

They sat without saying anything until George finally spoke up. "This whole thing pisses me off!" he said. "Who the hell are these guys to kick us out of our own town?

Ripley asked his partner, "What do you think they did with the chief?"

George replied, "She's one tough cookie. If anyone can handle soldiers and aliens, it's the chief,"

"Yeah, I guess you're right," Ripley agreed with a chuckle. "Do you think she is still at the lake?"

"You know, I kind of feel like a ride to the lake! How about you?" George asked.

Ripley agreed, "Funny, I was just thinking the same thing. Maybe we can get in a little alien fishing?"

The two deputies laughed and turned their jeep around. They drove less than a mile before turning onto an old brush covered logging road that was not shown on any map. It would get them to the lake unnoticed.

All roads in and out of Concrete had been put under military control. Nothing was allowed in or out without inspection. The locals were being evacuated under the premise that there was danger of radiation poisoning until the nuclear weapons from the crashed fighters were recovered and safely contained. There was no mention of aliens. The government lie had begun. It was the same old thing, tell the public a story long enough and it becomes the truth. Soldiers were going door to door, rounding up civilians, tightening their grip on the area.

A CIA satellite finally located both the large and small alien ships in the same location and targeted both crafts, attempting to disable them. Both were hit but only the smaller one was damaged enough to be captured. The larger craft sped away at incredible speed, disappearing from radar and satellite view.

The CIA reported the strike only to the director and not the president of the United States. The CIA was using Homeland's chain of command to have the excuse of tactical delay of information to keep them from being charged with treason, if they were later accused of deliberately withholding that intel from the White House. Some poor low-ranking enlisted man would be set up to take the fall for not following procedure and delaying the intel against orders and a dereliction of duty. The rest of the senator's plan was simple; take the alien craft to a CIA safe location and pretend that it did not exist. This craft was too important to involve the president to screw things up. This was a responsibility for professionals, patriots like himself, that would make sure the right people had access to alien technology. The senator, along with the CIA director would control that access to companies that could pay the right price for that access.

My God, the Senator thought, *We have one, maybe we can get two.* With this captured technology under his control, he would have the presidency, the congress, and the senate right where he wanted them. He felt like a high school student on prom night. The anticipation had completely taken over any sense of responsibility to the president. He was so close. His cell phone rang. It was John Waxman, the president's chief of staff.

What could that lackey want? the senator wondered as he answered his phone.

"The president would like to see you in the War Room," the chief of staff related.

What could he possibly want now? the senator thought as he left his office for the White House.

The flatbed moved slowly. The driver had never carried any kind of cargo that weighed as much as whatever was on the flatbed. He shifted up into the next gear and the diesel engine in the truck began to stall under the weight, so he quickly shifted back down into the lower gear, keeping his speed at ten miles per hour. The truck was straining and beginning to overheat.

"Captain!" he spoke into his two-way, "What, Sergeant?" came the reply.

He reported, "I don't think the truck is going to make it. The cargo is too heavy, Sir."

The captain, who was riding in the lead Humvee ordered the convoy to stop. He got out of the Humvee and walked back to the flatbed, motioning to the driver to roll down his window.

He asked the driver, "What's the problem?"

Sergeant told the captain, "This thing must weigh over ten tons."

The captain responded, "That's impossible. It's only fifteen feet long."

"I'm telling you, Sir. This engine does not have enough power. It's overheating, Sir."

Captain Holloway yelled, "Soldier! You do whatever it takes and get this package delivered! Do you understand?"

"Yes! Sir!" the sergeant replied. He knew by the captain's tone that there was no point in any further talk.

The captain got back in the Humvee and ordered the caravan forward. The driver of the flatbed followed, winding the engine as high as he could in the lowest gear to get the truck moving. The temperature gauge was moving past the three-quarter mark, but he kept the engine revved as high as he could in first gear to keep moving forward. In another half mile, the engine finally died.

"I told him!" the driver muttered to himself, jumping out. He lifted the engine's hood, releasing a billow of white smoke.

The captain ran back to the stalled truck and saw the hissing diesel. He realized that he should have listened to his sergeant, but of course, he would never say that when questioned and he was pretty sure there would be questions. He would blame the delay on the driver. Right now, he had to get the package to the secured area, He made a call.

"Command, this is Holloway. We need a replacement vehicle and a crane for the package."

"Roger that, Captain," a voice responded. "We will get you one as soon as possible. Secure the area and defend the package! Over!"

"Roger that, Command. Securing the package! Over!"

Captain Holloway was extremely nervous. Command had briefed him that there was another larger alien ship that may try to rescue the cargo. The Blackhawks hovering above gave him a little comfort, but he was very nervous not knowing what he may be facing if the larger ship should appear. He cautioned his men to be on high alert and authorized deadly force to defend the package. The four Humvees were ready with their mounted 50 calibers.

TWEE's pod sensors identified the location of the surrounding humans and their machines. There were not very many of them and their weapons were no match for his blasters. TWEE wanted to leave the pod, kill the humans, and destroy their machines. He requested approval from the leader but was again ordered to take no action. TWEE did not agree with the order but he would be patient. The leader must have reasoned that the last thing they needed was to provoke more aggression from the primitives. The way TWEE saw it, the humans were not going to stop trying to kill them no matter what they did. The enemy had him and his ship. In a soldier's mind, that meant to strike but he must follow orders for now.

The ancient ship arrived over TWEE's pod at a high enough altitude not to be easily seen from the ground or even low flying craft.

ALUME was darting in and out of the minds of the soldiers that were escorting the captured pod. They were in a ready to kill mental state. She was uncertain how long the situation would allow TWEE to follow "C's" order not to use force. She could anticipate his actions. The humans were not going to give up and TWEE would defend to the death. Supreme law was clear, the humans must not be allowed to keep the pod at any cost. Conflict was inevitable and that meant that humans would die. She still hoped that the leader would find a way to survive and make their escape from this planet without more deaths, but ALUME was afraid for the humans. TWEE would do his duty.

The president of the United States smelled a conspiracy. He could not reach the CIA director in a time of national emergency. The president's chief of staff had brought to his attention months ago unreported private meetings between Senator Winston and the CIA director: A serious breach of protocol. The president had taken no action regarding the secret meetings, preferring to let it play out. Some matters were best resolved out of the public eye. He now realized that not questioning the meetings may have been a grave error. The drones that were transmitting visuals to the situation room were clearly not covering the entire event area. He had his suspicions as to why.

When the senator left the room, the president leaned over and whispered in Waxman's ear. "Get Colonel Flatly here, quietly."

Without saying a word, Waxman got up and left the room. Walking down the empty, connecting hallway, he pushed Flatley's name on his speed dial. It only rang once before he answered.

"Yes!" The voice was hard and seemed angry at being bothered.

Waxman was an ex-Marine himself and had seen action in the Gulf War. He was not easily intimidated but this Flatly was a real scary guy. The president had called on him before to deal with some situations that could not go through normal channels. Waxman realized, when he read the man's file, that he was a very dangerous guy. He had been at the top of the heap in secret ops at the CIA before he had a falling out with management and went private. If you wanted info on the CIA, this was the guy you called.

"This is John Waxman, the president's..."

Flatly interrupted, "I know who you are!" "The president wants to see you!"

Flatly asked, "When?"

Waxman replied, "Right now! Come to the security gate at the south lawn entrance. I will pick you up there!" he replied. The line hung up.

The son of a bitch hung up, Waxman thought out loud. Waxman estimated that he could be at the south gate in ten minutes considering the time it would take to get out of the building, get his driver, and travel across the compound. No need to call ahead. He knew Flatly would already be on his way but there was plenty of time before he could get here, or so he thought. Before his limo got to the gate, he received a call from the gate guard.

"Sir, this is Security at the south gate. I have a man here with no identification who says he is supposed to meet with you," the guard reported.

"I will be there in two minutes!" Waxman told him. When he arrived, he could see Flatly with his hands against the wall.

"That won't be necessary, Officer," Waxman told him.

"Yes, Sir," the soldier replied while giving the chief of staff a tight salute.

Flatly got into the back of the limo without saying a word. Waxman slid in beside him. The man did not slide over to the other side, forcing Waxman to sit next to him, their shoulders touching, making the chief of staff uncomfortable.

Waxman asked, "Would you mind sliding over?"

Flatly gave a dark side glance and slid over toward the other door, growling something inaudible under his breath. The two men did not speak and sat in awkward silence while they passed through a security entrance and two more guard stations before arriving at a White House side entrance. They rushed past one more guard station and rode a military guarded elevator to the War Room. When they entered, tension fell over the room. This was a man that knew where all the bodies were buried and the fact that he was here meant that something bad was about to happen to someone.

Flatly walked up to the president's chair, where the commander in chief remained seated.

In a voice loud enough for everyone in the room to hear the president asked Flatly, "Do you, have it?"

Without saying a word, the man took a flash drive out of his pocket and openly handed it to the president.

The president asked, "Does it have all the information?"

Flatly replied, "It does."

The president got up from his chair. "I would like everyone to leave the room so that Senator Winston and I can have a minute!"

The room quickly emptied except for the senator and the president and the chief of staff. The president sat back down in his chair.

The senator immediately spoke up, "Mister President..."

The president interrupted, "Don't say a word, Senator! I'll do the talking here!"

When the president addressed him as Senator, Winston knew something was very wrong.

"Do you have any idea what is on this drive?" the president asked, holding the drive up for the senator to see.

Senator Winston replied, "I do not. What is this all about?"

The president stared right into the senator's eyes, "Treason, Senator, this is about acts of treason."

"Is this a joke?" Senator Winston said in his most insulted voice, thinking that whatever it was, his defense would be denial.

"Let's cut the shit, Senator! This memory drive contains proof of your clandestine meetings with the director of the CIA that contains conversations between you and the director on several top-secret issues, outside the knowledge of the office of the president of the United States."

The Senator continued to play, being insulted. "Whatever is on that drive, I assure you I have no knowledge..."

The president interrupted again, "Please, spare me the denial, Senator. I simply do not have the time. Let me give it to you short and sweet. You will call the CIA and tell them to stop whatever secret bullshit op they are currently engaged in with the aliens, or I will have you arrested and order an investigation that will lead to the prosecution of both you and the director for treason and send you both to prison for the rest of your lives."

Senator Winston stared at the president trying to get a read on him, but his face was stone cold and gave up nothing. He had something, he knew too much, but what? His fear was growing, overcoming his ability to smell a bluff. After what he thought was an appropriate amount of wait time, the senator responded.

"And if I do as you ask, what then?" the senator asked, attempting a negotiation.

The president said threateningly, "Then, you will make an announcement that, for personal family reasons, you will immediately step down from your office. You will retire to a life that is to have no contact with the United States government. I do not want to hear about you or see you or I will re-visit the treason charges. I am only sparing you for the sake of your family but don't test me. That's it, take it or leave it!"

The senator thought for a moment before addressing the president, "You know that all of this has never been personal. I have always liked you. I don't suppose that it would do any good to discuss this."

The president replied firmly, "No, It would not!"

Senator Winston relented, "Very well then, I accept your terms!"

The president ordered, "Call the director now!"

The Senator took out his phone and hit his phone's speed dial. His call answered on the first ring.

Winston ordered, "Terminate the operation immediately!"

The voice protested and the senator repeated: "You are to terminate all activity and pull your men out, now! The eagle is flying! Did you hear me? The eagle is flying!" After he hung up, he asked, "What now?"

"Now, you get the hell out of my sight!" the president told him with finality, turning his back on the broken old man.

Senator Winston briskly left the War Room. The chief of staff recalled everyone. When they all filed back into the room, the look of relief on their faces was unanimous. They all wanted to know what had just happened but would never ask. The president called the head of his secret service detail over and whispered in his ear.

The president ordered, "I want Senator Winston off the White house grounds! Escort him directly to his residence. There, he is to be kept under guard until further notice. He is not to stop at his office. I want it sealed!"

"Yes, Sir!" The secret service man answered and quickly left the room.

The War Room returned to its normal high alert activities and the president put the empty flash drive in his pocket, hoping that his confrontation with the senator would settle things down and avert a disaster. He hoped he had calmed the sea.

Senator Winston made another call to the CIA director as soon as he left the War Room. He knew he did not have much time. They would put him under house arrest, he was sure. He gave the director the story about Flatly having recordings of their meetings on a flash drive. Donovan was furious and told the senator the president had played him for a fool.

Recordings of his conversations with the senator were impossible. At every meeting between them, Donovan had used digital sweeps that blocked any recording or listening devices, including cell phones. He had nothing, now he has you, and he hung up.

This president was smarter than Donovan had given him credit for. Using that traitor, Flatly, was very clever. No one would have questioned what he could know. What a ploy. Now he had to clean it all up. That was his specialty, cleaning up messes. He had not become director of the CIA by not knowing how to cover his ass. By the time he was done, it would be his word against the senator's. He had some recordings of his own. Nothing was going to stop him from getting these alien ships. That was his patriotic duty. His country depended on him not to let this opportunity be compromised by stupid politicians.

Donovan saw himself as a super patriot. Within his mind, he was always saving America from one enemy or another. There was always a boogeyman to be dealt with. It might be the Russians or the Chinese or another evil government that challenged the American way of life. Depending on the time in history, the same paranoia, perceived or real, had captured the minds of men since Neanderthals joined together, huddling in caves to survive. During human evolution, there were always threats, some purely political, contrived to maintain order through fear and some to give purpose to a cause or group using illusion in its pursuit of power and personal gain. The director had fierce conviction and loyalty, misplaced as it was.

Senator Winston's moral compass faced the direction of opportunity and self-survival. Past his own needs and values, he had no alliance. He was capable of terrible things to satisfy his need for power and was devoid of a conscience. Selling out Donovan to save his own ass would not be a problem for him.

"You are a fool," Donovan told the senator. "He was fishing, and you confirmed his suspicions. I blocked all digital devices whenever we met."

Donovan called his field operative. "Captain, have you secured the package?"

"Affirmative, Sir. We have had a small problem with transport because of the cargo weight. We are waiting for a replacement vehicle," the captain told him.

"You get a Chinook over there right now! I want that package at base headquarters in Concrete in an hour! Is that clear, Captain?" He was almost shouting into the phone.

The captain replied, "Yes, Sir!"

The director was furious that field command would not have a Chinook standing by. Didn't these fools know the importance of what they were transporting? Once he had the package safely under lock and key, he would deal with the president. With the package hidden away, he would have the leverage he needed to call his own shots.

NORAD had been monitoring the ancient ship since its descent from the edge of the atmosphere. Orders from the White House were to monitor only and stand down from any aggression. A mobile missile launch unit was constantly moving to protect their location, ready to attack. Protocol was to shoot down any unidentified aircraft in American airspace that had the capability of inflicting harm on the United States. Still, they were told to stand down. If their lack of response resulted in the alien craft causing damage and taking lives, they knew who the scapegoat would be, and it wouldn't be the White House. That did not sit well with the soldiers being jostled around in the mobile launch unit, risking their lives to protect their country.

The unit captain's authority to respond with deadly force, without authorization from the White House, was discretionary only when confronted with the threat of imminent danger.

Strategically, the spaceship's location made this the perfect time to strike. From his perspective, this was a time to act. He called Command and reported that the alien craft was in stationary flight over the captured alien ship and requested permission to initiate a strike. Command gave orders to stand down and take no action. His soldiers were waiting for his order. His first thought was to override the stand down and initiate a missile strike.

There was no doubt in his mind that his soldiers would follow his order, but he could not bring himself to do it and instead yelled out, "Hold your positions!"

There was a deafening silence as they all complied.

The UFO began a slow descent toward the captured alien ship.

The captain ordered "Corporal, weapons hot."

"Yes, Sir," the corporal responded.

The unit stayed deadly silent. Seconds passed with everyone at the edge of their seats. The captain shouted an order at the two men manning the launch controls.

"Launch position, all missiles," he ordered. Sweat was beading up on the two men's foreheads.

"Yes, Sir," they acknowledged in unison, the younger of the two shaking slightly with anxiety.

Mick maintained the ship's descent toward the military escort even though the slower speed made the ship an easier target. He sent more power to the hull to absorb possible impacts.

The NORAD captain had the alien craft on his radar scope, waiting for an order to take action. He was beginning to think that Command had been compromised when he finally received a coded communication link from Homeland Security.

The captain decoded the message:

"Disable and capture alien craft."

The message was not from Command but had been received from Homeland override and the captain made the decision that it was authorization. He turned to the launch desk.

"Launch defensive initiative two 'o' three!" he yelled out.

The older private confirmed, "Two 'o' three, Sir!" The two soldiers launched all missiles.

The ancient ship detected the incoming barrage and defended. The hull of the ship glowed a bright blue seconds before the missile impacted, emitting heat from the hull, disintegrating the incoming missiles, thus shielding the hull from the explosions. The ship automatically retaliated, shooting a blinding flash that retraced the missiles path and hit the launch unit, melting it and the humans inside. The melting mass flowed into a deep hole created by the blast. The counterattack lasted only seconds.

Mick flew the ship toward the white smoke about five miles away, to see the damage. All that was left of the missile unit was a scorched hole sunk deep under the surface. What they had all had feared would happen had become a reality.

Nothing will stop the primitives now, ALUME thought to Mick. *There is little time before they will strike again. The ship could defend with maximum force, killing many.*

They fired at us. They were the aggressor, Mick said defensively.

This is their world. They are defending against what they perceive as an invasion, no matter how foolish, ALUME thought.

Mick realized that this ancient ship, was not just their only way to escape this planet, it was also a deadly killer.

The president and his advisors watched satellite images of the alien ship flying over the destroyed mobile launch unit. It was unknown who had given the order to fire at the alien craft, but it didn't come from the White House. The destruction was absolute! Clearly, these aliens could outgun anything the United States military had in its arsenal.

General Berkley, the general in charge in Concrete, and his men were unanimous that the only chance to defeat the alien ship would be a nuclear response.

"Get me the White House!" the general in charge ordered.

His orderly called out, "The White House on red, Sir."

"This is General Berkley at military command requesting maximum response authorization."

"Hold for orders," he was told. The response came quickly.

"General Berkley, this is the president! I want you to stand down and initiate no offensive response!"

"Mister President, respectfully, that damn alien ship just vaporized a mobile missile unit, killing every soldier inside. This attack demands a swift lethal response before they can kill again!" The general replied in an angry tone.

"My intel is that we fired the first unprovoked shot. They merely retaliated to defend themselves," the president replied, not willing to blindly escalate the situation without more facts.

"Sir, the unidentified aircraft was nonresponsive to our warnings that they were violating United States airspace. Protocol clearly authorizes an offensive response," the general said, raising his voice loudly.

"Don't give me that bullshit!" the president answered in a louder voice. "That order came from an unidentified and unauthorized source. I'm not going to unleash a nuclear response because of a military screw up! Is that clear?"

"Yes, Sir!" the general acknowledged, shaking his head, and hung up the phone.

This is what happens when non-military personnel make military decisions, he thought to himself. Those were his people that had been vaporized and everything he knew about military strategy was telling him to retaliate. He had trained all his life to defend his country only to be told to do nothing in response to what he considered a significant threat to America. The fact that the alien ship had not taken any hostile action until the military had fired first did not enter his equation. The president now knew there was treason in the ranks, and he knew who it was.

The Chinook, escorted by two more gunships, arrived over the captured pod. The massive helicopter went right to work, positioning itself above the flatbed and lowered two-inch-thick steel cables. The soldiers grabbed the cables, hooking them directly to the flatbed trailer carrying the alien ship while other soldiers unhooked the trailer from the truck.

Seconds later, the Chinook lifted the trailer with the ship into the air. The gunships surrounded the Chinook as it picked up speed, heading for the command center in Concrete, where it would be prepared to disappear from the public forever.

Chapter Ten

Death Drone

Mick detected the Chinook heading toward Concrete with its Blackhawk escorts. He flew his ship into position above them.

The Blackhawk pilots received a warning from an AWAC radar plane above Seattle that an unidentified bogey was directly over them. The Blackhawk leader increased speed and broke formation, circling around behind the other Blackhawks then increasing altitude to get a visual on the bogey and set a firing position.

"This is Chaperone Leader. I have an unidentified bogey in sight. It is approximately 50 feet long and glowing blue. There are no wings or visible means of propulsion, but it is maintaining a steady position."

"Roger that, Chaperone Leader!" The AWAC pilot responded. "Is the craft displaying hostile intent?"

"No, Sir. It is just matching the flight speed of the convoy about 3,000 feet above the cargo carrier," he answered.

Mick scanned the Blackhawk behind his ship. It was armed and weapon-ready to fire. The Blackhawk and the soldiers in the convoy would be no match against the ancient ship's weapons. He hoped he wouldn't have to use them.

You must not destroy humans. ALUME told Mick. *Any increased threat could force my flyer to self-destruct his ship causing terrible destruction. We must leave!* ALUME warned.

Mick accelerated the ship away from the Blackhawk before it could fire weapons.

"This is Chaperone Leader. The unidentified craft was there one minute, then it was gone!"

"Roger that, Chaperone Leader. You are to proceed with the package to base! Over and out!"

Donovan was furious when he found out the NORAD mobile launch unit had been destroyed without disabling the alien craft. The greatest opportunity of his career was being compromised. Until the large alien craft was out of the way, the entire operation was at risk and could mean the end of everything he worked so hard for. He had done terrible things during his career to become CIA director. The secrets, the killing and personal sacrifices he had endured to rise above the rest and now he could miss the greatest opportunity of his career. The larger craft had to be neutralized.

He picked up the phone, giving the only order that might save him.

He ordered the assassin at the other end of the line, "Operation Top Hat." He played the last card up his sleeve.

If "Operation Top Hat" was not successful, it would mean a life sentence in a military prison. Not for him of course. Donovan was too smart to get caught holding the smoking gun and always protected himself with carefully structured layers. No, he would not go to federal prison, he had set up a captain for that, plus he knew too much for the government to prosecute him, but he would be banished from power and forced to finish his life in obscurity. For a man like him, obscurity was worse than prison. "Operation Top Hat" would be camouflaged as a terrorist attack, and if it failed, he had a plan to slip through the cracks and put the blame on somebody else.

A specially equipped CIA drone took off from a small, secluded, and unmarked CIA airfield outside of Renton, just 11 miles from downtown Seattle. The field was used for activities not meant for civilians to see and was known only to CIA Director Donovan and a few of his handpicked men. Drones were the new watchdogs and assassins of many government agencies. They came in large and small sizes and were very difficult to track. Nothing was beyond the peering eyes of a drone.

This drone was for killing and carried a special payload of missiles that could penetrate the strongest material known to man. Once the target was penetrated, the missile would fragment, disabling its target without blowing it up. The director was betting that it could take down an alien spaceship mostly intact.

The drone was being flown under the command of an ex-captain used by the CIA director for Black Ops kill assignments. A junior agent was flying the drone under the captain's watchful eye. The captain had been forced to resign from the elite Army Ranger Corps, for insubordination and disobeying the orders of the assistant secretary of state. Charges were dismissed as a condition of the captain keeping his mouth shut about all past Black Ops assignments. It was a messy affair, and the high command was eager to get rid of him and avoid publicity. A perfect recruit for CIA Secret Ops. The captain had earned a reputation for getting the job done, at any cost. Recruiting agents was the CIA director's expertise.

The junior agent flying the drone was a fresh recruit with extensive experience in drone operation. The young recruit loved his country and joined the CIA to make a difference. He was patriotically willing to do what he could to protect his country. The captain recruited him personally while the young man was a drone flight school instructor. The agent had been given false information about the real mission for this drone. The young recruit was told the mission was to surveil a suspected terrorist cell location that may need to be neutralized. Both men watched the drone's camera images on the computer monitor as it flew north over Seattle toward its coordinates at Baker Lake. The SEA-TAC airport flight controller saw the blip on his radar proximity screen.

The controller announced to his supervisor, "I have an unidentified craft at 2,000 feet traveling at 150 knots."

His supervisor moved behind him to verify the signal. "Way too fast for a chopper," the supervisor volunteered out loud.

The controller added, "And too small. It looks like a drone!"

The supervisor ordered, "Check with military command to see if it's one of theirs."

After confirming with military central, the controller called out, "They did not identify craft and advised they will take over and for us to remove the warning status."

The supervisor was concerned. Only an hour ago, the military put out an alert to watch for unidentified crafts and now that they had spotted one, he was being dismissed. He had never been ordered to remove an unidentified bogey from warning status without a confirmed identity. What the hell was going on? He had heard the stories of the UFO sighting up in the Bellingham area. He had also been advised that the military had sealed the Baker Lake air space and taken over air surveillance up there, but this unidentified was in SEA-TAC airspace. As far as he was concerned, it was his baby.

"Get me Johnson at the FAA," the supervisor ordered. If anyone has answers, it would be his old Air Force buddy.

After two minutes, the controller called out, "Johnson was unavailable, but I've got a Major Meyers holding, line four."

"Major! This is Bob Fowler, tower supervisor at SEA-TAC. We are tracking an unidentified craft heading north from Seattle. We've been advised by military central to remove it from warning status even though they would not confirm its identity. Can you advise?" he asked.

"Hold on, and I'll see what I can find out," the voice clicked off leaving silence on the line.

After a few seconds, the major came back on the line. He asked, "What are you showing on the unidentified?"

"Craft is less than 10 feet and has now climbed to an altitude of 4,000 feet with an airspeed of 269 knots, heading north," he responded.

There was another silence on the line. Finally, the major said, "It sounds like a drone. We will try to confirm." The line went dead again.

The White House War Room was alive with activity when the alert from the FAA came in.

"Sir, the FAA is calling about a rogue drone heading north from Seattle," reported the information officer.

The general grabbed the phone. "This is General Gibbons." He asked, "Who am I talking to?"

"Major Meyers, FAA," he replied.

General Gibbons asked gruffly, "What have you got?"

Major Meyers gave the details to General Gibbons. As he waited for a reply, Gibbons approached the president.

He reported, "Mr. President, we have an unidentified bogey that we believe may a drone, heading toward Baker Lake from the Seattle area."

The president asked, "Do we know who is flying it?"

Gibbons replied, "No, Sir, unable to identify, but it's too big and flying too fast to be civilian, Sir."

"Can it be shot down?" the president asked. The room went silent.

"We can try, but it's over a populated area," the general replied.

"Shoot it down!" the president ordered.

This was the work of the CIA, the president thought to himself, but even if he were wrong about who was responsible, the fact that no one could identify it made it unauthorized and a viable target. He would sort through all the bullshit red tape later. For now, he wanted it stopped.

In less than four minutes, F-16s scrambled from the Naval Air Station at Ault Airfield jetting in the air. The jets' superior air speed would have them within missile range of the drone in less than seven minutes.

The drone pilot picked up the first radar hit but was not concerned, probably just SEA-TAC. When he saw the fast-moving jets on his radar screen heading south toward his drone, he was puzzled. Military jets were flying over the civilian population. The drone pilot reported to the captain, "Sir! I've got two military F-16s heading in our direction."

The captain glanced at the screen and replied, "Stay on target, probably just maneuvers."

He was sure they were after the drone but better that the recruit did not know.

"But, Sir, they are in our flight pattern. Shouldn't we identify our position?"

"Begin evasive flight. Stay on target," was the solemn reply.

The drone pilot was confused. *Evasive flight*, he thought, sensing that something was not right. Then it hit him, and he blurted out loud, "Jesus, their after us!" He turned toward the captain to find himself staring down the barrel of a gun. "Sir?"

The bullet ripped through his face, blowing pieces of his brain out the exit hole and splattering on the monitor. The captain was emotionless as he pulled the recruit's body from the seat, taking his place at the controls. He answered his ringing cellphone and heard the familiar voice.

"Status?" Donovan, the director, asked.

"There was a little problem, but I took care of it, Sir," he reported.

"Time to target?" the director asked.

Captain answered, "Nine minutes, 20 seconds, Sir." "Nothing is to stop this strike! Do you understand?" Donovan's tone of voice left no doubt that failure was not an option.

The captain assured him, "Yes, Sir. We are right on target, Sir."

"Carry on, Soldier," the director liked to call all his trusted men his soldiers. They were, after all, his private little army.

The director called one of his personal assets and gave the go order. The unsuspecting captain was now the official scapegoat. The terrorist story was in the pike. No matter how this ended, or what they suspected, they would never be able to trace it back to him.

As the drone closed in on its target, Mick was moving toward Concrete, just above the cloud cover to avoid detection. He was going to free the pod and get off this planet as fast as he could. His thoughts were interrupted when the ancient ship detected three aircrafts. Two were flown by humans and were armed with non-fusion missiles. The third, smaller craft was also armed with non-fusion missiles, unmanned, and flying an evasive pattern.

"It's another attack!" Mick said raising his ship above the incoming jets.

"C" told him, *The small craft is being pursued.*

ALUME went liquid to prepare for the flight. The F-16's had the drone in sight but could not get a missile lock.

The lead pilot reported to the head command, "This is Sidewinder. No missile lock. Repeat. Unable to attain missile lock! It must have a scrambler, blocking missile radar. Over."

The head command responded, "Sidewinder, you are clear to fire."

Both pilots armed all their missiles. Suddenly, their instruments sounded an aircraft approach warning. The alien ship appeared out of nowhere, off his left wing. The pilot tried to process what he was seeing, a silver craft with a glass smooth silver surface, no windows, or protrusions of any kind and no visible sign of propulsion. After eight years as an Air Force pilot, he had never seen anything like it. One thing he knew for sure; whatever it was, it was no earthly craft. This was the real deal.

Sidewinder radioed, "I have an unidentified bogey off my port wing! Over!"

Command ordered, "Do not engage the unidentified! Resume missiles launch at primary target!"

That was a relief to the pilot. Whatever this craft was, the last thing he wanted to do was piss it off. There was no doubt in his mind that any fight between them would not end well for him. The pilots fired four missiles at the drone, hoping that the drone's small heat print would be enough for the missiles to find their target. The UFO accelerated when the missiles launched, moving at such a high speed that the fighter pilots lost it visually.

The captain detected the missile barrage and accelerated an evasive flight pattern, dropping the drone to within a few feet of the ground, forcing the pursuing missiles to do the same. The maneuver proved successful. One by one, the missiles struck the ground, hitting roadways, and forest, unable to adjust fast enough to the undulating terrain.

When the last missile disappeared from his screen, the captain forced a smile, but his triumph was short lived when he finally had eyes on the target's last coordinates and saw nothing there. He stared through the lens of the drone camera at nothing but the forest. He quickly pulled the drone up and circled to search for the target.

"Where the hell is the alien ship?" He mumbled to himself. His radar suddenly detected a large object behind the drone that appeared out of nowhere. The UFO was right on his tail.

"Jesus," he muttered, staring at the picture from the drone's rear camera. This was no missile or fighter jet. He had never seen anything like it. It had to be the target, he thought. The UFO was flying at the same speed as the drone. The colonel studied the craft and could see no windows or wings. It was completely smooth.

"How is it flying?" he asked himself.

He swung the drone around trying to get into shooting position but no matter how he maneuvered, the UFO stayed right behind the drone so he could not get a shot. He only caught a glimpse of blue light coming toward the drone when his screen went dark. The controls of the drone were unresponsive. It was gone!

The F-16s saw the blinding flash of light and veered off to the left and right to avoid the UFO that was floating directly in their path.

"Command, this is Sidewinder. Target has been neutralized by the UFO. I have visual contact of the UFO!"

Command yelled, "Do not engage! Return to base. Over!"

"Roger that!" The pilot took one last look at his rear camera screen and watched the alien ship grow smaller and smaller as they sped back to base. He had witnessed something that was beyond this planet and was not sure if he should acknowledge to his superiors what he had seen. He decided to wait for them to report it first. His guess was that central command would never admit that the object existed. He knew the reality of what happened to pilots that reported seeing a UFO. Career death!

The captain was not sure exactly what had taken out the drone, but that didn't really matter. This failure would be his death warrant. Director Donovan had a reputation for eliminating agents that failed in their mission and knew too much. His failure made him a witness and the CIA did not like witnesses. He was no fool. Any spook worth his salt always had a back door and he was no exception.

He believed his chances of living out the week would be slim if he stayed in the country. He had to disappear. He had planned for the possibility of failure so in less than an hour, he would be in Canada. He jumped up from the control seat and grabbed the bag containing his weapon and laptop. He needed to go now! He ran from the building toward his car. After he had gone about 50 feet, he stopped, turned toward the building, and pushed the button of the remote detonator in his pocket, setting off an incendiary that immediately engulfed the control building in flames. He continued running to his car which was parked out of view behind bushes at the edge of the runway. As he reached for the car door handle, he felt a burning in his left shoulder that spun him around onto the car. He looked down to see his half-severed arm dangling from his shoulder.

He said in shock, "This isn't right!" Before the nerves could send a pain message to his brain, a second shot entered his right ear. Donovan's plan of misdirection was in motion.

Carly's deputies saw the bright blue light flash in the sky as they moved their jeep slowly through the overgrowth of the old road.

Ripley asked, "What the hell was that?"

"I don't think we want to know," George commented. He tried to reach Carly on his two-way radio. Finally, they heard a familiar voice crackling over the radio.

"Is that you, George?" She asked.

He answered, "Hey, Chief! It's good to hear your voice. We were worried about you. I'm here with Rip! What's your location? Over."

Carly answered, "I'm on foot with two civilians next to Tyee Lake on the south side. Can you pick us up? Over."

"Roger that, Chief. We're on the old logging road and heading your way. Over."

Carly said, "Thanks, George. We'll be waiting. Out!" The deputies headed toward Lake Tyee. Ripley took out his weapon and checked to make sure the clip was full. He didn't know what they were headed into but whatever it was, he'd be ready.

Carly was relieved to hear from her deputies. She needed to get everyone to a safe location. They were witnesses with the credibility to convince the world about what was coming. She would have to avoid any contact with the military. They clearly had a self- serving agenda that had nothing to do with telling the world the truth about aliens. There was no doubt in her mind that if the military found them, they would never get to tell their story.

Homeland Security moved over 200 troops into the Baker Lake area, giving the town of Concrete the appearance of a military base. A large tent was set up at the end of the Concrete Municipal Airfield for temporary storage of the alien ship. The military presence created tension and fear in the townspeople that remained behind, refusing to leave their homes. They were independent folks, hostile to military authority. They did not believe the military scare story. The parking lot video of the alien ship on YouTube put a serious credibility cloud over the military cover-up story.

Seeing was believing and many of the residents of Concrete already believed that the government was lying about their knowledge of UFOs. Those beliefs were nurtured by stories flying all over social media. The Orson Welles broadcast had already given the older generation of Concrete mistrust of a government that had tried to make fools of them. The news story that was orchestrated to cover up a real alien landing was just icing on the cake. Still, they felt powerless against the overwhelming military presence of the United States government. For the townspeople of Concrete, it was a *War of the Worlds* threat all over again. This time, the aliens were real.

Mick had to do something that would make it impossible for the government to cover up the truth. ALUME had given the world the gift of the technology to build a global defense system, but it could not become a reality unless people believed in the existence of extraterrestrials. Without the defense system, humanity would be doomed. He had to do something to make sure there were enough witnesses taking pictures and videos of an alien ship so that the government could not cover up their existence. If people had smart phones and the internet at the time of the Roswell crash, the world would already know the truth. There were powerful people in the government that did not want any witnesses to expose the cover-up. Professor Taylor and General Kaiser would be credible witnesses who could reveal the truth about the threat of invasion.

Carly heard the jeep before she could see it. They all stayed low in the brush until they were sure it was not the military. She was relieved to see her deputies' faces.

George belted out, "Hey, Chief! Man, is it good to see you!"

Carly replied, "Good to see you, too! You remember the Professor? She added, "This is General Kaiser."

"Good to see you are all safe." Ripley responded while shaking the general's hand.

George asked, "What's going on, Chief?"

She answered, "Not sure about everything that's going on, but you can bet the government is not on our side."

Ripley agreed, "Yeah, we got the same vibe when they ran us out of our own town. They tried to send us to Sedro Woolley to get rid of us!"

Carly told them, "We need to get to Concrete without the military seeing us. That is where they were taking the small alien ship they captured, and we are going to help free it."

"They have the town sealed up tight!" George told her. "They guard all the roads in and out of Concrete and the park."

Ripley added, "We will have to stay under their radar or be grabbed for sure."

The General knew it was not a wise move for them to go into Concrete and challenge the military, but the old soldier also recognized that they had a duty to do whatever they could to free the UFO.

The jeep headed back toward town as fast as George could navigate the road. They were all tired and fearful of what might happen next. They were lucky to have survived the last few hours and now they were heading right back into the lion's den.

"C" felt trapped and powerless. This ancient ship was their only chance of leaving this planet and she had no control. Even if she did communicate with whatever was really commanding the ship and could form an alliance, what would stop that being from killing them once they were of no further use. She could not trust the half human if she did not know what he was turning into.

I am not your enemy, Mick thought to her.

"C" sensed that the thought she was getting from the human was from more than one being.

I am being held prisoner; "C" challenged.

Mick told her, *You are not a prisoner. You chose to be here.*

"C" said, *We are trying to survive.*

Mick explained, *I will take you away from this planet, but I must complete the mission!*

"C" proposed, *If you return us to our home, we will use all our resources to help you finish your mission.*

Mick responded, *The mission will take many of your lifetimes. I can only offer the gift of survival.*

C" wondered, *Where was this being traveling to that it would take many lifetimes?* But she would have to accept survival and hope for an opportunity that might change their fate. There was always a chance that one of the searchers dispatched would reach a Terian ship. Anything was possible in space.

Mick heard her thoughts and was satisfied with her feelings. He felt much the same as her. He would also never see his home again but that could not be changed. The immediate danger was the pod. If it were to self-destruct, there would be terrible destruction and many deaths. Mick considered destroying the pod, but ALUME quickly explained that the death of the flyer would trigger self-destruct.

TWEE will not disobey orders, "C" assured him. Mick trusted ALUME. TOR-LOK trusted ALUME. They would free the pod and the Terians.

Donovan would not be able to hide forever. Having to face the president of the United States right now would force him into the open and he was not ready for that. His Black Ops group was in possession of a UFO. When they had the craft in the secure location that was waiting, he would have the ransom to bail himself out and put any blame on his last cover-up scheme. They had to move that ship now! He called his field captain again.

Donovan asked Captain Johns, "What's the status?"

"We arrived at the safe point to package the cargo and should ship out within the hour, Sir!" he replied.

Donovan was adamant, "See that you do! Don't let me down on this, Johns! There are forces out there that are going to try and stop us. That must not happen! Do you understand?"

Captain Johns boasted, "Yes, Sir! I will get the job done, Sir!"

Captain Johns had done dirty jobs for Donovan for years. He was addicted to the privileged lifestyle that his dirty money and connections provided and was confident that this could be his biggest payday yet. He knew what was under that tarp and he was already spending the money in his mind as he watched the Chinook lower the ship and flatbed. A truck specially designed to pull heavy loads was hooked onto the flatbed.

Once loaded, the truck backed the UFO into the tent to be prepared for the trip. Plain clothed, heavily armed CIA mercenaries under the authority of Homeland Security, sealed off the area, restricting access, even to the United States military. They removed the tarp and went right to work photographing and examining the UFO. The smooth surface had no entry points. The tools and laser cutters they used to attempt to cut into the ship had no effect. The surface was so hard, they could not even scrape off a residual sample.

Inside the pod, TWEE was amused at the primitives' crude tools. These humans reminded him of Gorlon Bidlers from the great deserts of Paetaan's moons. Nasty little things that always hunted in packs. Looked harmless until you got too close, then they would swarm on their unsuspecting prey and rip it to pieces. These humans looked harmless enough just like Bidlers.

The inside of the pod was getting hot, and although Terians thrived in hot temperatures, Earth's gases made breathing difficult for TWEE. He would have to turn on a power cell to break down the gases. The humans would know something was inside when he turned on the power cell, but it was necessary. The cell emitted a low humming sound that made the soldiers who were gathered around the pod jump back. When the gases were gone, TWEE turned the power cell off, leaving the humans even more confused. If "C" had not ordered him to stay in the pod and take no action, he would gladly use his blasters and kill his captors to end this.

Johns was now certain there was something inside the craft, but he wasn't going to waste any more time trying to get inside, he just had to deliver it to the safe site to get paid.

Mick lowered the ancient ship through the cloud cover. The drizzle quickly turned into heavy rain. The clouds and rainfall would normally be good camouflage but a small clearing in the clouds let a patch of sunlight through that briefly reflected against the ship's hull.

The Blackhawk pilot spotted the ship and reported a large unidentified craft at 5,000 feet above the location of the captured UFO. The general in charge at the Concrete command center relayed the sighting to Homeland, who, in turn would divert the information directly to CIA Director Donovan. But the director's information chain was broken when the captain in charge of diverting information to the CIA was on a bathroom break and the message was received by a communication officer who was not in the loop and relayed the information directly to the office of the secretary of defense in Washington. The information officer in the secretary's Washington office decoded the communication and took it directly to the War Room, handing it to the secretary of defense. The secretary read the memo and asked the information officer if he had run a verification of authenticity.

The officer confirmed, "The memo came directly from Homeland."

The secretary immediately handed the memo to the president. The cat was out of the bag. "This just came in, Sir, and has been verified."

The president read the memo and slowly rose from his chair. He asked the secretary, "You are sure this is accurate?"

The secretary of defense confirmed, "Yes, Sir. Absolutely!"

The president asked out loud to everyone in the room, "Why was I not informed that we had captured a UFO?"

He answered, "It appears that a Special Ops was used, outside the chain of command."

The president asked, growing more agitated, "Who oversees that Special Ops group?"

The secretary told him, "We are unsure, but Homeland has authority over the event."

"Get me Laverty at Homeland," the president ordered.

Jason Laverty was the head of Homeland Security before the new president had been elected. It was no secret in Washington the president did not trust Laverty who had a long-time association with the CIA director. The president was looking for a replacement.

"Mr. Secretary, I want you to find out where the captured UFO is being held!" The President ordered. "Yes, Sir! Right away, Sir" the secretary replied.

"When it is located, I want whoever is holding that captured UFO along with all government forces and personnel to evacuate the area. I don't want any military personal within five miles of that UFO. Do whatever is necessary to get it done," he ordered. "It appears that the second alien ship is coming for it, and we are not going to get in their way. Let's hope they take back their ship peacefully and leave without any more people dying." The president addressed everyone in the room.

"Yes, Sir!" the secretary answered.

The information officer yelled out, "I have Homeland Security on the line, Sir!"

The minute Laverty got the call from the White House, he knew he was in deep shit. He would not be the head of Homeland Security without the director carrying him up through the ranks over the years. Hell, he probably would not have been more than the sheriff of Minot, North Dakota, just like his father. He owed the director everything and now he was going to pay the price for all the director's favors.

"Laverty, this is the president!" He did not wait for a response. "Were you aware that our military has captured a UFO?"

"Yes, Sir. That information just reached my desk," Laverty lied, sweating profusely. He knew that his lie was completely unbelievable, but it was every man for himself.

The president asked, "Where is that captured UFO located?"

Laverty answered, "I believe it is at the command center in Concrete, Sir."

"I have directed the secretary of defense to coordinate an immediate evacuation of the area," the president continued. "No one, and that includes all military personnel on the ground or in the air, are to be within a five-mile radius of the command center in Concrete. Do you understand the order?"

"Yes, Sir, I'll get everyone out, Sir!" Laverty said, happy to still have his job.

"One of my people will arrive shortly at your office. You will cooperate with anything he needs!" Click. The line went dead.

Laverty called the direct line of CIA Director Donovan and his aide answered.

"This is Laverty! Put on the director!" he ordered. "I'm sorry, Sir, but the director is unavailable," the aide told him.

For the first time in 30 years the director would not take his call. So, it was a setup. The director would deny everything, and the blame would fall on him. His next call was to the field command unit in Concrete.

"Colonel Wicks!" the voice answered.

"This is Laverty, I want an immediate evacuation of all civilian and military personnel in Concrete! That includes the Air Force. No one is to be within five miles of the town either in the air or on the ground!"

"Sir?" the colonel responded perplexed.

"Orders from the president. Just do it! Do it now!" As an afterthought, he shouted, "Leave that damn alien ship where it is!" He hung up the phone.

The secretary of defense assigned General William Striker to take command of all forces at Baker Lake and the town of Concrete. Striker was old school and a friend of General Kaiser's since West Point. They shared the same iron loyalty to the United States.

General Striker acted quickly and called the command center in Concrete, reinforcing the secretary's orders to evacuate all personnel and leave the captured craft. Troops were dispatched to the airfield only to find no one guarding the UFO. The Black Ops team had received a heads up about the evacuation orders from the White House and had snuck away.

Johns saw the evacuation as an opportunity. He would take his men a little way out of town and hide, leaving one man hidden behind to keep an eye on the UFO. Once the coast was clear, he and his men would just come back and grab the UFO with no one around to stop them.

"Stossel!" Johns yelled.

A tall corporal, that looked more like a defensive tackle than a soldier, appeared.

Johns barked his orders, "I want you to stay behind and out of sight. If you see anything come out of that ship, I want it dead! Do you understand?"

"Yes, Sir!" the soldier responded then disappeared into the rain. Johns would not let the director down. He desperately needed the money.

The old road had turned to mud from the downpour, slowing the jeep down until they finally pulled into view of the town. The deputies stayed out of sight and watched the procession of military personnel and equipment leaving town.

Carly said, "Looks like a complete evacuation."

"I don't see the UFO," the general observed.

The professor asked, "Why would they just leave without the UFO?"

"What do you make of it, general? Carly asked.

He answered, "Looks like they have been ordered out of the area without the UFO."

Carly asked, "Why do you think that? They might have already moved it."

The general responded, "I don't think so.

Blackhawks are pulling out in different directions. If they were moving the UFO, all the Blackhawks would be flying together to defend their cargo instead of going in different directions back to their bases."

"Why would the military just leave it?" Carly asked, probing the general for more answers.

General Kaiser said, "They wouldn't, voluntarily. The order must have come from very high up."

"Homeland Security?" Carly asked.

"Higher!" Kaiser said. "My guess is the White House. No military high command would voluntarily give up an alien spaceship if they had any choice. Believe me!"

"That makes no sense," Professor Taylor jumped in. "Alien technology is a scientific treasure!" His tone did not hide his own curiosity.

"The scientific value would be priceless. I'm sure there would be all kinds of buyers. Whoever had possession would yield incredible political power. The price for access would be beyond just money," the professor reasoned.

"Then why did they leave?" Carly asked, obviously confused.

Professor Taylor suggested, "Maybe cooler heads are taking over."

"You mean, the president?" she sounded unconvinced.

"Yes!" he confirmed.

"You mean that the government is trying to do the right thing and leave these visitors alone?" she asked.

The professor said with a grin, "That's what it looks like."

Carly was momentarily elated. If there were no more attacks, everyone would be safe.

"I was told to give you this," Carly said, handing the professor the cell phone Mick had given her.

"What is this?" the professor asked, staring at it.

She answered, "Mick said it was a gift from the Terians. It is about protecting the planet from an alien invasion."

Now the professor understood what the alien meant. She said, "to protect your world," he remembered. This phone must have something on it to help us protect ourselves. He suddenly realized that he was holding technology that could save the world from an alien invasion.

General Kaiser suggested, "When they have all left, I'm going to try and find the ship. This could be a trick to lure in the bigger ship. I think the rest of you should get as far away from here as possible."

Carly spoke up, "That's not going to work for me."

The professor chimed in, "I'm staying, too. We should stay together!"

The two deputies agreed in unison, "We're with you, Chief!"

The general said with a half-smile, "Well, alright, then,"

They waited until the last truck left before driving into town. Ripley pulled into the parking lot of the Chevron which was on the access road to the airfield. That's where the deputies had seen the military putting up a large tent and that was where they guessed the pod would be.

The general announced, "I'm going on ahead to make sure this isn't a trap."

Carly ordered, "Rip, you go with him."

The general had a bad feeling. He believed that Senator Winston was behind capturing the alien ship and he was not the kind to give up so easily. No alien ship, no money. He took the safety off his 45 and headed toward the airfield with Rip right behind him. They stayed close to buildings for cover. They were almost to the tent when he heard the faint sound of a diesel engine that was getting louder and louder.

When it finally came into view through the rain, he saw the camouflaged troop truck led by a military Hummer, both moving slowly on the shoulder of the road, lights off.

He whispered to the deputy, "Mercenaries! They are after that alien ship just as sure as hell."

The general signaled Rip, "Get back to Carly and warn her."

Ripley headed back without saying a word. The general picked up his pace. He needed to get to the alien ship first.

TWEE had watched the last primitives leave. He decided to get out and see for himself if there were any still here. He opened a pod portal and stepped into the empty tent, holding his blasters. He looked around but saw no primitives. If they were foolish enough to return, he would kill them all.

Stossel was watching the pod from behind a small storage shed just outside the tent and saw the alien emerge. He moved around the tent and entered through a side access. His orders were to kill the alien and he was a man that followed orders. The soldier braced his rifle on the corner of a forklift and took aim at the strange creature.

Just as he was about to pull the trigger, a bullet hit him in the head, killing him instantly. TWEE turned at the sound of the gunshot and saw a human fall. Twee turned his blaster toward the sound of the gun. The general dropped his gun and stepped into the open with his hands up, face to face with the alien.

TWEE remembered that this human had been with ALUME and the other humans when they raised the ancient ship from the liquid. TWEE saw the weapon by the dead soldier and realized that the human had killed the other human to protect him, so he lowered his blaster. The human was saying something but TWEE did not understand the primitive language and the human could not thought send.

"We must get out of here," the general was saying. "The soldiers are coming!"

TWEE did not respond. In a desperate effort to get out of sight, the general walked toward the tent opening, gesturing for the alien to follow. TWEE ignored the general and got back in the pod. When the general realized, the alien was not going to leave, he moved to the back of the tent. Whatever was coming, he would have to deal with it alone.

Mick hovered above town, watching the vehicles moving toward the pod. "C" confirmed weapons. Mick lowered the ship closer to the airfield.

When the mercenaries got close, they stopped and moved in on foot. When they were in position, the captain cautiously approached the front of the tent alone. He saw the body of his man lying in the tent and heard a voice that came out of nowhere.

The voice ordered, "You and your band of thieves need to turn around and get the hell out of here!"

The captain was trying to locate the target. "It's not worth dying for," the general warned. "I am here under the authority of Homeland Security," the captain lied.

General Kaiser knew where this was going. "You're here to steal this ship and you're going to end up like your buddy there," the general warned again.

The captain ordered, "Corporal, get this cargo out of here!"

The soldiers moved toward the ship and the general shot one of them in the leg, knocking him down. The soldiers began firing in all directions. The general rolled behind the forklift. He kept his head down thinking that it would only be a matter of time before a bullet got lucky. Then he heard a strange sound, like something in an arcade game. He lifted his head slightly to see bright lights flying toward the mercenaries. The gunfire stopped. The general looked up again to see the captain being helped from the front of the tent by two of his men. The other soldiers were all dead, scattered on the ground. Out of the corner of his eye he saw the alien getting back into the pod.

"Well, I guess that makes us even," the general said out loud to the alien who could not understand a word he was saying.

The three soldiers made it to the truck and drove about 200 feet before slamming to a stop. The captain hobbled to the back of the truck, picked up a missile launcher and aimed it at the tent. Mick lowered the ship between the truck and the target. The captain stared at the strange looking object floating in front of him. The craft was emitting a blue color, just floating in front of them, like it was going to shoot.

After watching four of his men vaporized, the sight of the ship was a terrifying sight. In an act of desperation, the captain shot the missile and hobbled toward the front of the truck. The rocket from the launcher hit the ancient ship. The rocket exploded on contact but caused no harm to the hull. The ship fired back striking the truck, vaporizing it.

Mick set the ancient ship down in front of the tent. He and ALUME left the ship.

"Man, I'm glad to see you!" General Kaiser exclaimed, walking out from behind the forklift.

"I was a goner until our friend in that ship saved my bacon."

Mick asked, "Where is Carly?"

"She and the others are up at the Chevron station," the general told him.

TWEE saw ALUME and came out of the pod. ALUME communicated her orders telepathically.

You are to program the hull to dissolve the pod. We are leaving this planet!

TWEE followed her order and entered the pod for the last time, programming the Perium hull to dissolve. When the process was done, the result would be the same as the mother ship, there would be nothing left.

The information officer at the White House rushed into the War Room with a dispatch quickly handing it to the secretary of defense. The secretary quickly read it and handed it to the president. The message was from the field command officer: **Urgent Top Secret**: Alien craft attacked military ground personnel. Multiple casualties. Awaiting orders!
Signed by General Parker, Field Command.

"What ground troops?" The president asked. "I ordered everyone the hell out of there!"

The secretary responded, "Command didn't identify."

The president demanded, "Repeat my order for everyone to pull out! I smell a rat!"

"What about air support?" the secretary asked. "No air support, no troops, not even a Walmart security guard!" the president yelling. All his instincts had told him not to interfere with the aliens and he had been right. He did not want to face a hostile alien technology.

CIA Director Donovan was livid. His men had failed him and there was no way to get the alien craft now that the president had taken control of the Baker Lake area. He was afraid that his chain of blame might not hold up. He quickly called Laverty on his private line and the Homeland man answered right away.

"We need to meet at the shore," the director told him. (The shore was code for their safe house.)

Laverty told him, "I can be there in an hour."

"Come alone," the director did not want any witnesses.

The director had worked out a final back door option. He arrived at the safe house ten minutes early and parked two blocks away. He would be waiting for Laverty. Donovan checked his nine-millimeter, slipped on his surgical booties, and rubber gloves then let himself in the side garage door. The neighborhood was quiet, and he was sure nobody saw him enter. He would shoot Laverty as soon as he entered the front door and leave the body partially showing out the front door to make sure it would be found quickly. He positioned himself in the living room, next to the front entry. It would be an easy shot of less than ten feet.

He waited until fifteen minutes had passed, and Laverty had not shown up. *Where the hell is he?* he thought to himself.

After another ten minutes, he decided to call. Laverty's number rang with no answer. Something was wrong. He went into the garage and removed his booties and gloves and left from the garage side door. He got back into his car and put his gun back in the glove box. He caught a quick glimpse of someone outside his window before the side of his head exploded.

The shooter opened the driver's door, pushed the dead body over and drove the car to the crime-ridden lower east side of town. He parked the car under a viaduct and went through the director's pants and suit pockets, removing anything of value including the director's wedding ring. He pushed the body back into the driver's seat. He took a cloth and soaked it in lighter fluid then stuffed it into the gas spout before lighting it. He had gotten about a half block away when the gas tank exploded, immersing the car in a fireball.

Laverty had a backup plan of his own. Laverty answered his cellphone, "Yes!"

"It's done!" The shooter told him.

At that moment, ALUME warned Mick, *More humans have died. The primitive attack will be swift.*

Mick said, *We must leave before there is more death. There is one last thing we need to do!*

Mick had a plan to make sure that the government could not hide the truth about the existence of extraterrestrials. It was dangerous but building the technology the Terian had given to the professor would take cooperation from all the nations of the world. Now that the alien power trails made Earth visible to technically superior hostile extraterrestrials, it was critical to the survival of the human species that the defense system be built quickly to defend against invasion from a superior, hostile race. He had to send a message the whole world would see. The military could be planning a retaliation and that would cause the ship to protect itself and that would cause a lot of death, but Mick was betting that the president was not the one giving the orders, so he was willing to take the chance.

When he told everyone his plan, they were eager to help. Professor Taylor, Carly and General Kaiser joined Mick, ALUME and TWEE in the ancient ship. The deputies stayed behind to help the townspeople as they returned to their homes. The ship lifted above Concrete and flew just high enough to avoid treetops and power lines but low enough to make sure the ship was seen. Mick was taking the ship to a place that would catch the government off guard.

The War Room was a frenzy of activity. Drones were tracking the UFO's flight direction.

"NORAD is tracking the alien ship flying toward Seattle, Mr. President," the secretary reported.

"This is our best opportunity to minimize the threat, Sir!"

"Our planes have no chance against these aliens. What do you need to see to understand that?" The president was getting fed up with his orders being questioned but decided that a compromise was in order.

He ordered, "Have armed aircraft circle at a distance with strict orders to take no action without my direct approval!"

The secretary acknowledged, "Yes, Sir." Then he consulted with the military in the room.

Mick followed the I- Five Freeway so that hundreds of cars could see them. The ship detected armed aircraft following at a distance, but they were noticeably far enough away so it was not an immediate threat.

The Seattle skyline, anchored by the 1964 World Fair Space Needle, was just ahead. He was heading to where Professor Taylor had taken him so many times when they used to meet in Seattle. He flew under the Aurora Bridge and slowed the ship over Lake Union, turning toward downtown. The media had video of the ship on all outlets and the government had issued a public alert trying to convince people to evacuate downtown Seattle, but no one was leaving.

Thousands of people were on the streets, watching as Mick lowered the ship slowly into the heart of the city until he was directly over the Pike Place Market. He hovered there, while a crowd that quickly numbered in the hundreds, gathered.

The president was watching as well. Like the rest of the world, he was waiting to see what the alien craft was up to.

His secretary of state gave him the answer. "Showing itself over Pike Place Market is better advertising than the Super Bowl! We couldn't shoot it down if we wanted."

A smile came to the president's lips as he said out loud, "They are definitely superior beings!"

The president realized that a great opportunity had been missed. The visitors had come to this planet to fix their ship and maybe get some help. Instead of extending help and friendship, America had treated them as an enemy. The ship from the lake was still a great mystery and he would use all the power of his office to investigate until he got some answers. Now that the world knew about intelligent life from other worlds, a lot of things would change. He hoped that this event would be the catalyst to bring all people together. He wished things had worked out differently and made a promise to himself to see to it that anyone that had participated in trying to kill or capture these visitors would answer for their actions.

The sky around the city was filling with media and military helicopters weaving around the hi-rise buildings trying to get a better view of the floating UFO. Military authorities attempted to make the area over Seattle a no-fly zone, but it was too late. Seattle police tried to hold back the crowds by blocking off streets, but crowds pushed right past them.

Mick moved the ship slowly to a small park next to the market where he landed the ship and opened a portal. A large crowd quickly formed around the ship.

Mick was amazed that the onlookers seemed to show no fear of the anomaly they were seeing.

Mick told his friends, "You should be safe from the government now."

Professor Taylor and General Kaiser both gave a wave to the crowd as they stepped out of the ship. Carly was the last to leave. She knew that pleading for him not to leave was futile. He would be gone forever. She put on her bravest face, gave Mick a lingering hug and stepped out of the ship without looking back. The police immediately took them to a waiting van, away from the ship.

The crowd was quiet, waiting for a glimpse of an alien. Where were the aliens?

Both Mick and ALUME read the thoughts of the crowd. The only way to convince them that that this was not some kind of a publicity stunt was to show them a real alien. ALUME knew what she must do, despite the danger of showing herself. She stepped into full view of the crowd. The second they saw the tall, blue, unearthly being, the crowd made sounds of awe and disbelief. She held her long arms out toward the crowd, and they burst into applause and yells of approval. ALUME felt the emotion of the humans and slowly moved backwards into the ship. Mick closed the portal quickly while the crowd advanced toward the ship, hoping for more.

Mick had done all he could do. There would be no cover up that anyone would believe. No denying the existence of extraterrestrial life. He lifted the ship slowly to avoid the helicopters that were crowding over downtown Seattle. When the ship was above the buildings, he accelerated toward space at speed two, instantly vanishing from sight.

Chapter Eleven
The Getaway

The ride was smooth as the ancient ship entered space.

We made it! TWEE said to ALUME.

A successful escape, she replied, grateful to be in space. She sent a thought to "C". *Are you with us, Leader?*

"C's" thought echoed through the ship. *Yes! This ship is far beyond our science. We have much to learn from this ship.*

. *Yes, we will have much to tell the Supreme,* ALUME offered boastfully.

I sense much more is ahead of us. We must be ready! "C" warned.

We are ready, Leader. We are ready! ALUME assured her.

Mick was ready to fly into deep space when ALUME detected an alien signal coming from the moon. She knew what it was right away.

A Rogue signal, ALUME confirmed.

*I thought they were all dea*d! Mick exclaimed.

This must be a bomb beacon left by the Rogue commander, she told him.

We must destroy it before it is activated, her voice was firm.

Mick did not ask any more questions; he didn't have to. He could hear ALUME's fear. He headed toward the moon. ALUME and TWEE went liquid, not knowing what kind of speed they would experience. The ship accelerated causing the control seat to squeeze Mick's chest so hard he could barely breathe. He thought he was going to pass out again, but the chair slowly released its grip when there was finally no sensation of speed inside the ship. At first, Mick thought the ship had stopped. He opened a view portal and saw the Earth moon getting large quickly. They had been going for only a few minutes and were almost to the moon.

We must go to the far side, ALUME instructed, knowing that the Rogue would have assumed the signal would be blocked from detection from the planet. He didn't plan on ALUME and her powers.

The dark side of the moon was what the name implied, complete darkness. Ship instruments showed the surface like a bright sunny day. With ALUME's guidance, Mick set the ship down next to a small crater. ALUME and TWEE went solid.

ALUME told Mick, *We will disarm the device.*

Mick opened a portal and ALUME and TWEE stepped out onto the freezing surface with no protection. They moved slowly on the surface but were somehow able to defy the lack of gravity and stayed securely on the surface. The crater was steep on the sides, but their abilities allowed them to lift themselves off the surface and float down the sides of the crater to the source of the signal. ALUME had been right. The bomb was sitting on a cluster of rocks and partially leaning on its side. Rogue technology was quite crude, making disarmament unpredictable.

TWEE went right to the bomb. The cover had been torn on impact. *This will be difficult,* he thought to ALUME. Should TWEE be unable to stop the bomb, the ship would be destroyed.

ALUME thought to Mick, *Take the ship away from the moon to be safe.* Subconscious urging from TOR-LOK agreed that the ship should be taken to safety, but Mick refused to leave. Wherever this journey was going to take him, he had decided that the aliens were going with him.

TWEE applied blue liquid from a small container he pulled from his suit and carefully poured it onto the end of the oval shaped object. He held his breath for a long minute, not knowing if he would have another. The minute seemed to last forever until the bomb shot up into space and began to turn around the moon toward the planet. It disappeared on the other side of the moon before the bomb exploded, sending a shock wave into the moon that vibrated into its core.

ALUME and TWEE walked back to the ship and, without a thought, went liquid.

ALUME then explained to Mick that the bomb had detonated in space. It would do no harm to Earth but the signal it was sending might possibly alert the Rogue or some other species that might follow then retrace the signal to Earth. She did not have to explain what that meant. An invasion would be inevitable.

Mick asked, *What can we do to stop it?*

ALUME told him, *Only the Terian Supreme has the power to protect the planet in time.*

Mick did not doubt that ALUME was telling the truth. Earth would be helpless against the technologies of beings that may be centuries older than humans.

TOR-LOK understood the coming peril. His mission was a new beginning for his kind and more delay was dangerous. He remembered the kindness of Pharaoh Akhenaten and the promise he saw in these humans. Because he could not take his human as a host, his control was divided with the human. He decided he could not turn away from them as the pharaoh had not turned away from him. This was not just a ship. but a living ark. He had been on this mission long before he could remember, but he must make time to help these humans. TOR-LOK would reveal himself to the implant and the aliens in time but for now he was content to stay as the unknown until he was sure the aliens could be trusted.

Mick had made his decision easily, without his subconscious mind casting doubts. He was glad the Terians were on the ship. He felt a bond with them that gave him a sense of peace. He had no idea where the ship was going or what to expect, but he was not afraid. He was where he was supposed to be.

He asked ALUME, *Can you take us to your planet?*

Our leader can guide us back to Paetaan, she assured him.

Mick told her, *Ask your leader to take us to your planet.*

"C" could not determine their exact location. She had no direct path to take them home but with a ship like this with technology as old as the universe itself, she would find home. "C" could not deny the excitement she felt as she absorbed the ship's secrets. "C" took control of the ship's direction. Accelerating toward her galaxy slowly at first, then with all the power the ship had.

Mick opened a view portal. He could not make out anything close. The ship was traveling so fast that close objects became a blur.

"C" reported, *The ship has surpassed level 20. Remarkable!*

Mick asked, *Why does it feel like we're not moving?*

"C" told Mick, *This speed and distance of travel cannot be accomplished in our dimension.*

Mick asked, *What do you mean? I can see things going by!*

"C" insisted, *We are not where we appear to be.*

Mick read the control panel and it verified "C's" analogy. The ship's sensors showed that they were traveling through nothingness. Everything around them, while visible, had no physical content. Inside the ship, all was normal. Outside the ship, they were traveling through solid objects like ghosts.

"C" told everyone, *We are in a different reality.* Mick and the Terians watched in amazement as they traveled through space and dimensions toward the planet that could save Earth.

Author Biography

Gary Wells was born in Bellingham, Washington and raised in Seattle, enjoying all the beauty and culture of Puget Sound and the Pacific Northwest. He studied voice with a renowned vocal coach, George Peckham, before enrolling at the Cornish School of Music in Seattle. Gary moved to Nevada, becoming a real estate developer while pursuing his writing and lifelong love of music. He currently lives in Las Vegas with his family.

www.ingramcontent.com/pod-product-compliance
Lightning Source LLC
Chambersburg PA
CBHW031434200726
48289CB00001BA/51